CITY FOR LOVE

This is a story of Paris . . .

The Paris of sidewalk cafes and cheap hotels, prostitutes and cab drivers, socialites and shopkeepers.

The Paris of Ravic. A brilliant surgeon hounded out of Germany by the Nazis and forced to practice secretly—to "ghost" difficult operations for wealthy society doctors.

The Paris of Joan Madou. An actress, fascinating, vivacious, passionate, disloyal, who becomes Ravic's mistress.

This is the story of their love. Tempestuous, tragic, and ultimately inspiring, it could only have happened in Paris—and only at a time when the whole world trembled on the brink of flames.

ARCH OF TRIUMPH

"A vivid picture of a crisis in history, a gallery of brilliant portraits of individuals, a study of human motives . . . a work of art."
—Cleveland Plain Dealer

⊘

Great Reading from SIGNET

ARCH
OF
TRIUMPH

Erich Maria Remarque

Translated from the German by
Walter Sorell and Denver Lindley

A SIGNET BOOK

NEW AMERICAN LIBRARY

PUBLISHER'S NOTE

This novel is a work of fiction. Names, characters, places, and incidents either are the product of the author's imagination or are used fictitiously, and any resemblance to actual persons, living or dead, events, or locales is entirely coincidental.

Copyright © 1945 by Erich Maria Remarque

Coyright renewed © 1972 by Paulette Goddard Remarque

All rights reserved

Cover photo copyright © 1984 by CBS/Bob Greene.

Published by arrangement with Paulette Remarque

First Printing, July, 1950

3 4 5 6 7 8 9 10 11

PRINTED IN THE UNITED STATES OF AMERICA

Chapter 1

THE WOMAN VEERED toward Ravic. She walked quickly, but with a peculiar stagger. Ravic first noticed her when she was almost beside him. He saw a pale face, high cheek-bones and wide-set eyes. The face was rigid and masklike; it looked hollowed out, and her eyes in the light from the street lamps had an expression of such glassy emptiness that they caught his attention.

The woman passed so close she almost touched him. He reached out and seized her arm with one hand; the next moment she tottered and would have fallen, if he had not supported her.

He held her arm tight. "Where are you going?" he asked after a moment.

The woman stared at him. "Let me go!" she whispered.

Ravic did not answer. He still held her arm tight.

"Let me go!" The woman barely moved her lips.

Ravic had the impression that she did not see him at all. She was looking through him, somewhere into the empty night. He was only something that had stopped her and toward which she spoke. "Let me go!"

Ravic saw at once she was no whore. Neither was she drunk. He did not hold her arm so tight now. She could have freed herself easily, but it did not occur to her. Ravic waited awhile. "Where can you really want to go at night, alone at this time in Paris?" he quietly asked once more and released her arm.

The woman remained silent. But she did not walk on. Once stopped, she seemed unable to move again.

Ravic leaned against the railing of the bridge. He could feel the damp porous stone under his hands. "Perhaps down there?" He motioned with his head backward and down at the Seine, which moved restlessly toward the shadows of the Pont de l'Alma in a gray and gradually fading glimmer.

16

The woman did not answer.

"Too early," Ravic said. "Too early and much too cold in November."

He took out a package of cigarettes and fumbled in his pockets for matches. He saw there were only two left in the little box and he bent down cautiously in order to shelter the flame with his hands against the soft breeze from the river.

"Give me a cigarette, too," the woman said in an almost toneless voice.

Ravic straightened up and held the package toward her. "Algerian. Black tobacco of the Foreign Legion. Probably it's too strong for you. I have nothing else with me."

The woman shook her head and took a cigarette. Ravic held the burning match for her. She smoked hastily, inhaling deeply. Ravic threw the match over the railing. It fell through the dark like a little shooting star and went out only when it reached the water.

A taxi drove slowly across the bridge. The driver stopped. He looked toward them and waited for a moment, then he stepped on the accelerator and drove along the wet dark-gleaming Avenue George V.

Ravic felt suddenly tired. He had been working all day and had not been able to sleep. And so he had gone out again to drink. But now, unexpectedly, in the wet coolness of the late night, tiredness fell over him like a sack.

He looked at the woman. What had made him stop her? Something was wrong with her, that much was clear. But what did it matter to him? He had already seen plenty of women with whom something was wrong, particularly at night, particularly in Paris, and it made no difference to him now and all he wanted was a few hours' sleep.

"Go home," he said. "What are you doing on the streets at this hour? You'll only get into trouble."

He turned up the collar of his coat and was about to walk away. The woman looked at him as though she did not understand. "Home?" she repeated.

Ravic shrugged his shoulders. "Home, back to your apartment, to your hotel, call it what you like, somewhere. You don't want to be picked up by the police?"

"To the hotel! My God!" the woman said.

Ravic paused. Once more someone who does not know where to go, he thought. He could have foreseen it. It was always the same. At night they did not know where to go and

"I don't know. Anything at all."

"Two calvados," Ravic said to the waiter, who was in and rolled-up shirtsleeves. "And a package of Chesterfi

"Haven't any," the waiter announced. "Only Fren

"Well then, a pack of Laurens green."

"We don't have green either. Only blue."

Ravic looked at the waiter's arm, on which wa naked woman walking on clouds. The waiter, the next morning they were gone before you were awake. Then they knew where to go. The old cheap desperation that came with the dark and left with it. He threw his cigarette away. As if he himself did not know it and know it to the point of weariness!

"Come, let's go somewhere and have a drink," he said.

It was the simplest solution. Afterwards he could pay and leave and she could decide what to do.

The woman made an uncertain movement and stumbled. Ravic caught hold of her arm. "Tired?" he asked.

"I don't know. I guess so."

"Too tired to sleep?"

She nodded.

"That can happen. Come along, I'll hold onto you."

They walked up the Avenue Marceau. Ravic felt the woman leaning on him. She did not lean as if she were tired—she leaned as if she were about to fall and had to support herself.

They crossed the Avenue Pierre Ier de Serbie. Behind the intersection of the Rue de Chaillot the street opened up and floating and dark in the distance, the mass of the Arc de Triomphe emerged out of the rainy sky.

Ravic pointed to the narrow lighted entrance of a cellar drinking place. "In here—we'll still be able to get something."

It was a bistro frequented by drivers. A few cabdrivers and two whores were sitting inside. The drivers were playing cards. The whores were drinking absinthe. With a quick glance they took stock of the woman. Then they turned indifferently away. The older one yawned audibly; the other began lackadaisically making up her face. In the background a busboy, with the face of a weary rat, sprinkled sawdust around and began to sweep the floor. Ravic and the woman sat down at a table near the entrance. It was more convenient; he could then leave more easily. He did not remove his coat. "What do you want to drink?" he asked.

glance, clenched his fist and made his muscles jump. The woman on the clouds wriggled her belly lasciviously.

"All right, blue," Ravic said.

The waiter grinned. "Maybe we still have one green left." He shuffled off.

Ravic's eyes followed him. "Red slippers on his feet," he said, "and a nautch girl on his arm! He must have served in the Turkish navy."

The woman put her hands on the table. She did it as if she never wanted to lift them again. Her hands had been well cared for but that meant nothing. Still they were not too well cared for. Ravic saw that the nail of the right middle finger was broken; it seemed to have been torn off without having been filed. In some places the polish was chipped.

The waiter brought the glasses and a package of cigarettes.

"Laurens green. Found one after all."

"I thought you would. Were you in the navy?"

"No. Circus."

"Better still." Ravic handed a glass to the woman. "Here, drink this. It's the best thing at this hour. Or would you like coffee?"

"No."

"Drink it all at once."

The woman nodded and emptied the glass. Ravic studied her. She had a colorless face, almost without expression. The mouth was full but pale, the contours appeared blurred. Only the hair was very beautiful—of a lustrous natural blond. She wore a Basque beret and under her raincoat a blue tailored suit. The suit had been made by a good tailor, but the green stone in the ring on her hand was much too big to be real.

"Do you want another?" Ravic asked.

She nodded.

He beckoned the waiter. "Two more calvados. But bigger glasses."

"Bigger glasses? More in them, too?"

and not been able to sleep much at night—then one saw a lot on the way.

The waiter brought the drinks. Ravic took the penetrating and aromatic smelling apple brandy and placed it carefully in front of the woman. "Drink this too. It doesn't help much, but it warms you up. And whatever's the matter—don't take it too hard. There's nothing that remains serious for long."

The woman looked at him. She did not drink.

"It's true," Ravic said. "Particularly at night. Night exaggerates."

The woman still stared at him. "You don't have to comfort me," she said.

"All the better."

Ravic looked around for the waiter. He had had enough. He knew this type. Probably Russian, he thought. The minute they sit down somewhere, while they're still wet, they become arrogant.

"Are you Russian?" he asked.

"No."

Ravic paid and rose to say goodbye. At the same moment the woman got up, too. She did it silently and naturally. Ravic looked at her uncertainly. All right, he thought then, I can do it just as well outside.

It had begun to rain. Ravic stopped in front of the door. "Which way are you going?" He was determined to take the opposite direction.

"I don't know. Somewhere."

"But—where do you live?"

The woman made a quick movement. "I can't go there! No, no! I can't do that! Not there!"

Suddenly her eyes were full of a wild fear. She has quarreled, Ravic thought, has had some sort of row and has run away. By tomorrow noon she will have thought it over and will go back.

"Don't you know anyone to whom you could go? An acquaintance? You could call them up from the bistro."

"You must go somewhere," Ravic said impatiently. "You can't stay in the streets in this rain."

The woman drew her raincoat tighter around her. "You are right," she said as though she had suddenly come to a decision. "You are quite right. Thanks. Don't trouble about me any more. I'll find a place all right. Thank you." With one hand she pulled the collar of her coat together. "Thank you for everything." She glanced up at Ravic with an expression of misery, and tried unsuccessfully to smile. Then she walked away through the misty rain unhesitatingly and with soundless steps.

Ravic stood still for a moment. "Damn it," he grumbled, surprised and irresolute. He did not know how it happened or what it was, the hopeless smile, or the look, or the empty street or the night—he knew only that he could not let this woman go alone through the mist, this woman who suddenly looked like a lost child.

He followed her. "Come with me," he said gruffly. "We'll find something for you."

They reached the Etoile. The square lay before them in a drizzling grayness, huge and unbounded. The mist was thicker now and one could no longer see the streets that branched off. There was only the broad square with the scattered dim moons of the street lamps and with the monumental stone arch which receded into the mist as though it would prop up the melancholy sky and protect beneath itself the faint lonely flame on the tomb of the Unknown Soldier, which looked like the last grave of mankind in the midst of night and loneliness.

They walked across the square. Ravic walked fast. He was too tired to think. Beside him he heard the soft, pattering steps of the woman following him silently, with head bent, hands hidden in the pockets of her coat, a small alien flame of life—and suddenly in the late loneliness of the square, strangely she seemed to belong to him for a moment although he did not know anything about her, or just for that reason. She was

He rang the bell. "Is there a vacant room?" he asked the boy who opened the door.

The boy stared at him sleepily. "The concierge is not here," he mumbled finally.

"I see that. I asked you if there was a vacant room."

The boy shrugged his shoulders helplessly. He saw that Ravic had a woman with him; but he could not understand why he wanted another room. According to his experience this was not why women were brought in. "Madame is asleep. She'd fire me if I woke her up," he said. He scratched himself vigorously.

"All right. Then we'll have to see for ourselves."

Ravic tipped the boy, took his key, and walked upstairs, followed by the woman. Before he unlocked his door, he examined the door next to it. There were no shoes in front of it. He knocked twice. Nobody answered. He carefully tried the knob. The door was locked. "This room was empty yesterday," he muttered. "We'll try it from the other side. The landlady has probably locked it for fear the bedbugs will get away."

He unlocked his room. "Sit down for a minute." He pointed to a red horsehair sofa. "I'll be back right away."

He opened a large window leading to a narrow iron balcony and climbed over the connecting trellis to the adjacent balcony, where he tried the door. It too was locked. He came back resignedly. "It's no use. I can't get you another room here."

The woman sat in the corner of the sofa. "May I sit here for a moment?"

Ravic looked at her closely. Her face was crumpled with fatigue. She seemed hardly able to get up again. "You may stay here," he said.

"Just for a moment—"

"You can sleep here. That's the easiest thing."

The woman did not seem to hear him. Slowly, almost automatically she moved her head. "You should have left me ~he street. Now—I think I won't be able—"

he had nowhere else to go. This is a hotel for refugees. Something like this happens almost every day. You can take the bed, I'll sleep on the sofa. I'm used to it."

"No, no—I'll just stay where I am. If I may only sit here, that's all."

"All right, just as you like."

Ravic took off his coat and hung it on a hook. Then he took a blanket and a cushion from his bed and moved a chair close to the sofa. He fetched a bathrobe from the bathroom and hung it over the chair. "Here," he said, "this is what I can give you. If you like, you can have pajamas too. You'll find some in the drawer over there. I won't trouble about you any more. You may use the bathroom now. I've got to do something in here."

The woman shook her head.

Ravic stood in front of her. "But we'll take off your coat," he said. "It's pretty wet. And let me have your hat too."

She gave him both. He put the cushion in the corner of the sofa. "That's for your head. Here is a chair so that you won't fall off when you go to sleep." He moved it closer to the sofa. "And now your shoes! Soaked through, of course! A good way to catch cold." He took off her shoes, got a pair of short woolen socks out of the drawer and slipped them over her feet. "Now, that's better. During critical times have an eye for comfort. That's an old soldier's maxim."

"Thanks," the woman said. "Thanks."

Ravic went into the bathroom and turned on the tap. The water gushed into the basin. He undid his tie and stared absent-mindedly at himself in the mirror. Challenging eyes in deep-shadowed sockets; a narrow face, dead tired, only the eyes giving it life; lips too soft for the furrow running from the nose to the mouth—and above the right eye, disappearing into the hair, a long jagged scar—

The telephone bell cut into his thoughts. "Damn it!' For an instant he had forgotten everything. There were such moments of complete oblivion. And there was still the wo___

He carefully put the receiver down and for a few seconds remained seated on the arm of the sofa. "I've got to go," he said, "right now."

The woman rose immediately. She swayed a little and leaned on the chair.

"No, no—" For a moment Ravic was touched by this obedient readiness. "You can stay here. Go to sleep. I will be gone for an hour or two, I don't know exactly how long. Do stay here." He got into his coat. He had a passing thought. And at once forgot it. The woman would not steal. She was not the type. He knew it too well. And there wasn't much she could steal.

He was already at the door when the woman asked, "Can't I go with you?"

"Impossible. Stay here. Take whatever you need. The bed, if you want. There's cognac over there. Go to sleep—"

He turned away. "Leave the light on," the woman said suddenly and quickly.

Ravic took his hand from the knob. "Afraid?" he asked.

She nodded.

He pointed to the key. "Lock the door behind me. But don't leave the key in the lock. There's another key downstairs with which I can get in."

She shook her head. "It's not that. But please leave the light on."

"I see!" Ravic looked at her sharply. "I wasn't going to turn it off anyway. Leave it on. I know that feeling. I've gone through such times, too."

At the corner of the Rue des Acacias he got a taxi. "Drive to Rue Lauriston. Fast!"

The driver made a U-turn and drove into the Avenue Carnot and then into the Avenue de la Forge. As he crossed the Avenue de la Grande Armée a small two-seater raced toward them from the right. The two cars would have collided, had not the street been wet and smooth. But when the two-seater's brake took hold it skidded into the middle of the street just past the radiator of the taxi. The light car whirled facing the huge gate to Hades—a small green insect out of which a pallid fist rose menacingly toward the night sky.

The cabdriver turned around. "Have you ever seen anything like that?"

"Yes," Ravic said.

"But with such a hat. Why does anyone with such a hat have to drive so fast at night?"

"It was his right of way. He was on the main road. Why are you cursing?"

"Of course he was right. That's just why I am cursing."

"What would you have done if he had been wrong?"

"I would have cursed just the same."

"You seem to make life easy for yourself."

"I wouldn't have cursed like that," the driver explained and turned into the Avenue Foch. "Not so surprised, you understand?"

"No. Drive slower at intersections."

"That's what I was going to do. That damn oil on the street. But what makes you ask me if you don't want to listen to an answer?"

"Because I'm tired," Ravic replied impatiently. "Because it's night. Also, if you like, because we are sparks in an unknown wind. Drive on."

"That's something else." The driver touched his cap with a certain respect. "That I understand."

"Listen," Ravic said with suspicion. "Are you Russian?"

"No. But I read a lot while waiting for customers."

I'm out of luck with Russians today, Ravic thought. He leaned his head back. Coffee, he thought. Very hot black coffee. Let's hope they have plenty of it. My hands have to be damned steady. If they aren't—Veber will have to give me a shot. But I'll be all right. He pulled the window down and slowly and deeply breathed in the moist air.

Chapter 2

THE SMALL operating room was lighted bright as day. It looked like a very hygienic slaughterhouse. Pails with blood-drenched cotton stood here and there, bandages and tampons lay scattered, and the red was a loud and solemn protest against all the white. Veber was sitting at an enameled steel table in the anteroom, making notes; a nurse was boiling the instruments; the water bubbled, the light seemed to hum, and only the body on the table lay quite independent—nothing any longer mattered to it.

Ravic let the liquid soap run over his hands and began to wash. He did it with a furious sullenness as if he wished to rub off his skin. "Damn!" he muttered. "Damned confounded crap!"

The nurse looked at him with disgust. Veber glanced up. "Calm down, Nurse Eugénie. All surgeons swear. Particularly if something has gone wrong. You should be used to it."

The nurse threw a handful of instruments into the boiling water. "Professor Perrier never swore," she explained in an offended tone.

"Professor Perrier was a brain specialist. A most subtle mechanic, Eugénie. We work in the abdomen. That's something else." Veber closed his notebook and got up. "You did your best, Ravic. But after all one can't win against quacks."

"Oh yes—sometimes you can." Revic dried his hands and lit a cigarette. The nurse opened the window in silent disapproval. "Bravo, Eugénie," Veber praised her. "Always according to rules."

"I have responsibilities. I don't want to be blown up."

"That's nice, Eugénie. And reassuring."

"Some have none. And some don't want to have any."

"Some have none. And some don't want to have any." Ravic." Veber laughed. "We'd

Ravic turned around. He looked at the dutiful nurse. She returned his look fearlessly. The steel-rimmed glasses made her bleak face somehow untouchable. She was a human being like himself, but to him she appeared more alien than a tree. "Pardon me," he said, "you are right, nurse."

Under the white light on the table lay what a few hours before had been hope, breath, pain, and quivering life. Now it was only an insensible cadaver—and the human automaton called Nurse Eugénie, with responsibilities and respect for herself, proud of never having taken a false step, covered it up and rolled it away. These are the ones who live forever, Ravic thought—life does not love them, these souls of wood—therefore it forgets them and lets them live on and on.

"So long, nurse," Veber said. "Take a good sleep today."

"Goodbye, Doctor Veber. Thank you, doctor."

"Goodbye," Ravic said. "Excuse my swearing."

"Good morning," Eugénie replied icily.

Veber smiled. "A character of cast iron."

Outside a gray day was dawning. Garbage trucks rattled through the streets. Veber turned up his collar. "Nasty weather! Can I give you a lift, Ravic?"

"No, thanks, I'd rather walk."

"In this weather? I can drop you. It's not out of my way."

Ravic shook his head. "Thank you, Veber."

Veber gave him an appraising look. "Strange that you still get worked up when someone dies under the knife. Haven't you been at it for the last fifteen years? You should be used to it by now!"

"Yes, I am. And I'm not worked up."

Veber stood before Revic, broad and heavy. His big round face shone like a Normandy apple. His black, trimmed mustache, wet with rain, glittered. The buick standing at the curb also glittered. Presently Veber would drive home comfortably in it—to a rose-colored doll's house in the suburbs with a neat glittering woman in it and two neat glittering children and a neat glittering life. How could one explain to him something of that breathless tension when the knife began the first cut and the narrow red trace followed the light pressure, when the body, under clips and forceps, opened like a multiple curtain, when organs which destroyed tissues, in lumps, in tumors, in scissures—and the fight began, the silent, mad fight during which one could use no other weapon than a thin blade and a needle and a steady hand—how could one explain what it meant when then all at once a dark shadow rushed through the blinding white of stark concentration, a majestic derision that seemed to render the knife dull, the needle brittle, and the hand heavy—and when this invisible, enigmatic pulsing—life—then ebbed away under one's powerless hands, collapsed, draw into this ghostly vortex which one could never reach or hold—and when a face that had a moment ago breathed and borne a name turned into a rigid, nameless mask—this senseless, rebellious helplessness: how could one explain it—and what was there to explain?

Ravic lit another cigarette. "Twenty-one years old," he said.

With his handkerchief Veber wiped the shiny drops from his mustache. "You worked marvelously, Ravic. I couldn't have done it. That you couldn't save what a quack had botched up—is something that does not concern you. Where would we be if we thought otherwise?"

"Yes," Ravic said. "Where would we be?"

Veber put his handkerchief back. "After all you have gone through, you should be damned tough by now."

Ravic looked at him with a trace of irony. "One is never tough. But one can get used to a lot of things."

"That's what I mean."

"Yes, and to some things never. But that is difficult to realize. Let's take for granted that it was the coffee. Maybe it actually was the coffee that made me so edgy. And we confuse it with excitement."

"The coffee was good, wasn't it?"

"Very good."

"I know how to make coffee. I had an idea you'd need it, that's why I made it myself. It was different from the black water Eugénie usually produces, wasn't it?"

"No comparison. You're a master at making coffee."

Veber stepped into his car. He trod on the starter and leaned out of the window. "Couldn't I drop you? You must be tired?"

Like a seal, Ravic thought absent-mindedly. He is like a healthy seal. But what does that mean? Why does it occur to me? Why always these double thoughts? "I'm no longer tired," he said. "The coffee woke me up. Sleep well, Veber."

Veber laughed. His teeth glistened beneath his black mustache. "I won't go to bed now. I'll work in my garden. I'll plant tulips and daffodils."

Tulips and daffodils, Ravic thought. In neat, separate beds with neat graveled paths between. Tulips and daffodils—the peach-colored, golden storm of spring. "So long, Veber," he said. "You will take care of the rest, won't you?"

"Naturally. I'll call you up in the evening. Sorry the fee will be low. Not even worth mentioning. The girl was poor and, as it seems, had no relatives. We'll see about that."

Ravic dismissed it with a gesture.

"She gave a hundred francs to Eugénie. Apparently that was all she had. That will be twenty-five francs for you."

"Never mind," Ravic said impatiently. "So long, Veber."

"So long. Till tomorrow morning at eight."

Ravic walked slowly along the Rue Lauriston. Had it been summer, he would have sat down on a bench in the Bois in the morning sun and, with vacant mind, would have stared into the water and the young woods, until the tension left him. Then he would have driven to the hotel and gone to bed.

He entered a bistro at the corner of the Rue Boissière. A few workers and truckdrivers stood at the bar. They drank hot, black coffee, dipping brioches into it. Ravic watched them for a time. This was ordinary, simple life, a life to seize hold of, to work with: tiredness in the evening, eating, a woman, and a heavy dreamless sleep.

"A kirsch," he said.

The dying girl had worn a cheap narrow chain of imitation gold around her right ankle—one of those little follies that are possible only when one is young, sentimental, and without taste. A chain with a little plate and an inscription: *Toujours Charles*, riveted around her ankle so that one could not take it off—a chain that told a story of Sundays in the woods near the Seine, of being in love and of ignorant youth, of a small jeweler somewhere in Neuilly, of nights in September in an attic—and then suddenly the staying away, the waiting, the fear—Toujours Charles who never showed up again, then the girl friend who knew an address, the midwife somewhere, a table covered with oilcloth, piercing pain and blood, blood, a bewildered old woman's face, arms pushing you quickly into a cab to be rid of you, days of misery and of hiding, and finally the ride to the hospital, the last hundred francs crumpled in the hot moist hand—too late.

The radio began to blare. A tango, to which a nasal voice sang idiotic words. Ravic caught himself performing the whole operation over again. He checked every move. Maybe, some hours earlier there might have been a chance. Veber had had him called. He had not been in the hotel. So the girl had to die because he had been loafing on the Pont de l'Alma. Veber could not perform such operations himself. The idiocy of chance. The foot with the golden chain, limp, turned inward. "Come into my boat, the moon is shining," the crooner quavered in falsetto.

Ravic paid and left. Outside he stopped a taxi. "Drive to the Osiris."

The Osiris was a large middle-class brothel with a huge bar in Egyptian style.

"We're just closing," the doorman said. "There is no one inside."

"No one?"

"Only Madame Rolande. The ladies have all gone."

"All right."

The doorman ill-humoredly stamped on the pavement with his galoshes. "Why don't you keep the taxi? It won't be easy to get another one later. We're closed."

"You said that once before. I'll get another taxi all right."

Ravic put a package of cigarettes into the doorman's breast pocket and walked through the small door past the cloakroom into the big room. The bar was empty; it gave the usual impression of the remains of a bourgeois symposium—pools of spilled wine, a couple of overturned chairs, butts on the floor, and the smell of tobacco, sweet perfume, and flesh.

"Rolande," Ravic said.

She stood in front of a table on which was a pile of pink silk underwear. "Ravic," she said without surprise. "Late. What do you want—a girl or something to drink? Or both?"

"Vodka. The Polish."

Rolande brought the bottle and a glass. "Help yourself. I still have to sort and list the laundry. The laundry wagon will be here any minute. If one doesn't keep track of everything that gang will steal like a flock of magpies. The drivers, you understand. As presents for their girls."

Ravic nodded. "Turn the music on, Rolande. Loud."

"All right."

Rolande put the plug in. The sound of drums and brass went thundering through the high empty room like a storm. "Too loud, Ravic?"

"No."

Too loud? What was too loud? Only the quiet. The quiet in which one burst as though in a vacuum.

"All through." Rolande came to Ravic's table. She had a buxom figure, a clear face, and calm black eyes. The black Puritan dress she wore characterized her as the *gouvernante;* it distinguished her from the almost naked whores.

"Have a drink with me, Rolande."

"All right."

Ravic fetched a glass from the bar and poured. Rolande pulled the bottle back when her glass was half filled. "Enough. I won't drink more."

"Half-filled glasses are disgusting. Leave what you don't drink."

"Why? That would be wasteful."

Ravic glanced up. He saw the reliable intelligent face and smiled. "Waste! The old French fear. Why save? You are not saved from anything."

"This is business. That's something else."

Ravic laughed. "Let's drink a toast to it! What would the world be without business ethics! A pack of criminals, indealists, and sluggards."

"You need a girl," Rolande said. "I can call up Kiki. She is very good. Twenty-one years old."

"So. Twenty-one years too. Thats not for me today." Ravic refilled his glass. "What do you actually think of, Rolande, before you fall asleep?"

"Mostly of nothing. I am too tired."

"And when you aren't tired?"

"Of Tours."

"Why?"

"An aunt of mine owns a house with a shop there. I hold two mortgages on it. When she dies—she is seventy-six—I'll get the house. Then I'll make a café out of the shop. Light wallpaper with flower designs, a band, three men, piano, violin, cello, in the rear a bar. Small and fine. The house is situated in a good district. I think I'll be able to furnish it for nine thousand five hundred francs, even with curtains and lamps. Then I'll put aside another five thousand for the first few months. And naturally I'll have the rent from the first and second floors. That's what I think about."

"Were you born in Tours?"

"Yes. But no one knows where I've been since. And if the business prospers, no one will bother about it either. Money covers everything."

"Not everything. But a lot."

Ravic felt the heaviness behind his eyes that slowed down his voice. "I think I have had enough," he said and took a few bills out of his pocket. "Will you marry in Tours, Rolande?"

"Not right away. But in a few years. I have a friend there."

"Do you go there occasionally?"

"Rarely. He writes sometimes. To another address of course. He's married, but his wife is in the hospital. Tuberculosis. One or two more years at the most, the doctors say. Then he'll be free."

Ravic got up. "God bless you, Rolande. You have sound common sense."

She smiled appreciatively. She believed he was right. Her clear face showed not a trace of tiredness. It was fresh as if she had just got up from sleep. She knew what she wanted. Life held no secrets for her.

Outside it had become bright day. The rain had stopped. The pissoirs stood like armored turrets at the street corners. The doorman had disappeared, the night was wiped out, the day had begun, and a bustling crowd thronged the entrances to the subway—as if they were holes into which they flung themselves as sacrifice to some dark deity.

The woman started up from the sofa. She did not cry out—she just started up with a low suppressed sound, propped herself on her elbows, and stiffened.

"Quiet, quiet," Ravic said. "It's me. The man who brought you here a few hours ago."

The woman breathed again. Ravic saw her only indistinctly; the glow of the electric bulbs blended with the morning creeping through the windows in a yellowish, pale, sickly light. "I think we can turn these off now," he said and turned the switch.

He felt again the soft hammers of drunkenness behind his forehead. "Do you want breakfast?" he asked. He had forgot-

21

ten the woman and then when he got his key he had believed she had left. He would have liked to be rid of her. He had drunk enough, the backdrop of his consciousness had shifted, the clanging chain of time had burst asunder, and memories and dreams stood around him, strong and fearless. He wanted to be alone.

"Do you want some coffee?" he asked. "It's the only thing that's any good here."

The woman shook her head. He looked more closely at her.

"What's the matter? Has anybody been here?"

"No."

"But something must be the matter. You stare at me as if I were a ghost."

The woman moved her lips. "The smell—" she said.

"Smell?" Ravic repeated uncomprehendingly. "Vodka hardly smells, neither does kirsch or cognac. And cigarettes you smoke yourself. What's there about that to be scared of?"

"I don't mean that."

"What is it then, for God's sake?"

"It is the same—the same smell—"

"Heavens, it must be ether," said Ravic, suddenly understanding. "Is it ether?"

She nodded.

"Have you ever been operated on?"

"No—it is—"

Ravic did not listen further. He opened the window. "It will be gone in a minute. Smoke a cigarette meanwhile."

He went into the bathroom and turned on the faucets. He saw his face in the mirror. A few hours ago he had stood here in the same way. In the interim a human being had died. It did not matter. Thousands of people died every moment. There were statistics about it. It did not matter. For the one individual, however, it meant everything and was more important than the still revolving world.

He sat down on the edge of the tub and took off his shoes. That always stayed the same. Objects and their silent compulsion. The triviality, the stale habit in all the delusive lights of passing experience. The flowering shore of the heart by the waters of love—but whatever one was, poet, demigod, or idiot—every few hours one was called down from his heavens to urinate. One could not escape it! The irony of

22

"No."

"Well, I have. But it will be gone in an hour. Here, a brioche."

"I can't eat."

"Of course you can. You only imagine you can't. Try something."

She took the brioche. Then she put it back again. "I really can't."

"Then drink your coffee and have a cigarette. That's a soldier's breakfast."

"Yes."

Ravic ate. "Aren't you hungry yet?" he asked after a while.

"No."

The woman put out her cigarette. "I think—" she said and stopped.

"What do you think?" Ravic asked without interest.

"I should be going now."

"Do you know your way? This is near the Avenue Wagram."

"No."

"Where do you live?"

"In the Hôtel Verdun."

"It's a few minutes from here. I can direct you outside. Anyway, I'll have to take you past the porter."

"Yes—but it's not that."

She was silent again. Money, Ravic thought. "I can easily help you out, if you are hard up." He took his wallet out of his pocket.

"Don't! What's that for?" the woman said brusquely.

"Nothing." Ravic put the wallet back.

"Excuse me—" She rose. "You were—I have to thank you—it would have been—the night—alone, I wouldn't have known . . ."

Ravic remembered what had happened. It would have been ridiculous if the woman had made any claim on him—but he had not expected her to thank him, and it was far more disturbing.

"I really would not have known . . ." the woman said. She was still standing before him, undecided. Why doesn't she go? he thought.

"But now you know?" he said just to say something.

"No." She looked at him frankly. "I do not know yet. I

only know that I must do something. I know that I cannot escape."

"That's a lot." Ravic took his coat. "I'll take you down now."

"It's not necessary. Only tell me—" She hesitated, searching for words. "Perhaps you know—what must be done—if . . ."

"If?" Ravic said after a while.

"If someone dies," the woman blurted and suddenly collapsed. She wept. She did not sob, she merely wept, almost soundlessly.

Ravic waited until she was calmer. "Has someone died?"

She nodded.

"Last night?"

She nodded again.

"Did you kill him?"

The woman stared at him. "What? What did you say?"

"Did you do it? When you ask me what to do you must tell me."

"He died!" the woman cried. "He died! Suddenly he was—"

She covered her face.

"Was he sick?" Ravic asked.

"Yes—"

"Did you have a doctor?"

"Yes—but he did not want to go to the hospital—"

"Did you have a doctor yesterday?"

"No. Earlier. Three days ago. He had—he ranted against the doctor and refused to see him again—"

"Didn't you call another doctor afterwards?"

"We didn't know any. We have only been here three weeks. This one—the waiter got us this one—and he did not want him any more—he said—he thought he would be better off without him—"

"What was the matter with him?"

"I don't know. The doctor said pneumonia—but he didn't believe him—he said all doctors are crooks—and he was really feeling better yesterday. Then suddenly—"

"Why didn't you take him to the hospital?"

"He did not want to go. He said—he—I would betray him when he was away—he—you don't know him—there was nothing to be done—"

"Is he still at the hotel?"

"Yes."

"Did you tell the owner of the hotel what had happened?"

"No. Suddenly when he grew silent—and everything was so silent, and his eyes, I couldn't bear it and ran away—"

Ravic thought about the night. For a moment he was embarrassed. But it had happened and it was unimportant: to him and to the woman. Particularly to the woman. This night nothing really had mattered to her and only one thing was important: that she got through it. Life consisted of more than sentimental similes. The night Lavigne had heard that his wife was dead he had spent in a brothel. The whores had saved him; a priest could not have helped him through it. Whoever understood this, understood it. There was no explanation for it. But responsibilities went along with it.

His took his coat. "Come! I'll go with you. Was it your husband?"

"No," the woman said.

The patron of the Hôtel Verdun was fat. He hadn't a single hair on his skull, but to make up for it he had a dyed black mustache and bushy black eyebrows. He was standing in the lobby; behind him a waiter, a chambermaid, and a cashier with a flat bosom. It was evident that he already knew everything. He burst into abuse as soon as he saw the woman enter. His face paled, he waved his fat little hands in the air, and he sputtered with rage, indignation and, as Ravic saw, relief. When he came to "police, aliens, suspicion, and prison," Ravic interrupted him.

"Do you come from Provence?" he asked.

The patron stopped short. "No. What do you mean?" he asked in surprise.

"Nothing," Ravic replied. "I only wanted to interrupt you. An utterly senseless question is the best way. You would have gone on talking for another hour."

"Who are you, sir? What do you want?"

"That's the first intelligent sentence you've said up to now."

The hotelkeeper calmed down. "Who are you?" he asked more quietly, careful not to insult an influential man under any circumstances.

"I'm the doctor," Ravic replied.

The patron saw that there was no danger here. "There is no

need of a doctor now," he burst out anew. "This is a case for the police!"

He stared at Ravic and the woman. He expected fear, protest, and entreaties.

"That's a good idea. Why aren't they already here? You've known for several hours that the man is dead!"

The patron did not answer.

"I'll tell you why," Ravic took one step forward. "You don't want a scandal because of your guests. Many people would move out if they heard about such things. But the police must come, that's the law. It's up to you to hush it up. But that wasn't what bothered you. You were afraid the mess would be left in your lap. You needn't have been. Besides you were worried about your bill. It will be paid. And now I want to see the corpse. Then I'll take care of everything else."

He walked past the hotelkeeper. "What is the room number?" he asked the woman.

"Fourteen."

"You don't have to come with me. I can do it alone."

"No. I don't want to stay here."

"It would be better for you not to see any more."

"No, I will not stay here."

"All right. Just as you like."

It was a front room with a low ceiling. A few chambermaids, porters, and waiters were crowded around the door. Ravic pushed them aside. There were two beds in the room; in the one next to the wall, the body of the man was lying. He lay there yellow and stiff, with curled black hair, in red silk pajamas. His hands were folded; a small cheap wooden Madonna on whose faces were traces of lipstick stood on the table beside him. Ravic picked it up—on its back was stamped "Made in Germany." Ravic examined the face of the dead man; there was no rouge on his lips nor did he seem to have been that type. The eyes were half open; one more than the other, which gave the body an expression of indifference, as if it had grown stiff in eternal boredom.

Ravic bent over the corpse. He took stock of the bottles on the table near the bed and examined the body. No trace of violence. He drew himself up. "Do you know the name of the doctor who was here?" he asked the woman.

"No."

He looked at her. She was very pale. "First of all you sit down over there. On that chair in the corner. And stay there. Is the waiter who called the doctor for you here?"

His eyes skimmed over the faces at the door. There was the same expression on each of them: horror and greed. "François was on this floor," said the charwoman, who was holding a broom like a spear in her hand.

"Where is François?"

A waiter pushed his way through the crowd. "What was the name of the doctor who was here?"

"Bonnet. Charles Bonnet."

"Do you know his telephone number?"

The waiter fumbled for it in his pockets. "Passy 2743."

"Good." Ravic saw the face of the patron emerging from the crowd. "Let's close the door first. Or do you want the people from the street to come in, too?"

"No! Get out! Get out! Why do you stand around here stealing my time for which you get paid?"

The patron chased the employees out of the room and closed the door. Ravic took the receiver from the hook. He called Veber and talked to him for a short while. Then he called the Passy number. Bonnet was in his consultation room. He confirmed what the woman had said. "The man has died," Ravic said. "Could you come over and make out the death certificate?"

"That man threw me out in the most insulting manner."

"He can't very well insult you now."

"He didn't pay my fee. Instead he called me an avaricious quack."

"Would you come so that your bill can be paid?"

"I could send someone."

"You'd better come yourself. Otherwise you will never get your money."

"I'll come," Bonnet said after some hesitation. "But I won't sign anything before I'm paid. It amounts to three hundred francs."

"All right. Three hundred. You'll get it."

Ravic hung up. "I'm sorry you had to listen to this," he said to the woman. "But there was no alternative. We need the man."

The woman already had some money in her hand. "It doesn't matter," she replied. "Such things are not new to me. Here is the money."

"There is no hurry about that. He'll be here right away. Then you can give it to him."

"Couldn't you yourself sign the death certificate?" the woman asked.

"No," Ravic said. "We need a French physician for that. It is best to have the one who treated him."

When the door closed behind Bonnet the room became suddenly quiet. Much quieter than if just one man had left the room. The noise of cars on the streets sounded somehow tinny, as though bounced against a wall of heavy air through which it could penetrate only with difficulty. After the confusion of the past hours the presence of the dead man was now there for the first time. His powerful silence filled the cheap small room and it did not matter that he wore bright red silk pajamas—he reigned even as a dead clown might reign—because he no longer moved. What lived, moved—and what moved could have power, grace, and absurdity—but never the strange majesty of which will never move again, but only decay. What was completed alone possessed it, and the man reached completion only in death—and for a short while.

"You were not married to him, were you?" Ravic asked.

"No. Why?"

"The law. His estate. The police will want to make a list—of what belonged to you and—to him. You must keep what belongs to you. What is his, will be retained by the police. For his relatives should they show up. Had he any?"

"Not in France."

"You had been living with him, hadn't you?"

The woman did not answer."

"For a long time?"

"For two years."

Ravic looked around. "Haven't you any suitcases?"

"I have—they were over there against the wall—last night."

"I see, the patron." Ravic opened the door. The charwoman with the broom started back. "Mother," he said, "for your age you are much too inquisitive. Get me the patron."

The charwoman was about to protest.

"You're right," Ravic interrupted her. "At your age one has nothing but inquisitiveness left. Nevertheless, get me the patron."

The old woman mumbled something and disappeared, pushing the broom before her.

"I'm sorry," Ravic said, "but it can't be helped. It may seem vulgar, yet we'd better do it right now. It's simpler, even though you may not understand it at the moment."

"I do," the woman said.

Ravic looked at her. "You understand?"

"Yes."

The hotelkeeper entered, a paper in his hand. He did not knock at the door.

"Where are the suitcases?" Ravic asked.

"First the bill. Here. You've got to pay the bill first."

"First the suitcases. No one has as yet refused to pay your bill. The room is still rented. And next time knock at the door before you enter. Let me have the bill and get us the suitcases."

The man gave him a furious look. "You'll get your money all right," Ravic said.

The patron left. He slammed the door.

"Have you any money in the suitcases?" Ravic asked the woman.

"I—no, I don't think so."

"Do you know where there might be any money? In his suit? Or wasn't there any?"

"He had money in his wallet."

"Where is it?"

"Under—" The woman hesitated. "He kept it under his pillow most of the time."

Ravic got up. He carefully lifted the pillow on which the head of the dead man rested and drew forth a black leather wallet. He gave it to the woman. "Take out the money and everything that is important to you. Quickly. There is no time left for sentimentality. You've got to live. What other purpose could it serve? To molder at police headquarters?"

He looked out the window for a minute. A truck driver was having a row with the driver of a grocer's wagon drawn by two horses. He was berating him with the full superiority conferred by a heavy motor. Ravic turned around again.

"Ready?"

"Yes."

"Give the wallet back to me."

He pushed it under the pillow. He noticed that it was thinner than it had been. "Put the things into your bag," he said.

She did it obediently. Ravic picked up the bill and perused it. "Have you already paid a bill here?"

"I don't know. I think so."

"This is a bill for two weeks. Did he pay—" Ravic hesitated. It struck him as strange to speak of the dead man as Mr. Raszinsky. "Were the bills always paid promptly?"

"Yes, always. He often said that—in our situation it is important always to pay promptly when you have to."

"That scoundrel of a patron! Have you any idea where the last bill might be?"

"No. I only know that he kept all his papers in the small suitcase."

There was a knock at the door. Ravic could not help smiling. The porter brought in the suitcases. The patron came in after him. "Are these all?" Ravic asked the woman.

"Yes."

"Naturally these are all," the hotelkeeper growled. "What did you expect?"

Ravic picked up the smaller suitcase. "Have you got a key to this? No? Where can the keys be?"

"In his suit. In the wardrobe."

Ravic opened the wardrobe. It was empty. "Well?" he asked the patron.

The patron turned to the porter. "Well?" he spat.

"The suit is outside," stammered the porter.

"Why?"

"To be brushed and cleaned."

"He does not need that any more," Ravic said.

"Bring it in at once, you damned thief," the patron yelled.

The porter gave him a funny look, winked, and left. He returned immediately with the suit. Ravic shook the jacket, then the trousers. There was a clinking sound. Ravic hesitated a moment. Strange, going through the pockets of a dead man's trousers. At if the suit had died with him. And strange to feel that way. A suit was just a suit.

He took the keys out of the pocket and opened the suitcase. On top lay a canvas folder. "Is this it?" he asked the woman.

She nodded.

Ravic found the bill at once. The bill was receipted. He showed it to the patron. "You have overcharged for a whole week."

"What of it!" he shouted. "And the trouble! The mess! The excitement! All that is nothing? My gall bladder is acting

32

up again, that ought to be included, too! You yourself said that my guests might leave. The damage is much greater! And the bed? The room that must be fumigated? The bedclothes that are filthy?"

"The bedclothes are on the bill. Also a dinner for twenty-five francs that he was supposed to have eaten last night. Did you eat anything last night?" he asked the woman.

"No. But couldn't I just pay for it? It is—I'd like to get it over with quickly."

To get it over with quickly, Ravic though. We know that feeling. And then—the silence and the dead man. The thud of silence. Better so—even if it is ugly. He picked up a pencil from the table and began to figure. Then he handed the bill to the patron. "Do you agree?"

The latter glanced at the final figure. "Do you think I am crazy?"

"Do you agree?" Ravic repeated.

"Who are you anyway? Why are you meddling?"

"I am a brother," Ravic said. "Do you agree?"

"Plus ten per cent for service and taxes. Otherwise not."

"All right." Ravic added on the figures. "You'll have to pay two hundred and ninety-two francs," he said to the woman.

She took three hundred-franc notes out of her bag and gave them to the patron, who grabbed them and turned to go. "The room must be vacated by six o'clock. Otherwise it will count as another day."

"We get eight francs change," Ravic said.

"And the concierge?"

"That we'll settle ourselves."

Sullenly the patron counted out eight francs on the table. "*Sales ètrangers*," he muttered and left the room.

"The pride of some French hotelkeepers consists in their hatred of foreigners from whom they make their living." Ravic noticed the tip-conscious porter hovering at the door. "Here—"

The porter looked first at the bill. "*Merci, monsieur*," he announced then and left.

"Now we still have the police to deal with and then he can be taken away," Ravic said, looking toward the woman. She was sitting quietly in the corner among the suitcases, in the slowly gathering dusk. "When one is dead, one becomes very important—when one is alive, nobody cares." He looked at the woman again. "Would you like to go downstairs? There must be a writing room downstairs."

She shook her head.

"I'll go with you. A friend of mine will come to settle the matter with the police. Doctor Veber. We may wait for him downstairs."

"No, I'd like to stay here."

"There's nothing to do. Why do you want to stay here?"

"I don't know. He—won't be here much longer. And I often—he wasn't happy with me. I was often away. Now I will stay."

She spoke calmly, without sentimentality.

"He won't know that now," Ravic said.

"It isn't that—"

"All right. Then we'll have a drink here. You need it." Ravic did not wait for an answer. He rang the bell. Surprisingly the waiter appeared promptly. "Bring us two large cognacs."

"In here?"

"Yes. Where else?"

"Very well, sir."

The waiter brought two glasses and a bottle of Courvoisier. He started toward the corner where the bed glimmered whitely in the dusk. "Shall I turn on the light?" he asked.

"No. But you can leave the bottle here."

The waiter put the tray on the table and departed as quickly as he could.

Ravic took the bottle and filled the glasses. "Drink this, it will do you good."

He expected the woman would refuse and he would have to persuade her. But she emptied the glass without hesitation.

"Is there anything else of value in the suitcases that aren't yours?"

"No."

"Something you would like to keep? That could be useful to you? Why don't you take a look?"

"No. There is nothing in them. I know."

"Not even in the small suitcase?"

"Maybe. I don't know what he kept in it."

Ravic picked up the suitcase, and put it on the small table near the window. A few bottles; some underwear; a few notebooks; a box of water colors; brushes; a book; in a compartment of the canvas folder two bank notes wrapped in

34

tissue paper. He held them up to the light. "Here is a hundred dollars," he said. "Take it. You can live on this for a while. We'll put the suitcase with your belongings. It could just as well have been yours."

"Thank you," the woman said.

"Possibly you find all this disgusting. But it has to be done. It is important to you. It will give you a little time."

"I don't find it disgusting. Only I couldn't have done it myself."

Ravic filled the glasses again. "Have another drink."

She emptied the glass slowly. "Do you feel better now?" he asked.

She looked at him. "Neither better nor worse. Nothing." The dusk enveloped her. Sometimes the red reflections of the neon lights flickered across her face and hands. "I can't think at all," she said, "as long as he is here."

The two ambulance men turned back the blanket and put the stretcher down near the bed. Then they lifted the body. They did it quickly and in a businesslike manner. Ravic stood close to the woman to be at hand in case she fainted. Before the men covered the body, he bent down and took the small wooden Madonna from the night table. "I think that belongs to you," he said. "Don't you want to keep it?"

"No."

He gave it to her. She did not take it. He opened the smaller suitcase and put it in.

The ambulance men covered the corpse with a cloth. Then they lifted the stretcher. The door was too narrow and the corridor outside was not very wide. They tried to get it through; but it was impossible. The stretcher hit against the wall.

"We must take him off," said the older man. "We can't turn the corner this way."

He looked at Ravic. "Come," Ravic said to the woman. "We'll wait downstairs."

She shook her head.

"All right," he said to the man. "Do what you think necessary."

Both men lifted the body, holding it by the feet and shoulders, and put it on the floor. Ravic wanted to say something. He watched the woman. She did not move. He kept silent. The men carried the stretcher into the hall. Then they came back into the dusk and carried the body out into the dimly lit corridor. Ravic followed them. They had to lift the stretcher very high in order to go down the stairs. Their faces swelled and became red and wet with perspiration under the weight, and the dead body swung heavily above them. Ravic's eyes followed them until they reached the foot of the stairs. Then he went back.

The woman was standing near the window, looking out. The car was parked on the street. The men pushed the stretcher into it like bakers pushing bread into the oven. Then they climbed up on their seats, the motor roared as if someone were crying out from underground, and the car shot around the corner in a sharp curve.

The woman turned around. "You should have left before," Ravic said. "Why did you have to see the end of it?"

"I could not. I could not leave before him. Don't you understand that?"

"Yes. Come. Have another drink."

"No."

Veber had turned on the light when the ambulance and police came. The room seemed bigger now that the body was gone. Bigger and strangely dead; as though the body had gone out and death alone was left.

"Do you want to stay here in the hotel? I imagine not."

"No."

"Do you have any friends here?"

"No, no one."

"Do you know a hotel where you'd like to live?"

"No."

"There is a small hotel in the neighborhood, similar to this one. Clean and decent. The Hôtel de Milan. We might find something for you there."

"Couldn't I go to the hotel where—to your hotel?"

"The International?"

"Yes. I—there is—I know it by now somehow—it is better than one entirely unknown—"

"The International is not the right hotel for women," Ravic said. That would be the finishing touch, the thought. In the same hotel. I am not a nurse. And besides—maybe she thinks I already have some sort of responsibility. That could be. "I can't advise you to go there," he said in a harsher voice than he intended. "It is always overcrowded. With refugees. Stay at the Hôtel de Milan. If you don't like it there, you may move whenever you like.''

The woman looked at him. He felt she knew what he was thinking and he was embarrassed. But it was better to be embarrassed for an instant and to be left alone later.

"Good," the woman said. "You are right."

Ravic ordered the suitcases carried down to a taxi. The Hôtel de Milan was only a few minutes' ride. He rented a room and went upstairs with the woman. It was a room on the second floor, with wallpaper of rose-garlands, a bed, a wardrobe and a table with two chairs. "Is this all right?" he asked.

"Yes. Very good."

Ravic eyed the wallpaper. It was terrible. "At least it seems to be clean in here," he said. "Bright and clean."

"Yes."

The suitcases were brought upstairs. "Now you have everything here."

"Yes, thanks. Many thanks."

She sat down on the bed. Her face was pale and expressionless. "You should go to bed. Do you think you will be able to sleep?"

"I'll try."

He took an aluminum tube out of his pocket and shook a few tablets out of it. "Here is something to make you sleep. With water. Do you want to take it now?"

"No, later."

"All right. I'll go now. I'll look you up one of these days. Try to sleep as soon as possible. Here is the address of the funeral parlor in case something comes up. But don't go there. Think of yourself. I'll come around." Ravic hesitated a moment. "What's your name?" he asked.

"Madou. Joan Madou."

"Joan Madou. All right. I'll remember it." He knew he would not remember it and he would not look her up. But because he knew it he wished to keep up appearances. "I'd better write it down," he said and took a prescription pad out of his vest pocket. "Here—write it yourself. That's simpler."

She took the pad and wrote down her name. He looked at it, tore the sheet off, and stuck it in a side pocket of his coat. "Go to bed right away," he said. "Tomorrow everything will seem different. It sounds stupid and trite, but it is true:

all you need now is sleep and a little time. A certain amount of time that you have to get through. Do you know that?"

"Yes, I know."

"Take the tablets and sleep well."

"Yes, thank you. Thanks for everything. I don't know what I would have done without you. I really don't know."

She offered her hand. It was cool to the touch and she had a firm clasp. Good, he thought. There is some determination here already.

Ravic stepped into the street. He inhaled the moist, soft wind. Automobiles, people, a few early whores already at the corners, brasseries, bistros, the smell of tobacco, apéritifs and gasoline—quick, fluctuating life. How sweet it could taste in passing! He looked up at the hotel front. A few lighted windows. Behind one of them the woman was sitting now and staring straight ahead. He took the slip with her name out of his pocket, tore it up, and threw it away. Forget. What a word, he thought. Full of horror, comfort, and apparitions! Who could live without forgetting? But who could forget enough? The ashes of memory that ground one's heart. Only when one had nothing more to live for, was one free.

He went to the Place de l'Etoile. A great crowd filled the square. Searchlights had been placed behind the Arc de Triomphe. They illuminated the tomb of the Unknown Soldier. A huge blue-white-red flag waved in the wind in front of it. It was the celebration of the twentieth anniversary of the 1918 Armistice. The sky was overcast and the beam of the searchlights threw the shadow of the flag against the floating clouds, dull and blurred and torn. It looked like a ragged flag which gradually melted into the slowly darkening sky. Somewhere a military band was playing. It sounded weak and thin. There was no singing. The crowd stood silent. "Armistice," an old woman said at Ravic's side. "I lost my husband in the last war. Now it's my son's turn. Armistice. Who knows what next year will bring. . . ."

Chapter 4

THE FEVER CHART over the bed was new and clean. Only the name was on it. Lucienne Martinet. Buttes-Chaumont. Rue Clavel.

The girl's face on the pillow was gray. She had been operated on the night before. Ravic carefully listened to her heart. Then he straightened up. "Better," he said. "The blood transfusion worked a minor miracle. If she lasts one more day she has a chance."

"Fine," Veber said. "Congratulations. It didn't look as if she had. A pulse of a hundred forty and a blood pressure of eighty; caffeine, coramine—that was damn close."

Ravic shrugged his shoulders. "That's nothing to be congratulated for. She came earlier than the other girl. The one with the gold chain around her ankle. That was all."

He covered the girl up. "This is the second case within a week. If it goes on you'll have a hospital for mishandled abortions from the Buttes-Chaumont. Wasn't the other girl from there, too?"

Veber nodded. "Yes. And from the Rue Clavel. They probably knew each other and went to the same midwife. She even came about the same time in the evening as the other girl. It's a good thing I was able to get hold of you at the hotel. I was afraid you wouldn't be in."

Ravic looked at him. "When one lives in a hotel one usually isn't in at night, Veber. Hotel rooms in November aren't particularly cheerful."

"I can imagine that. But then why do you go on living in a hotel?"

"It's a comfortable and impersonal way of living. One's alone and one isn't alone."

"Is that what you want?"

"Yes."

39

"You could have all that in another way too. If you'd rent a small apartment, it would be just the same."

"Maybe." Ravic bent over the girl again.

"Don't you think so, too, Eugénie?" Veber asked.

The nurse glanced up. "Mr. Ravic will never do it," she said coldly.

"Doctor Ravic, Eugénie," Veber corrected. "I've told you a hundred times. He was chief surgeon in a great hospital in Germany. Far more important than I am."

"Here—" the nurse began and straightened her glasses.

Veber quickly stopped her. "All right! All right! We know all that. This country doesn't recognize foreign degrees. Idiotic at that! But what makes you so sure he won't take an apartment?"

"Mr. Ravic is a lost man. He will never build a home for himself."

"What?" Veber asked in astonishment. "What's that you are saying?"

"There is no longer anything sacred to Mr. Ravic. That's the reason."

"Bravo," Ravic said from the girl's bedside.

"I have never heard anything like it!" Veber stared at Eugénie.

"Why don't you ask him yourself, Doctor Veber?"

Ravic smiled. "You hit the mark, Eugénie. But when there is no longer anything sacred to one, everything again becomes sacred in a more human way. One reveres the spark of life that pulses even in an earthworm and that forces it from time to time up to the light of day. That's not meant to be a comparison."

"You can't insult me. You have no faith." Eugénie energetically smoothed her white coat over her breast. "Thank God, I have my faith!"

Ravic straightened up. "Faith can easily make one fanatical. That's why all religions have cost so much blood." He grinned. "Tolerance is the daughter of doubt, Eugénie. That explains why you, with all your faith, are so much more aggressive toward me than I, lost infidel, am toward you."

Veber guffawed. "There you are, Eugénie. Don't answer! You'll get in even deeper!"

"My dignity as a woman—"

"Fine!" Veber interrupted. "Stick to that. That's always

good. I've got to leave now. I've still some things to do in the office. Come, Ravic. Good morning, Eugénie.''

"Good morning, Doctor Veber."

"Good morning, Nurse Eugénie," Ravic said.

"Good morning," Eugénie replied with an effort and only after Veber had turned around to look at her.

Veber's office was crowded with Empire furniture; white and gold and fragile. Photographs of his house and garden hung on the wall above his desk. A modern broad chaise longue stood against the wall. Veber slept on it when he stayed overnight. The private hospital belonged to him.

"What would you like to drink, Ravic? Cognac or Dubonnet?"

"Coffee, if there is any left."

"Of course." Veber placed the coffeepot on the desk and put the plug in. Then he turned to Ravic. "Can you substitute for me in the Osiris this afternoon?"

"Of course."

"You don't mind?"

"Not in the least. I've no other plans."

"Fine. Then I won't have to drive in again just to go there. I can work in my garden. I'd have asked Fauchon but he is on his vacation."

"Nonsense," Ravic said. "I've done it often enough."

"That's right. Nevertheless—"

"Nevertheless no longer exists nowadays. Not for me."

"Yes. It's idiotic enough that you are not permitted to work here officially and have to hide out as a ghost surgeon."

"But Veber! That's an old story now. It is happening to all physicians who fled Germany."

"Just the same! It's ridiculous! You perform Durant's most difficult operations and he makes a name for himself."

"Better than if he did them himself."

Veber laughed. "I'm a fine one to talk. You do mine too. But after all, I am a gynecologist and not a specialist in surgery."

The coffeepot began to hum. Veber turned it off. He took cups out of a closet and poured the coffee. "One thing I really don't understand, Ravic," he said. "Why do you go on living in that depressing hole, the International? Why don't you rent one of those nice new apartments in the neighborhood of the Bois? You could buy some furniture anywhere cheap. Then at least you'd know what's your own!"

"Yes," Ravic said. "Then I would know what was my own!"

"See! Why don't you do it?"

Ravic took a gulp of his coffee. It was bitter and very strong. "Veber," he said, "you are a magnificent example of the convenient thinking of our time. In one breath you are sorry because I work illegally here—and at the same time you ask me why I don't rent a nice apartment—"

"What's one got to do with the other?"

Ravic smiled patiently. "If I take an apartment I must be registered with the police. I would need a passport and a visa for that."

"That's right. I hadn't thought of that. And in hotels you don't need any?"

"There too. But, thank God, there are a few hotels in Paris that don't take registration too seriously." Ravic poured a few drops of cognac into his coffee. "One of them is the International. That's why I live there. I don't know how the landlady arranges it. But she must have good connections. Either the police really don't know about it or they are bribed. At any rate I have lived there for quite a long time undisturbed."

Veber leaned back. "Ravic!" he said. "I didn't know that. I only thought you weren't permitted to work here. That's a hell of a situation!"

"It's paradise. Compared with a German concentration camp."

"And the police? If they do come some day?"

"If they catch us we get a few weeks' imprisonment and are deported across the border. Mostly into Switzerland. In case of a second offense we get six months in prison."

"What?"

"Six months," Ravic said.

Veber stared at him. "But that's impossible! That's inhuman!"

"That's what I thought, too. Until I experienced it."

"How do you mean experienced? Has that ever happened to you?"

"Not once. Three times. Just as to hundreds of others as well. In the beginning, when I knew nothing about it and counted on so-called humaneness. After that I went to Spain— where I didn't need any passport—and got a second lesson in applied humaneness. From German and Italian fliers. Then later when I returned to France I, of course, knew the ins and outs of it.''

Veber got up. "But for heaven's sake"—he figured it out—"then you have been imprisoned over a year for nothing.''

"Not as long as that. Only two months.''

"How is that? Didn't you say in the case of a second offense it was six months?''

Ravic smiled. "There are no second offenses when one is experienced. One is deported under one name and simply returns under another. If possible, at another point on the frontier. That's how we avoid it. Since we have no papers it can only be proven if someone recognizes us personally. That very rarely happens. Ravic is my third name. I've used it for almost two years. Nothing has happened in that time. It seems to have brought me luck. I'm beginning to like it more every day. By now I've almost forgotten my real name.''

Veber shook his head. "And all this simply because you are not a Nazi!''

"Naturally. Nazis have first-class papers. And all the visas they want.''

"Nice world we live in! And the government doesn't do a thing!''

"There are several million men out of work for whom the government has to care first. Besides it's not only in France. The same thing is happening everywhere.''

Ravic got up. "Adieu, Veber. I'll look in on the girl again in two hours. And once more at night.''

Veber followed him to the door. "Listen, Ravic," he said. "Why don't you come out to our house sometime? For dinner.''

"Certainly." Ravic knew he would not go. "Sometime soon. Adieu, Veber.''

"Adieu, Ravic. And do come, really.''

Ravic went into the nearest bistro. He sat by a window so that he could look out upon the street. He loved that—to sit without thinking and watch the people passing by. Paris was the city where one could best spend one's time doing nothing.

The waiter wiped the table and waited. "A Pernod," Ravic said.

"With water, sir?''

"No." Ravic deliberated. "Don't bring me a Pernod.''

There was something he had to wash away. A bitter taste.

For that the sweet anise wasn't sharp enough. "Bring me a calvados," he said to the waiter. "A double calvados."

"Very well, sir."

It was Veber's invitation. That tinge of pity in it. To grant someone an evening with a family. The French rarely invite foreigners to their homes; they prefer to take them to restaurants. He had not yet been to Veber's. It was well meant but hard to bear. One could defend oneself against insults; not against pity.

He took a gulp of the apple brandy. Why did he have to explain to Veber his reasons for living in the International? It wasn't necessary. Veber had known all he need know. He knew that Ravic was not permitted to operate. That was enough. That he worked with him nevertheless, was his affair. In this way he made money and could arrange for operations he did not dare perform himself. No one knew about it—only he and the nurse—and she kept quiet. It was the same with Durant. Whenever he had an operation to perform he stayed with the patient until he went under the anesthetic. Then Ravic came and performed the operation for which Durant was too old and incompetent. When the patient awoke later on, there was Durant, the proud surgeon, at his bedside. Ravic saw only the covered patient; he knew only the narrow iodine-stained area of the body bared for the operation. He very often did not know even on whom he operated. Durant gave him the diagnosis and he began to cut. Durant paid Ravic about one-tenth of what he received for an operation. Ravic didn't mind. It was better than not operating at all. With Veber he worked on a more friendly basis. Veber paid him a quarter of the proceeds. That was fair.

Ravic looked through the window. And what besides? There wasn't much else left. But he was alive, that was enough. At a time when everything was tottering he had no wish to build up something that was bound shortly to fall into ruins. It was better to drift than to waste energy; that was the one thing that was irreplaceable. To survive meant everything—until somewhere a goal again became visible. The less energy that took, the better; then one would have it afterwards. The antlike attempt to build up a bourgeois life again and again in a century that was falling to pieces—he had seen that ruin many. It was touching, ridiculous, and heroic at the same time—and useless. It made one weary. An avalanche couldn't be stopped once it had started to move: whoever tried, fell beneath it. Better to wait and later to dig out the victims. On long marches one had to travel light. Also when one was fleeing—

Ravic looked at his watch. It was time to look at Lucienne Martinet. And then go to the Osiris.

The whores in the Osiris were waiting. Although they were examined regularly by an official physician, the madame was not content with that. She could not afford to have anyone contract a disease in her place; for that reason she had made an arrangement with Veber to have the girls privately re-examined each Thursday. Sometimes Ravic substituted for him.

The madame had furnished and equipped a place on the first floor as an examination room. She was proud of the fact that for more than a year none of her customers had caught anything in her establishment; but in spite of all the girls' precautions seventeen cases of venereal disease had been caused by customers.

Rolande, the *gouvernante*, brought Ravic a bottle of brandy and a glass. "I think Marthe has got something," she said.

"All right. I'll examine her carefully."

"I haven't let her work since yesterday. Naturally, she denies it."

"All right, Rolande."

The girls came in in their slips, one after the other. Ravic knew almost all of them; only two were new.

"You don't have to examine me, doctor," said Léonie, a red-haired Gascon.

"Why not?"

"No clients the whole week."

"What does madame say to that?"

"Nothing. I made them order a lot of champagne. Seven, eight bottles a night. Three businessmen from Toulouse. Married. All three of them would have liked to, but none of them dared because of the others. Each was afraid if he came with me the others would talk about it at home. That's why they drank; each thought he would outlast the others." Léonie laughed and scratched herself lazily. "The one who didn't pass out wasn't able to stand up."

"All right. Nevertheless. I've got to examine you."

"It's all right with me. Have you a cigarette, doctor?"

"Yes, here."

Ravic took a swab and colored it. Then he pushed the glass slide under the microscope.

"You know what I don't understand?" Léonie said, watching him.

"What?"

"That you still feel like sleeping with a woman when you do these things."

"I don't understand it either. You're all right. Now who's next?"

"Marthe."

Marthe was pale, slender, and blond. She had the face of a Botticelli angel, but she spoke the argot of the Rue Blondel.

"There is nothing wrong with me, doctor."

"That's fine. Let's have a look at you."

"But there is really nothing wrong."

"All the better."

Suddenly Rolande was standing in the room. She looked at Marthe. The girl stopped talking. She looked at Ravic apprehensively. He examined her thoroughly.

"But it is nothing, doctor. You know how careful I am."

Ravic did not reply. The girl continued to talk—hesitated and began again. Ravic swabbed a second time and examined it.

"You are sick, Marthe," he said.

"What?" She jumped up. "That can't be true."

"It is true."

She looked at him. Then she broke out suddenly—a flood of curses and maledictions. "That swine! That damned swine! I didn't trust him anyway, the slippery trickster! He said he was a student and he ought to know, a medical student, that scoundrel!"

"Why didn't you take care?"

"I did, but it went so quickly, and he said that he, as a student—"

Ravic nodded. The old story—a medical student who had treated himself. After two weeks he had considered himself cured without making a test.

"How long will it take, doctor?"

"Six weeks." Ravic knew it would take longer.

"Six weeks? Six weeks without any income? Hospital? Do I have to go to the hospital?"

"We'll see about that. Maybe we can treat you at home later—if you promise—"

"I'll promise anything! Anything! Only not the hospital!"

"You've got to go at first. There's no other way."

The girl stared at Ravic. All prostitutes feared the hospital. The supervision was very strict there. But there was nothing else to do. Left at home she would furtively go out after a few days, in spite of all promises, and look for men in order to make money and infect them.

"The madame will pay the expenses," Ravic said.

"But I! I! Six weeks without any income! And I have just bought a silver fox on installments! Then the installment will be due and everything will be gone."

She cried. "Come, Marthe," Rolande said.

"You won't take me back! I know!" Marthe sobbed louder. "You won't take me back! You never do it! Then I'll be on the streets. And all because of that slippery dog—"

"We'll take you back. You were good business. Our clients like you."

"Really?" Marthe looked up.

"Of course. And now come."

Marthe left with Rolande. Ravic looked after her. Marthe would not come back. Madame was much too careful. Her next stage was perhaps the cheap brothels in the Rue Blondel. Then the street. Then cocaine, the hospital, peddling flowers or cigarettes. Or, if she were lucky, some pimp who would beat and exploit her and later throw her out.

The dining room of the Hôtel International was in the basement. The lodgers called it the Catacombs. During the day a dim light came through several large, thick, opalescent-glass panes which faced on the courtyard. In the winter it had to be lighted all day long. The room was at once a writing room, a smoking room, an auditorium, an assembly room, and a refuge for those emigrants who had no papers—when there was a police inspection they could escape through the yard into a garage and from there to the next street.

Ravic sat with the doorman of the Scheherazade night club, Boris Morosow, in a section of the Catacombs that the landlady called the Palm Room; on a splindly legged table a solitary miserable palm languished there in a majolica pot. Morosow was a refugee from the first war and had lived in Paris for the last fifteen years. He was one of the few Russians who did not claim to have served in the Czar's Guard and who did not speak of his aristrocratic family.

They were sitting and playing chess. The Catacombs were empty except for one table at which a few people were sitting and drinking and talking in loud voices, breaking into a toast every few minutes.

Morosow looked around angrily. "Can you explain to me, Ravic, why there is such a rumpus here tonight? Why don't these refugees go to bed?"

Ravic smiled. "The refugees in that corner don't concern me, Boris. That is the Fascist section of the hotel. Spain."

"Spain? Weren't you there, too?"

"Yes, but on the other side. Moreover as a doctor. These are Spanish monarchists with Fascist trimmings. The remnants of them. The others have gone back a long time ago. These haven't quite been able to make up their minds yet. Franco was not genteel enough for them. The Moors who butchered Spaniards naturally did not disturb them."

Morosow placed his chessmen. "Then they probably are celebrating the massacre at Guernica. Or the victory of Italian and German machine guns over the miners in Estremadura. Never before have I seen those fellows here."

"They have been here for years. You didn't see them because you never eat here."

"Do you eat here?"

"No."

Morosow grinned. "All right," he said. "Let's skip my next question and your answer, which certainly would be insulting. For all I care, they could have been born here in this hole. If they would only lower their voices. Here—the good old queen's gambit."

Ravic moved the pawn opposite. They made the first moves quickly. Then Morosow began to brood. "There is a variant by Alekhine—"

Ravic saw that one of the Spaniards was coming over. He was a man with close-set eyes and he stopped by their table. Morosow looked at him ill-humoredly. The Spaniard did not stand quite straight. "Gentlemen," he said politely, "Colonel Gomez requests you to drink a glass of wine with him."

"Sir," Morosow replied with equal politeness, "we are just playing a game of chess for the Championship of the Seventeenth Arrondissement. We express our grateful thanks, but we can't come."

The Spaniard did not move a muscle. He turned to Ravic formally as if he were at the court of Philip II. "You rendered a friendly service to Colonel Gomez some time ago. He would like to have a drink with you in token of appreciation before his departure."

"My partner," Ravic replied with the same formality, "has just explained to you that we must play this game today. Give my thanks to Colonel Gomez. I am very sorry."

The Spaniard bowed and went back. Morosow chuckled. "Just like the Russians in the first years. Stuck to their titles and manners as if they were life preservers. What friendly service did you render to this Hottentot?"

"Once I prescribed a laxative for him. The Latin people have a high regard for good digestion."

Morosow winked at Ravic. "The old weakness of democracy. A Fascist in the same situation would have prescribed arsenic for a democrat."

The Spaniard returned. "My name is Navarro. First Lieutenant," he declared with the heavy earnestness of a man who has drunk too much and does not know it. "I am the aide-de-camp of Colonel Gomez. The colonel is leaving Paris tonight. He is going to Spain to join the glorious army of Generalissimo Franco. That's why he would like to drink with you to Spain's freedom and to Spain's army."

"Lieutenant Navarro," Ravic said briefly, "I'm not a Spaniard."

"We know that. You are a German." Navarro showed the shadow of a conspiratorial smile. "That's just the reason for Colonel Gomez's wish. Germany and Spain are friends."

Ravic looked at Morosow. The irony of the situation was marked. Morosow kept from smiling. "Lieutenant Navarro," he said, "I regret that I must insist on finishing this game with Doctor Ravic. The results must be cabled to New York and Calcutta tonight."

"Sir," Navarro replied coldly, "we expected you to decline. Russia is Spain's enemy. The invitation was directed to Doctor Ravic only. We had to invite you too since you were with him."

Morosow placed a knight he had won on his huge flat hand and looked at Ravic. "Don't you think there has been enough of this buffoonery?"

"Yes." Ravic turned around. "I think the simplest thing is that you go back, young man. You have needlessly insulted Colonel Morosow, who is an enemy of the Soviets."

He bent over the chessboard without waiting for an answer. Navarro stood undecided for a moment. Then he left.

"I don't know whether you noticed that I have just promoted you to the rank of colonel, Boris," Ravic said. "As far as I know you were a miserable lieutenant colonel. But it seemed unbearable to me that you should have the same military rank as this Gomez.''

"Don't talk so much, old boy. I've just messed up Alekhine's variant because of these interruptions. That bishop seems to be lost." Morosow looked up. "My God, here comes another one. Another aide-de-camp. What a people!''

"It is Colonel Gomez himself." Ravic leaned back comfortably. "This will be a discussion between two colonels."

"Short one, my son."

The colonel was even more formal than Navarro. He apologized to Morosow because of his aide-de-camp's error. The apology was accepted. Now Gomez invited them to drink together to Franco as a sign of reconciliation since all obstacles had been removed. This time Ravic refused.

"But sir, as a German and an ally—" The colonel was obviously confused.

"Colonel Gomez," said Ravic, who was gradually becoming impatient, "leave the situation as it is. Drink to whomever you like and I'll play chess."

The colonel tried to puzzle it out. "Then you are a—"

"You'd better make no statements," Morosow interrupted him briefly. "It would only lead to conflict."

Gomez became more and more confused. "But you as a White Russian and an officer of the Czar must be against—"

"We don't have to be anything at all. We are old-fashioned creatures. We have different political opinions and, nevertheless, don't break each other's skulls."

Finally it seemed to dawn upon Gomez. He stiffened. "I see," he declared sharply. "Decadent, democratic—"

"My friend," Morosow said, suddenly becoming dangerous, "get out! You should have got out years ago! To Spain. To fight. Germans and Italians fought for you there instead. Adieu."

He got up. Gomez took one step back. He stared at Morosow, disconcerted. Then he abruptly turned around and went back to his table. Morosow sat down again. He sighed and rang for the waitress. "Bring us two double calvados, Clarisse."

Clarisse nodded and disappeared. "Stout, soldierly souls!" Ravic laughed. "A simple mind and a complicated conception of honor make life very difficult when one is drunk, Boris."

"That I see! Here comes the next one already. Who is it this time? Franco himself?"

It was Navarro. He stopped two steps away from the table and addressed Morosow. "Colonel Gomez regrets to be unable to present his challenge. He is leaving Paris tonight. Besides, his mission is too important to risk difficulties with the police." He turned toward Ravic. "Colonel Gomez still owes you the fee for a consultation." He threw a folded five-franc bill on the table and was about to turn away.

"One moment," Morosow said. Clarisse was just then at his side with a tray. He took a glass of calvados, briefly contemplated it, shook his head, and put it back. Then he took one of the water glasses from the tray and negligently tossed it in Navarro's face. "That's to sober you up," he declared calmly. "Remember in the future that one doesn't throw money. And now get away from here, you medieval idiot!"

Navarro stood still in astonishment. He dried his face. The other Spaniards approached. There were four of them. Morosow got up slowly. He was more than a head taller than the Spaniards. Ravic remained sitting. He looked at Gomez. "Don't make yourself ridiculous, you comic-opera characters," he said. "None of you is sober. Within a few minutes you'll be lying here with broken bones. Even if you were sober you would stand no chance." He got up, seized Navarro by the elbows, lifted him, and put him down so near to Gomez that Gomez had to step aside. "And now leave us alone. We did not ask you to annoy us." He took the five-franc bill from the table and put it on the tray. "That's for you, Clarisse. From these gentlemen here."

"The first time I ever got anything from them," Clarisse declared. "Thanks."

Gomez said something in Spanish. The five turned around and went back to their table. "It's a pity," Morosow said. "I'd have liked to beat up those fellows. Sorry that it can't be done because of you, you illegal foundling. Don't you sometimes regret that you can't do it?"

"Not with those. There are others I'd like to get hold of."

A few words in Spanish became audible from the table in the corner. The five rose. A threefold *viva* resounded. The glasses were set down clinking. There was the sound of one breaking. Then the martial group filed out of the room.

"I almost threw this good calvados in his face." Morosow

51

took the glass and emptied it. "And that's the sort that governs Europe now! Were we too such fools once?"

"Yes," Ravic said.

They played for an hour. Then Morosow looked up. "There is Charles," he said. "He seems to be looking for you."

The boy from the concierge's box was coming toward them. He held a little package in his hand. "This was left for you," he said to Ravic.

"For me?"

Ravic examined the package. It was small and wrapped in white tissue paper, tied with a string. There was no address on it. "I'm not expecting any packages. It must be a mistake. Who brought it?"

"A woman—a lady—" the boy stammered.

"A woman or a lady?" Morosow asked.

"Just—just in between."

Morosow grinned. "Pretty sharp."

"There's no name on it. Did she say it was for me?"

"Not just like that. Not your name. She said it was for the doctor who lives here. And—you know the lady."

"Did she say that?"

"No," the boy blurted. "But the other night she was with you."

"From time to time ladies do come in with me," Ravic said. "But you should know that the first virtue of a hotel employee is discretion. Indiscretion is only for cavaliers of the great world."

"Go ahead and open the package, Ravic," Morosow said. "Even if it isn't for you. We've done worse in our deplorable lives."

Ravic laughed and opened it. He unwrapped a small object. It was the wooden Madonna he had seen in the room of the woman—he tried to remember—what was her name?—Madeleine—Mad—he had forgotten it. A name something like that. He examined the tissue paper; there was no slip in it. "All right," he said to the boy. "It's for me."

He placed the Madonna on the table. It looked strange among the chessmen. "A Russian?" Morosow asked.

"No. I thought so, too, at first."

Ravic noticed that the red of the lipstick had been washed off. "What on earth shall I do with it?"

"Put it anywhere. Many things can be put just anywhere.

52

There's plenty of room for everything in this world. Only not for human beings."

"They will have buried the man meanwhile—"

"Is she the one?"

"Yes.

"Did you ever bother to see her again?"

"No."

"Strange," Morosow said, "we always think we've helped and yet we stop just when it's hardest for the other."

"I'm no charitable institution, Boris. And I have seen worse than that and done nothing. Why should it be harder for her now?"

"Because now she's alone. Up to now the man was there even though he was dead. He was above the earth. Now he's below it—gone, not here any more. This"—Morosow pointed at the Madonna—"is not thanks. It is a cry for help."

"I slept with her. Without knowing what had happened. I want to forget that."

"Nonsense! It is the least important thing in the world as long as there is no love in it. I knew a woman who said it was easier to sleep with a man than to call him by his first name." Morosow leaned forward. His large bald head reflected the light. "I will tell you something, Ravic—we ought to be friendly to people if we can and as long as we possibly can because we're still going to commit a few so-called crimes in our lives. At least I will. And probably you too."

"Yes."

Morosow put his arm around the pot containing the meager palm. It trembled slightly. "We all feed on one another. Such occasional little sparks of kindliness—that's something one shouldn't allow to be taken away. It strengthens one for a difficult life."

"All right, I'll go to see her tomorrow."

"Fine," Morosow said. "That's what I meant. And now stop talking so much. Who has white?"

Chapter 5

THE PATRON recognized Ravic immediately. "The lady is in her room," he said.

"Can you call her and say that I am downstairs?"

"Her room has no telephone yet. I am sure you may go up."

"What is the number?"

"Twenty-seven."

"I don't remember her name. What is it?"

The patron showed no surprise. "Madou. Joan Madou," he added. "I don't think it is her real name. Probably a stage name."

"Why stage name?"

"She registered as an actress. It sounds like it, doesn't it?"

"I don't know. I knew an actor who called himself Gustave Schmidt. In reality his name was Alexander Maria Count of Zambona. Gustave Schmidt was his stage name. Didn't sound like one, did it?"

The patron would not concede defeat. "Nowadays so many things happen," he declared philosophically.

"So much doesn't actually happen. When you study history you'll find that we are living in a relatively calm era."

"Thanks, it's enough for me."

"For me, too. But one has to find consolation wherever one can. Number twenty-seven, you said?"

"Yes, sir."

Ravic knocked. No one answered. He knocked once more and heard an indistinct voice. When he opened the door he saw the woman. She was sitting on the bed, which stood against the partition wall. She was dressed and wore the blue tailored suit in which Ravic had first seen her. She would have looked less forlorn had she been lying somewhere, negligently attired in a dressing gown. But this way, dressed for no one and nothing, out of mere habit which now had no meaning, there was something about her that touched Ravic's heart. He was familiar with it—he had seen hundreds of people sitting this way—refugees driven helplessly into foreign countries. A little island of uncertain existence—that was how they sat, now knowing where to go—and only habit kept them alive.

He closed the door behind him. "I hope I'm not disturbing you," he said and at once felt how meaningless the words were. What was there that could still disturb this woman? There was nothing that could disturb her.

He put his hat on a chair. "Were you able to settle everything?" he asked.

"Yes. There wasn't much."

"No trouble?"

"No."

Ravic sat down in the only armchair in the room. The springs squeaked and he could feel that one was broken.

"Did you intend to go out?" he asked.

"Yes. Sometime later. Nowhere in particular—just to go. What else can one do?"

"Nothing. That's right, for a few days. Don't you know anyone in Paris?"

"No."

"No one?"

The woman raised her head with a tired movement. "No one—except you, the patron, the waiter, and the chambermaid." She smiled faintly. "That's not many, is it?"

"No. Did Mr.—" Ravic tried to remember the name of the dead man. He had forgotten it.

"No," the woman said. "Raszinsky had friends here, but I've never seen them. He fell ill as soon as we arrived."

Ravic had not intended to stay long. Now, seeing the woman sitting that way, he changed his mind. "Have you had dinner already?" he asked.

"No. I am not hungry."

"Have you eaten anything at all today?"

"Yes. This noon. It's easier during the day. In the evening—"

Ravic looked around. The small bare room smelled of cheerlessness and November. "It's time you get out of here," he said. "Come. We'll go and have something to eat."

He expected the woman to object. She seemed so indifferent that nothing could arouse her. But she stood up at once and reached for her raincoat.

"That won't do," he said. "The coat is too thin. Haven't you a warmer one? It is cold outside."

"It was raining before—"

"It is still raining. But it is cold. Can't you put something on underneath? Another coat or at least a sweater?"

"I have a sweater."

She went toward the larger suitcase. Ravic noted that she had hardly unpacked anything. She got a black sweater out of the suitcase, took her jacket off, and pulled on the sweater. She had beautiful straight shoulders. Then she took the Basque beret and put on her jacket and coat. "Is this better?"

"Much better."

They went down the stairs. The patron was no longer there. In his stead the concierge sat beside the keyboard. He was sorting letters and smelled of garlic. A spotted cat sat motionless beside him and watched him.

"Do you still have the feeling that you can't eat anything?" Ravic asked outside.

"I don't know. Not much, I think."

Ravic hailed a taxi. "Well, then we'll drive to the Belle Aurore. One doesn't have to eat a full dinner there."

The Belle Aurore was not crowded. It was already too late for that. They found a table in the small upstairs room with the low ceiling. Besides them, there was only one couple, sitting by the window and eating cheese—and a solitary thin man, with a mountain of oysters in front of him. The waiter came and eyed the checked tablecloth critically. Then he decided to change it.

"Two vodkas," Ravic ordered. "Cold.

"We'll drink something and eat hors d'oeuvres," he said to the woman. "I think that's best for you. This restaurant is famous for its hors d'oeuvres. There's hardly anything else here. Anyhow you seldom get to eat anything else. There are dozens of them, warm and cold, and they're all very good. We'll try them."

The waiter brought the vodka and got his pad ready. "A carafe of vin rosé," Ravic said. "Have you Anjou?"

"Anjou, open, rosé. Very well, sir."

"Fine. A large carafe in ice. And the hors d'oeuvres."

The waiter left. At the door he almost collided with a woman in a red-feathered hat, who was rushing up the stairs.

She pushed him aside and approached the thin man with the oysters. "Albert," she said. "You swine—"

"Sh, sh—" Albert gestured and turned around.

"Don't sh, sh me." The woman put her wet umbrella across the table and sat down determinedly. Albert did not seem to be surprised. "Chérie," he said and began to whisper.

Ravic smiled and lifted his glass. "We'll drink this straight down. *Salute.*"

"*Salute,*" Joan Madou said and drank.

The hors d'oeuvres were rolled in on a small wagon. "What would you like?" Ravic looked at the woman. "I think it will be simplest if I fill a plate for you."

He piled a plate full and handed it to her. "It won't matter if you don't like any of it. There are more wagons to come. This is just the beginning."

He filled a plate for himself and began to eat, not concerning himself further about her. Suddenly he felt very hungry. When he looked up after a while he saw that she too was eating. He shelled a langoustine and held it out to her. "Try this. It's better than languoste. And now the pâté maison. With a crust of white bread. So, that's not bad at all. And a little of the wine with it. Light, dry, and cool."

"You are going to a lot of trouble for me," Joan Madou said.

"Yes—like a headwaiter," Ravic laughed.

"No. But you are going to a lot of trouble for me."

"I don't like to eat alone. That's all there is to it. Just like you."

"I'm not a good companion."

"You are," Ravic replied. "For dining, you are. For dining you are a first-rate companion. I can't bear garrulous people. Or those with loud voices."

He looked across the room toward Albert. The red-feathered hat was just explaining to him very audibly why he was such a swine, at the same time rhythmically rapping on the table with her umbrella. Albert was listening and did not seem impressed.

Joan Madou smiled briefly. "Neither can I."

"Here comes the next wagon with supplies. Would you like to have something at once or do you want a cigarette first?"

"A cigarette first."

"All right. Today I have different cigarettes, not those with black tobacco."

He gave her a light. She leaned back and inhaled the smoke deeply. Then she looked straight at him. "It is good to sit this way," she said and for a moment it seemed to him that she was going to cry.

They drank coffee in the Colisée. The large room facing the Champs Elysées was overcrowded, but they secured a table downstairs in the bar. The upper part of the walls was glass behind which parrots and cockatoos hovered and multi-colored tropical birds soared to and fro.

"Have you thought about what you're going to do?" Ravic asked.

"No, not yet."

"Did you have anything definite in mind when you came here?"

The woman hesitated. "No, nothing in particular."

"I'm not asking out of curiosity."

"I know that. You think I should do something. That's what I want, too. I say so to myself every day. But then—"

"The landlord told me you were an actress. I didn't ask him. He told me when I asked for your name."

"Had you forgotten it?"

Ravic glanced up. She looked at him calmly. "Yes," he said. "I left the slip of paper in my hotel and couldn't recall it at the moment."

"Do you know it now?"

"Yes. Joan Madou."

"I'm not a good actress," the woman said. "I only played small parts. Nothing at all in the last few years. Also I don't speak French well enough."

"What do you speak then?"

"Italian. I was brought up in Italy. And some English and Romanian. My father was Romanian. He is dead. My mother is British; she is still living in Italy; I don't know where."

Ravic only half listened. He was bored and he no longer knew what to talk about. "Have you done anything else?" he asked, just for the sake of asking. "Besides those small parts you played?"

"Only what went with them. Some dancing and singing."

Ravic looked at her doubtfully. She didn't seem suited for that. There was something pale and vague about her and she was not attractive.

"That may be easier to try here," he said. "For that you need not speak perfectly."

"No. But first I have to find something. It is difficult if one doesn't know anyone."

Morosow, Ravic suddenly thought. The Scheherazade. Naturally! Morosow ought to know about such things. The idea revived him. Morosow had dragged him into this dull evening—now the woman could be passed on to him and Boris would have a chance to show what he could do. "Do you know Russian?" he asked.

"A little. A few songs. Gypsy songs. They are similar to Romanian ones. Why?"

"I know someone who knows about these things. Maybe he can help you. I'll give you his address."

"I don't think there's much point to it. Agents are the same everywhere. Recommendations are of little help."

Ravic realized she thought he wanted to get rid of her in the easiest way. Since that was so, he protested. "The man I mean is not an agent. He is the doorman of the Scheherazade. That's a Russian night club on Montmartre."

"Doorman?" Joan Madou lifted her head. "That is something else," she said. "Doormen are much better informed than agents. That may be something. Do you know him well?"

Ravic looked at her in surprise. Suddenly she had spoken like a professional. "He is a friend of mine," he said. "His name is Boris Morosow and he has been with the Scheherazade for the last ten years. There's always a pretty big show. They change the numbers frequently. He's on good terms with the manager. If there's no spot for you in the Scheherazade he will be sure to know of something else. Will you try it?"

"Yes. When?"

"It would be best around nine o'clock in the evening. He's not busy then and he will have time for you. I'll tell him about it." Ravic looked forward to seeing Morosow's face. Suddenly he felt better. The slight burden of responsibility he had still felt had disappeared. He had done what he could and now it was up to her. "Are you tired?" he asked.

Joan Madou looked straight into his eyes. "I'm not tired," she said. "But I know that it is no pleasure to sit here with me. You came out of pity and I thank you for it. You took me out of my room and you spoke to me. That means a great deal to me, since I've hardly spoken to anyone for days. Now

59

I'll go. You have done more than enough for me. What would have become of me otherwise?''

My God, Ravic thought, now she is starting that. He looked uncomfortably at the glass wall before him. A fat dove was trying to ravish a cockatoo. The cockatoo was so bored that she did not even shake him off. She merely went on eating and ignored him.

"It was not pity."

"What else?"

The dove gave it up. He hopped down from the broad back of the cockatoo and began to clean his feathers. The cockatoo indifferently lifted her tail and defecated.

"We'll both drink a cognac now," Ravic said. "That's the best answer. But believe me I'm not really such a philanthropist. There are many evenings when I sit around by myself. Do you consider that particularly interesting?"

"No, but I'm a bad partner. That's worse."

"I've given up looking for partners. Here's your cognac. *Salute!''*

"Salute.''

Ravic put his glass down. "So. And now we'll leave this menagerie. You wouldn't like to go back to your hotel, would you?"

Joan Madou shook her head.

"All right. Then let's go somewhere else. Let's go to the Scheherazade. We'll have a drink there—we both seem to need it—and at the same time you can find out what's going on there."

It was almost there o'clock in the morning. They stood in front of the Hôtel de Milan. "Have you had enough to drink?" Ravic asked.

Joan Madou hesitated. "I thought I had enough when I was there, in the Scheherazade. But now here, looking at this door—it wasn't enough."

"Something can be done about that. Maybe we can still get something here in the hotel. Otherwise we'll go to some bar and buy a bottle. Come."

She looked at him. Then she looked at the door. "Very well," she said with determination. Yet she continued to stand there. "To go up there," she said, "In that empty room—"

"I'll go with you. And we'll take a bottle with us."

60

The doorman woke up. "Have you anything to drink?" Ravic asked.

"Champagne cocktail?" the doorman asked immediately, businesslike, but still yawning.

"Thank you. Something stronger. Cognac, a bottle."

"Courvoisier, Martell, Hennessy, Bisquit Dubouchée?"

"Courvoisier."

"Very well, sir. I'll take the cork out and bring the bottle up."

They walked upstairs. "Have you got your key?" Ravic asked the woman.

"The room is not locked."

"Your money and your papers might be stolen if you don't lock it."

"That could happen even if I locked it."

"That's true with these keys. Although it isn't quite as easy then."

"Maybe. But I don't want to come in alone from outside and take a key and open a door in order to enter an empty room—that's as if I were opening a tomb. It is enough already to have to enter this room—in which nothing awaits one but a few suitcases."

"Nothing awaits us anywhere," Ravic said. "We always have to bring everything with us."

"That may be. But there is at least sometimes a merciful illusion. Here there's nothing—"

Joan Madou flung her Basque beret and coat on the bed and looked at Ravic. Her eyes were light and large in her pale face and as though fixed in a furious desperation. She stood thus for a moment. Then she began to walk in the small room back and forth, with long strides, hands in the pockets of her jacket, resiliently swinging her body when she turned. Ravic watched her attentively. Suddenly she had strength and a catlike grace, and the room seemed much too narrow for her.

There was a knock. The doorman brought in the cognac. "Would the lady and gentleman care to eat something?" he asked. "Cold chicken, a sandwich—"

"That would be a waste of time, brother." Ravic paid and shoved him out of the room. Then he poured two glasses full. "Here. It is simple and barbaric—but the more primitive the better in difficult situations. Refinement is something for quiet times. Drink this."

"And then?"

"Then you will drink another."

"I have tried that. It didn't help. It is not good to be drunk when one is alone. Things just become sharper."

"One only has to be drunk enough. Then it works."

Ravic sat on a narrow wobbly chaise longue which stood by the wall opposite the bed. He hadn't seen it before. "Was this here when you moved in?" he asked.

She shook her head. "I had it put there. I didn't like to sleep in the bed. It seemed so pointless. A bed, and to have to undress and all that. What for? Mornings and in the daytime it was somehow possible. But nights—"

"You must have something to do." Ravic lit a cigarette. "It's too bad we didn't meet Morosow in the Scheherazade. I didn't know that today was his day off. Do go there tomorrow night. About nine o'clock. I'm sure he'll find something for you. Even if it's work in the kitchen. Then at least you would be busy at night. That's what you want, isn't it?"

"Yes." Joan Madou stopped walking. She drank her glass of cognac and sat down on the bed. "I've walked about, outside, every night. As long as one walks everything is easier. Only when one sits down and the ceiling falls on one's head—"

"Didn't anything ever happen to you on the street? Nothing stolen?"

"No. I probably don't look as if I had anything one could steal." She held her empty glass out to Ravic. "And as for the other—I waited for it often enough. At least to have someone speak to me! To be something more than mere nothing, mere walking! That at least eyes would look at one, eyes and not just stones. That one would not run around like an outcast! Like someone on a strange planet!" She threw her hair back and took the glass that Ravic handed her. "I don't know why I'm talking about it," she said. "I don't want to. Maybe it is because I was silent all those days. Maybe because today for the first time—" She interrupted herself. "Don't listen to me—"

"I'm drinking," Ravic said. "Say whatever you want. It is night. No one hears you. I am listening to myself. Everything will be forgotten by tomorrow."

He leaned back. Somewhere in the house there was the sound of rushing water. The radiator rattled and the rain knocked with soft fingers at the window.

"When one comes back and switches off the light—and

62

the darkness falls on one like chloroform on a wad of cotton, and one turns on the light again and stares and stares—"

I must be drunk already, Ravic thought. Earlier than usual today. Or it may be the faint light. Or both. This is not the same insignificant, faded woman any longer. This is someone else. Suddenly there are eyes. There is a face. Something is looking at me. It must be the shadows. The soft fire behind my forehead that is illuminating her. The first glow of drunkenness.

He did not listen to what Joan Madou said. He knew about all that and no longer wanted to know about it. To be alone—the eternal refrain of life. It wasn't better or worse than anything else. One talked too much about it. One was always and never alone. A violin, suddenly—somewhere out of a twilight—in a garden on the hills around Budapest. The heavy scent of chestnuts. The wind. And dreams crouched on one's shoulders like young owls, their eyes becoming lighter in the dusk. A night that never became night. The hour when all women were beautiful.

He looked up. "Thank you," Joan Madou said.

"Why?"

"Because you've let me talk without listening. It helped me. I needed it."

Ravic nodded. He noticed that her glass was empty again. "All right," he said. "I'll leave the bottle here for you."

He got up. A room. A woman. Nothing else. A pale face in which there was no longer any radiance. "Do you really want to go?" Joan Madou asked. She looked around as if someone were hidden in the room.

"Here is Morosow's address. His name, so that you won't forget it. Tomorrow night at nine." Ravic wrote it on a prescription pad. Then he tore the sheet off and put it on the suitcase.

Joan Madou had got up. She reached for her coat and beret. Ravic looked at her. "You needn't see me down."

"I don't mean to do that. I just don't want to stay here. Not now. I want to walk around somewhere."

"But you'll have to come back again later anyhow. The same thing all over again. Why don't you stay here? Now that you've already overcome it."

"It will be morning soon. When I come back it will be morning. Then it will be easier."

Ravic went to the window. It was still raining. Streamers, wet and gray, drifted with the wind around the yellow halos of the street lamps. "Come," he said, "we'll have another drink and then you'll go to bed. This is no weather for walking."

He picked up the bottle. Suddenly Joan Madou was close at his side. "Don't leave me here," she said quickly and urgently, and he felt her breath. "Don't leave me here alone, tonight. I don't know why, but not tonight! Tomorrow I'll have courage but tonight I can't be alone, I'm weary and weak and spent, I have no strength left, you shouldn't have taken me out—not tonight—I can't be alone now!"

Ravic carefully put the bottle on the table and loosened her hands from his arm. "Child," he said, "we have to get used to everything sometime." He glanced at the chaise longue. "I could sleep on that. There is no point in going anywhere else now. I need a few hours' sleep. I have to operate at nine in the morning. I could sleep here just as well as at my own place. It wouldn't be my first night watch. Would that do?"

She nodded. She was still standing close beside him.

"I must be out by seven-thirty. Damned early. It will wake you up."

"That doesn't matter. I'll get up and make breakfast for you, everything—"

"Nothing of the sort," Ravic said. "I'll have my breakfast in some café like a sensible workingman; coffee with rum and croissants. I can do everything else in the hospital. It will delight me to ask Eugénie for a bath. All right, let's stay here. Two lost souls in November. You take the bed. If you like I can go down and stay with the old doorman till you're ready."

"No," Joan Madou said.

"I won't run away. Besides we'll need some things. Pillows, blankets, and such."

"I can ring for him."

"I can do that myself." Ravic looked for the button. "It's better if a man does it."

The doorman came quickly. He had another bottle of cognac in his hand. "You overrate us," Ravic said. "Many thanks. We belong to the postwar generation. A blanket, a pillow, and some sheets. I've got to sleep here. Too cold and too much rain outside. I had a bad case of pneumonia and it's only two days since I left bed. Could you arrange that?"

"Naturally, sir. I thought something of the sort myself."

"All right." Ravic lit a cigarette. "I'll go out into the hall. I'll look at the shoes in front of the doors. That's an old hobby of mine. I won't run away," he said, noticing Joan Madou's expression. "I'm not Joseph of Egypt. I'll not leave my coat behind."

The doorman returned with the things. He stopped abruptly when he saw Ravic standing in the hall. Then his face brightened. "It's not often one sees anything like that," he said.

"I rarely do it myself. Only on birthdays and Christmas. Let me have those things. I'll take them inside. What's that?"

"A hot-water bottle. Because of your pneumonia."

"Excellent! But I keep my lungs warm with cognac." Ravic pulled a few bills out of his pocket.

"I'm sure you have no pajamas, sir. I could get you a pair."

"Thanks, brother." Ravic looked at the old man. "They'd certainly be too small for me."

"On the contrary, they would fit you. They are perfectly new. Confidentially, an American once gave them to me as a gift. He had received them from a lady. I don't wear such things. I wear nightshirts. They are perfectly new, sir."

"All right, bring them up. Let's have a look at them."

Ravic waited in the hall. Three pairs of shoes stood before the doors. A pair of high boots with stretchable elastic sides. Thunderous snores emerged from the room behind. The others were a pair of brown men's shoes and a pair of high-buttoned patent leather shoes. They both stood in front of one door and seemed strangely forlorn although they were together.

The doorman brought the pajamas. They were marvelous pajamas. Blue artificial silk with gold stars on them. Ravic contemplated them for a while, speechless. He understood the American.

"Magnificent, aren't they?" the doorman asked proudly.

The pajamas were new. They were still in the box of the Grands Magasins du Louvre where they had been bought. "It's a pity," Ravic said. "I'd like to have seen the lady who chose them."

"You may have them for tonight. You don't have to buy them, sir."

"How much do I owe you?"

"Whatever you think."

Ravic drew his hand from his pocket. "This is too much sir," the doorman said.

"Aren't you a Frenchman?"

"I am. From Saint-Nazaire."

"Then you've been spoiled by the Americans. Besides—nothing is too much for those pajamas."

"I'm glad you like them. Good night, sir. I'll call on the lady for them tomorrow."

"I'll return them myself tomorrow morning. Wake me at seven-thirty. But knock quietly. I'll hear you. Good night."

"Look at that," Ravic said to Joan Madou, showing her the pajamas. "A costume for Santa Claus. This doorman is a magician. I'll even put the things on. It takes both courage and unselfconsciousness to be ridiculous."

He arranged the blankets on the chaise longue. It didn't matter to him whether he slept in his hotel or here. In the hall he had seen a passable bathroom and had got a new tooth-brush from the doorman. All the other things didn't matter. The woman was somehow like a patient.

He filled a tumbler with cognac and set it at the bedside with one of the small glasses the doorman had brought. "I think that will be enough for you," he said. "It's simpler this way. I won't need to get up and refill it. I'll take the bottle and the other glass over here with me."

"I don't need the small glass. I can drink from the other."

"That's even better." Ravic arranged himself on the chaise longue. He was glad the woman wasn't fussing about whether he was comfortable. She had what she wanted—thank God, she wasn't displaying any superfluous house-wifely qualities.

He filled his glass and put the bottle on the floor. "*Salute!*"

"*Salute!*" Joan Madou said. "And thanks."

"That's all right. I wasn't in the mood for walking in the rain anyway."

"Is it still raining?"

"Yes."

The gentle knocking penetrated the quiet on the outside—as though something wanted to come in, gray, cheerless, and formless, something that was saddder than sadness—a remote anonymous memory, an endless wave drifting in toward them and trying to take back and bury what it had once washed up on an island and forgotten—a little bit of humankind and light and thought.

"A good night for drinking—"

"Yes—and a bad night for being alone."

Ravic remained silent for a while. "We have to get used to it," he said then. "All that held things together before is now destroyed. Today we have fallen apart like a necklace of glass beads whose string is broken. Nothing is solid any more." He refilled his glass. "As a boy I slept in a meadow one night. It was summer and the sky was very clear. Before I fell asleep I saw Orion on the horizon, standing above the woods. Then I woke up in the middle of the night—and suddenly Orion was standing high above me. I have never forgotten that. I had learned that the earth is a planet and rotates; but I had learned it as one learns something from books and does not quite realize. But now, for the first time I felt that it really was like that. I felt that the earth was silently flying through the immensities of space. I felt it so strongly that I almost believed I had to hold onto something in order not to be hurled off. Probably it happened because emerging from a deep sleep and bereft for a moment of memory and habit, I looked into the huge, displaced sky. Suddenly the earth was no longer firm—and since then it has never become wholly firm again—"

He emptied his glass. "It makes some things more difficult and others easier." He looked at Joan Madou. "I don't know how far you've gone. When you are tired enough, just don't answer any more."

"Not yet. Soon. There's a spot somewhere that is still awake. Awake and cold."

Ravic put the bottle down on the floor beside him. From the warmth of the room a brown tiredness trickled slowly into him. The shadows came. The flapping of wings. A strange room, night, and outside like remote drums the monotonous beating of the rain—a hut and a little light on the verge of chaos, a small fire in a meaningless wilderness—an unknown face toward which one spoke—

"Have you ever felt that, too?" he asked.

She remained silent awhile. "Yes. Not exactly. Differently. When for days I had not spoken to anyone and walked for nights—and there were people everywhere—who were at home somewhere. Only I wasn't. Then everything slowly became unreal—as if I were drowned and walking through a strange city under water—''

Outside someone came up the stairs. Keys jingled and a door clicked shut. Immediately afterwards water gushed from a faucet.

"Why do you stay in Paris if you don't know anyone?" Ravic asked. He felt that he was getting very sleepy.

"I don't know. Where else shall I go?"

"Haven't you any place to go back to?"

"No. One cannot go back."

The wind chased a shower of drops across the window. "Why did you come to Paris?" Ravic asked.

Joan Madou did not answer. He thought she had already fallen asleep. "Raszinsky and I came to Paris because we wanted to separate," she said then.

Ravic heard it without surprise. There were hours when nothing surprised one. In the room opposite, the man who had just come in began to vomit. They heard his muffled gasps through the door. "Then why were you so desperate?" Ravic asked.

"Because he was dead! Dead! Suddenly he was no more! Never to be called back again! Dead! No chance to make things right! Don't you understand?" Joan Madou sat up in bed and stared at Ravic.

"Yes," he said and thought: It is not true. Not because he was dead. Because he left you before you could leave him. Because he left you alone before you were ready.

"I—I should have been different to him—I was—"

"Forget it. Regret is the most useless thing in the world. One cannot recall anything. And one cannot rectify anything. Otherwise we would all be saints. Life did not intend to make us perfect. Whoever is perfect belongs in a museum."

Joan Madou did not answer. Ravic watched her drink and lie back on her pillow. There was still something—but he was too tired to think about it. Besides, it made no difference to him. He wanted to sleep. Tomorrow he had to operate. All this no longer concerned him. He put the empty glass on the floor next to the bottle. Strange where one sometimes gets oneself, he thought.

Chapter 6

LUCIENNE MARTINET was sitting by the window when Ravic came in. "How does it feel," he asked, "to be out of bed for the first time?"

The girl looked at him and then out at the gray afternoon and back at Ravic. "Not very good weather today," he said.

"It is," she replied. "For me it is."

"Why?"

"Because I don't have to go out."

She sat crouched in her chair, a cheap cotton kimono with poppies on it drawn around her shoulders, a slender insignificant being with poor teeth—but to Ravic she was for the moment more beautiful than Helen of Troy. She was a piece of life he had rescued with his own hands. It was nothing to be particularly proud of; one he had lost shortly before; the next he might lose, too; and in the end one lost all of them and oneself too. But this girl, for the moment, was saved.

"It's no fun to drag around hats in weather like this," Lucienne said.

"Did you deliver hats?"

"Yes. For Madame Lanvert. That shop in the Avenue Matignon. We had to work until five. Then I had to deliver hat boxes to the customers. Now it is five-thirty. By this time I would be on my way." She looked out of the window. "Too bad it isn't raining harder. It was better yesterday. It poured. Now someone else has to go through it."

Ravic sat down opposite her on a seat by the window. Strange, he thought. One always expects people to be unreservedly happy after escaping death. They hardly ever are. Nor is this one. A minor miracle happened to her and the only thing that interests her about it is that she doesn't have to walk through the rain. "How did you happen to come to just this hospital, Lucienne?" he asked.

She looked at him warily. "Someone told me about it."

"Who?"

"An acquaintance."

"What acquaintance?"

The girl hesitated. "An acquaintance who was here, too. I brought her here. Up to the door. That's why I knew about it."

"When was that?"

"A week before I came."

"Was it the one who died during the operation?"

"Yes."

"And nevertheless you came here?"

"Yes," Lucienne said indifferently. "Why not?"

Ravic did not say what he had intended to say. He looked into the small cold face that had once been soft and that life had so quickly made hard. "Did you go to the same midwife, too?" he asked.

Lucienne did not answer. "Or to the same doctor? You needn't be afraid of telling me. After all I don't know who it was."

"Mary went there first. A week earlier. Ten days earlier."

"And you went there later in spite of the fact that you knew what had happened to her?"

Lucienne raised her shoulders. "What could I do? I had to risk it. I didn't know of anyone else. A child—what would I do with a child?" She looked out of the window again. On a balcony opposite stood a man in suspenders, holding an umbrella. "How much longer will I have to stay here, doctor?"

"About one week."

"One week more."

"That's not long. Why?"

"It costs and costs—"

"Maybe we can make it a day or two less."

"Do you think I can pay it off in installments? I haven't enough money. It is expensive, thirty francs a day."

"Who told you that?"

"The nurse."

"Which one? Eugénie of course—"

"Yes. She said the operation and the bandages would cost extra. Is that very expensive?"

"You have paid for the operation."

"The nurse said it hadn't been nearly enough."

"The nurse doesn't know much about that, Lucienne. You'd better ask Doctor Veber later."

70

"I'd like to know soon."

"Why?"

"Then I can plan the length of time I'll have to work to pay it off." Lucienne looked at her hands. Her fingers were thin and pricked. "I've another month's rent to pay," she said. "When I came here, it was the thirteenth. I should have given notice on the fifteenth. Now I shall have to pay for another month. For nothing."

"Haven't you got anyone to help you?"

Lucienne glanced up. Suddenly her face seemed ten years older. "You know about that yourself, doctor. He was just angry. He didn't know I was so ignorant. Otherwise he wouldn't have had anything to do with me."

Ravic nodded. Things like this weren't new to him. "Lucienne," he said, "we could try to get something from the woman who did the abortion. It was her fault. All you need do is to give us her name."

The girl straightened up quickly. Suddenly she was all resistance. "Police? No! Then I'd get mixed up in it myself."

"Without police. We would only threaten."

She laughed bitterly. "You won't get anything from her that way. She is made of iron. I had to pay her three hundred francs. And for that—" She smoothed her kimono. "Some people just haven't any luck," she said without resignation as if she spoke of someone else and not of herself.

"On the contrary," Ravic replied. "You had a lot of luck."

He saw Eugénie in the operating room. She was polishing nickel-plated instruments. It was one of her hobbies. She was so absorbed in her work that she did not hear him come in.

"Eugénie," he said.

She turned around, startled. "Oh you! Do you always have to frighten people?"

"I don't think I have that much personality. But you shouldn't frighten the patients with your stories about fees and costs."

Eugénie drew herself up, the polishing rags in her hand. "Naturally that whore had to blab right away."

"Eugénie," Ravic said, "there are more whores among women who have never slept with a man than among those who make their difficult living that way. Not to mention the married ones. Besides, the girl wasn't blabbing. You just spoiled the day for her. That's all.''

"What of it? Sensitive and leading that sort of life!''

You walking moral catechism, Ravic thought. You disgusting model of conscious virtue—what do you know of the forlornness of this little milliner who courageously went to the same midwife who had ruined her friend—and to the same hospital in which the other had died—and who has nothing to say except: What else could I have done? And: How can I pay for it?

"You should marry, Eugénie," he said. "A widower with children. Or the owner of a funeral parlor.''

"Mr. Ravic," the nurse replied with dignity, "will you kindly not concern yourself with my private affairs? Otherwise I'll have to complain to Doctor Veber.''

"You do that anyway all day long." Ravic was pleased to see two red spots appear over her cheekbones. "Why are pious people so rarely loyal, Eugénie? Cynics have the best character; idealists are the least bearable. Doesn't that make you think?''

"Thank God, no.''

"That's what I thought. I am going now to the children of sin. To the Osiris. Just in case Doctor Veber should need me.''

"I hardly think Doctor Veber will need you.''

"Virginity does not quite bestow clairvoyance. He might need me. I'll be there until above five. Then at my hotel.''

"Nice hotel, that den of Jews!''

Ravic turned around. "Eugénie, all refugees are not Jews. Not even all Jews are Jews. And many of whom you wouldn't believe it are Jews. I even knew a Jewish Negro once. He was a terribly lonely man. The only thing he loved was Chinese food. That's how life is.''

The nurse did not answer. She was polishing a nickel plate that was completely spotless.

Ravic was sitting in the bistro on the Rue Boissière, staring through the rainy windows when he saw the man. It was like a blow in the solar plexus. In the first moment he felt only the shock without realizing what it was—but in the next second he had pushed the table aside, jumped from his seat, and thrust himself ruthlessly toward the door through the crowded place . . .

Someone caught him by the arm and held onto him. He

turned around. "What?" he asked uncomprehendingly. "What?"

It was the waiter. "You did not pay, sir."

"What?—Oh yes—I'll be back—" He pulled his arm free. The waiter flushed. "We don't allow that here. You have to—"

"Here—"

Ravic pulled a bill out of his pocket, flung it at the waiter, and thrust the door open. He pushed past a group of people and ran around the corner to the right, along the Rue Boissière.

Someone yelled behind him. He recollected himself, stopped running, and walked on as quickly as he could without being conspicuous. It is impossible, he thought, it is absolutely impossible. I must be mad, it is impossible! The face, that face, it must be a resemblance, some kind of damned devilish resemblance, an idiotic trick played by my nerves—it cannot be in Paris, that face, it is Germany, it is in Berlin, the window was swept by rain, one couldn't see through it clearly, I must have been mistaken, certainly . . .

He pushed himself through the crowd letting out from a movie, hastily, searching every face he passed; he peered beneath hats, he met irritated and astonished looks, he went on, to other faces, other hats, gray, black, blue, he passed them, he turned back, he stared at them—

He stopped at the intersection of the Avenue Kléber. He suddenly remembered, a woman, a woman with a poodle— and immediately behind her he had seen that man.

He had long since passed the woman with the poodle. Quickly he walked back. Seeing the woman with the dog from a distance, he stopped at the curb. He clenched his fists in his pockets, and he painstakingly watched every passer-by. The poodle stopped at a lamppost, sniffed, and lifted its hind leg with infinite deliberation. Then he ceremoniously scratched the pavement and ran on. Ravic suddenly felt his neck wet with perspiration. He waited another few minutes—the face did not appear. He looked into the parked cars. No one was in them. He turned back again and walked quickly to the subway at the Avenue Kléber. He ran down into the entrance, bought a ticket, and walked along the platform. There were a good many people there. Before he got through searching, a train thundered in, stopped, and disappeared in the tunnel. The platform was empty.

Slowly he walked back to the bistro. He sat down at the

table at which he had been sitting. The glass half full of calvados was still there. It seemed strange that it was still standing there.

The waiter shuffled toward Ravic. "Excuse me, sir, I didn't know—"

"Never mind!" Ravic said. "Bring me another calvados."

"Another?" The waiter looked at the half-filled glass on the table. "Don't you want to drink that first?"

"No. Bring me another."

The waiter lifted the glass and smelled it. "Isn't it good?"

"It's all right, only I want another."

"Very well, sir."

I was mistaken, Ravic thought. This rain-swept window, partly blurred—how could anything be positively recognized? He stared through the window. He stared attentively, like a hunter lying in wait, he watched every person passing by—but, at the same time, gray and sharp, a moving picture flashed shadowlike across it, a shred of memory . . .

Berlin. A summer evening in 1933. The house of the Gestapo Blood; a bare room without windows; the sharp light of naked electric bulbs; a red-stained table with binding straps; the night-tortured clarity of his brain that had been startled out of unconsciousness a dozen times by being half choked in a pail of water; his kidneys so beaten they no longer ached; the distorted, helpless face of Sybil before him; a couple of torturers in uniform holding her—and a smiling face and a voice explaining in a friendly way what would happen to Sybil if a confession were not forthcoming—Sybil who three days later was reported to have been found hanged. . . .

The waiter appeared and put the glass on the table. "This is another brand, sir. Didier from Caen, older."

"All right. Thanks."

Ravic emptied his glass. He got a package of cigarettes out of his pocket, took one out and lit it. His hands were not yet steady. He flung the match on the floor and ordered another calvados. That face, that smiling face which he thought he had just seen again—he must have been mistaken. It was impossible that Haake was in Paris. Impossible! He shook off the memories. It was senseless to drive oneself mad about it as long as one couldn't do anything. The time for that would come when everything back there collapsed and one could return. Till then . . .

He called the waiter and paid. But he could not help searching every face on the streets.

He was sitting with Morosow in the Catacombs.

"Do you think it was he?" Morosow asked.

"No. But he looked it. A crused sort of resemblance. Or my memory is no longer to be trusted."

"Bad luck that you were in the bistro."

"Yes."

Morosow remained silent awhile. "Makes one damn jumpy, doesn't it?" he said then.

"No. Why?"

"Because one doesn't know."

"I know."

Morosow did not reply.

"Ghosts," Ravic said. "I thought I'd be over that by now."

"One never is. I went through the same thing. Especially at the beginning. During the first five or six years. I'm still waiting for three of them who are in Russia. There were seven. Four have died. Two of them were shot by their own party. I've been waiting now for more than twenty years. Since 1917. One of the three who is still alive must be seventy by now. The other two, about forty or fifty. They're the ones I still hope I'll get. They are for my father."

Ravic looked at Boris. He was over sixty, but a giant. "You will get them," he said.

"Yes." Morosow opened and closed his big hands. "That's what I'm waiting for. That's why I live more carefully. I don't drink so often now. It may take some time yet. And I've got to be strong. I don't want to shoot or knife them."

"Neither do I."

They sat for a while. "Shall we play a game of chess?" Morosow asked.

"Yes. But I don't see any board free."

"There, the professor is through playing. He played with Levy. As usual he won."

Ravic went for the board and the chessmen. "You've played a long time, professor," he said. "The whole afternoon."

The old man nodded. "It distracts you. Chess is more perfect than any game of cards. At cards you have good luck or bad luck. It isn't sufficiently diverting. Chess is a world in itself. While one is playing, it takes the place of the outside world.'' He raised his inflamed eyes. ''Which is not so perfect.''

Levy, his partner, suddenly bleated. Then he was silent, turned around, frightened, and followed the professor.

They played two games. Then Morosow got up. ''I've got to go. To open doors for the cream of humankind. Why don't you drop in any more at the Scheherazade?''

''I don't know. Just chance.''

''How about tomorrow night?''

''I can't tomorrow. I am having dinner at Maxim's.''

Morosow grinned. ''For an illegal refugee you have a lot of nerve to hang out in the most elegant places in Paris.''

''They are the only ones where you are entirely safe, you secure owner of a Nansen passport. One who behaves like a refugee is soon caught. You still should remember that much.''

''All right. With whom are you going then? With the German Ambassador as another protection?''

''With Kate Hegstroem.''

Morosow whistled. ''Kate Hegstroem,'' he said. ''Is she back?''

''She is arriving tomorrow morning. From Vienna.''

''Fine. Then I'll be seeing you later in the Scheherazade anyway.''

''Maybe not.''

Morosow dismissed the thought. ''Impossible! The Scheherazade is Kate Hegstroem's headquarters when she is in Paris. You know that as well as I do.''

''This time it's different. She'll be going into the hospital. To be operated on one of the next few days.''

''That's just why she will come. You don't understand women.'' Morosow narrowed his eyes. ''Or don't you want her to come?''

''Why not?''

''It just occurs to me that you haven't been with us since you sent us that woman. Joan Madou. Seems to be not just chance.''

''Nonsense. I don't even know that she is still with you. Could you use her?''

''Yes. First she was in the chorus. Now she has a short solo number. Two or three songs.''

''Has she got adjusted meanwhile?''

''Naturally. Why not?''

"She was damned desperate. Poor devil."

"What?" Morosow asked.

"I said poor devil."

Morosow smiled. "Ravic," he replied in a fatherly manner with a face in which suddenly there were steppes, space, knowledge, and all the experience in the world, "don't talk nonsense. That woman is quite a bitch."

"What?" Ravic asked.

"A bitch. No prostitute. A bitch. If you were a Russian you would understand."

Ravic shook his head. "Then she must have changed a lot. So long, Boris! God bless your eyes!"

Chapter 7

"WHEN DO I have to be at the hospital, Ravic?" Kate Hegstroem asked.

"Tomorrow night. We'll operate the day after."

She stood before him, slim, boyish, self-assured, pretty, and no longer quite young.

"This time I'm afraid," she said. "I don't know why. But I'm afraid."

"You needn't be. It is a routine matter."

Ravic had removed her appendix two years before. At that time they had taken a liking to each other and since then had been friends. Sometimes she disappeared for months and then one day she would suddenly return. She was something like a mascot to him. Her appendectomy was the first operation he had performed in Paris. She had brought him luck. Since that time he had continued to work and had had no further difficulties with the police.

She went over to the window and looked out. There lay the courtyard of the Hôtel Lancaster. A huge old chestnut tree stretched its naked arms upward toward the wet sky. "This rain," she said. "I left Vienna and it was raining. I awoke in Zurich and it was raining. And now here—" She pushed the curtains back. "I don't know what's the matter with me. I think I'm growing old."

"One always thinks that when one isn't."

"I should be different. I was divorced two weeks ago. I should be gay. But I am tired. Everything repeats itself, Ravic. Why?"

"Nothing repeats itself. We repeat ourselves, that's all."

She smiled and sat down on a sofa that stood beside the artificial fireplace. "It's good to be back," she said. "Vienna has become a military barracks. Disconsolate. The Germans have trampled it down. And with them the Austrians. The

Austrians too, Ravic. I thought that would be a contradiction of nature: an Austrian Nazi. But I've seen them.''

"That is not surprising, Kate. Power is the most contagious disease."

"Yes. And the most deforming. That's why I asked for a divorce. This charming idler whom I married two years ago suddenly became a shouting stormtroop leader who made old Professor Bernstein wash the streets while he stood by and laughed. Bernstein who, a year ago, had cured him of an inflammation of the kidneys. Pretending that the fee had been too high.'' Kate Hegstroem drew in her lips. "The fee which I'd paid, not he.''

"Be glad you are rid of him.''

"He asked two hundred fifty thousand schillings for the divorce.''

"Cheap,'' Ravic said. "Anything you can settle with money is cheap.''

"He got nothing.'' Kate Hegstroem raised her oval face, which was flawlessly cut like a gem. "I told her what I thought about him, his party, and his leader—and that from now on I would say this publicly. He threatened me with the Gestapo and the concentration camp. I laughed at him. I am still an American and under the protection of the Embassy. Nothing would happen to me—but to him because he was married to me.'' She laughed. "He had not thought of that. He made no trouble from then on.''

Embassy, defense, protection, Ravic thought. That was like something from another life. "I wonder that Bernstein is still able to practice,'' he said.

"He no longer can. He examined me secretly when I had the first hemorrhage. Thank God, I can't have a child. A child by a Nazi—'' She shuddered.

Ravic rose. "I must go now. You will be examined once more by Veber in the afternoon. Just for form's sake.''

"I know. Nevertheless—I am afraid this time.''

"But, Kate—it isn't the first time. It's simpler than the removal of your appendix.'' Ravic took her lightly around her shoulder. "You were my first operation here. That's like one's first love. I'll take good care of you.''

"Yes,'' she said and looked at him.

"All right, then. Adieu, Kate. I'll call for you at eight tonight.''

"Adieu, Ravic. I'm going now to buy an evening dress at

Mainbocher. I must get rid of this tiredness. And the feeling of being caught in a spider web. That Vienna," she said with a bitter smile. "The city of dreams—"

Ravic went down in the elevator and walked through the hall past the bar. A few Americans were sitting there. In the center a huge bunch of red gladioli stood on a table. In the gray diffused light suddenly they had the pale color of old blood and only when he came closer did he notice that they were perfectly fresh. It was merely the light from outside that made them appear so. He looked at them for some time.

There was much commotion on the second floor of the International. A number of rooms stood open, the maids and the valet were running to and fro, and the proprietress was directing all this from the corridor.

Ravic came down the stairs. "What's going on here?" he asked.

The proprietress was a buxom woman with a huge bosom and a too small head with short black curls. "The Spaniards have left," she said.

"I know. But why are you tidying up the rooms so late in the night?"

"We need them tomorrow morning."

"New German refugees?"

"No, Spanish."

"Spanish?" Ravic asked for a moment, not understanding what she meant. "How is that? Haven't they just left?"

The landlady looked at him with her bright black eyes and smiled. It was a smile of simplest understanding and simplest irony. "The others are coming back," she said.

"Which others?"

"The opposition. But that's always so." She called a few words to the girl who was doing the cleaning. "We are an old hotel," she said then with a certain pride. "Our guests like to return to us. They wait for their old rooms. Naturally a number of them have been killed meanwhile. But the others have waited in Biarritz and Saint-Jean-de-Luz until rooms were vacant."

Ravic looked at the landlady, astonished. "When were they here before?" he asked.

"But Mr. Ravic!" She was surprised that he did not understand right away. "Of course during that time when Primo de Rivera was dictator in Spain. They had to escape then and they lived here. When Spain became republican they went back and the monarchists and Fascists came here. Now the latter have gone back and the republicans are returning. Those that are still left. A merry-go-round."

"Yes, indeed," Ravic said. "A merry-go-round."

The landlady looked into one of the rooms. A colored print of the former King Alfonso hung over the bed. "Take that down, Jeanne," she called.

The girl brought the picture. "Here. Put it over here." The landlady leaned the picture against the wall to her right and walked on. In the next room hung a picture of Generalissimo Franco. "This one too. Put it with the others."

"Why didn't these Gomez people take their pictures with them?" Ravic asked.

"Refugees rarely take pictures with them when they go back," the landlady declared. "Pictures are a comfort in a foreign land. When one returns one no longer needs them. Also the frames are too inconvenient to travel with and the glass breaks easily. Pictures are almost always left in hotels."

She put two other portraits of the fat generalissimo, one of Alfonso, and a smaller one of Queipo de Llano with the others in the corridor. "The holy pictures can be left inside," she decided when she discovered a Madonna in glaring colors. "Saints are neutral."

"Not always," Ravic said.

"In difficult periods God always has a chance. I have even seen atheists praying here." With an energetic movement the landlady adjusted her left breast. "Haven't you ever prayed when the water was up to your neck?"

"Naturally. But I'm not an atheist. I am only a reluctant believer."

The valet came up the stairs. He carried a pile of pictures across the corridor. "Are you going to redecorate?" Ravic asked.

"Of course. One must have much tact in the hotel business. That's what really gives a house a good reputation. Particularly with our kind of customers who, I can actually say, are very sensitive about these things. One hardly expects someone to enjoy a room in which his archenemy looks down on him proudly in bright colors and sometimes even out of a gold frame. Am I not right?"

"One hundred per cent."

The landlady turned toward the valet. "Put these pictures

here, Adolphe. No, you'd better put them in the light against the wall, one next to the other, so that we can see them."

The man growled and bent down to prepare the exhibition. "What will you hang in there now?" Ravic asked, interested. "Deer and landscapes and eruptions of Vesuvius and the like?"

"Only if there aren't enough. Otherwise I'll put back the old pictures."

"Which old ones?"

"Those from before. Those the gentlemen left here when they took over the government. Here they are."

She pointed at the left wall of the corridor. The valet had set up the new pictures in a row opposite those which had been taken out of the rooms. There were two of Marx, three of Lenin with the half of one pasted over with paper, a picture of Trotsky, and a few black and white prints of Negrin and other republican leaders of Spain, in smaller frames. They were less conspicuous and none of them was so resplendent with color and decorations and emblems as the pompous row of Alfonsos, Primos, and Francos which stood opposite them on the right. It was a strange sight: those two rows of opposed philosophies silently staring at each other in the dimly lit corridor and between them the French landlady with the tact, experience, and the ironic wisdom of her race.

"I saved these things at that time," she said, "when those gentlemen checked out. Governments don't last long these days. You see I was right—now they come in handy. One has to be farsighted in the hotel business."

She gave orders where to hang the pictures. She sent back the picture of Trotsky. She was not sure about him. Ravic examined the print of Lenin with the half pasted over. He scratched off part of the paper along the line of Lenin's head—and from under the piece of paper emerged another head, Trotsky's, smiling at Lenin. Very likely a follower of Stalin had pasted it over. "Here," Ravic said. "Another hidden Trotsky. From the good old days of friendship and fraternity."

The landlady took the picture. "We can throw this one away. It is completely valueless. One half of it persistently insults the other half." She gave it to the valet. "Keep the frame, Adolphe. It is good oak wood."

"What will you do with the rest?" Ravic asked. "With the Alfonsos and Francos?"

"They'll go into the cellar. You can never tell whether or not you will need them again one day."

"Your cellar must be a wonderful place. A contemporary mausoleum. Have you still other pictures there?"

"Oh naturally; we have other Russian ones—a few simpler pictures of Lenin in cardboard frames, as a last resource, and then those of the last Czar. From Russians who died here. A wonderful original in oil and in a heavy gold frame from a man who committed suicide. Then there are the Italian pictures. Two Garibaldis, three kings, and a somewhat damaged newspaper cut of Mussolini from the days when he was a socialist in Zurich. Certainly that thing has only curiosity value. No one would like to have it hung up."

"Have you German pictures too?"

"Still a few of Marx; they are the most common; one Lassalle, one Bebel—then a group picture with Ebert, Scheidemann, Noske, and many others. In that picture Noske had been smeared with ink. The gentleman told me that he became a Nazi."

"That's right. You may hang it with the socialistic Mussolini. You have none from the opposite side in Germany, eh?"

"We have! We have one Hindenburg, one Kaiser Wilhelm, one Bismarck, and"—the landlady smiled—"even one of Hitler in a raincoat. It's a pretty complete collection."

"What?" Ravic said. "Hitler? Where did you get him?"

"From a homosexual. He came in 1934 when Roehm and the others were killed here. He was full of fear and prayed a lot. Later a rich Argentinean took him along. His first name was Putzi. Do you want to see the picture? It is in the cellar."

"Not now. Not in the cellar. I'd rather see it when all the rooms in the hotel are filled with the same sort of pictures."

The landlady looked sharply at him for a moment. "Ah so," she said then. "You mean when they come as refugees."

Boris Morosow was standing in front of the Scheherazade in his uniform with the gold braid and he opened the door of the taxi. Ravic stepped out. Morosow smiled. "I thought you weren't coming."

"I didn't intend to."

"I forced him, Boris." Kate Hegstroem embraced Morosow. "Thank God, I am back again with you!"

"You have a Russian soul, Katja. Heaven knows why you had to be born in Boston. Come, Ravic." Morosow thrust the entrance door open. "Man is great in his intentions, but weak in carrying them out. Therein lie our misery and our charm."

The Scheherazade was decorated like a Caucasian tent. The waiters were Russians in Red Circassian uniforms. The orchestra was composed of Russian and Romanian gypsies. People sat at small tables which stood by a banquette that ran along the wall. The tables had plate-glass tops illuminated from below. The place was dim and quite crowded.

"What would you like to drink, Kate?" Ravic asked.

"Vodka. And have the gypsies play. I've had enough of the 'Vienna Woods' played in march time." She slipped her feet out of her shoes and lifted them onto the banquette. "Now I'm not tired any more, Ravic," she said. "A few hours of Paris have already changed me. But I still feel as if I had escaped from a concentration camp. Can you imagine that?"

He looked at her. "Approximately," he replied.

The Circassian brought a small bottle of vodka and glasses. Ravic filled them and handed one to Kate Hegstroem. She drained the glass quickly and thirstily and put it back. Then she looked around. "A moth-eaten hole," she said and smiled. "But at night it becomes a cave of refuge and of dreams."

She leaned back. The soft light from under the glass top of the table illuminted her face. "Why, Ravic? Everything becomes more colorful at night. Nothing appears difficult then, you think you are able to do anything, and what one cannot achieve is made up for by dreams. Why?"

He smiled. "We have our dreams because without them we could not bear the truth."

The orchestra began to tune their instruments. A few empty fifths and a few runs on a violin fluttered through the room. "You don't look like a man who would deceive himself with dreams," Kate Hegstroem said.

"You can deceive yourself with truth too. That's an even more dangerous dream."

The orchestra started to play. In the beginning there were the cymbals only. The soft muted hammers plucked a melody out of the darkness, low, almost inaudible, threw it high into a soft glissando and passed it hesitantly on to the violins.

The gypsy approached their table slowly across the dance floor. He stood there, smiling, the violin at his shoulder, with bold eyes and an ardently greedy face. Without his violin he might have been a cattle dealer—with it he was a messenger of the steppes, of spacious evenings, of horizons, and of all that never becomes reality.

Kate Hegstroem felt the melody like fountain water in April on her skin. Suddenly she was full of echoes; but there was no one who called her. Scattered voices murmured, vague shreds of memory fluttered, sometimes there was a shimmering like brocade, but they all whirled away and there was no one who called her. No one called.

The gypsy bowed. From under the table Ravic slipped a bill into his hand. Kate Hegstroem moved in her corner. "Have you ever been happy, Ravic?"

"Often."

"I don't mean that. I mean really happy, breathlessly, unthinkingly, with everything you have."

Ravic looked into the agitated small face before him that knew only one interpretation of happiness, the most vacillating of all, love, and none of the others. "Often, Kate," he said and meant something quite different and knew it was not that either.

"You don't want to understand me. Or to talk about it. Who is that now singing with the orchestra?"

"I don't know. I haven't been here for a long time."

"You can't see the woman from here. She is not with the gypsies. She must be sitting somewhere at a table."

"Then very likely it's a guest. That happens often here."

"A strange voice," Kate Hegstroem said. "At once sad and rebellious."

"That's the songs."

"Or I am it. Suddenly. Do you understand what she is singing?"

"*Ja vass lovbill*—I love you. It's a song by Pushkin."

"Do you know Russian?"

"Only as much as Morosow has taught me. Mostly curses. Russian is an excellent language for curses."

"You don't like to talk about yourself, do you?"

"I don't even like to think about myself."

She sat awhile. "Sometimes I think the old life has gone," she said then. "The freeness from care, the expectation—all that was before."

Ravic smiled. "It's never gone, Kate. Life is much too great a thing to be gone before we stop breathing."

She did not listen to what he said. "There is a fear often," she said. "A sudden unexplainable fear. As if the world

85

outside may suddenly have collapsed when we leave here. Do you know that, too?"

"Yes, Kate. Everyone knows that. It is a European disease. For the last twenty years."

She fell silent. "But that is no longer Russian," she said then and listened to the music.

"No. That is Italian. *Santa Lucia Luntana*."

The spotlight moved from the violinist to the table beside the orchestra. Now Ravic saw the woman who was singing. It was Joan Madou. She was sitting alone, with one elbow resting on the table, looking straight ahead as if she were in thought and no one else there beside her. Her face was very pale in the white light. It no longer had anything of the flat, blurred look that he knew. Suddenly it was of an exciting forlorn beauty and he remembered having seen it once, fleetingly, like that—the night in her room—but then he had thought it was the soft deception of drunkenness and also it had faded away immediately thereafter and disappeared. Now it was there, wholly, and even more.

"What's the matter, Ravic?" Kate Hegstroem asked.

He turned around. "Nothing. I know that song. A Neapolitan heart-wringer."

"Memories?"

"No. I have no memories."

He said it more vehemently than he had intended. Kate Hegstroem looked at him. "Sometimes I really wish I knew what is the matter with you, Ravic."

He made a defensive motion. "Nothing more than with anyone else. Today the world is full of involuntary adventures. Every refugee hotel is crowded with them. And everyone's story would have been a sensation for Alexandre Dumas or Victor Hugo; now we begin to yawn even before he starts to tell it. Here is another vodka for you, Kate. Nowadays the greatest adventure is a simple life."

The orchestra began to play a blues. They played dance music rather badly. A few guests started dancing. Joan Madou rose and walked toward the exit. She walked as if the place were empty. Ravic suddenly recalled what Morosow had said about her. She passed quite close to Ravic's table. It seemed to him that she saw him, but her eyes at once swept on indifferently beyond him, and she left the room.

"Do you know that woman?" asked Kate Hegstroem, who had been watching him.

"No."

Chapter 8

"Do you see that, Veber?" Ravic asked. "Here—and here—and here—"

Veber bent over the clamped-open incision. "Yes."

"These small nodules here—and here—that's not a swelling nor is it an adhesion—"

"No—"

Ravic straightened up. "Cancer," he said. "A clear, unmistakable case of cancer! This is the damnedest operation I've performed in years. The speculum doesn't show anything, the pelvic examination an insignificant softness at one side only, a slight swelling, the possibility of a cyst or of a fibroma, nothing of importance, but we have to make an abdominal approach, so we cut and suddenly find carcinoma."

Veber looked at him. "What do you want to do?"

"We can make a frozen section. To get a microscopic report. Is Boisson still in the laboratory?"

"Certainly."

Veber gave an order to the infirmière to call up the laboratory. She went out quickly on noiseless rubber soles.

"We should go on cutting," Ravic said. "Do a hysterectomy. There's no point in doing anything else. The damnedest part of it is that she doesn't know. How's the pulse?" he asked the anesthetist.

"Regular. Ninety."

"Blood pressure?"

"One hundred twenty."

"All right." Ravic looked at Kate Hegstroem's body which, head low, lay on the operating table in the Trendelenburg position. "She should know beforehand. She should give her consent. We simply can't just go ahead like this. Or can we?"

"Not according to the law. On the other hand—we have already begun."

"That we had to do. We could not do the abortion without an abdominal approach. This is quite another operation. To remove the uterus is different from an abortion."

"I believe she trusts you, Ravic."

"I don't know. Maybe. But would she agree—" He adjusted the rubber apron under the white coat with his elbow. "Nevertheless—first I could try to explore further. Then we can still decide whether to do the hysterectomy. Knife, Eugénie."

He lengthened the incision to the navel and clamped the smaller blood vessels. Then he stopped the larger ones with double knots, took another knife, and cut through the yellow fascia. He fixed the muscles underneath with the back of the knife, then he pulled up the peritoneum, opened and clipped it. "The retractor."

The assistant nurse held it ready. She threw the weighted chain between Kate Hegstroem's legs and hooked on the bladder plate.

"Dressings!"

He pressed in the damp warm dressing, laid open the abdominal cavity and carefully applied the grasping forceps. Then he glanced up. "Look here, Veber—and here—the broad ligament. This thick hard mass. Impossible to apply the Kocher forceps. It has gone too far."

Veber stared at the spot which Ravic pointed out. "Look at that," Ravic said. "We cannot clamp the arteries. Brittle. It's spreading here too. Hopeless—"

He carefully snipped off a small piece. "Is Boisson in the laboratory?"

"Yes," the infirmière said. "I have telephoned. He is waiting."

"All right. Have this sent to him. We can wait for the report. It won't take more than ten minutes."

"Tell him to telephone," Veber said. "Immediately. We'll suspend the operation."

Ravic straightened up. "How is the pulse?"

"Ninety-five."

"Blood pressure?"

"One hundred fifteen."

"All right. Veber, we don't need to decide whether to operate with or without consent. There's nothing more we can do."

Veber nodded.

"We'll have to sew her up," Ravic said. "Remove the fetus, that's all. Sew her up and say nothing."

He stood there for a moment and looked at the open body beneath the white sheets. The piercing light made the sheets appear even whiter, like new-fallen snow, under which yawned the red crater of the gaping wound. Kate Hegstroem, thirty-four years old, capricious, slender, tanned, filled with the will to live—sentenced to death by this nebulous invisible touch that was destroying her tissues.

He bent over the body again. "We still have to—"

The child. A groping life, blind, still grew in this disintegrating body. Doomed with it. Still feeding, sucking, eager, only a drive toward growth, something that would one day want to play in gardens, that would want to become somebody, an engineer, a priest, a soldier, a murderer, a human being, something that would want to live, to suffer, to be happy and to go to pieces—the instrument carefully slid along the invisible wall, found the resistance, broke it cautiously, removed it—ended it. Ended the unconscious struggles, ended the unbreathed breath, the unlived joyousness, lamentations, growth. Nothing now but a bit of dead pallid flesh and dripping blood.

"Any report from Boisson yet?"

"Not yet. It should be here any minute now."

"We can wait another few minutes."

Ravic stepped back. "Pulse?"

He glanced over the shield into Kate Hegstroem's eyes. They were open and she looked at him—not with a glazed expression, but as if she saw him and knew everything. For a moment he thought she was conscious. He took a step forward and halted. Impossible. What was he thinking of? It was an accident: the light. The pupils had reacted to light during the narcosis. "How is her pulse?"

"One hundred. Blood pressure, one hundred twelve. It's going down!"

"Time's getting short," Ravic said. "Boisson should be ready by now."

There was the subdued ringing of the telephone downstairs. Veber turned toward the door. Ravic did not look up. He waited. He heard the door being opened. The nurse entered. "Yes," Veber said. "Carcinoma."

Ravic nodded and went back to work. He lifted the forceps

and the clips. He removed the retractor; the dressings. Eugénie, at his side, mechanically counted the instruments.

He began stitching. Lightly, methodically, painstakingly, completely concentrated and without a single thought. The grave closed, the layers of flesh were drawn together to the last, outermost one; he put on the clips for the skin and straightened up. "Finished."

Eugénie stepped on the lever bringing the operating table to a horizontal position and covered Kate Hegstroem. Scheherazade, Ravic thought, the day before yesterday, a dress from Mainbocher, have you ever been happy, often, I am afraid, a routine matter, let the gypsies play. He looked at the clock above the door. Twelve o'clock. Noon. Outside, office and factory doors were opening now and healthy people streaming out. Lunch time. The two nurses rolled the level stretcher out of the operating room. Ravic tore the rubber gloves from his hands, went into the washroom, and began to wash.

"Your cigarette," Veber said, washing himself at the other basin. "You'll burn your lips."

"Yes, thanks. Who will tell her, Veber?"

"You will," Veber declared unhesitatingly.

"We'll have to explain to her why we had to operate. She expected us to do it from the inside. We can't tell her what it really was."

"Something will occur to you," Veber said confidently.

"You think so?"

"Of course. After all, you've got until tonight."

"And you?"

"She wouldn't believe anything I'd say. She knows that you operated and she'll want to hear about it from you. She would only be suspicious if I told her."

"That's right."

"I still don't understand it," Veber said. "How it could develop in such a short time."

"It can. I wish I knew what to tell her."

"You'll think of something, Ravic. A cyst of some sort or a fibroma."

"Yes," Ravic said. "Some sort of cyst or fibroma."

At night he went to the hospital again. Kate Hegstroem was sleeping. She had awakened in the evening, had vomited, spent a restless hour, and had then fallen asleep again.

"Did she ask anything?"

"No," said the red-cheeked nurse. "She was still drowsy and asked no questions."

"I think she'll sleep until morning. In case she wakes up and asks questions, tell her everything went well. She's to go back to sleep. Give her something if necessary. If she should become restless, call Doctor Veber or me. I'll leave word at the hotel where to find me."

He stood in the street like someone who had for once escaped. A few hours' grace before he had to lie to a trusting face. Suddenly the night seemed warm and shimmering. The gray scab of life was once again mercifully covered over by a few borrowed hours which flew up like doves. They too were lies—one had to pay for everything—they were a postponement only; but what wasn't? Was not everything postponement, merciful postponement, a bright flag which covered the remote, black, inexorably nearing gate?

He went into a bistro and took a seat at one of the marble tables at the window. The room was smoky and full of noise. The waiter came. "A Dubonnet and a package of Colonials."

He opened the package and lighted one of the black cigarettes. At the table next to him some Frenchmen were discussing their corrupt government and the Munich pact. Ravic only half listened. Everyone knew that the world was apathetically sliding into a new war. No one did anything to stop it—postponement, another year's postponement—that was all they managed to struggle for. Postponement here too, again and again.

He emptied the glass of Dubonnet. The sweetish dull flavor of the apéritif filled his mouth with a flat distaste. Why had he ordered it? He called the waiter. "A fine."

He looked through the window and shook his thoughts off. If there was nothing to be done, one shouldn't drive oneself crazy. He recalled the time when he had learned this lesson. One of the great lessons of his life.

It was in August, 1916, near Ypres. The company had returned from the front the day before. It had been a quiet section in which they were used for the first time since they had been set into the field. Nothing had happened. Now they were lying in the warm August sun around a small fire, frying potatoes they had found in the fields. A minute later nothing was left. A sudden artillery attack—a shell had hit the middle of the fire—when he came to himself again, whole, uninjured, he found two of his comrades dead—and farther away his

91

friend Messmann, whom he had known from the time when both began to walk, with whom he had played, gone to school, from whom he had been inseparable—lying there with his belly torn open, his intestines coming out—

They carried him on a tent litter to the field hospital, by the nearest path through a cornfield up a slope. Four men carried him, one at each corner, and he was lying in the brown tent litter, his hands pressed against the white, fat, bloody intestines, his mouth open, his eyes uncomprehendingly fixed. . . .

Two hours later he died. For one of them he had screamed.

Ravic remembered how they had returned. He had sat in the barracks, dull and bewildered. It was the first time he had seen anything like that. Katczinsky had found him there, the group leader, a shoemaker in private life. "Come," he had said. "They have beer and whisky in the Bavarian canteen today. Sausages too." Ravic had stared at him. He could not understand such callousness. Katczinsky had watched him for a while. Then he had said, "You are coming with me. Even if I have to beat you up. Today you'll eat and get drunk and go to a cat-house." He had not answered. Katczinsky had sat down beside him. "I know what's the matter with you. I know too what you think of me now. But I have been here two years and you two weeks. Listen! Can anything still be done for Messmann?"—"No."—"Don't you know that we would risk everything if there were a chance to save him?" He had looked up. Yes. He knew that. He knew that about Katczinsky. "Well. He is dead. There is nothing to be done any more. But in two days we'll have to get out of here for the front. This time it won't be so quiet there. Crouching here now and thinking of Messmann, the thing eats into you. Ruins your nerves. Makes you jittery. Perhaps just enough to slow you down during the next attack out there. Just half a second late. Then we carry you back as we did Messmann. Whom does it help? Messmann? No. Someone else? No. It kills you, that's all. Now do you understand?"—"Yes, but I can't."—"Shut up, you can! Others could too. You aren't the first."

It had become better after that night. He had gone with him; he had learned his first lesson. Help when you can; do everything then—but when you can no longer do anything, forget it! Turn away! Pull yourself together. Compassion is meant for quiet times. Not when life is at stake. Bury the dead and devour life! You'll still need it. Mourning is one thing, facts are another. One doesn't mourn less when one sees the facts and accepts them. That is how one survives.

Ravic drank his cognac. The Frenchmen at the next table were still talking about their government. About France's failure. About England. About Italy. About Chamberlain. Words, words. The only ones who did something were the others. They were not stronger, only more determined. They were not braver, they only knew that the others wouldn't fight. Postponement—but what did they do with it? Did they arm themselves, did they make up for lost time, did they pull themselves together? They watched the others going ahead arming themselves—and waited, passively hoping for a new postponement. The story of the herd of seals. Hundreds of them on a beach; among them the hunter killing one after the other with a club. Together they could easily have crushed him—but they lay there, watching him come to murder, and did not move; he was only killing a neighbor—one neighbor after the other. The story of the European seals. The sunset of civilization. Tired shapeless *Götterdämmerung*. The empty banners of human rights. The sellout of a continent. The onrushing deluge. The haggling for the last prices. The old dance of despair on the volcano. Peoples again slowly being driven into a slaughterhouse. The fleas would save themselves when the sheep were being sacrificed. As always.

Ravic pressed out his cigarette. He looked around. What did it all mean? Hadn't the evening been like a dove before, like a soft gray dove? Bury the dead and devour life. Time is short. To survive was everything. A time would come when one was needed. One should keep oneself whole and ready for that. He called the waiter and paid.

The lights in the Scheherazade were lowered when he entered. The gypsies were playing and the spotlight flooded the table beside the orchestra where Joan Mudou sat.

Ravic stopped inside the door. One of the waiters approached him and moved a table into position. But Ravic remained standing and looked at Joan Madou.

"Vodka?" the waiter asked.

"Yes. A carafe."

Ravic sat down. He poured vodka into his glass and drank it quickly. He wanted to get rid of the thoughts he had had outside. The grimace of the past and the grimace of death—a belly torn open by shells and one eaten up by cancer. He noticed that he was sitting at the same table where he had sat with Kate Hegstroem two days before. Another table was vacated beside him. He did not move there. It made no difference. Whether he was sitting at this table or at the next—it did not help Kate Hegstroem. What had Veber said once? Why do you get upset when an operation is hopeless? You do what you can and you go home, otherwise where would it lead? Yes, where would it lead? He heard Joan Madou's voice coming from the orchestra. Kate Hegstroem was right—it was an agitating voice. He reached for the carafe with the limpid brandy. One of those moments when colors fade and life turns gray under powerless hands. The mystic ebb. The silent caesura between breaths. The bit of time slowly consuming one's heart. *Santa Lucia Luntana*, sang the voice by the orchestra. It came to him as though across an ocean—from a forgotten far shore where something bloomed.

"How do you like her?"

"Whom?" Ravic glanced up. The manager stood at his side. He motioned to Joan Madou.

"Much. Very much."

"She isn't exactly a sensation. But quite good between the other numbers."

The manager moved along. For a moment his pointed beard stood out black against the white light. Then he disappeared in the darkness.

The spotlight died away. The orchestra began to play a tango. The illuminated table plates emerged again and above them the blurred faces. Joan Madou rose and made her way among the tables. She had to stop several times because couples were going to the dance floor. Ravic looked at her and she looked at him. Her face betrayed no surprise. She came straight toward him. He got up and pushed the table aside. A waiter came to his aid. "Thanks," he said. "I'll do it myself. All we need is another glass."

He moved the table back again and filled the glass which the waiter had brought. "Here, this is vodka," he said. "I don't know whether you drink that."

"Yes. We have drunk it before. In the Belle Aurore."

"That's right."

We were here before too, he thought. Ages ago. Three weeks ago. Then you were sitting here in your raincoat, huddled, nothing but a bit of misery and defeat in the half-dark. Now—"*Salute*," he said.

A gleam crossed her face. She did not smile; only her face became brighter. "I haven't heard that for a long time," she said. *"Salute."*

He emptied his glass and looked at her. The high brows, the wide-set eyes, the mouth—all that had formerly been blurred and separate, without context, now combined to shape a bright, mysterious face—a face whose openness was its secret. It neither hid nor revealed anything. It promised nothing and thereby everything. Odd, I haven't seen this before, he thought. But perhaps it was not there. Perhaps it was then completely filled with confusion and fear.

"Have you a cigarette?" Joan Madou asked.

"Only the Algerians. Those with the strong black tobacco."

Ravic was about to call the waiter. "They are not too strong," Joan Madou said. "Once you gave me one. On the Pont de l'Alma."

"That's true."

It is true and it isn't true, he thought. That was a pale, hunted creature, not you. There were many other things as well between us and suddenly none of them is true any longer. "I was here once before," he said. "Day before yesterday."

"I know. I saw you."

She didn't ask about Kate Hegstroem. She sat in the corner, calm and relaxed, and smoked, and was completely absorbed in her smoking. Then she drank, calmly and slowly, and was completely absorbed in her drinking. She seemed to do everything she did wholly, however unimportant it was. At that time she was completely desperate too, Ravic thought—and now she wasn't at all any more. Suddenly she had warmth and a self-evident, assured placidity. He did not know whether it was due to the fact that nothing moved her life at the moment—he only felt it shine unpremeditatedly upon him.

The carafe of vodka was empty. "Shall we go on drinking the same?"

"What was it you gave me to drink then?"

"When? Here? I think we mixed them all up."

"No, not here. That first evening."

Ravic reflected. "I can't remember any more. Wasn't it cognac?"

"No. It looked like cognac but it was something else. I tried to get it. But I couldn't."

"Why do you want it? Was it so good?"

"Not because of that. It was the warmest thing I ever drank in my life."

"Where did we drink it?"

"In a small bistro near the Arc. We had to go down a few steps. Cabdrivers and a few girls were there. The waiter had a woman tattooed on his arm."

"Now I know. It must have been calvados. Apple brandy from Normandy. Have you tried that?"

"I don't think so."

Ravic called the waiter. "Have you any calvados?"

"No. Sorry. No one ever asks for it."

"This place is too elegant for it. It must have been calvados. It's a shame we can't find out. The simplest thing would be to go to that place again. But that's not possible now."

"Why?"

"Don't you have to stay here?"

"No. I'm through."

"Fine. Do you want to go there?"

"Yes."

Ravic had no trouble finding the bistro. It was fairly empty. The waiter with the woman tattooed on his arm glanced at each of them in turn; then he shuffled out from behind his counter and wiped a table. "This is progress," Ravic said. "He didn't do that then."

"Not this table," Joan Madou said. "That one, there."

Ravic smiled. "Are you superstitious?"

"Sometimes."

The waiter stood beside them. "That's it," he said, making the tattooing jump. "That's where you sat last time."

"Do you still remember?"

"Perfectly."

"You should be a general," Ravic said. "With such a memory."

"I never forget anything."

"Then I wonder how you can live. But do you also remember what we drank last time?"

"Calvados," the waiter said without hesitating.

"Right. We'd like to repeat it now." Ravic turned to Joan Madou. "How simply problems are solved sometimes. Now we'll see if it tastes just the same."

The waiter brought the glasses. "Double. You ordered double calvados then."

"You're gradually giving me an uncanny feeling, my good man. Do you also remember how we were dressed?"

"Raincoats. The lady wore a basque beret."

"It's a pity you have to be here. You belong in vaudeville."

"I used to be," the waiter replied, astonished. "Circus. I told you that. Did you forget?"

"Yes. It's disgraceful, but I did."

"This gentleman has a bad memory," Joan Madou said to the waiter. "He is an expert in forgetting just as you are an expert in not forgetting."

Ravic glanced up. She looked at him. He smiled. "Perhaps not, after all," he said. "And now we'll taste the calvados. *Salute!*"

"Salute!"

The waiter remained standing. "What one forgets one misses later in life, sir," he declared. The topic was not yet exhausted as far as he was concerned.

"Correct. And what one doesn't forget makes one's life a hell."

"Not mine. It's gone. Then how can it make one's life a hell?"

Ravic glanced up. "Just because of it, brother. But you're a happy man, not just an artist. Is it the same calvados?" he asked Joan Madou.

"It is better."

He looked at her. He felt a warmth rising in him. He knew what she meant; but it was disarming that she said it. She did not seem to be concerned with what effect it might have. She sat in this bare-looking place as if she were all by herself. The light from the unshaded electric bulbs was merciless. Under them, two whores sitting a few tables away looked like their own grandmothers. But the glare had no effect on her. What had shone before in the subdued light of the night club held its own here too. The cool bright face which didn't ask for anything, which simply existed, waiting—it was an empty face, he thought; a face that could change with any wind of expression. One could dream into it anything. It was like a beautiful empty house waiting for carpets and pictures. It had all possibilities—it could become a palace or a brothel. It depended on the one who filled it. How limited by comparison was all that is already completed and labeled—

He noticed that she had emptied her glass. "My respects,"

he said. "That was a double calvados. Do you want another one?"

"Yes. If you have time."

Why shouldn't I have time? he thought. Then it occurred to him that she had seen him with Kate Hegestroem last time. He looked up. Her face didn't betray anything.

"I have time," he said. "I have to operate tomorrow at nine, that's all."

"Can you do it if you stay up so late?"

"Yes. This has nothing to do with it. It's habit. Nor do I operate every day."

The waiter refilled their glasses. He brought a package of cigarettes with the bottle and put it on the table. It was a package of Laurens green. "These are what you had last time, aren't they?" he asked Ravic triumphantly.

"I have no idea. You know more than I do. I believe you."

"He's right," Joan Madou said. "It was Laurens green."

"You see! The lady has a better memory than you have, sir."

"That's yet to be proved. Anyway, we can use the cigarettes."

Ravic opened the package and held it out to her. "Do you still live in the same hotel?" he asked.

"Yes. Only I took a larger room."

A few cabdrivers entered. They sat down at one of the near-by tables and began a loud discussion.

"Would you like to leave?" Ravic asked.

She nodded.

He called the waiter and paid. "Are you sure you don't have to go back to the Scheherazade?"

"No."

He took her coat. She did not put it on. She simply hung it around her shoulders. It was an inexpensive mink, possibly an imitation—but it did not look cheap on her. Only what is not worn with assurance is cheap, Ravic thought. He had seen cheap crownsables.

"Now I'll take you to your hotel," he said when they stood outside the entrance in the light drizzle.

She turned toward him slowly. "Aren't we going to your place?"

Her face was just below his, partly turned up to him. The

98

light from the lamp in front of the door shone full on it. Fine beads of moisture glittered on her hair.

"Yes," he said.

A taxi approached and stopped. The driver waited awhile. Then he clicked his tongue, the gears grated, and he drove away.

"I've been waiting for you. Did you know?" she asked.

"No."

Her eyes gleamed in the light from the street lamp; one could look through them and see no end. "I've seen you today for the first time," he said. "You are not the same woman as before."

"No."

"And all that was before never happened."

"No. I have forgotten it."

He felt the light ebb and flow of her breath. Invisibly and tenderly, it was vibrating toward him, without heaviness, ready and full of confidence—a strange life in a strange night. Suddenly he felt his blood. It mounted and mounted and it was more than that: life, a thousand times cursed and welcomed, often lost and rewon—an hour ago still a barren landscape, arid, full of rocks, and without consolation—and now gushing, gushing as if from many fountains, resounding and close to the mysterious moment in which one had not believed any more—one was the first man again, on the shore of the ocean and out of the waves emerged, white and radiant, question and answer in one, it mounted and mounted, and the storm began above his eyes.

"Hold me," she said.

He looked down into her face and put his arm around her. Her shoulders came closer to him like a ship coming to anchor in a harbor. "Must one hold you?" he asked.

"Yes."

Her hands lay close together against his chest. "I'll hold you," he said.

She nodded.

Another taxi came to a squeaking stop beside the curb. The driver, unmoved, looked over at them. On his shoulder sat a little dog in a knitted vest. "Taxi?" he croaked from behind a long flaxen mustache.

"Look," Ravic said. "That man knows nothing. He doesn't know that wings have touched us. He looks at us and doesn't see that we have changed. That is the crazy thing about the world: you may turn into an archangel, a fool or a criminal—no one will see it. But when a button is missing—everyone sees that."

"It is not crazy. It is good so. It leaves us to ourselves."

Ravic looked at her. Us—he thought—what a word! The most mysterious in the world.

"Taxi?" the driver croaked patiently, but louder, and lit a cigarette.

"Come," Ravic said. "He won't let us go. He is experienced in his trade."

"I don't want to ride. Let's walk."

"It is beginning to rain."

"That isn't rain. That is mist. I don't want a taxi. I want to walk with you."

"All right. But I'd like to make that man understand that something has happened here."

Ravic walked over and spoke to the driver. The man smiled a beautiful smile, greeted Joan with a gesture that Frenchmen alone achieve at such moments, and drove away.

"How did you explain it to him?" she asked when Ravic returned.

"With money. The simplest thing. Like all people who work nights he's a cynic. He understood immediately. He was benevolent with a touch of amiable contempt."

She smiled. He put his arm around her shoulders. She leaned against him. He felt something open up in him and spread, warm and soft and wide, something that drew him down as though with many hands, and made it suddenly unbearable that they were standing side by side on their feet, those small platforms, absurdly upright, balancing, instead of forgetting and sinking down, yielding to the call of the skin, the call behind the millenniums when there did not as yet exist brains and thoughts and suffering and doubt, but only the dark happiness of the blood—

"Come," he said.

They walked along the empty gray street through the light rain, and when they reached its end, the square lay before them again, huge and unbounded and, out of the flowing silver, suspended aloft, rose the massive grayness of the Arc.

Chapter 9

RAVIC RETURNED to the hotel. Joan Madou had still been sleeping when he had left that morning. He had thought he would be back in an hour. It was now three hours later.

"Hello, doctor," someone said on the stairs.

Ravic looked at the man. A pale face, a bush of wild black hair, glasses. He did not recognize him.

"Alvarez," the man said. "Jaime Alverez. Don't you remember?"

Ravic shook his head.

The man bent down and pulled up his trouser leg. A long scar ran along his shinbone up to his knee. "Do you remember now?"

"Did I operate on that?"

The man nodded. "On a kitchen table behind the front. In a temporary field hospital before Aranjuez. A little white cottage in an almond grove. Do you remember now?"

Suddenly Ravic scented the heavy aroma of almond blossoms. He smelled it as if it had ascended the dark staircase, sweet, putrid, inextricably mixed with the sweeter and more putrid scent of blood.

"Yes," he said. "I remember."

The wounded had been lying on the moonlit terrace, beside one another in rows. A few German and Italian planes had accomplished that. Children, women, peasants, torn by bomb fragments. A child without a face; a pregnant woman torn open to her breast; an old man who anxiously held the fingers torn off one hand in his other hand because he thought they could be sewed on. Over all that the heavy night odor and the clear dew falling.

"Is your leg quite all right again?" Ravic asked.

"Just about. I can't bend it completely." The man smiled. "But it was good enough to get me across the Pyrenees. Gonzalez is dead."

Ravic no longer knew who Gonzalez was. But now he recalled a young student who had assisted him. "Do you know what happened to Manolo?"

"Imprisoned. Shot."

"And Serna? The brigade commander?"

"Dead. Before Madrid." The man smiled again. It was a rigid automatic smile that came suddenly and was without emotion. "Mura and La Pena were taken prisoners. Shot."

Ravic no longer knew who Mura and La Pena were. He had left Spain after six months when the front was broken and the field hospital disbanded.

"Carnero, Orta, and Goldstein are in a concentration camp," Alvarez said. "In France. Blatzky too is safe. Hidden across the frontier."

Ravic recalled only Goldstein. There had been too many faces at that time. "Do you live here in the hotel now?" he asked.

"Yes. We moved in yesterday. Over there." The man pointed at the rooms on the second floor. "We were kept in the camp down at the frontier for a long time. Finally we were released. We still had some money." He smiled again. "Beds. Real beds. A good hotel. Even pictures of our leaders on the walls."

"Yes," Ravic said without irony. "It must be pleasant after all that over there."

He said goodbye to Alvarez and went to his room.

The room had been cleaned and was empty. Joan had gone. He looked around. She had not left anything behind. He had not expected her to.

He rang. After a while the maid came. "The lady left," she said before he could ask her.

"I see that myself. How did you know anyone was here?"

"But Mr. Ravic," the girl said without adding anything and with an expression as if her honor had been offended.

"Did she have breakfast?"

"No. I haven't seen her. Otherwise I would have thought of it. I know that from before."

Ravic looked at her. He did not like the concluding sentence. He pulled a few francs out of his pocket and put them into the girl's apron pocket. "All right," he said. "Do the same next time. Bring breakfast only when I explicitly tell you to do so.

And don't come up to clean the room before you know for sure that it is empty."

The girl smiled understandingly. "Very well, Mr. Ravic."

He looked after her uneasily. He knew what she thought. She believed Joan was married and did not want to be seen. In former days he would have laughed about it. Now he did not like it. But why not? he thought. He shrugged his shoulders and went to the window. Hotels were hotels. That could not be changed.

He opened the window. A cloudy moon hung above the houses. Sparrows chirped in the eaves. On the floor below two voices squabbled. That would be the Goldberg family. The man was twenty years older than his wife. A wholesale corndealer from Breslau. His wife was having an affair with the refugee Wiesenhoff. She thought no one knew it. The only one who did not know it was Goldberg.

Ravic closed the window. He had operated on a gall bladder that morning. An anonymous gall bladder for Durant. He had cut open for Durant part of an unknown male belly. A fee of two hundred francs. Afterwards he had gone to see Kate Hegstroem. She had a fever. Too much fever. He had been with her for an hour. She had slept restlessly. It was nothing alarming. But it would have been better if there had been no fever.

He stared through the window. The strange empty feeling of afterwards. The bed that no longer had any meaning. The day that mercilessly tore yesterday into pieces like a jackal tearing the hide of an antelope. The woods of the night, miraculously grown in the dark, now endlessly remote again, merely a fata morgana in the wasteland of hours. . . .

He turned around. On his table he found Lucienne Martinet's address. She had been released from the hospital a short time before. She had given them no peace until they released her. Two days ago he had been with her. It was not necessary to look her up again; but he had nothing else to do and decided to go there.

The house was in the Rue Clavel. Downstairs was a butcher's shop in which a strong woman was swinging a cleaver and selling meat. She was in mourning. Her husband had died two weeks before. Now the woman reigned in the shop, with a helper. Ravic saw her as he passed by. She was apparently about to go calling. She wore a hat with a long black crepe veil and was quickly chopping off a pig's leg to oblige an acquaintance. The veil waved about the open carcass, the cleaver glittered and came crashing down.

"With one blow," the widow said in a satisfied tone and flung the leg on the scale.

Lucienne lived in a small room on the top floor. She was not alone. A fellow of about twenty-five slouched on a chair. He wore a bicyclist's cap and was smoking a homemade cigarette which stuck to his upper lip when he talked. He remained sitting as Ravic entered.

Lucienne lay in bed. She was bewildered and blushed. "Doctor—I didn't know you would come today." She looked at the young man. "This is—"

"Someone," the boy interrupted her gruffly. "It isn't necessary to toss names around." He leaned back. "So you are the doctor!"

"How are you, Lucienne?" Ravic asked without taking any notice of him. "You're wise to stay in bed."

"She could have been up long ago," the boy declared. "There's no longer anything wrong with her. When she doesn't work it runs up expenses."

Ravic turned around and looked at him. "Leave us alone," he said.

"What?"

"Get out. Out of the room. I'm going to examine Lucienne."

The boy burst out laughing. "You can do that just as well with me here. We aren't so fine. And why examine? You were here only the day before yesterday. That costs for an extra visit, eh?"

"Brother," Ravic said calmly, "you don't look as if you would pay it. Besides, whether it will cost anything is a different matter. And now get out."

The boy grinned and sprawled his legs comfortably. He wore tapered patent leather shoes and violet socks.

"Please, Bobo," Lucienne said. "I'm sure it will only take a moment."

Bobo did not pay any attention to her. He stared at Ravic. "It suits me fine that you're here," he said. "Now I can put you straight right away. My dear man, if you think perhaps you can bleed us for hospital bills, operations, and all that— nothing doing! We didn't ask to have her sent to the hospital— not to mention the operation—so it's no go with the money angle. You ought to be glad we don't ask for compensation!

For an unauthorized operation.'' He showed a row of stained teeth. ''That's some surprise, isn't it? Yes, sir, Bobo knows his way around; he can't be easily gypped.''

The boy looked very much contented. He felt he had got out of that brilliantly. Lucienne became pale. She looked anxiously from Bobo to Ravic.

''You understand?'' Bobo asked triumphantly.

''Was he the one?'' Ravic asked Lucienne. She did not answer. ''So that's it,'' he said and studied Bobo.

A tall thin fellow with a rayon scarf around his skinny throat, in which the Adam's apple was moving up and down. Drooping shoulders, too long a nose, a degenerate chin—the picture-book conception of a suburb pimp.

''So what's it?'' Bobo asked, challenging.

''I think I've told you often enough now to get going. I want to examine her.''

''*Merde*,'' Bobo replied.

Slowly Ravic walked toward him. He had had enough of Bobo. The boy jumped up, stepped back, and suddenly had a thin rope of about two yards' length in his hands. Ravic knew what he intended to do with it. When Ravic came closer he was going to jump aside, then get swiftly behind him and slip 'the rope over his head so that he could strangle him from behind. It would work if the other person did not know about it or attempt to box.

''Bobo,'' Lucienne called. ''Bobo, don't!''

''You young scum!'' Ravic said. ''That miserable old rope trick—don't you know any better?'' He laughed.

Bobo was nonplused for a moment. His eyes became uncertain. In an instant Ravic had ripped his jacket down over his shoulders with both hands so that he could not lift his arms. ''This is one you did not know, eh?'' he said, quickly opened the door, and shoved the surprised and helpless fellow roughly out of the room. ''If that's the sort of thing you like, become a soldier, you would-be apache! But don't molest grown-up people.''

He locked the door from inside. ''So, Lucienne,'' he said. ''Now let's have a look at you.''

She trembled. ''Calm, calm. It's over.'' He took the worn-out cotton quilt and put it on the chair. Then he rolled back the green blanket. ''Pajamas. Why that? They're less comfortable. You should not move much yet, Lucienne.''

She remained silent for a moment. "I only put them on today," she said.

"Haven't you got any nightgowns? I can have two of them sent to you from the hospital."

"No, not because of that. I put them on because I knew—" she looked at the door and whispered "—that he would come. He said I was no longer sick. He wouldn't wait any longer."

"What? It's a pity. I didn't know that before." Ravic looked at the door angrily. "He'll wait."

Lucienne had the véry white skin of anemic women. The veins lay blue under the thin epidermis. She was well built, with delicate bones, slender, but nowhere too bony. One of the innumerable girls, Ravic thought, who make one wonder why nature puts on such a show of grace—since one knows what will become of almost all of them—overworked drudges who soon lose their figures through the wrong and unhealthy ways of life.

"You will have to stay in bed pretty much for another week, Lucienne. You may get up and walk around here. But be careful; don't lift anything. And don't climb any stairs for the next few days. Have you got someone to take care of you? Besides this Bobo?"

"The landlady. But she too has started to grumble."

"Someone else?"

"No. Before there was Marie. She is dead."

Ravic took stock of the room. It was poorly furnished and clean. A few fuchsias stood in the window. "And Bobo?" he said. "Well, he appeared again after everything was over—"

Lucienne did not answer.

"Why don't you throw him out?"

"He isn't so bad, doctor. Only wild—"

Ravic looked at her. Love, he thought. That too is love. The old miracle. It not only casts a rainbow of dreams against the gray sky of facts—it also sheds romantic light upon a heap of dung—a miracle and a mad mockery. Suddenly he had the strange feeling of having become, in a remote way, an accomplice. "All right, Lucienne," he said. "Don't worry about it. First become healthy."

Relieved, she nodded. "And that about the money," she blurted out, embarrassed, "that isn't true. He only said so. I'll pay everything. Everything. In installments. When will I be able to work again?"

"In about two weeks, if you're not foolish. And nothing with Bobo! Absolutely nothing, Lucienne! Otherwise you might die, you understand?"

"Yes," she replied without conviction.

Ravic covered her slender body with the blanket. When he looked up he noticed that she was weeping. "Couldn't it be sooner?" she said. "I can sit while I work. I must—"

"Perhaps. We'll see. It depends on how well you take care of yourself. You should tell me the name of the midwife who did the abortion, Lucienne."

He saw the defense in her eyes. "I won't go to the police," he said. "Certainly not. I'll only try to get the money back you paid her. Then you could be calmer. How much was it?"

"Three hundred francs. You'll never get it from her."

"One can try. What's her name and where does she live? You'll never need her again, Lucienne. You can no longer have any children. And she can't do anything to you."

The girl hesitated. "There in the drawer," she said then. "At your right in the drawer."

"This slip here?"

"Yes."

"All right. I'll go there one of the next few days. Don't be afraid." Ravic put on his coat. "What's the matter?" he asked. "Why do you want to get up?"

"Bobo. You don't know him."

He smiled. "I think I know worse than him. Stay right in bed. To judge by what I have seen we need not be concerned. So long, Lucienne. I'll drop in on you soon again."

Ravic turned the key and latch simultaneously, and quickly opened the door. No one stood in the corridor. Nor had he expected it; he knew Bobo's type.

Downstairs the assistant was now standing in the butcher's shop, a man with a sallow face and without the ardor of the proprietress. He was chopping listlessly. Since the master's death he had become noticeably more tired. His chances of marrying his master's wife were small. A brushmaker in the bistro opposite announced this in a loud voice and also that she would drive him too into the grave before that happened. The assistant had already lost much weight, he said. But the widow had blossomed mightily. Ravic drank a cassis and paid. He had expected to find Bobo in the bistro; but Bobo was not there.

*　　*　　*

Joan Madou quickly left the Scheherazade. She opened the door of the taxi in which Ravic was waiting. "Come," she said. "Let's get away from here. Let's go to your place."

"Has something happened?"

"No. Nothing. It's just that I've had enough of nightclub life."

"Just a moment." Ravic called to the woman who stood before the entrance, selling flowers. "Granny," he said. "Let me have all your roses. How much are they? But don't be exorbitant."

"Sixty francs. For you. Because you gave me that prescription for my rheumatism."

"Did it help?"

"No. How can it, as long as I have to stand in the wet at night?"

"You're the most sensible patient I ever met in my life."

He took the roses. "Here is my apology for having left you to wake up alone this morning," he said to Joan and put the flowers on the floor of the taxi. "Would you like to have a drink somewhere?"

"No, I'd like to go to your place. Put the flowers here on the seat. Not on the floor."

"They are all right down there. One should love flowers, but not make too much fuss about them."

She turned her head quickly. "You mean one shouldn't spoil what one loves?"

"No. I only mean that one shouldn't dramatize beautiful things. Besides, at the moment it is better if there are no flowers between us."

Joan looked at him doubtfully for a moment. Then her face brightened. "Do you know what I did today? I lived. Lived again. I breathed. Breathed again. I existed. Existed again. For the first time. I had hands again. And eyes and a mouth."

The driver maneuvered the taxi out from among the other cars in the small street. Then he started with a jerk. The jolt threw Joan toward Ravic. He held her in his arms for a moment and felt her closeness. It was like a warm wind as if she were melting away the crust of the day, the strange defensive coolness within him, while she sat there and spoke, carried away by her feelings and by herself.

"The whole day—it threw itself over my neck and against my breast as though to make me grow green and put out leaves and blossoms—it held me and held me and did not let me go—and now here I am—and you—''

Ravic looked at her. She sat leaning forward on the dirty leather seat and her shoulders shone out of her black evening gown. She was open and outspoken and without shame, she said what she felt and he found himself poor and dry in comparison.

I was performing operations, he thought. I forgot you. I was with Lucienne. I was somewhere in the past. Without you. Then when the evening came a certain warmth came slowly with it. I was not with you. I thought of Kate Hegstroem.

''Joan,'' he said and put his hands on her hands, which she had rested on the seat. ''We can't go to my place now, I've got to go first to the hospital. Only for a few minutes.''

''Have you got to look after the woman you operated on?''

''Not the one of this morning. Someone else. Would you like to wait somewhere for me?''

''Must you go right away?''

''It would be better. I don't want to be called later.''

''I can wait for you. Have we enough time to go by your hotel?''

''Yes.''

''Let's go there first. Then you'll come later. I can wait for you.''

''All right.'' Ravic gave the driver his address. He leaned back and felt the top of the seat against his neck. His hands were still on Joan's hands. He felt that she was waiting for him to say something. Something about him and her. But he could not. She had already said too much. It was not so much, he thought.

The cab stopped. ''You go on,'' Joan said. ''I'll manage here all right. I'm not afraid. Just give me your key.''

''The key is in the hotel.''

''I'll have them give it to me. I've got to learn to do that.'' She took the flowers from the floor. ''With a man who leaves me while I sleep and comes again when I don't expect it—there are many things I'll have to learn. Let me start right away.''

''I'll come up with you. We won't overdo anything. It's bad enough to have to leave you alone again immediately.''

She laughed. She looked very young. ''Please wait a moment,'' Ravic said to the driver.

The man slowly closed one eye. ''Even longer.''

"Let me have the key," Joan said as they walked upstairs.

"Why?"

"Let me have it."

She opened the door. Then she stopped. "Beautiful," she said into the dark room into which a bleak moon shone through the clouds outside the window.

"Beautiful? This hole?"

"Yes, beautiful! Everything is beautiful."

"Maybe right now. Now it's dark. But—" Ravic reached for the switch.

"Don't. I'll do it myself. And now go. And don't wait till tomorrow noon to come back."

She stood in the doorway in the dark. The silver light from the window was behind her shoulders and her head. She was indistinct and exciting and mysterious. Her coat had slipped down; it lay at her feet like a heap of black foam. She leaned against the door-frame and one of her arms caught a long shaft of light from the corridor. "Go and come again," she said and closed the door.

Kate Hegstroem's fever had gone down. "Has she been awake?" Ravic asked the drowsy nurse.

"Yes. At eleven. She asked for you. I told her what you instructed me to say."

"Did she say anything about the bandages?"

"Yes. I told her you had to make an incision. A light operation. You'd explain it to her tomorrow."

"That was all?"

"Yes. She said everything was all right as long as you considered it right. I was to give you her regards if you came again tonight and tell you that she has confidence in you."

"So—"

Ravic stood awhile and looked down at the nurse's parted black hair. "How old are you?" he asked.

She raised her head in astonishment. "Twenty-three."

"Twenty-three. And how long have you been nursing?"

"For the last two and a half years. In January it was two and a half years."

"Do you like your profession?"

The nurse smiled all over her apple face. "I like it very much," she declared chattily. "Of course some of the patients are trying, but most of them are nice. Madame Brissot gave me a beautiful, almost new silk dress as a present yesterday. And last week I got a pair of patent leather shoes from Madame Lerner. The one who later died at home." She smiled again. "I hardly have to buy any clothing. I almost always get something. If I can't use it I exchange it with a friend of mine who has a shop. That's why I'm well off. Madame Hegstroem too is always very generous. She gives me money. Last time it was a hundred francs. For only twelve days. How long will she be here this time, doctor?"

"Longer. A few weeks."

The nurse looked happy. Behind her clear unlined forehead she was calculating how much she would get. Ravic bent over Kate Hegstroem once more. She was breathing quietly. The slight odor from the wound mingled with the dry perfume of her hair. Suddenly he could not stand it. She had confidence in him. Confidence. The flat cut-up abdomen in which the beast was feeding. Sewn up without the possibility of doing anything. Confidence.

"Good night, nurse," he said.

"Good night, doctor."

The chubby nurse sat down in the chair in a corner of the room. She dimmed the light on the side toward the bed, wrapped her feet in a blanket, and reached for a magazine. It was one of those cheap magazines containing detective stories and movie pictures. She adjusted herself comfortably and began to read. Beside her on a little table she had put an opened box of chocolate wafers. Ravic saw her take one without looking up. Sometimes one doesn't comprehend the simplest things, he thought—that in the same room one person should be lying deadly ill and the other not at all concerned about it. He closed the door. But isn't it the same with me? Am I not going from this room into another in which—

The room was dark. The door to the bathroom was ajar. There was a light beyond it. Ravic hesitated. He did not know whether Joan was still in the bathroom. Then he heard her breathing. He walked through the room to the bathroom. He did not say anything. He knew she was here and was not asleep, but she too said nothing. Suddenly the room was full of silence and expectancy and tension—like a vortex which silently called—an unknown abyss, beyond thought, from which rose the poppy clouds and the dizziness of a red tumult.

He closed the door of the bathroom. In the clear light of

the white bulbs everything was familiar and known to him again. He turned on the taps of the shower. It was the only shower in the hotel. Ravic had paid for it himself and had had it installed. He knew that in his absence it was still being shown to the patron's French relatives and friends as a remarkable sight.

The hot water ran down his skin. In the next room Joan Madou was lying and waiting for him. Her skin was smooth, her hair surged over the pillow like an impetuous wave, and her eyes shone lucidly even when the room was dark, as if they caught the meager light of winter stars from outside the window and reflected it. She lay there, subtle and changeable and exciting because there was nothing left of the woman whom one had known an hour ago, she was everything that enticement and temptation could give without love—and yet all of a sudden he felt something like an aversion to her—a strange resistance mixed with a violent and sudden attraction. He looked around involuntarily—if the bathroom had had a second exit, he thought it possible that he would have dressed and gone out to drink.

He dried himself and hesitated for a while. Strange, what had fluttered in from nowhere! A shadow, a nothing. Perhaps it was because he had been with Kate Hegstroem. Or because of what Joan had said in the taxi earlier. Much too quick and much too easy. Or simply because someone was waiting—instead of his waiting. He tightened his lips and opened the door.

"Ravic," Joan said out of the dark. "The calvados is on the table by the window."

He stood still. He realized that he had been tense. He could not have stood many things she might have said. This one was right. His tension eased into loose, light certainty. "Did you find the bottle?" he asked.

"That was easy. It was standing right here. But I opened it. I discovered a corkscrew somewhere among your things. Give me another glass."

He poured two glasses and brought one to her. "Here—" It was good to feel the clear apple brandy. It was good that Joan had found the right word.

She leaned her head back and drank. Her hair fell over her shoulders and in this moment she seemed to be nothing but drinking. Ravic had noticed this in her before. She gave herself completely to whatever she did. It occurred to him vaguely that therein lay not only fascination, but also danger. Such women were nothing but drinking, when they drank; nothing not love when they loved; nothing but desperation when they were desperate; and nothing but forgetfulness when they forgot.

Joan put down the glass and laughed suddenly. "Ravic," she said. "I know what you are thinking."

"Really?"

"Yes. You felt already half married just now. So did I. To be abandoned at the door is not exactly an enviable experience. Left alone with roses in one's arms. Thank God, the calvados was here. Don't be so careful with the bottle."

Ravic refilled her glass. "You are a wonderful person," he said. "It's true. There in the bathroom I could hardly stand you. Now I find you wonderful. *Salute!*"

"*Salute.*"

He drank his calvados. "It is the second night," he said. "The dangerous night. The charm of the unknown is gone and the charm of familiarity has not yet come. We'll survive it."

Joan put her glass down. "You seem to know quite a lot about it."

"I know nothing at all. I just talk. One never knows anything. Everything is always different. Now too. It never is the second night. It is always the first. The second would be the end."

"Thank God! Otherwise where would it lead? Into something like arithmetic. And now come. I don't want to go to sleep yet. I want to drink with you. The stars stand naked up there in the cold. How easily one can freeze when one is alone! Even when it is hot. Never when there are two."

"Two together can actually freeze to death."

"Not we."

"Naturally not," Ravic said and in the dark she did not see the expression that crossed his face. "Not we."

Chapter 10

"What was the matter with me, Ravic?" Kate Hegstroem asked.

She was lying in her bed, slightly raised, with two pillows under her head. The room had the odor of Eau de Santé and perfume. The window was slightly opened at the top. Clear, somewhat chilly air streamed in from the outside and mingled with the warmth of the room as if it were not January but already April.

"You were feverish, Kate. For a few days. Then you slept. Almost twenty-four hours. Now the fever has gone and everything is fine. How are you feeling?"

"Tired. Still always tired. But different from before. Not so tense any more. I have hardly any pain."

"You will have some later. Not very much, and we'll take care of it so you'll be able to stand it. But it won't stay the way it is now. You know that yourself—"

She nodded. "You have cut me up, Ravic—"

"Yes, Kate."

"Was it necessary?"

"Yes."

He waited. It was better to let her ask. "How long will I have to be in bed?"

"A few weeks."

She remained silent for a while. "I think it will be good for me. I need quiet. I'd had enough. I realize it now. I was tired. I did not want to admit it. Did this have something to do with it?"

"Certainly. Most certainly."

"Also the fact that I had hemorrhages from time to time? Between periods?"

"That too, Kate."

"Then it's a good thing that I have time. Maybe it was

necessary. To have to get up now and face all that again—I don't think I could do it."

"You don't have to. Forget about it. Think only of the very next thing. For instance, of your breakfast."

"All right." She smiled faintly. "Then pass me the mirror."

He gave her the hand mirror from the night table. She studied herself attentively in it.

"Are these flowers from you, Ravic?"

"No. From the hospital."

She put the mirror on the bed. "Hospitals don't send lilacs in January. Hospitals send asters or something like that. Neither do hospitals know that lilacs are my favorite flowers."

"Here they do. Here you are a veteran, Kate." Ravic got up. "I have to go now. I'll come back about six o'clock to look after you."

"Ravic—"

"Yes."

He turned around. Now it will come, he thought. Now she will ask.

She extended her hand. "Thanks," she said. "Thanks for the flowers. And thanks for looking out for me. I always feel safe with you."

"All right, Kate. All right. There was nothing really to look out for. And now fall asleep again if you can. In case you should have pains call the nurse. I'll see that you get medicine. This afternoon I'll be back."

"Veber, where is the brandy?"

"Was it as bad as that? Here's the bottle. Eugénie, get us a glass."

Eugénie reluctantly went for a glass. "That's a thimble," Veber protested. "Get us a decent glass. Or wait, it might break your hand, I'll do it myself."

"I don't know why it is, Doctor Veber," Eugénie declared bitingly, "whenever Mr. Ravic comes in, you—"

"All right, all right," Veber interrupted her. He poured a glass of cognac. "Here, Ravic. What does she believe?"

"She does not ask anything," Ravic said. "She trusts me without asking questions."

Veber glanced up. "You see," he replied triumphantly. "I told you so."

Ravic emptied his glass. "Has a patient ever expressed his thanks to you when you couldn't do anything for him?"

"Often."

"And believed everything?"

"Naturally."

"And how did you feel about it?"

"Relieved," Veber said in astonishment. "Very much relieved."

"I feel like vomiting. Like a fraud."

Veber laughed. He put the bottle aside again. "Like vomiting," Ravic repeated.

"That's the first human feeling I ever discovered in you," Eugénie said. "Except, naturally, for the way you express yourself."

"You are not a discoverer, you are a nurse, Eugénie, you often forget that," Veber declared. "The affair is settled, Ravic, isn't it?"

"Yes. For the time being."

"All right. She told the nurse this morning that she wants to go to Florence as soon as she leaves the hospital. Then we're in the clear." Veber rubbed his hands. "The doctors over there can take care of it then. I don't like it when someone dies here. It always hurts the reputation."

Ravic rang the bell at the apartment door of the midwife who performed the abortion for Lucienne. After some time a sinister-looking man opened. He kept the latch in his hand when he saw Ravic. "What do you want?" he growled.

"I want to speak to Madame Boucher."

"She has no time."

"That doesn't matter. I'll wait awhile."

The man was about to close the door. "If I can't wait I'll be back in a quarter of an hour," Ravic said. "But not alone. With someone who will certainly be able to see her."

The man stared at him. "What does that mean? What do you want?"

"I told you. I want to speak to Madame Boucher."

The man pondered. "Wait," he said and then closed the door.

Ravic studied the peeling brown paint on the door, the tin letter box and the enameled label with the name. A great deal of misery and fear had passed through this door. A few senseless laws which forced so many lives into the hands of quacks instead of doctors. No more children were born because of it. Whoever did not want a child found a way, law or no law. The only difference was that the lives of some thousands of mothers were ruined every year.

The door was opened again. "Are you from the police?" the unshaven man asked.

"If I were from the police I wouldn't be waiting here."

"Come in."

The man showed Ravic through a dark corridor into a room crowded with furniture. A plush sofa and a number of gilt chairs, an imitation Aubusson carpet, walnut Vertikows and pastoral prints on the walls. In front of the window stood a metal stand with a bird cage and a canary in it. Wherever there was any space there were chinaware and plaster figurines.

Madame Boucher came in. She was enormously fat and wore a kind of billowing kimono which was not quite clean. She was a monster, but her face was smooth and pretty, with the exception of her eyes, which darted restlessly. "Monsieur?" she asked in a businesslike tone and remained standing.

Ravic got up. "I come in behalf of Lucienne Martinet. You performed an abortion for her."

"Nonsense!" the women replied immediately with complete calm. "I don't know any Lucienne Martinet and I don't perform abortions. You must be mistaken or someone has told you a lie."

She acted as if the affair were settled and was about to leave. But she didn't go. Ravic waited. She turned around. "Something else?"

"The abortion was a failure. The girl had serious hemorrhages and almost died. She had to have an operation. I operated on her."

"It's a lie!" Madame Boucher suddenly hissed. "It's a lie! Those rats! They fool around trying to fix themselves up and then get other people into trouble! But I'll show her! Those rats! My lawyer will settle that. I am well known and a taxpayer and I'll see whether such an impudent little slut that whores around—"

Ravic studied her, fascinated. Her expression did not change during the outburst. It remained smooth and pretty—her mouth only was drawn in and spat like a machine gun.

"The girl wants very little," he interrupted the woman. "She only wants back the money she paid you."

Madame Boucher laughed. "Money! Pay back? When did I get any from her? Has she a receipt?"

"Naturally not. You wouldn't give any receipts."

"Because I've never seen her! And would anyone believe her?"

"Yes. She has witnesses. She was operated on in Doctor Veber's hospital. The diagnosis was clear. A report exists about it."

"You may have a thousand reports! Where does it say that I touched her? Hospital! Doctor Veber! It's a scream! Such a rat goes to an elegant hospital! Haven't you got anything else to do?"

"I have. Listen. The girl paid you three hundred francs. She can sue you for compensation."

The door was opened. The sinister man entered. "Something wrong, Adèle?"

"No. Sue for compensation? If she goes to court she herself will be sentenced. First of all she, that's certain because she admits that an abortion was done for her. That I did it still has to be proved. That she can't."

The sinister man bleated. "Quiet, Roger," Madame Boucher said. "You may go."

"Brunier is outside."

"All right. Tell him to wait. You know—"

The man nodded and left. With him went a strong smell of cognac. Ravic sniffed. "That's an old cognac," he said. "At least thirty, forty years old. Lucky man who drinks something like that early in the afternoon."

Madame Boucher shared at him for a moment, flabbergasted. Then she slowly drew in her lips. "That's right. Do you want some?"

"Why not?"

In spite of her fat she was at the door with surprising speed and silentness. "Roger."

The sinister man came in. "You've been drinking the good cognac again! Don't lie! I smell it! Bring the bottle! Don't talk, bring the bottle!"

Roger brought the bottle. "I gave Brunier some. He forced me to drink with him."

Madame Boucher did not answer. She closed the door and fetched a curved glass from the walnut Vertikow. Ravic looked at it with disgust. The head of a woman was engraved on it. Madame Boucher poured and put the glass in front of him on the tablecloth, which was adorned with peacocks. "You seem to be a sensible person, sir," she said.

Ravic could not deny her a certain respect. She was not of

iron, as Lucienne had told him; she was worse—of rubber. You could break iron. Not rubber. Her argument against collecting damages was sound. "Your operation was a failure," he said. "It had serious consequences. This should be reason enough for you to refund the money."

"Do you pay money back if a patient dies after an operation?"

"No. But sometimes we don't take any money for an operation. For instance from Lucienne."

Madame Boucher looked at him. "You see—then why is she making such a fuss? She should be glad."

Ravic lifted his glass. "Madame," he said, "my respects. One can't get the better of you."

The woman slowly put the bottle on the table. "Sir, many have already tried it. But you seem to be more sensible. Do you think this business is fun? Or all the money mine? The police get almost a hundred francs of those three hundred. Do you believe that I could work otherwise? One of them is sitting outside now to get money. I have to bribe them, always bribe them; there's no other way. I tell you that here, alone, between the two of us, and should you want to make use of it somehow, I'd deny it and the police would pay no attention. You may believe that."

"I believe it."

Madame Boucher cast a quick look at him. When she saw that he did not mean it ironically, she moved a chair closer to him and sat down. She moved the chair like a feather—beneath her fat she seemed to have enormous strength. She refilled his glass with the cognac reserved for bribes. "Three hundred francs looks like a good deal of money—but there are more expenses than just the police. The rent—naturally higher for me than for someone else—laundry, instruments—for me twice as expensive as for physicians—commissions, bribes—I must be on good terms with everyone—drinks, presents at New Year and on birthdays for the officials and their wives—that's something, sir! Sometimes hardly anything is left."

"I don't question that."

"Then what?"

"That the sort of thing can happen that happened to Lucienne."

"Does it never happen with doctors?" Madame Boucher asked quickly.

"Not so often by far."

"Sir." She straightened up. "I'm honest. I tell every one of the girls who come here that something might happen. And none of them leaves. They beg me to do it. They cry and are desperate. They would commit suicide if I didn't help them. What scenes have been staged here! They roll on the rug and entreat me! Do you see the corner of that Vertikow where the veneer is chipped off? A well-to-do lady did that in her desperation. I took care of her. Do you want to see something? Ten pounds of plum jam she sent me yesterday are in the kitchen. Out of pure gratitude although she had paid. I'll tell you something, sir—" Madame Boucher's voice rose and became fuller "—you may call me an abortionist—others call me their benefactress and angel."

She got up. The kimono billowed around her majestically. The canary began to sing in his cage as if by command. Ravic got up. He had a feeling for melodrama. But he knew too that Madame Boucher did not exaggerate. "All right," he said. "I'll go now. For Lucienne you weren't exactly a benefactress."

"You should have seen her before! What more does she want? She's healthy—the child is done with—that was all she wanted. And she doesn't have to pay for the hospital."

"She'll never be able to have a child again."

Madame Boucher hesitated a second only. "All the better," she declared, unmoved. "Then she will be overjoyed, that little whore."

Ravic realized that there was nothing to be done. "*Au revoir, madame,*" he said. "It has been interesting here with you."

She came close to him. Ravic would have liked to avoid shaking hands with her. But that was not her intention. She lowered her voice in a confidential manner. "You are sensible, sir. More sensible than most doctors. It's a pity that you—" She hesitated and looked at him encouragingly. "Sometimes one needs for certain cases—an understanding physician could then be of great help—"

Ravic did not object. He wanted to hear more. "It would not harm you," Madame Boucher added. "Just in special cases—" She studied him like a cat that pretends to love birds. "There are well-to-do clients among them sometimes—naturally always payment in advance and—we are safe, completely safe from the police—I assume you could very well

120

use a few hundred francs on the side—" She tapped him on his shoulder. "A good-looking man like you—"

She seized the bottle with a broad smile. "Well, what do you think?"

"Thanks," Ravic said and kept her from pouring. "No more. I can't stand much." He refused with great reluctance, for the cognac was excellent. The bottle had no label and certainly came from a first-class private cellar. "I'll think the other matter over. I'll come again sometime. I'd like to see your instruments. Maybe I can give you some advice as far as they are concerned."

"I'll show you my instruments when you come again. Then you'll show me your papers. Confidence for confidence."

"You've already shown me some confidence."

"Not the least." Madame Boucher smiled. "I only made you a proposition which I can deny at any time. You're not a Frenchman, one can hear that, although you speak well. Nor do you look it. You're probably a refugee." She smiled more broadly and looked at him with cool eyes. "One wouldn't believe you and would be, at best, interested in the French diploma which you haven't got. Outside in the hall sits a police official. If you want to, you can denouce me right away. You won't do it. But you can think over my proposition. You wouldn't give me your name and address, would you?"

"No," Ravic said, feeling beaten.

"I thought not." Madame Boucher really looked like a huge well-fed cat now. "Au revoir, monsieur. Consider my offer. I've often before thought of working with the assistance of a refugee doctor."

Ravic smiled. He knew why. A refugee doctor would be completely at her mercy. If anything happened he would be guilty. "I'll think it over," he said. "Au revoir, madame."

He walked along the dark corridor. Behind one of the doors he heard someone moaning. He assumed that the rooms were arranged like small cabins with beds. The women would stay there before they tottered home.

A slim man with a trimmed mustache and an olive-colored skin sat in the hall. He studied Ravic attentively. Roger sat at his side. He had another bottle of the old cognac on the table. He tried to hide it instinctively when he saw Ravic. Then he grinned and dropped his hand. "Bon soir, docteur," he said and showed his stained teeth. It seemed he had been eavesdropping at the door.

"Bon soir, Roger." It seemed to Ravic appropriate to be intimate. This indestructible woman had almost changed him from an outspoken enemy into an accomplice within half an hour in there. And so it was actually a relief to be not too formal with Roger who, after all that, had something astonishingly human about him.

Downstairs he met two girls. They were looking from door to door. "Sir," one of them asked with determination, "does Madame Boucher live here in this house?"

Ravic hesitated. But what point was there in saying anything? It would not help at all. They would go. Then too he could not give them any other directions. "On the third floor. There is a name plate on the door."

The luminous dial of his watch shone in the dark like a tiny imitation sun. It was five o'clock in the morning. Joan should have come at three. It was still possible that she would come. Also possible that she was too tired and had gone straight to her hotel.

Ravic stretched out to go back to sleep. But he could not fall asleep. He lay awake for a long time and looked at the ceiling where the red band from the electric signs on the roof opposite ran at regular intervals. He felt empty and did not know why. It was as if the warmth of his body were slowly seeping through his skin, and as if his blood wanted to lean against something that was not there and that it fell and fell into a soft nothingness. He crossed his hands behind his head and lay quiet. Now he knew he was waiting. And he knew it was not only his consciousness that waited for Joan Madou—his hands waited and his veins and a strangely alien tenderness within him.

He got up, put on his dressing gown and sat down by the window. He felt the warmth of the soft wool on his skin. The robe was old; he had had it with him for many years. He had slept in it on his flights; he had warmed himself in it during the cold nights in Spain when, dead tired, he had come back from the field hospital to his barracks. Juana, twelve years old, with eyes eighty years old, had died under it in a wrecked hotel in Madrid—with the single wish sometime to own a dress of the same soft wool and to forget how her mother had been ravished and her father trampled to death.

He looked around. The room, a few suitcases, some belongings, a handful of well-read books—a man needed few things to live. And it was good not to get used to many things when life was unsettled. Again and again one had to abandon them or they were taken away. One should be ready to leave every day. That was the reason he had lived alone—when one was on the move one should not have anything that could bind one. Nothing that could stir the heart. The adventure—but nothing more.

He looked at the bed. The crumpled colorless linen. It did not matter that he waited. He had often waited for women. But he felt that he had waited differently—simply, clearly, and brutally. Also sometimes with the anonymous tenderness that enchases desire with silver—but for a long time not as he waited today. Something had crept into him to which he had not paid any attention. Did it stir again? Did it move? How long ago was it? Did something call again out of oblivion, out of blue depths, did it again blow across him like the breath of meadows, full of peppermint, with a row of poplars against the horizon and the smell of woods in April? He did not want to possess anything. He did not want to be possessed. He was on the move.

He got up and began to dress. One must remain independent. Everything began with small dependencies. One did not notice them much. And suddenly one was entangled in the net of habit. Habit for which many names existed—love was one of them. One should not grow accustomed to anything. Not even to a body.

He did not lock the door. If Joan came she would not find him. She could stay if she wanted to. He deliberated for a second whether to leave a note. But he did not want to lie; nor did he want to tell her where he had gone.

He returned about eight o'clock in the morning. He had walked in the cold under the street lights of early dawn and had felt clear and relaxed. But as he stood in front of the hotel he felt again the tenseness.

Joan was not there. Ravic assured himself that he had not expected anything else. But his room seemed to him emptier than usual. He looked around and searched for a sign of her having been there. He found nothing.

He rang for the maid. She came after a while. "I'd like some breakfast," he said.

She looked at him. She said nothing. He didn't want to ask her any questions. "Coffee and croissants, Eve."

"Very well, Mr. Ravic."

He looked at the bed. If Joan had come one could not very well have expected her to lie down in a crumpled empty bed. Odd, how dead everything became that had to do with the body when there was no longer any warmth—a bed, underwear, even a bath. It was repulsive when it had lost its warmth.

He lighted a cigarette. She might have assumed that he had been called to see a patient. But then he could have left a note. Suddenly he thought himself a good deal of an idiot. He wanted to be independent and succeeded only in being inconsiderate. Inconsiderate and foolish like an eighteen year old who wants to prove something to himself. There was more dependency in this than if he had waited.

The girl brought his breakfast. "Shall I do the bed now?" she asked.

"Why now?"

"In case you still want to go to sleep. One sleeps better in a freshly made bed."

She looked at him without expression. "Was someone here?" he asked.

"I don't know. I only came at seven."

"Eve," he said, "how does it feel to have to make a dozen strangers' beds every morning?"

"It's all right, Mr. Ravic. As long as the people don't want anything else. But there are always a few who want more. Though the brothels are so cheap in Paris."

"In the morning one can't go into a brothel, Eve. And some guests feel particularly strong in the morning."

"Yes, especially the old ones." She shrugged her shoulders. "You lose the tip if you don't do it, that's all. Then too some make complaints every minute afterwards—that the room is not clean or that you are fresh. Naturally, out of anger. You can't do anything about it. That's how life is."

Ravic pulled a bill out of his pocket. "Let's make life somewhat easier today, Eve. Buy yourself a hat with that. Or a woolen jacket."

Eve's eyes lost their dull expression. "Thank you, Mr. Ravic. Today is starting well. Then should I make your bed later?"

"Yes."

She looked at him. "The lady is a very interesting lady," she said. "The lady who keeps coming here now."

"One more word and I'll take the money away from you."

124

Ravic pushed Eve out of the door. "The old lechers are waiting for you. Don't disappoint them."

He sat down at the table and ate. The breakfast did not taste particularly good. He got up and continued to eat standing. It tasted better.

The sun hung red above the roofs. The hotel was waking up. Old man Goldberg on the floor below began his morning concert. He coughed and groaned as if he had six lungs. The refugee Wiesenhoff opened his window and whistled a parade march. On the upper-floor water gushed. Doors were slammed. Ravic stretched himself. The night had gone. The corruption of the dark was done with. He decided to remain alone for a few days.

Outside the newspaper boys were calling out the morning news. Incidents at the Czechoslovakian frontier. German troops at the Sudeten line. The Munich pact jeopardized.

Chapter 11

THE BOY did not scream. He just stared at the doctors. He was still too stunned to feel any pain. Ravic glanced at the crushed leg. "How old is he?" he asked the mother.

"What?" the woman asked uncomprehendingly.

"How old he is?"

The woman with the kerchief over her head moved her lips. "His leg!" she said. "His leg! It was a truck."

Ravic listened to his heart. "Has he been sick?"

"His leg!" the woman said. "It is his leg!"

Ravic straightened up. The heart was beating quickly like a bird's, but there was nothing alarming in the sound. During anesthesia he would have to watch the boy, who looked emaciated and rachitic. He had to start immediately. The torn leg was full of street dirt.

"Will you cut my leg off?" the boy asked.

"No," Ravic said without believing it.

"It's better if you cut it off instead of its being stiff."

Ravic looked attentively at the precocious face. There was not yet any sign of pain in it. "We'll see," he said. "Now we'll have to put you to sleep. It's very simple. You needn't be afraid. Be quite calm."

"One minute, sir. The number is FO 2019. Will you put it down for my mother?"

"What? What, Jeannot?" his mother asked, startled.

"I noticed the number. The number of the car. FO 2019. I saw it close in front of me. There was a red light. It was the driver's fault."

The boy began to breathe laboriously. "The insurance company must pay. The number—"

"I wrote it down," Ravic said. "Be calm. I wrote everything down." He motioned to Eugénie to start the anesthetic.

"My mother must go to the police. The insurance company must pay—" Large beads of perspiration appeared on his face as suddenly as if it had been rained on. "If you amputate the leg they pay more—than if it—remains stiff—"

His eyes were sunk in blue-black circles which stood out from his skin like dirty ponds. The boy moaned and tried quickly to say something. "My mother—doesn't understand—help—her—" He could no longer go on. He began to scream, dull, repressed screams as if a tortured animal cowered within him.

"How is the world outside, Ravic?" Kate Hegstroem asked.

"Why do you want to know that, Kate? Rather think of something pleasanter."

"I feel as though I have been here for weeks already. Everything else is so remote. As if submerged."

"Let it remain submerged for a while."

"No. Otherwise I'll be afraid that this room is the last ark and that the deluge is already below the window. What's going on outside, Ravic?"

"Nothing new, Kate. The world goes on eagerly preparing for suicide and at the same time deluding itself about what it's doing."

"Will there be war?"

"Everyone knows that there will be war. What one does not yet know is when. Everyone expects a miracle." Ravic smiled. "Never before have I seen so many politicians who believe in miracles as at present in France and England. And never so few as in Germany."

She remained lying silent for a while. "To think that it should be possible—" she said then.

"Yes—it seems so impossible that it will happen some day. Just because one considers it so impossible and doesn't protect oneself against it. Do you have pain, Kate?"

"Not so much that I can't stand it." She adjusted her pillow under her head. "I'd like to get away from all this, Ravic."

"Yes—" he replied without conviction. "Who wouldn't like to?"

"When I get out of here I'll go to Italy. To Fiesole. I have a quiet old house there with a garden. I want to stay there for a while. It will still be cool. A veiled serene sun. At noon the early lizards on the south walls. In the evening the bells of Florence. And at night the moon and the stars behind the cypresses. There are books in the house and there is a big stone fireplace with wooden benches around it. The andirons for the wood are set up in such a manner as to hold a stand where one can put one's glass. Red wine is warmed that way. No people. Only an old couple to keep one's things in order.''

She looked at Ravic. "Beautiful," he said. "Quiet, a fireplace, books, and peace. In former days that sort of thing was considered bourgeois. Today it's the dream of a lost paradise.''

She nodded. "I want to stay there for a while. A few weeks. Maybe even a few months. I don't know yet. I want to become calm. And then I'll return and pack and go to America.''

Ravic heard supper trays being carried in the corridor. The rattling of a few dishes. "You are right, Kate," he said.

She hesitated. "Can I still have a child, Ravic?''

"Not right away. You've got to become much stronger first.''

"I don't mean that. Can I have it sometime? After this operation? Isn't—''

"No," Ravic said. "We didn't remove anything. Not a thing!''

She took a deep breath. "That's what I wanted to know.''

"But it will still take a long time, Kate. Your entire organism must change first.''

"It does not matter how long it takes." She smoothed her hair. The stone on her hand glittered in the dark. "It is ridiculous that I am asking for that, isn't it? Just now.''

"No. That happens often. More often than one would think.''

"Suddenly I have had enough of all this. I want to go back and marry, for good, the old-fashioned way, and have children and be calm and praise God and love life.''

Ravic looked out of the window. The wild red of the sunset hung over the roofs. The electric signs were drowned in it like bloodless shadows of colors.

"It must seem absurd to you, after all you know about me," Kate Hegstroem said behind him.

"No, not at all.''

"I've thought about it these last two days. And I feel younger and lighter than I have for longer than I can remember. When I'm over there I'll forget the years here like a senseless dream.''

Joan Madou came at four o'clock at night. Ravic woke up when he heard someone at the door. He had gone to sleep, not expecting her. He saw her standing in the open door. She tried to force her way through with an armful of giant chrysanthemums. He did not see her face. He only saw her figure and the huge bright blossoms. "What is that?" he said. "A forest of chrysanthemums. For heaven's sake, what does it mean?"

Joan got the flowers through the door and flung them with a flourish onto the bed. The blossoms were wet and cool and the leaves smelled of autumn and earth. "Presents," she said. "Since I know you I'm beginning to get presents."

"Take them away. I'm not dead yet. To lie under flowers—what's more, chrysanthemums—the good old bed of the Hôtel International really looks like a coffin."

"No!" Joan snatched up the flowers from the bed with a violent movement and threw them on the floor. "You mustn't—" She straightened up. "Don't talk like that! Ever!"

Ravic looked at her. He had forgotten how they had met. "Forget it," he said. "I didn't mean anything."

"Don't talk like that ever again. Not even as a joke. Promise!"

He saw her lips trembling. "But—" he said. "Does it really frighten you so?"

"Yes. It is even worse. I don't know what it is."

Ravic got up. "I'll never make a joke about it again. Are you satisfied now?"

She nodded, leaning on his shoulder. "I don't know what it is. I simply can't stand it. It's like a hand reaching out of the dark. It is fear—blind fear as if it were lying in wait somewhere for me." She pressed close to him. "Don't let it happen."

Ravic held her tight in his arms. "No—I won't let it happen."

She nodded again. "You can do it—"

"Yes," he said with a voice full of sadness and derision, thinking of Kate Hegstroem. "I can. Of course I can—"

She moved in his arms. "I was here yesterday—"

Ravic did not move. "You were?"

"Yes."

He was silent. Suddenly something perished. How childish

129

he had been! Waiting or not waiting—to what purpose? A foolish game with someone who did not play games.

"You were not here—"

"No."

"I know I shouldn't ask you where you were—"

"No."

She freed herself from his embrace. "I'd like to take a bath," she said in a changed voice. "Outside it's snowing. I'm cold. Can I still do it? Or will it wake up the hotel?"

Ravic smiled. "Don't ask about the consequences if you want to do something. Otherwise you'll never do it."

She looked at him. "One should ask in trifling matters. Never in great ones."

"Also correct."

She went into the bathroom and let the water run. Ravic sat down by the window and reached for a box of cigarettes. Outside over the roofs stood the red reflection of the town where silently the snow drifted. A taxi whined through the streets. The chrysanthemums gleamed palely on the floor. A newspaper was lying on the sofa. He had brought it along in the evening. Fighting at the Czechoslovakian frontier. Fighting in China. An ultimatum. An overthrown cabinet. He took the paper and pushed it under the chrysanthemums.

Joan came out of the bathroom. She was warm and crouched on the floor beside him among the flowers. "Where were you last night?" she asked.

He reached her down a cigarette. "Do you really want to know?"

"Yes."

He hesitated. "I was here," he said then, "and waited for you. I thought you weren't coming and then I left."

Joan waited. Her cigarette glowed in the dark and died away again.

"That's all," Ravic said.

"Did you go out to drink?"

"Yes—"

Joan turned around and looked at him. "Ravic," she said, "did you really go away because of that?"

"Yes."

She put her arms on his knees. He felt her warmth through the dressing gown. It was her warmth and the warmth of the gown which was more familiar to him than many years of his

130

life, and suddenly it seemed to him as if both had belonged together for a long time and as if Joan had returned to him from somewhere out of his life.

"Ravic, I've come to you every night. You ought to have known that I'd come yesterday too. Didn't you go out because you didn't want to see me?"

"No."

"You can tell me when you don't want to see me."

"I would tell you."

"Wasn't it that?"

"No, it was really not that."

"Then I'm happy."

Ravic looked at her. "What did you say?"

"I'm happy," she repeated.

He fell silent for a while. "Do you really know what you're saying?" he asked.

"Yes."

The pale radiance from outside was mirrored in her eyes. "One shouldn't say something like that lightly, Joan."

"I'm not saying it lightly."

"Happiness," Ravic said. "Where does it start and where does it end?"

His foot touched the chrysanthemums. Happiness, he thought. The blue horizons of youth. The golden-bright balance of life. Happiness! My God, where was it now?

"It starts with you and ends with you," Joan said. "That is quite simple."

Ravic did not reply. What is she talking about? he thought. "Soon you will tell me that you love me," he said then.

"I love you."

He made a gesture. "You hardly know me, Joan."

"What has that to do with it?"

"Much. Love—that means someone you want to grow old with."

"I don't know anything about that. It is someone you cannot live without. That's what I know."

"Where is the calvados?" Ravic asked.

"On the table. I'll get it for you. Stay where you are."

She brought the bottle and a glass and put them on the floor with the flowers. "I know that you don't love me," she said.

"Then you know more than I do—"

She looked up quickly. "You will love me," she said.

"Fine. Let us drink to that."

"Wait." She filled the glass and drained it. Then she filled it again and handed it to him. He took it and held it for a moment. All this is not true, he thought. A half dream in the waning night. Words spoken in the dark—how can they be true? Genuine words need much light. "How do you know all that so precisely?" he asked.

"Because I love you."

How she handles that word, Ravic thought. Without deliberation, like an empty bowl. She fills it with something and calls it love. With how many things had it been filled already! With fear of being alone—with stimulation through another ego—with the boosting of one's self-reliance—with the glittering reflection of one fantasy—but who really knows? Wasn't what I said about growing old together the stupidest thing of all? Isn't she far more right with her spontaneousness? And why do I sit here on a winter night, between wars, and spout words like a schoolmaster? Why do I resist, instead of plunging myself into it disbelievingly?

"Why do you resist?" she repeated.

"What?"

"Why do you resist?" she repeated.

"I don't resist—what should I resist?"

"I don't know. Something within you is closed up and you don't want to let anything or anyone in."

"Come," Ravic said, "let me have another drink."

"I am happy and I wish you were happy, too. I am completely happy. I wake up with you and I go to sleep with you. I don't know anything else. My head is made of silver when I think of both of us and sometimes it is like a violin. The streets are full of us as if we were music, and from time to time people break in and talk and pictures flash by like a movie, but the music remains. That always remains."

A few weeks ago you were still unhappy, Ravic thought, and you did not know me. An easy happiness. He emptied his glass of calvados. "Have you been happy often?" he asked.

"Not often."

"But sometimes. When was the last time your head was made of silver?"

"Why do you ask me?"

"Just to ask something. Without a reason."

"I have forgotten. And I don't want to know any more. It was different."

She smiled at him. Her face was bright and open like a flower with few leaves that hid nothing. "Two years ago," she said. "It did not last long. In Milan."

"Were you alone at that time?"

"No. I was with someone else. He was very unhappy and jealous and did not understand."

"Naturally not."

"You would understand. He made terrible scenes." She made herself comfortable, pulled a pillow down from the sofa and pushed it behind her back. "He called me a whore and faithless and ungrateful. It wasn't true. I was faithful as long as I loved him. He didn't understand that I did not love him any longer."

"One never understands that."

"Yes, you would understand. But I would always love you. You are different and everything is different with us. He wanted to kill me." She laughed. "They always want to kill. A few months later the other one wanted to kill me. But they never do it. You would never want to kill me."

"Only with calvados," Ravic said. "Pass the bottle. The conversation, thank God, is becoming more human. A few minutes ago I was pretty frightened."

"Because I love you?"

"We won't start that again. That's like parading about in a frock coat and a powdered wig. We are together—for shorter or longer, who knows? We are together, that's enough. Why do we have to label it?"

"I don't like that 'for shorter or longer.' But those are only words. You won't leave me. These too are only words, and you know it."

"Naturally. Has anyone you loved ever left you?"

"Yes." She looked at him. "One always leaves the other. Sometimes the other is quicker."

"And what did you do?"

"Everything!" She took the glass out of his hands and finished it. "Everything! But it didn't help. I was terribly unhappy."

"For long?"

"For a week. About a week."

"That isn't long."

"It's an eternity if you are really unhappy. I was so unhappy with every part of me that everything was exhausted after a week. My hair was unhappy, my skin, my bed, even

133

my clothes. I was so filled with unhappiness that nothing else existed. And if nothing else exists any more, unhappiness ceases to be unhappiness—because there is nothing left with which to compare it. Then it is nothing but complete exhaustion. And then it is over. Slowly one starts to live again."

She kissed his hand. He felt the soft cautious lips. "What are you thinking of?" she asked.

"Of nothing. Nothing but that you are of a wild innocence. Completely corrupt and not corrupt at all. The most dangerous thing in the world. Give me back the glass. I'll drink to my friend Morosow, the connoisseur of the human heart."

"I don't like Morosow. Can't we drink to someone else?"

"Naturally you don't like him. He has keen eyes. Let's drink to you."

"To me?"

"Yes, to you."

"I'm not dangerous," Joan said. "I'm in danger, but not dangerous."

"The fact that you think so is part of it. Nothing will ever happen to you. *Salute.*"

"*Salute.* But you don't understand me."

"Who wants to understand? That's the cause of all misunderstandings in the world. Pass me the bottle."

"You drink too much. Why do you want to drink so much?"

"Joan," Ravic said, "the day will come when you will say: Too much! You drink too much, you'll say and believe that you desire my good only. In reality, you will simply want to prevent my excursions into a sphere which you cannot control. *Salute!* Today we celebrate. We have gloriously escaped pathos which stood like a fat cloud outside the window. We slew it with pathos. *Salute!*"

She straightened up. She propped herself with her hands on the floor and looked at him. Her eyes were wide open, the bathrobe had slipped down from her shoulders, her hair was thrown back on the nape of her neck, and there was something of a bright young lioness about her in the dark. "I know," she said calmly, "you're laughing at me. I know it and I don't mind. I feel that I'm alive; I feel it in my whole being, my breath is different and my sleep is no longer dead, my joints have purpose again and my hands are no longer empty, and it does not matter to me what you think about it and what you may say about it, I let myself fly and I let myself run and I throw myself into it, without a thought, and I am happy and I am neither cautious nor afraid of saying it, even if you do laugh at me and make fun of me—''

Ravic was silent for a while. "I'm not making fun of you," he then said. "I'm making fun of myself, Joan—''

She leaned toward him. "Why? There is something in the back of your head that resists. Why?"

"There is nothing that resists. I am just slower than you are."

She shook her head. "It's not only that. There's something that wants to remain alone. I feel it. It's like a barrier."

"There's no barrier. That is merely fifteen more years of life than you have had. Not everyone's life is like a house that belongs to him and that he can go on decorating ever more richly with the furniture of his memory. Some people live in hotels, in many hotels. The years close behind them like hotel doors—and the only thing that remains is a little courage and no regrets."

She did not answer for some time. He did not know whether she had listened to him or not. He looked out of the window and calmly felt the deep glow of the calvados in his veins. The beat of the pulses was still and became a widespread quietness in which the machine guns of ceaselessly ticking time were silent. The moon rose, a blurred red, over the roofs like the cupola of a mosque, half hidden by clouds, emerging slowly while the earth sank into the drifting snow.

"I know," Joan said, her hands on his knees and her chin on her hands, "it's foolish to tell you these earlier things about myself. I could be silent or I could lie, but I don't want to. Why should I not tell you everything about my life and why should I make more out of it? I'd rather make less out of it because it is laughable to me now and I don't understand it any more and you may laugh about it and also about me too."

Ravic looked at her. One of her knees was crushing a few of the large white blossoms against the newspaper he had bought. A strange night, he thought. Somewhere now there is shooting and men are being hunted and imprisoned and tortured and murdered, some corner of a peaceful world is being trampled upon, and one knows it, helplessly, and life buzzes on in the bright bistros of the city, no one cares, and people go calmly to sleep, and I am sitting here with a woman between pale chrysanthemums and a bottle of calvados, and the shadow of love rises, trembling, lonesome, strange and sad, it too an exile from the safe gardens of the past, shy and wild and quick as if it had no right—

"Joan," he said slowly and wanted to say something entirely different, "it is good that you are here."

She looked at him.

He took her hands. "You understand what that means? More than a thousand other words—"

She nodded. Suddenly her eyes were filled with tears. "It doesn't mean anything," she said. "I know."

"That's not true," Ravic replied and knew that she was right.

"No, nothing at all. You must love me, beloved. That's all."

He did not answer.

"You must love me," she repeated. "Otherwise I'm lost."

Lost—he thought. What a word! How easily she uses it. Who is really lost does not talk.

Chapter 12

"DID YOU take my leg off?" Jeannot asked.

His thin face was bloodless and white like the wall of an old house. His freckles stood out very large and dark as though they did not belong to his face but were drops of paint sprinkled over it. The stump of his leg lay under a wire basket over which the blanket was drawn.

"Have you any pain?" Ravic asked.

"Yes. In my foot. My foot hurts very much. I asked the nurse. The old dragon wouldn't tell me."

"The leg has been amputated," Ravic said.

"Above the knee or below the knee?"

"Ten centimeters above it. Your knee was crushed and could not be saved."

"Good," Jeannot said. "That makes about fifteen per cent more from the insurance company. Very good. An artificial leg is an artificial leg, whether above or below the knee. But fifteen per cent more is something you can put into your pocket every month." He hesitated for a moment. "For the time being you'd better not tell my mother. She can't see it anyway with this parrot cage over the stump."

"We won't tell her anything, Jeannot."

"The insurance company must pay an annuity for life. That's correct, isn't it?"

"I think so."

His face twisted into a grimace. "They'll be surprised. I am thirteen years old. They'll have to pay for a long time. Do you know yet which insurance company it is?"

"Not yet. But we have the number of the car. You kept it in mind. The police have been here already. They want to question you. You were still asleep this morning. They'll come again tonight."

Jeannot deliberated. "Witnesses," he said then. "It's important that we have witnesses. Have we any?"

"I think your mother has two addresses. She had the slips of paper in her hand."

The boy became restless. "She'll lose them. If only she hasn't lost them already. You know how old people are. Where is she now?"

"Your mother sat at your bedside all night and until noon today. Only then were we able to send her away. She'll come back again soon."

"Let's hope she'll still have them. The police—" He made a weak gesture with his emaciated hand. "Cheats," he murmured. "They are all cheats. In cahoots with the insurance companies. But if one has good witnesses—when will she come back?"

"Soon. Don't get excited about it. It'll be all right."

Jeannot moved his mouth as if he were chewing something. "Sometimes they pay the whole amount at once. A settlement instead of an annuity. We could start a business with it, mother and I."

"Now rest," Ravic said. "You'll have time to think about it later."

The boy shook his head. "You will," Ravic repeated. "You must be rested when the police come."

"Yes, you're right. What shall I do?"

"Sleep."

"But then—"

"They'll wake you up."

"Red light. I'm sure it was a red light."

"Certainly. And now try to sleep. There is a bell in case you should need anything."

"Doctor—"

"Yes?" Ravic turned around.

"If everything works out—" Jeannot lay on his pillow and something like a smile flitted across his twisted, precocious face. "Sometimes one is lucky after all, isn't one?"

The evening was humid and warm. Tattered clouds floated low over the city. In front of Fouquet's restaurant, circular coke-ovens had been set up. A few tables and chairs stood around them. Morosow was sitting at one of them. He beckoned to Ravic. "Come, have a drink with me."

Ravic sat down beside him. "We sit too much in rooms," Morosow declared. "Has that ever occurred to you?"

"But you don't. You're always standing in front of the Scheherazade."

"My boy, spare me your miserable logic. Evenings I'm a sort of two-legged door at the Scheherazade, but not a human being in the open. We live in rooms too much, I say. We think too much in rooms. We make love too much in rooms. We despair too much in rooms. Can you despair in the open?"

"And how!" Ravic said.

"Only because we live too much in rooms. Not if one is used to the open. One despairs more decently in a landscape than in a two-room-and-kitchenette apartment. More comfortably, too. Don't contradict me! To contradict shows an occidental narrowness of the mind. Who actually wants to be right? Today is my day off and I wish to absorb life. By the way, we also drink too much in rooms."

"We also urinate too much in rooms."

"Get away with your irony. The facts of life are simple and trivial. Only our imagination gives life to them. It makes the laundry pole of facts a flagstaff of dreams. Am I right?"

"No."

"Of course not. I don't even want to be."

"Of course you are right."

"Good, brother. We also sleep too much in rooms. We become pieces of furniture. Stone buildings have broken our spines. We have become walking sofas, dressing tables, safes, leases, salaries, kitchen pots, and water toilets."

"Correct. Walking party platforms, ammunition factories, institutes for the blind and asylums for the insane."

"Don't keep interrupting me. Drink, be quiet and live, you murderer with the scalpel. See what has become of us. As far as I know, only the old Greeks had gods of drinking and the joy of life: Bacchus and Dionysus. Instead of that we have Freud, inferiority complexes and the psychoanalysis. We're afraid of the too great words in love and not afraid of much too great words in politics. A sorry generation!" Morosow winked.

Ravic winked, too. "Good old cynic with dreams," he said. "Are you engaged in improving the world again?"

Morosow grinned. "I'm engaged in feeling it, you romantic without illusions, for a short time on earth, called Ravic."

Ravic laughed. "For a very short time. This is now my third life as far as names go. Is this Polish vodka?"

"Estonian. From Riga. The best. Pour—and then let us sit calmly here and stare at the most beautiful street in the world and praise this mild evening and casually spit in the face of despair."

The fire in the coke-ovens crackled. A man with a violin took up a position by the curb and began to play *Auprès de ma blonde*. Passers-by jostled him, the bow scraped, but the man continued to play as if he were alone. It sounded thin and empty. The violin seemed to be freezing. Two Moroccans went from table to table and offered garish carpets of artificial silk.

The newspaper boys passed with the latest editions. Morosow bought the *Paris Soir* and the *Intransigeant*. He read the headlines and pushed the newspapers aside. "They are all damned counterfeiters," he growled. "Have you ever observed that we are living in the age of counterfeiters?"

"No. I thought we were living in the age of cans."

"Cans? How so?"

Ravic pointed at the newspapers. "Cans. We don't have to think any more. Everything is pre-meditated, pre-chewed, pre-felt. Cans. All you have to do is open them. Delivered to your home three times a day. Nothing any more to cultivate yourself, or let grow and boil on the fire of questions, of doubt, and of desire. Cans." He grinned. "We don't live easily, Boris. Just cheaply."

"Cans with false labels." Morosow lifted the papers. "Counterfeiting! Take a look at that! They build their ammunition factories because they want peace; their concentration camps because they love the truth; justice is the cover for every factional madness; political gangsters are saviors; and freedom is the big word for all greed for power. Counterfeit money! Counterfeit spiritual money! The lie as propaganda. Kitchen Machiavellism. Idealism in the hands of the underworld. If at least they would be honest—" He crushed the newspapers together and threw them away.

"Very likely we are reading too many newspapers in rooms," Ravic said and laughed.

"Naturally. In the open one only needs them to start a fire—"

Morosow stopped abruptly. Ravic was no longer sitting beside him. He had jumped up and was pushing his way through the crowd in front of the café in the direction of the Avenue George V.

Morosow sat for a second, astonished. Then he pulled some money out of his pocket, threw it onto a china plate beside the glasses, and followed Ravic. He did not know what had happened but he followed him anyhow, to be at hand if he should need him. He saw no police. Neither did he see any plain-clothes detectives hunting Ravic. The sidewalks were packed with people. Good for him, Morosow thought. If a policeman recognized him, he can easily escape. He saw Ravic again only when he had reached the Avenue George V. The traffic lights changed at that moment and the jammed lines of cars dashed forward. Notwithstanding, Ravic tried to cross the street. A taxi almost knocked him down. The cabdriver was furious. Morosow grabbed Ravic's arm from behind and pulled him back. "Are you mad," he cried. "Do you want to commit suicide? What's the matter?"

Ravic did not answer. He stared across the street. The traffic was very dense. Car after car, four rows deep. It was impossible to get through.

Morosow shook him. "What happened, Ravic? The police?"

"No." Ravic did not take his eyes from the passing cars.

"What is it? What is it, Ravic?"

"Haake—"

"What?" Morosow's eyes narrowed. "What does he look like? Quick! Quick, Ravic!"

"A gray coat—"

The shrill whistle of the traffic policeman came from the middle of the Champs Elysées. Ravic dashed across between the last cars. A dark gray coat—that was all he knew. He crossed the Avenue George V and the Rue Bassano. Suddenly there were dozens of gray coats. He cursed and walked on as quickly as he could. The traffic had stopped at the Rue Galilée. He rapidly crossed it and ruthlessly pushed his way through the crowd, along the Champs Elysées. He came to the Rue de Presbourg, crossed it, and suddenly stood still. Before him was the Place de l'Etoile, huge, confusing, full of traffic, with streets branching off in all directions. Gone! No one could be found here.

He turned around slowly, scrutinizing the faces of the crowd—but his excitement was gone. Suddenly he felt very empty. He must have been mistaken again—or Haake had escaped him a second time. But could one be mistaken twice?

Could someone disappear from the surface of the earth twice? There were the side-streets. Haake could have turned into one of those. He looked along the Rue de Presbourg. Cars, cars, and people, people. The busiest hour of the evening. There was no point in searching along them. Too late again.

"Nothing?" Morosow asked when he caught up with him.

Ravic shook his head. "I am probably seeing ghosts again."

"Did you recognize him?"

"I thought so. Only just a minute ago. Now—now I don't know at all."

Morosow looked at him. "There are many faces that look alike, Ravic."

"Yes, and some that one never forgets."

Ravic stood still. "What do you want to do?" Morosow asked.

"I don't know. What can I do now?"

Morosow stared into the crowd. "Damned bad luck! Just at this time. Close of business. Everything crowded—"

"Yes—"

"And, moreover, the light! Half-darkness. Could you see him well?"

Ravic did not answer.

Morosow took his arm. "Listen," he said. "Running around in the streets and cross-streets is pointless. While you are looking through one street you will think he is in the next one. Not a chance. Let's go back to Fouquet's. That's the best place. You can keep a better lookout from there than by running around. In case he comes back, you'll be able to see him from there."

They sat down at an outside table which was open to the street in two directions. For a long time they sat in silence. "What do you intend to do if you meet him?" Morosow asked finally. "Do you know yet?"

Ravic shook his head.

"Think about it. It's better for you to know beforehand. There's no sense in being taken by surprise and doing something foolish. Particularly not in your situation. You don't want to be imprisoned for years."

Ravic looked up. He did not answer. He only looked at Morosow.

"It wouldn't matter to me," Morosow said. "If it were me. But it does matter to me in your case. What would you have done if he had been the one and you had got hold of him across the street at the corner?"

"I don't know, Boris. I really don't know."

"You have nothing on you, have you?"

"No."

"If you had attacked him without planning it, you would have been separated in a minute. By now you would be at police headquarters and he would probably have got away with a few black-and-blue marks. You know that, don't you?"

"Yes." Ravic stared into the street.

Morosow deliberated. "At best you might have tried to push him under an automobile at the intersection. But that wouldn't have been sure either. He might have got away with a couple of scratches."

"I won't push him under an automobile," Ravic replied without taking his eyes from the street.

"I know that. I wouldn't do it, either."

Morosow was silent for a while. "Ravic," he said then. "If he was the one and if you meet him you must be dead sure what to do, you know that? You'll have only one chance."

"Yes, I know." Ravic continued to stare into the street.

"If you should see him follow him. But don't do anything else. Only follow him. Find out where he lives. Nothing else. All the rest you can work out later. Take your time. Do nothing foolish. Do you hear?"

"Yes," Ravic said absent-mindedly and stared into the street.

A man selling pistachio nuts came to their table. He was followed by a boy with toy mice. He made them dance on the marble table top and run up his sleeve. The violin player appeared for the second time. Now he wore a hat and played *Parlez moi d'amour*. An old lady with a syphilitic nose was hawking violets.

Morosow looked at his watch. "Eight," he said. "It's senseless to wait any longer, Ravic. We've been sitting here for over two hours already. The man won't come back now. Everyone in France is eating supper somewhere at this hour."

"Why don't you go, Boris? Why are you sitting around here with me anyhow?"

"That has nothing to do with it. I can sit here with you as

143

long as we like. But I don't want you to drive yourself crazy. It's senseless for you to sit here for hours. The chances of meeting him are now the same everywhere. No, now they are greater in any restaurant, in any night club, in any brothel."

"I know, Boris." Ravic stared into the street. The traffic had become less dense.

Morosow put his large hairy hand on Ravic's arm. "Ravic," he said, "listen. If you are destined to meet that man, you'll meet him—and if not, then you can wait for him for years. You know what I mean. Keep your eyes open—everywhere. And be prepared for anything. But otherwise go on living as if you were mistaken. That's the only thing you can do. Otherwise you will ruin yourself. I lived through the same thing once. About twenty years ago. I kept thinking I saw one of my father's murderers. Hallucinations." He emptied his glass. "Damned hallucinations. And now come with me. We'll go somewhere and have something to eat."

"You go and have something to eat, Boris. I'll come later."

"Do you intend to stay here?"

"Just for another moment. Then I'll go to the hotel. I have something to do there."

Morosow looked at him. He knew what Ravic wanted to do in the hotel. But he also knew that he couldn't do anything else. This was Ravic's business alone. "All right," he said. "I'll be at the Mère Marie. Later at Bublishki's. Call me or come there." He raised his bushy eyebrows. "And don't run any risks. Don't be a hero for nothing! And a damned idiot. Don't shoot unless you are sure you can escape. This is no child's play and no gangster movie."

"I know that, Boris. Don't worry."

Ravic went to the Hôtel International and started back immediately. On his way he passed the Hôtel de Milan. He looked at his watch. It was eight-thirty. He could still find Joan at home.

She came toward him. "Ravic," she said surprised. "You've come here?"

"Yes—"

"You've never been here, do you know that? Since the day you brought me here."

He smiled absent-mindedly. "That's true, Joan. We lead a strange life."

"Yes. Like moles. Or bats. Or owls. We see each other only when it is dark."

She walked through the room with long lithe strides. She wore a dark-blue tailored dressing gown, drawn tight about her hips with a belt. The black evening gown which she wore at the Scheherazade was lying on the bed. She was very beautiful and infinitely remote.

"Don't you have to go, Joan?"

"No. Not for half an hour. This is the best time for me. The hour before I have to leave. You see what I have? Coffee and all the time in the world. And now even you are here. I have calvados too."

She brought the bottle. He took it and put it, unopened, on the table. Then he took her hands. "Joan," he said.

The light in her eyes dimmed. She stood close to him. "Tell me at once what it is—"

"Why? What should it be?"

"Something. There is always something the matter when you are this way. Did you come because of that?"

He felt her hands trying to pull away from him. She did not move. Even her hands did not move. It was only as if something in them wanted to pull away from him. "You can't come tonight, Joan. Not tonight and perhaps not tomorrow and not for a few days."

"Do you have to stay at the hospital?"

"No. It is something else. I can't talk about it. But it is something that has nothing to do with you and me."

She stood there for a while, motionless. "All right," she said then.

"You understand?"

"No. But if you say so, it is right."

"You aren't angry?"

She looked at him. "My God, Ravic," she said. "How could I ever be angry with you about anything?"

He looked up. It was as though a hand had pressed hard on his heart. Joan had spoken with purpose, but nothing she could have done would have touched him more. He paid little heed to what she murmured and whispered during the night; it was forgotten as soon as dawn stood gray outside the window. He knew that the rapture of those hours in which she crouched or lay at his side was as much rapture over herself, and he took it for intoxication and the shining avowal of the moment, but never for more. Now for the first time, like a flier who, through an opening of gleaming clouds on which the light plays hide-and-seek, suddenly perceives the earth below, green, brown, and solid, he saw more. He saw devotion behind the rapture, feeling behind the intoxication, simple confidence behind the rush of words. He had expected suspicion, questions, and lack of understanding—but not this. It was always the little things that brought revelation—never the big ones. The big ones were too tied up with dramatic gestures and the temptation to lie.

A room. A hotel room. A few suitcases, a bed, light, the black solitude of night and past outside the window—and here a bright face with gray eyes and high brows and the bold sweep of the hair—life, pliant life, openly turned toward him like an oleander bush toward the light—here it was, here it stood, waiting, silent, calling to him: Take me! Hold me! Had he not said a long time ago: I'll hold you?

He stood up. "Good night, Joan."

"Good night, Ravic."

He was sitting in front of the Café Fouquet. He was sitting at the same table as before. He sat there for hours, buried in the darkness of his past in which only a single feeble light burned: the hope for revenge.

They had arrested him in August, 1933. He had kept two friends of his who were wanted by the Gestapo hidden at his place for two weeks and he had then helped them to escape. One of them had saved his life in 1917, at Bixschoote in Flanders and had brought him back under cover of machine-gun fire when he had been lying in No Man's Land, slowly bleeding to death. The other was a Jewish writer whom he had known for years. He had been brought up for examination; they wanted to find out in which direction the two had escaped, what papers they had on them and who would be of help to them on the road. Haake had examined him. After he had fainted the first time he had tried to shoot or strike down Haake with his own revolver. He had jumped into a crashing red darkness. It had been a useless attempt against four strong, armed men. For three days out of unconsciousness, slow awakening, out of frantic pain Haake's cool smiling face emerged. For three days the same questions—for three days the same body, bruised all over, almost incapable of further suffering. And then on the afternoon of the third day Sybil was brought in. She did not know about anything. He was shown to her to force a confession from her. She was a beautiful, luxury-loving creature who had lived a carefree superficial life. He had expected her to scream and break down. She did not break down. She turned on the torturers. She used deadly words. Deadly for her and she knew it. Haake had ceased smiling. He had cut short the examination. Next day he had explained to Ravic what would happen to her in the concentration camp for women if he did not confess. Ravic had not answered. Haake had explained to him what would happen to her before that. Ravic had not confessed to anything because there was nothing to confess. He had tried to convince Haake that this woman could not know anything. He had told him that he only knew her superficially. That she had meant little more in his life than a beautiful picture. That he could never have confided anything to her. All this had been true. Haake had only smiled. Three days later Sybil was dead. She had hanged herself in the concentration camp for women. A day later one of the fugitives was brought back. It was the Jewish writer. When Ravic saw him he could no longer recognize him, not even by his voice. It took another week before he was finally dead under Haake's examination. Then came the concentration camp for Ravic. The hospital. The escape from the hospital.

The silver moon stood above the Arc de Triomphe. The street lamps along the Champs Elysées flickered in the wind. The lights of night were reflected in the glasses on the table. Unreal, Ravic thought, unreal the one and the other. Unreal these glasses, this moon, this street, this night, and this hour that touches me with its breath, strange and familiar as if it had been here before, in another life, on another star—unreal these memories of years that are past, submerged, alive and dead at the same time, only phosphorescing now in my brain and petrified into expectation—unreal this fluid rolling through the darkness of my veins, unresting, 98.6 in temperature, slightly salty in flavor, four liters of secrecy and drive, blood, and the reflection in ganglia, the invisible storehouse in nothingness, called memory. Star after star, rising year after year, one bright, the other bloody as Mars above the Rue de Berri, and many darkly gleaming and full of spots—the sky of memory beneath which the present restlessly carries on its confused life.

The green light of revenge. The city quietly floating in the late moonlight and in the drone of automobile motors. Long rows of houses, stretching endlessly, rows of windows and packed behind them bundles of fate, by the block. The heart-beat of millions of men, the incessant beat as of a millionfold motor, moving slowly, slowly along the street of life, with every throb a tiny millimeter closer to death.

He got up. The Champs Elysées was almost empty. Only a few whores loitered at the corners. He walked down the street, passed the Rue Pierre Charron, the Rue Marbeuf, the Rue Marignan to the Rond Point and back to the Arc de Triomphe. He stepped over the chains and stood before the tomb of the Unknown Soldier. The small blue flame flickered in the shadow. A withering wreath lay in front of it. He crossed the Etoile and went to the bistro where he thought he had first seen Haake. A few taxi drivers were still sitting there. He sat down by the window where he had been sitting before and drank his coffee. The street outside was empty. The drivers were talking about Hitler. They found him ridiculous and prophesied his immediate downfall should he dare to come near the Maginot Line. Ravic stared into the street.

Why am I sitting here? he thought. I could be sitting anywhere in Paris; the chances are the same. He looked at his watch. It was just before three. Too late. Haake—if it had been he—would not be roaming the streets at this time.

Outside he saw a whore strolling around. She looked inside through the window and walked on. If she comes back I'll go, he thought. The whore came back. He did not go. If she comes once more I'll certainly go, he decided. Then Haake is not in Paris. The whore returned. She beckoned with her head and passed by. He remained sitting. She returned once more. He did not go.

The waiter put the chairs on the tables. The cabdrivers paid and left the bistro. The waiter turned off the light above the counter. The room was plunged into murky darkness. Ravic looked around. "The check," he said.

Outside it had become windier and colder. The clouds floated higher and faster. Ravic walked by Joan's hotel and stopped. All was dark except one window where a lamp shimmered behind curtains. It was Joan's room. He knew that she hated to enter a dark room by herself. She had left the light on because she was not coming to him today. He looked up and suddenly he no longer understood himself. Why didn't he want to see her? The memory of the other woman had died long ago; only the memory of her death had remained.

And the other thing? What did it have to do with her? What did it still have to do even with himself? Wasn't he a fool to chase an illusion, the reflex of an entangled, blackened memory, a dark reaction—to begin anew stirring the dross of dead years, stirred up by mere chance, by an accursed resemblance—to allow a piece of the rotted past to break open again, the abscess of a barely healed neurosis—and thereby jeopardize everything he had built up in himself, his own self, that clear bit of life divorced from what he had been, the life he had created for himself and the only person close to him? What had the one to do with the other? Hadn't he taught himself that time and again? How else could he have escaped? And where would he be without it?

He felt that the lump of lead in his brain was melting away. He breathed deeply. The wind came along the street with swift blasts. He looked up at the lighted window again. There was someone to whom he meant something, someone to whom he was important, someone whose face changed when she looked at him—and he had been about to sacrifice that to a twisted illusion, to the impatient, disdainful arrogance born of a faint hope for revenge . . .

What did he really want? Why did he resist? What was he saving himself for? Life offered itself to him and he raised objections. Not because there was too little—because there was too much. Had the bloody thunderstorm of his past to sweep over him that he could recognize it? He moved his shoulders. Heart, he thought, heart! How it opened itself up! How it throbbed! Window, he thought, lonely window lit at night, reflection of another's life that had given itself up to him passionately, waiting, open, until he too should open. The flame of love—the Saint Elmo's fire of tenderness—the bright, swift, sheet lightning of the blood—one knew it, one knew everything about it, one knew so much that one thought this soft golden confusion could never flood one's brain again—and then suddenly one night one stood in front of a third-rate hotel and it rose like mist out of the asphalt and one felt it as though it had come from the other end of the earth, from blue cocoanut islands, from the warmth of a tropical spring, as though it had filtered through oceans, coral reefs, lava, and darkness and impetuously pierced its way into Paris, into the shabby Rue Poncelet, with the odor of hibiscus and mimosa, in a night filled with revenge and the past, the irresistible, indisputable, enigmatic resurrection of emotion . . .

The Scheherazade was crowded. Joan was sitting at a table with some people. She saw Ravic at once. He remained standing by the door. The place was full of smoke and music. She said something to the people at her table and came up to him quickly. "Ravic—"

"Are you still needed here?"

"Why?"

"I want to take you with me."

"But didn't you say—"

"That's over. Are you still needed here?"

"No. I'll just tell them that I'm going."

"Do it quickly—I'll wait for you in the taxi outside."

"Yes," she remained standing. "Ravic—"

He looked at her. "Did you come because of me?" she asked.

He hesitated a second. "Yes," he said in a low voice while her face moved close to his. "Yes, Joan. Because of you! Only because of you."

The taxi drove along the Rue de Liège. "What was the matter, Ravic?"

"Nothing."

"I was afraid—"

"Forget it. It was nothing—"

She looked at him. "I thought you would never come again."

He bent over her. He felt her trembling. "Joan," he said. "Don't think about anything and don't ask any questions. Do you see the light of the street lamps and the thousand colored signs out there? We are living in a dying age and this city quivers with life. We are torn from everything and we have nothing left but out hearts. I was in the land of the moon and I've come back, and here you are and you are life. Don't ask anything more. There are more secrets in your hair than in a thousand questions. Here before us is the night, a few hours and an eternity, until the morning rumbles against the windows. That people love each other is everything; a marvel and the most obvious thing in the world, this is what I felt today when the night melted away into a flowering bush and the wind smelled of strawberries and without love one is only a dead man on furlough, nothing but a scrap of paper with a few dates and a chance name on it and one might as well die—''

The light from the street lamps swept through the window of the taxi like the circling beam of a lighthouse through the darkness of a ship's cabin. Joan's eyes were alternately very translucent and very dark in her pale face. ''We shall not die,'' she whispered in Ravic's arms.

''No. Not we. Only time. Damned time. It always dies. We live. We always live. When you wake up it is spring and when you go to sleep it is fall and a thousand times in between it is winter and summer, and when we love each other enough we are immortal and indestructible like the heartbeat and the rain and the wind, and that is much. Day by day we are conquerors, beloved, and year by year we are defeated, but who wants to realize that and to whom does it matter? The hour is life, the moment is closest to eternity, your eyes glisten, star dust trickles through infinity, gods can age, but your mouth is young, the enigma trembles between us, the You and Me, Call and Answer, out of evenings, out of dusks, out of the ecstasies of all lovers, pressed from the remotest cries of brutal lust into golden storms, the endless road from the amoeba to Ruth and Esther and Helen and Aspasia, to blue Madonnas in chapels on the road, from jungle and animal to you, to you. . . .''

She lay in his arms, motionless, her face pale, in such surrender that she almost seemed absent—and he bent over her and spoke and spoke—and at the beginning he felt as though someone were looking over his shoulder, a shadow that talked soundlessly too, with a faint smile, and he bent deeper and felt her move toward him, and it was still there, and then it was gone. . . .

Chapter 13

"A SCANDAL," said the woman with the emeralds who was sitting opposite Kate Hegstroem. Her eyes sparkled. "A wonderful scandal! All Paris is laughing about it. Did you have any idea that Louis was a homosexual? Surely not! None of us knew; he kept it very well covered up. Lina de Newburg was considered his official mistress—and now imagine: a week ago he returned from Rome three days earlier than he had said and went to Nicky's apartment the same evening, intending to surprise him, and whom did he find there?"

"His wife," Ravic said.

The woman with the emeralds glanced up. Suddenly she looked as if she just had been told that her husband was bankrupt. "You already know the story?" she asked.

"No. But it must be like that."

"I don't understand." She stared at Ravic, irritated. "After all it was most improbable."

"That's just why."

Kate Hegstroem smiled. "Doctor Ravic has a theory, Daisy. He calls it the systematics of chance. According to it the most improbable is always practically the most logical."

"That's interesting." Daisy smiled politely and entirely uninterestedly. "It wouldn't have led to anything," she continued calmly, "if Louis had not made a terrific scene. He was completely beside himself. Now he is living in the Crillon. Wants to divorce her. Both are waiting for evidence." She leaned back in her chair, full of expectation. "What do you say?"

Kate Hegstroem looked quickly at Ravic. He was studying a branch of orchids which stood on the table between hatboxes and a basket of fruit containing grapes and peaches—white flowers like butterflies with lascivious, red-spotted hearts. "Unbelievable, Daisy," she said. "Really unbelievable!"

Daisy enjoyed her triumph. "I'm sure you couldn't have known that beforehand, could you?" she asked Ravic.

He carefully put the branch back into the narrow crystal vase. "No, certainly not that."

Daisy nodded in satisfaction and picked up her bag, her compact, and her gloves. "I've got to go. I'm late now. Louise is having a cocktail party. Her minister is coming. All sorts of rumors are going around." She rose. "By the way, Ferdy and Marthe have broken up again. She has sent her jewelry back to him. For the third time now. It still impresses him. The poor fool. He thinks he is loved for his own sake. He'll return everything to her and another piece as a reward. As always. He doesn't know—but she has already selected what she'd like to have at Ostertag's. He always buys there. A ruby brooch; big square stones, best pigeon-blood. She is smart."

She kissed Kate Hegstroem. "Adieu, my lamb. Now you are at least somewhat au courant. Can't you get out of here soon?" She looked at Ravic.

He caught Kate Hegstroem's look. "Not right away," he said. "Sorry."

He helped Daisy into her coat. It was a dark mink without a collar. A coat for Joan, he thought. Daisy made a very good appearance, slim, exquisite, with a short nose and delicate joints, well groomed and entirely without sex appeal. "Why don't you come for tea with Kate?" she said. "Only a few people are there on Wednesdays so we can chat undisturbed. I'm very much interested in operations."

"Gladly."

Ravic closed the door behind her and came back. "Beautiful emeralds," he said.

Kate Hegstroem laughed. "Well, that was my life before, Ravic. Can you understand that?"

"Yes. Why not? Wonderful if one can do it. It gives you protection against so much."

"I can't understand it any longer." She got up, and walked carefully to her bed.

Ravic smiled. "It makes very little difference where one lives, Kate. Some places are more comfortable than others, but it is never important. The only important thing is what one makes of it."

She put her long beautiful legs onto the bed. "Everything is inconsequential," she said, "when you have been in bed for a few weeks and can walk again."

Ravic took a cigarette. "You don't have to stay here any longer if you don't want to. You can live in the Lancaster if you take a nurse with you."

Kate Hegstroem shook her head. "I'll stay here until I can travel. Here I am protected against too many Daisies."

"Throw them out when they come," Ravic said. "Nothing is more tiring than listening to gossip."

She stretched herself cautiously on her bed. "Would you believe that Daisy is a wonderful mother in spite of her gossiping? She is bringing up her two children magnificently."

"That can happen," Ravic declared, unimpressed.

Kate Hegstroem smiled. She drew the blanket over her. "A hospital is like a convent," she said. "You learn to appreciate the simplest things again. Walking. Breathing. Seeing."

"Yes. Happiness lies all around us. We only have to pick it up."

She looked at him. "I really mean it."

"So do I, Kate. Only the simple things never disappoint us. And as far as happiness is concerned you can't start too far down."

Jeannot was lying on his bed, a heap of pamphlets scattered over his blanket.

"Why don't you put the light on?" Ravic asked.

"I can still see well enough. I have good eyes."

The pamphlets contained descriptions of artificial legs. Jeannot had got them together in every way he could. His mother had brought him the last ones. He showed Ravic a wonderfully colored folder. Ravic turned on the light. "This is the most expensive," Jeannot said.

"It is not the best," Ravic replied.

"But it is the most expensive. I'll explain to the insurance company that I must have it. Naturally I don't want it at all. Only the insurance company shall pay for it. I want a wooden stump and the money."

"The insurance company has its own physicians who check on everything, Jeannot."

The boy straightened up. "Do you think they won't allow me a leg?"

"They will. Perhaps not the most expensive. But they won't give you any money; they'll see to it that you really get it."

"Then I'll have to take it and sell it immediately. Of course I'll not get the full price. Do you think twenty percent off is enough? I'll offer it first for ten. Maybe we can talk with the shopkeeper in advance. What does it matter to the insurance company whether I take the leg? They must pay; nothing else really matters to them, or does it?''

''Of course not. You can try.''

''It would amount to something. We could buy the counter and the equipment for a small *crémerie* for that money.'' Jeannot smiled cunningly. ''Thank God, a leg like that with its joint and everything else is pretty expensive. A precision job. That's fine.''

''Has someone from the insurance company already been here?''

''No, not yet about the leg and the compensation. Only about the operation and the hospital. Do we have to hire a lawyer? What do you think? It was a red light! I'm quite positive. The police—''

The nurse came with the supper. She put it on the table beside Jeannot. The boy did not say anything until she had gone. ''They give you a lot to eat here,'' he declared then. ''I've never had so much. I can't finish it all by myself. My mother always comes and eats the rest. There is enough for both of us. She's saving money this way. The room here costs a great deal anyway.''

''That's paid by the insurance company. It makes no difference where you are.''

A gleam flitted across the gray face of the boy. ''I spoke to Doctor Veber. He'll give me ten per cent. He'll send the bill for what it costs to the insurance company. They pay it; but he'll let me have the ten per cent in cash.''

''You're efficient, Jeannot.''

''You've got to be efficient when you are poor.''

''That's right. Are you in pain?''

''In the foot I don't have any more.''

''Those are the nerves which are still there.''

''I know. It's funny just the same. To have pain in something that isn't there any more. Maybe the soul of my leg is still there.'' Jeannot grinned. He had cracked a joke. Then he removed the lid from his supper plates. ''Soup, chicken, vegetable, pudding. That's something for mother. She likes chicken. We didn't often have it at home.'' He leaned back comfortably. ''Sometimes I wake up at night and think we have to pay for everything here ourselves. That's how one thinks at night, the first moment. Then I remember that I'm lying here like the son of rich people and I have the right to ask for everything and can ring for the nurses and they must come and other people must pay for all that. Wonderful, isn't it?"

"Yes," Ravic said. "Wonderful."

He sat in the examination room of the Osiris. "Is there still someone there?" he asked.

"Yes," Léonie said. "Yvonne. She is the last."

"Send her in. You're all right, Léonie."

Yvonne was twenty-five years old, fleshly, blonde, with a broad nose and the short chubby hands and feet of many whores. She swayed into the room complacently and lifted the sleazy silk rag she wore.

"There," Ravic said. "Over there."

"Can't it be done here?" Yvonne asked.

"No. Why?"

Instead of answering Yvonne turned silently around and showed her hefty behind. It was blue with welts. She must have received a terrific thrashing from someone.

"I hope your client paid you well for it," Ravic said. "This is no joke."

Yvonne shook her head. "Not a centime, doctor. It was not a client."

"Then it was fun. I didn't know you liked that."

Yvonne again shook her head, a satisfied mysterious smile on her face. Ravic noticed that she enjoyed the situation. She felt important. "I'm not a masochist," she said. She was proud of knowing the word.

"What was it then? A row?"

Yvonne waited a second. "Love," she said then and stretched her shoulders voluptuously.

"Was he jealous?"

"Yes." Yvonne beamed.

"Does it hurt very much?"

"Something like this doesn't hurt." She sat down carefully. "Do you know, doctor, that Madame Rolande at first didn't want to let me work? Just one hour, I told her; try it only for one hour! You'll see! And now with the blue behind I have much more success than ever before."

"Why?"

"I don't know. There are fellows who are mad about it. It excites them. In the last three days I have made two hundred fifty francs more. How long will it show?"

"At least two or three weeks."

Yvonne clicked her tongue. "If this goes on I'll be able to buy a fur coat. Fox—perfectly matched catskins."

"If it doesn't last long enough your friend can easily help you out with another sound thrashing."

"That he won't do," Yvonne said vivaciously. "He is not like that. He is not a calculating beast, you know! He only does it out of passion. When it comes over him. Otherwise I could beg him on my knees, but he wouldn't do it."

"Character." Ravic glanced up. "You're all right, Yvonne."

She picked herself up. "Then the work can go on. An old one is already waiting for me downstairs. A man with a gray pointed beard. He always comes after these visits. To be the first because he wants to be sure. I've shown him my streaks. He is wild about them. He has no say at home. That's why. So he dreams about how he would like to thrash his old lady, I believe." She burst into clear bell-like laughter. "Doctor, the world is funny, isn't it?" She swayed out of the room complacently.

Ravic put aside the things he had used and stepped to the window. The dusk hung silver-gray above the buildings. The bare trees rose through the asphalt like the black hands of the dead. One had at times seen such hands in buried trenches. He opened the window and looked out. The hour of unreality, hovering between day and night. The hour of love in the small hotels—for those who were married and at evening presided with dignity over their families. The hour of apéritifs. The hour in which the earth caught its breath. The hour in which the Italian women in the lowlands of Lombardy were already beginning to say *felicissima notte*. The hour of despair and the hour of dreams.

He closed the window. Suddenly the room seemed to be much darker. Shadows had fluttered in and crouched in the corners, full of silent chatter. The bottle of cognac which Rolande had brought up sparkled on the table like a polished topaz. Ravic remained standing for a moment—then he went down.

The music box was playing and the big room was already brightly illuminated. The girls were sitting in their short pink-silk chemises in two rows on the hassocks. They all had their breasts bare. The customers wanted to see what they were buying. Half a dozen had arrived, mostly middle-aged tradesmen. They were the cautious experts; they knew when the examinations took place and came about this time to be positively sure of not risking a clap. Yvonne was with her old

157

gentleman. He sat at a table with a Dubonnet in front of him. She stood beside him, one foot on a chair, and drank champagne. She received ten per cent for each bottle. The man must be really crazy to spend so much. That was something only foreigners did. Yvonne was aware of it. She had an air of a benevolent circus trainer.

"Do you want another calvados?" Ravic asked.

Joan nodded. "Yes, let me have another."

He called the maître d'hôtel. "Have you still older calvados than this?"

"Isn't this good?"

"It is. But maybe you have still another in your cellar."

"I'll see."

The waiter went to the cashier's desk where the proprietress was asleep with her cat. From there he disappeared through a ground-glass door into the room where the owner lived among his accounts. After a while the waiter returned with an important, composed air and went downstairs into the cellar without glancing at Ravic.

"It seems to be working."

The waiter returned with a bottle which he held in his arms like a baby. It was a dirty bottle; not one of the picturesquely incrusted bottles for tourists, but simply one that was dirty from lying in the cellar for many years. He opened it cautiously, sniffed the cork, and then fetched two big glasses.

"Sir," he said to Ravic and poured a few drops.

Ravic took the glass and inhaled the odor. Then he drank, leaned back, and nodded. The waiter returned his nod solemnly and filled both glasses a third full.

"Just try this," Ravic said to Joan.

She took a sip and put the glass down. The waiter watched her. She looked at Ravic, astonished. "I've never tasted anything like that before," she said and sipped a second time. "One doesn't drink it—one just inhales it."

"That's it, madame," the waiter declared with satisfaction. "You've grasped it."

"Ravic," Joan said, "there's danger in what you're doing. After this calvados I'll never drink any other kind."

"Oh yes, you'll drink other kinds too."

"But I'll dream of this one."

"Fine. It'll make you a romantic. A calvados romantic."

"But then I won't like the other any more."

"On the contrary. It will taste even better than it really is.

It will be a calvados with the longing for another calvados. That in itself makes it less ordinary.''

Joan laughed. "That's nonsense. You know it yourself."

"Naturally it's nonsense. But we are living on nonsense. Not on the meager bread of facts. Otherwise, what would happen to love?"

"What has that to do with love?"

"A great deal. It takes care of its continuance. Otherwise we would love once only and reject everything else later. But as it is, the remnant of desire for the man one leaves behind, or by whom one is left behind, becomes the halo around the head of the new one. To have lost someone before in itself gives the new one a certain romantic glamour. The hallowed old illusion.''

Joan looked at him. "I find it abominable to hear you talk like this."

"I too."

"You shouldn't do it. Not even in fun. It turns a miracle into a trick."

Ravic did not answer.

"And it sounds as if you were already tired and were thinking about leaving me."

Ravic looked at her with a remote tenderness. "You need never think about that, Joan. When it comes to that, you will be the one who leaves me. Not I you. That much is sure."

She set her glass down hard. "What nonsense! I'll never leave you. Are you trying to talk me into something again?"

Those eyes, Ravic thought. As if behind them lightning were flashing. Soft, reddish lightning out of a thunderstorm of candles. "Joan," he said. "I don't want to talk you into anything. I'll tell you the story of the wave and the rock. It's an old story. Older than we are. Listen. Once upon a time there was a wave who loved a rock in the sea, let us say in the Bay of Capri. The wave foamed and swirled around the rock, she kissed him day and night, she embraced him with her white arms, she sighed and wept and besought him to come to her. She loved him and stormed about him and in that way slowly undermined him, and one day he yielded, completely undermined, and sank into her arms."

He took a sip of calvados. "And?" Joan asked.

"And suddenly he was no longer a rock to be played with, to be loved, to be dreamed of. He was only a block of stone at the bottom of the sea, drowned in her. The wave felt disappointed and deceived and looked for another rock.''

"And?" Joan looked at him suspiciously. "What does that mean? He should have remained a rock."

"The wave always says that. But things that move are stronger than immovable things. Water is stronger than rocks."

She made an impatient gesture. "What has all this to do with us? That's only a story without meaning. Or you're making fun of me again. When it comes to that, you'll leave me, that's the one thing I'm sure of."

"That," Ravic said, laughing, "will be your last statement when you go. You'll explain to me that I've left you. And you'll find reasons for it—and you'll believe them—and you'll be right before the oldest law court in the world: Nature."

He called the waiter. "Can we buy this bottle of calvados?"

"You want to take it with you?"

"Exactly."

"Sir, that's against our rules. We don't sell bottles."

"Ask the patron."

The waiter returned with a newspaper. It was the *Paris Soir*. "The patron will make an exception," he explained, as he pressed the cork tight and wrapped the bottle in the *Paris Soir* after first removing the sports page and putting it, folded, into his pocket. "Here, sir. You had best keep it in a dark cool place. It comes from the estate of the patron's grandfather."

"Good." Ravic paid. He took the bottle and looked at it. "Sunshine that has lain all through a hot summer and a blue fall on apples in an ancient wind-swept orchard of Normandy, come with us. We need you! There is a storm raging somewhere in the universe."

They stepped out into the street. It had begun to rain. Joan stopped. "Ravic! Do you love me?"

"Yes, Joan. More than you think."

She leaned against him. "Sometimes it doesn't look like it."

"On the contrary. Otherwise I'd never tell you such things."

"You'd better tell me other things."

He looked into the rain and smiled. "Love is not a pond into which one can always look for one's reflection, Joan. Love has its ebb and flow. And wrecks and sunken cities and octopuses and storms and chests with gold and pearls. But the pearls lie deep."

"I don't know anything about that. Love is belonging together. Forever."

Forever, he thought. The old fairy tale. When one can't even hold the minute.

Shivering, she buttoned her coat. "I wish it were summer," she said. "I've never longed for it as I have this year."

She took her black evening gown out of the wardrobe and flung it on the bed. "How I hate this sometimes. Always the same black dress! Always the same Scheherazade! Always the same! Always the same!"

Ravic looked up. He didn't say anything.

"Don't you understand?" she asked.

"Oh yes—"

"Why don't you take me away from here, beloved?"

"Where to?"

"Anywhere."

Ravic unwrapped the bottle of calvados and drew the cork. Then he fetched a glass and filled it. "Come," he said. "Drink this."

She shook her head. "It doesn't help. Sometimes it doesn't help to drink. Sometimes nothing helps. I don't want to go there tonight, to those idiots."

"Stay here."

"And then?"

"Phone that you are sick."

"Nevertheless, I'll have to go tomorrow. It will be even worse then."

"You could be sick for a few days."

"That's just the same." She looked at him. "What can it be? What's wrong with me, Ravic? Is it the rain? Is it this wet darkness? Sometimes it's like lying in a coffin. These gray afternoons that drown me. I had forgotten it a while ago, I was happy being with you in that little restaurant—why did you have to talk about things like leaving and being left? I don't want to know or hear anything about that. It makes me sad, it holds pictures out to me which I don't want to see, and it makes me restless. I know you don't mean it this way, but it hits me. It hits me and then rain and darkness come. You don't know that. You are strong."

"Strong?" Ravic repeated.

"Yes."

"How do you know that?"

"You have no fear."

"I haven't any fear left. That's not the same, Joan."

She wasn't listening to what he said. She walked across the room with her long strides for which the room was too small. She always walked as if she were walking against a nonexistent wind. "I want to get away from all this," she said. "Away from this hotel, this night club with those greedy eyes, away from it all." She stopped. "Ravic! Must we live the way we live? Can't we live like other people who love each other? Can't we be together and have things that belong to us around us, and evenings and security, instead of these suitcases and empty days and these hotel rooms where one is a stranger?"

Ravic's face was indecipherable. There it comes, he thought. He had expected it any time. "Do you actually see that for us, Joan?"

"Why not? Other people have it! Warmth, belonging together, a few rooms, and when one closes one's door the restlessness has gone and it doesn't creep through the walls as it does here."

"Do you really see that?" Ravic repeated.

"Yes."

"A neat little apartment with a neat little bourgeois life. A neat little security on the edge of the abyss. Do you really see that?"

"You could just as well call it something else," she said defiantly. "Something not quite so—contemptuous. When one is in love one finds other names for it."

"It remains the same, Joan. Do you really see that? Neither of us is made for it."

She stopped. "I am."

Ravic smiled. There were tenderness, irony, and a shadow of sadness in it. "Joan," he said, "not you either. You even less than I. But that isn't the only reason. There is still another."

"Yes," she replied with bitterness. "I know."

"No, Joan. You don't know. But I'll tell you. It will be better so. You shouldn't think what you are thinking now."

She still stood before him. "Let's get it over quickly," he said. "And don't ask many questions afterwards."

She did not answer. Her face was empty. Suddenly it was again the face she had had formerly. He took her hands. "I live illegally in France," he said. "I have no papers. That's the real reason. That's why I'll never be able to rent an apartment. Nor can I marry if I love someone. I need proofs

162

of my identity and visas for that. I don't have them. I'm not even permitted to work. I must do it clandestinely. I can never live otherwise than now."

She stared at him. "Is that true?"

He shrugged his shoulders. "There are a couple of thousand people who are living in a similar way. I'm sure you know that, too. Everyone knows it nowadays. I am one of them." He smiled and let her hands go. "A man without a future, as Morosow calls it."

"Yes—but—"

"I'm even very well off. I work, I love, I have you—what are a few inconveniences?"

"And the police?"

"The police don't bother too much about it. If they happened to catch me, I'd only be deported, that's all. But that's improbable. And now go and telephone your night club that you won't come. We'll have this evening for ourselves. The whole evening. Tell them that you're sick. If they want a certificate I'll get you one from Veber." She did not go. "Deported," she said as if she could understand it only slowly. "Deported? From France? And then you would be away?"

"For a short while only."

She did not seem to hear him. "Away!" she repeated. "Away? And what would I do then?"

Ravic smiled. "Yes," he said. "What would you do then?"

She sat there, leaning on her elbows as if paralyzed. "Joan," Ravic said, "I have been here for two years and it has not happened."

Her face did not change. "And if it should happen in spite of that?"

"Then I would be back soon. In a week or two. It's like a trip, nothing more. And now call the Scheherazade."

She got up hesitantly. "What shall I say?"

"That you have bronchitis. Speak a little hoarsely."

She walked over to the telephone. Then she came quickly back. "Ravic—"

He freed himself carefully. "Come," he said. "Let's forget it. It's really a blessing. It protects us against becoming rentiers of passion. It keeps love pure—it remains a flame—and doesn't become the stove for the family cabbage. Now go and telephone."

She lifted the receiver. He looked at her while she spoke. At first her heart wasn't in it; she still looked at him as if he

163

were going to be arrested immediately. But then she began gradually to lie, easily and casually. She was actually lying more than was necessary. Her face became alive and reflected the pain in her chest which she was describing. Her voice became more tired and steadily hoarser and finally was punctuated by coughs. She was no longer looking at Ravic; she looked straight ahead and was completely absorbed in her role. He watched her silently and then drank a big gulp of calvados. No complexes, he thought. A mirror which gives a wonderful reflection—but which holds nothing.

Joan put the receiver down and smoothed her hair. "They believed everything."

"You did it first rate."

"They said I should stay in bed. And if it wasn't completely gone by tomorrow, for heaven's sake, stay there then."

"You see! That takes care of tomorrow too."

"Yes," she said, gloomy for a second. "If you take it that way." Then she came to him. "You frightened me, Ravic. Tell me it isn't true. You often say things just for the sake of saying them. Tell me it isn't true. Not the way you said it."

"It isn't true."

She leaned her head on his shoulder. "It can't be true. I don't want to be alone again. I'm nothing when I'm alone. You must stay with me. I'm nothing without you, Ravic."

Ravic looked down at her. "Joan," he said. "Sometimes you are like the janitor's daughter and sometimes Diana of the woods. And sometimes both."

Her head did not move on his shoulder. "What am I now?"

He smiled. "Diana with the silver bow. Invulnerable and deadly."

"You should tell me that more often."

Ravic remained silent. She had not understood what he meant. Nor was it necessary. She took what she liked the way she liked and did not bother about anything else. But wasn't it just this that attracted him? Whoever wanted someone who was like himself? And who would ask for morals in love? That was an invention of the weak. And the dirge for the victims.

"What are you thinking of?" she asked.

"Nothing."

"Nothing?"

"Something," he said. "We'll go away from here for a

few days, Joan. There where the sun is. To Cannes or Antibes. To hell with all caution! To hell too with all dreams of three-room apartments and the vulture cry of the middle class! And to hell with the darkness and the cold and the rain! Aren't you Budapest and the odor of blooming chestnuts at night when the entire city, hot and longing for summer, is sleeping with the moon?''

She had straightened up quickly. ''Do you really mean that?''

''Yes.''

''But—the police—''

''To hell with the police. It is no more dangerous there than here. Resorts for tourists are not so painstakingly checked. Particularly not the expensive hotels. Have you never been there?''

''No. Never. I was only in Italy and on the Adriatic. When are we leaving?''

''In two or three weeks. That's the best time.''

''But have we any money?''

''We have some. In two weeks we'll have enough.''

''We could live in a small pension,'' she said hastily.

''You don't belong in a small pension. You belong in a hole like this or a first-rate hotel. We'll live in the Cap Hôtel in Antibes. Besides, it's very sensible. Those hotels are entirely safe and no one asks for papers there. In the next few days I have to carve open the stomach of someone of importance, a governor or minister; he'll provide the money we still need.''

Joan got up quickly. Her face was changed. ''Come,'' she said. ''Let me have more of that old calvados, Ravic! It really seems to be a calvados of dreams.'' She went to the bed and lifted the evening gown. ''My God! And I only have these two old black rags!''

Chapter 14

ANDRE DURANT was honestly incensed. "There's no working with you any more," he declared.

Ravic shrugged his shoulders. He had learned from Veber that Durant was to receive ten thousand francs for the operation. Unless he arranged with him in advance how much he was to get, Durant would send him only two hundred francs. That's what he had done last time.

"Half an hour before the operation. I would never have thought it of you, Doctor Ravic."

"Neither would I," Ravic said.

"You know you can always rely on my generosity. I don't understand why you are so businesslike now. At the very moment when the patient knows that we have his life in our hands it is painful for me to talk about money."

"It isn't for me," Ravic replied.

Durant looked at him for a while. His wrinkled face with the white goatee expressed dignity and indignation. He adjusted his gold-rimmed pince-nez. "How much were you thinking of?" he asked reluctantly.

"Two thousand francs."

"What?" Durant looked as though he had been shot and could not yet believe it. "Ridiculous," he then said briefly.

"All right," Ravic replied. "You can easily find someone else. Take Binot; he is excellent."

He reached for his coat and put it on. Durant stared at him. His dignified face labored. "Wait a minute," he said when Ravic picked up his hat. "You can't let me down like that! Why didn't you tell me this yesterday?"

"Yesterday you were in the country and I could not reach you."

"Two thousand francs! Do you know that even I won't ask that much? The patient is a friend of mine whom I can only charge for my expenses."

Durant looked like the Heavenly Father in a child's book. He was seventy years old, a fairly good diagnostician, but a poor surgeon. His excellent practice had been based mainly on the work of his former assistant, Binot, who, two years ago, had finally succeeded in making himself independent. Since that time Durant had engaged Ravic for his more difficult operations. Ravic was known for making the smallest incisions and working in such a fashion that hardly any scar was left. Durant was an excellent connoisseur of Bordeaux wines, a favorite guest at elegant parties, and his patients came mostly from there.

"If I had known that," he murmured.

He had always known it. That was why before important operations he remained for one or two days in his house in the country. He wanted to avoid talking about the price before the operation. Afterwards it was simpler—then he could hold out hopes for the next time—and then the next time it was the same thing. This time to the astonishment of Durant, instead of coming in at the last moment Ravic had arrived half an hour before the appointed time for the operation and so had got hold of him before the patient was anesthetized. There was no possibility of using this as a reason for breaking off the discussion.

The nurse put her head through the open door. "Shall we begin the anesthetic, professor?"

Durant looked at her. Then imploringly and compassionately at Ravic. Ravic answered his look compassionately but firmly. "What do you think, Doctor Ravic?"

"The decision rests with you, professor."

"Just a minute, nurse. We do not yet see the procedure quite clearly." The nurse withdrew. Durant turned toward Ravic. "Now what?" he asked reproachfully.

Ravic put his hands in his pockets. "Postpone the operation until tomorrow—or for an hour and take Binot."

Binot had performed almost all of Durant's operations for twenty years and had made no headway because Durant had systematically cut him off from almost all chance of becoming independent and had always characterized him as a better-class underling. He hated Durant and would demand at least five thousand francs, Ravic knew that much. Durant knew it, too.

"Doctor Ravic," he said. "Our profession shouldn't be involved in this sort of business discussion."

"I agree with you."

"Why don't you leave it to my discretion to settle this matter? Haven't you always been satisfied up to now?"

"Never," Ravic said.

"You never told me that."

"Because it wouldn't have done any good. Besides, I wasn't very much interested. This time I am interested. I need the money."

The nurse came in again. "The patient is restless, professor."

Durant stared at Ravic. Ravic stared back. It was difficult to get money from a Frenchman, that he knew. More difficult than from a Jew. A Jew sees the transaction; a Frenchman only the money he is going to hand out.

"One minute, nurse," Durant said. "Take the pulse, blood pressure and temperature."

"I have done that."

"Then start the anesthetic."

The nurse left. "All right then," Durant said. "I'll give you a thousand."

"Two thousand," Ravic corrected him.

Durant did not consent. He stroked his goatee. "Listen, Ravic," he said then with warmth. "As a refugee who isn't allowed to practice—"

"I should not perform any operations for you," Ravic interrupted him calmly. Now he expected to hear the traditional comment that he ought to be grateful to be tolerated in the country.

But Durant forewent that. He could see that he wasn't getting anywhere and time pressed. "Two thousand," he said bitterly, as if each word were a bank note fluttering out of his throat. "I'll have to pay it out of my own pocket. I thought you would remember what I've done for you."

He waited. Strange, Ravic thought, that bloodsuckers like to moralize. This old cheat with the rosette of the Legion of Honor in his buttonhole reproaches me for being exploited by him, instead of being ashamed. And he even believes it.

"Well, two thousand," Durant said. "Two thousand," he repeated. It was as if he had said home, love, God, green asparagus, young partridges, old St. Emilion. Gone!—"Well, can we start now?"

The man had a fat potbelly and thin arms and legs. Ravic happened to know who he was. His name was Leval and he was a high official whose department handled refugee matters. Veber had told him this as a special joke. Leval was a name known to every refugee in the International.

Ravic made the first cut quickly. The skin opened like a book. He clipped it tight and looked at the yellowish fat which popped up. "We'll take a few pounds off as a free gift. Then he can eat them on again," he said to Durant.

Durant did not answer. Ravic removed the layers of fat in order to get close to the muscles. There he lives now, the little god of the refugees, he thought. The man who holds hundreds of little fates in his hand, in this whitish swollen hand which lies here now lifeless. The man who had ordered the deportation of old Professor Meyer who hadn't enough strength left to walk once more the road to Calvary and who had simply hanged himself in a closet of the Hôtel International the day before his deportation. In the closet because there was no hook elsewhere. He could do it; he was so emaciated that a clothes hook was strong enough to hold him. Not much more than a bundle of clothes with a bit of strangled life inside—that was what the maid had found in the morning. If this potbelly had had mercy, Meyer would still be alive. "Clips," he said. "Tampon."

He continued to cut. The precision of the sharp knife. The sensation of a clean incision. The abdominal cavity. The white coils of the intestines. The man who lay there with his belly opened up had his moral principles, too. He had felt human compassion for Meyer; but he had also felt something that he called his patriotic duty. There was always a screen behind which one could hide—a superior who in turn had his superior—orders, instructions, duties, commands—and finally the many-headed monster, morale, necessity, hard reality, responsibility, or whatever it was called—there was always a screen behind which to evade the simple law of humanity.

There was the gall bladder. Rotten and sick. Hundreds of *tournedos Rossini* have done this to him, of tripe *à la mode de Caen*, of heavy canards pressés, pheasants, young chickens, fat sauces, together with bad temper and with thousands of pints of good Bordeaux wines. Professor Meyer had had no such worries. If one should blunder now, cut too far, cut too deep—then in a week would a better man sit in that stuffy room that smelled of files and moths, where trembling refugees awaited their life or death sentences? A better one—but maybe someone worse. This unconscious sixty-year-old body here on the table under the bright lights undoubtedly considered himself humane. Surely he was a kind husband, a good father—but the minute he entered his office he was transformed into a tyrant hiding behind the phrases, "We can't do that"—and "Where would it get us if"—and so on. France would not have perished if Meyer had continued to eat his meager meals—if the widow Rosenthal had been allowed to go on waiting for her dead son in a maid's room in the International—if the tubercular drygoods dealer, Stallman, had not been imprisoned for six months because of illegal entry, to be released only to die before he could be shipped across the border.

Fine, the incision was fine. Not too deep. Not too wide. Catgut. The knot. The gall bladder. He showed it to Durant. It shone greasily in the white light. He threw it into the pail. Let's go on. Why did they sew with reverdin in France? Out with the clip! The warm belly of an average official with a salary of thirty or forty thousand francs a year. How could he pay ten thousand for this operation? Where did he earn the rest? This potbelly had played marbles too. That was a good stitch. Stitch after stitch. Two thousand francs was still written across Durant's face although his pointed beard was hidden. It was in his eyes. A thousand francs in each eye. Love spoils one's character. Would I otherwise have squeezed this rentier and shaken his faith in the divinely appointed world order of exploitation? Tomorrow he'll sit unctuously at this potbelly's bedside and accept grateful speeches for his work. Careful, there was one more clip. The potbelly means one week at Antibes for Joan and me. A week of light in the rain of ashes of our times. A blue piece of sky before the thunderstorm. Now the seam of the peritoneum. Especially fine for the two thousand francs. I should sew it up with a pair of scissors inside in memory of Meyer. The humming white light. Why does one think so disconnectedly? Newspapers, probably. Radio. The incessant rattling of liars and cowards. The lack of concentration through avalanches of words. Confused brains. Exposed to all the demagogic trash. No longer used to chewing the hard bread of knowledge. Toothless brains. Nonsense. So that's done now. There's still the flabby skin. In a few weeks he can again deport trembling refugees. If he doesn't die. But he won't. People like him die at eighty, honored, self-respecting, and with proud grandchildren. That's done with. The end. Take him away!

Ravic drew the gloves from his hands and the mask from his face. The high official glided out of the operating room on soundless wheels. Ravic gazed after him. Leval, he thought, if you only knew! That your thoroughly legal gall bladder had provided me, an illegal refugee, with a few highly illegal days on the Riviera!

He began to wash. Beside him Durant washed his hands slowly and methodically. The hands of an old man with high blood pressure. While carefully rubbing his fingers he rhythmically chewed with his lower jaw, slowly and as if grinding corn. When he stopped rubbing he also stopped chewing. As soon as he started again the chewing began too. This time he washed particularly slowly and deliberately, Ravic thought.

"What are you still waiting for?" Durant asked after a while.

"For your check."

"I'll send you the money as soon as the patient pays. That will be a few weeks after he is released from the hospital."

Durant began to dry his hands. Then he seized a bottle of Eau de Cologne d'Orsay and rubbed it on. "You have that much confidence in me, haven't you?" he asked.

Cheat, Ravic thought. Still wants to squeeze out a little humiliation. "You said the patient was a friend of yours who would only pay the expenses."

"Yes," Durant replied unobligingly.

"Well—the expenses amount to a few francs for the materials and the nurses. You own the hospital. If you charge a hundred francs for everything—you may deduct that and let me have it later."

"The expenses, Doctor Ravic," Durant declared, straightening up, "are, I'm sorry to say, considerably higher than I had thought. The two thousand francs for you are a part of them. Therefore I must also charge the patient for that." He sniffed the Eau de Cologne on his hands. "You see."

He smiled. His yellow teeth formed a lively contrast to his snow-white beard. As if someone had made water in the snow, Ravic thought. Nevertheless he'll pay. Veber will give me the money on the strength of it. I won't do this old goat the favor of begging him for it now.

"All right," he said. "If it is so difficult for you, then send it later."

"It is not difficult for me. Although your demand came suddenly and as a surprise. It's for the sake of order."

"All right, then we'll do it for the sake of order; it's all the same."

"It's absolutely not the same."

"The effect is the same," Ravic said. "And now excuse me. I want to get a drink. Adieu."

"Adieu." Durant said, surprised.

Kate Hegstroem smiled. "Why don't you come with me, Ravic?"

She stood before him, slender, sure of herself, with long legs, her hands in the pockets of her coat. "The forsythia must be in bloom by now in Fiesole. A yellow fire along the garden wall. A fireplace. Books. Peace."

Outside a truck thundered along the pavement. The glass frames of the pictures tinkled in the small reception room of the hospital. They were photographs of the Cathedral of Chartres.

"The quiet at night. Far away from everything," Kate Hegstroem said. "Wouldn't you love that?"

"Yes. But I couldn't stand it."

"Why not?"

"Quiet is only good when one is quiet oneself."

"I am not quiet myself."

"You know what you want. That's almost the same thing."

"Don't you know what you want?"

"I don't want anything."

Kate Hegstroem slowly buttoned her coat. "Now what is that, Ravic? Happiness or despair?"

He smiled impatiently. "Probably both. As always, both. One shouldn't think about it too much."

"What else should one do?"

"Be happy." She looked at him.

"One doesn't need anyone else for that," he said.

"One always needs someone else for that."

He remained silent. What am I talking about? he thought. Travel chatter, goodbye embarrassment, mealy sermons. "Not for the little happiness of which you once spoke," he said. "They bloom everywhere like violets around burnt-down houses. One who doesn't expect anything will not be disappointed—that's a good basis. Then anything else that comes along adds a bit to it."

"It's nothing at all," Kate Hegstroem replied. "It only seems so when one lies in bed and thinks cautiously. Not any

172

more when one can walk around. Then ones loses it again. One wants more."

An oblique ray of light fell through the window across her face. It left her eyes in shadow; just her mouth bloomed in it alone.

"Do you know a doctor in Florence?" Ravic asked.

"No. Do I need one?"

"There's always a chance some trifling matter may turn up afterwards. Anything. It would make me more comfortable to know that you have a doctor there."

"I feel very well. And I'll come back if anything should happen."

"Of course. This is just a precaution. There is a good physician in Florence. Professor Fiola. Will you remember that? Fiola."

"I'll forget it. It isn't at all important, Ravic."

"I'll write him. He'll take care of you."

"But why? There is nothing wrong with me."

"Professional precaution, Kate. Nothing else. I'll write him to call you up."

"If you like." She took her bag. "Adieu, Ravic. I'm leaving. Maybe I'll go right to Cannes from Florence. And from there to New York on the *Conte di Savoia*. If you happen to come to America you'll find a woman in a country house with a husband and children and horses and dogs. I leave the Kate Hegstroem you've known here. She has a small grave in the Scheherazade. Have a drink over it now and then when you're there."

"All right. With vodka."

"Yes. With vodka." She stood undecided in the dark of the room. Now the ray of light fell behind her on one of the photographs of Chartres. The high altar with the cross. "Strange," she said. "I should be happy. I'm not—"

"That's true of every farewell. Even farewell to despair."

She stood before him, hesitating, full of soft life, determined and a little sad. "The simplest thing when saying goodbye always is to go," Ravic said. "Come, I'll go out with you."

"Yes."

The air was mild and humid. The sky hung above the roofs like glowing iron. "I'll call a taxi, Kate."

"No. I'll walk to the corner. I'll find one there. It's the first time I've been out."

"How does it feel?"

"Like wine."

"Don't you want me to call a cab for you?"

"No, I'll walk."

She looked down the wet street. Then she smiled. "In some corner there is a bit of fear left. Does that go with it, too?"

"Yes. That goes with it."

"Adieu, Ravic."

"Adieu, Kate."

She stood for another second as though she wanted to say something. Then she walked down the stairs with careful steps, slender, still supple, along the street toward the violet-colored evening and toward her destruction. She did not turn back again.

Ravic went back. As he passed the room which Kate Hegstroem had occupied, he heard music. Surprised, he stopped. He knew that there was no new patient there as yet.

He cautiously opened the door and saw the nurse kneeling in front of a record player. She was startled when she heard Ravic and got up. The victrola was playing an old record: *Le dernier valse*.

The girl smoothed her dress. "Miss Hegstroem gave me the victrola as a present," she said. "It's an American make. One can't buy it here. Nowhere in Paris. It's the only one here. I was trying it out immediately. It plays five records automatically."

She beamed with pride. "It's worth at least three thousand francs. And all the records with it. There are fifty-six. Besides there is a radio built in. That's luck."

Luck, Ravic thought. Happiness. Again. Here it was a record player. He stopped and listened. The violin flew up from the orchestra like a dove, plaintive and sentimental. It was one of those languishing airs that sometimes touch our hearts more than all the nocturnes of Chopin. Ravic looked around. The bed was stripped and the mattress put up. The laundry was piled by the door. The windows stood open. The evening stared into the room ironically. A fading scent of perfume and the dying strains of a waltz were what was left of Kate Hegstroem.

"I can't take everything with me at once," the nurse said. "It is too heavy. I'll take the victrola along first and then I'll come back twice and get the records. Maybe even three times. It's wonderful. One could open a café with it."

"A good idea," Ravic said. "Be careful not to break anything."

Chapter 15

RAVIC CAME AWAKE very slowly. For a short while he still lay in the strange twilight between dream and reality—the dream was still there, paler and more tattered—and at the same time he realized already that he was dreaming. He was in the Black Forest, close to the German frontier, at a small station. There was the sound of a waterfall near by. The scent of pines came from the mountains. It was summer and the valley was full of the smell of resin and meadows. The railway tracks shone red in the evening sun—as if they had been traversed by a train from which blood was dripping. What am I doing here? Ravic thought. What am I doing here in Germany? I have been in France. I have been in Paris. He floated over a soft iridescent wave which showered more sleep upon him. Paris—now it was melting away, it was only a haze, it disappeared. He was not in Paris. He was in Germany. But why had he come back here?

He walked across the small platform. The conductor was standing by a newsstand. He was reading the *Voelkischer Beobackter*, a middle-aged man with a fat face and very blond eyebrows. "When does the next train leave?" Ravic asked.

The conductor looked at him lazily. "Where are you going?" Suddenly Ravic felt a wave of hot panic. Where was he? What was the name of this place? What was the name of the station? Should he say Freiburg? Damn it, why didn't he know where he was? He looked along the platform. No sign. Nowhere the name of the place. He smiled. "I am on furlough," he said.

"Where do you want to go?" the conductor asked.

"I am just riding around. I got off the train here by chance. I liked the way it looked from the window. Now I don't like it any more. I can't stand waterfalls. Now I want to go on."

"Where do you want to go? You must know where you want to go."

"Day after tomorrow I have to be in Freiburg. I've got time until then. It's fun to ride along aimlessly."

"This line doesn't go to Freiburg," the conductor said and looked at him.

What nonsense is this? Ravic thought. Why do I ask at all? How did I come here? "I know," he said. "I've plenty of time. Do they have kirsch anywhere here? Genuine Black Forest kirsch?"

"There in the station restaurant," the conductor said, still looking at him.

Ravic walked slowly across the platform. His steps resounded on the cement under the open roof of the station. He saw two men sitting in the first- and second-class waiting room. He felt their looks on his back. A few swallows flew along under the roof of the station. He made believe he was watching them and looked out of the corner of his eye at the conductor, who was folding up his newspaper. Then he followed Ravic. Ravic went to the restaurant. The place smelled of beer. No one was there. He left the place. The conductor was standing outside. He saw Ravic come out and went into the waiting room. Ravic walked faster. He had made himself suspect, he knew that suddenly. At the corner of the building he turned around. No one was on the platform. He walked hastily through between the express room and the empty baggage office. He ducked under the baggage platform, on which a few milk cans stood, and crept along past the express room window, behind which a telegraph instrument was ticking, until he reached the other side of the building. Cautiously he turned around. Then he quickly crossed the tracks and ran through a blooming meadow toward the pine woods. The powdery heads of the dandelions flew up as he ran across the meadow. When he reached the pines he saw the conductor and the two men standing on the platform. The conductor was pointing at him and the two men began to run. He jumped backward and forced his way through the pines. The coniferous branches beat against his face. He ran in a big circle and then stood still lest his whereabouts be discovered. He heard the men breaking through the pines and continued to run. Every moment he listened. Sometimes he did not hear anything; then all he could do was wait. Afterwards there would be a crackling again, and he too continued to creep, on hands and knees now, to make less noise. He clenched his hands into fists and held his breath while listening; he felt a convulsive desire to jump up and rush away—but this would disclose where he was. He could move only when the others moved. He lay in a thicket between blue liverleaves. *Hepatica triloba,* he thought. *Hepatica triloba,* the liverleaf. The woods seemed endless. Now there was crackling everywhere. He felt perspiration breaking out of all his pores as if his body were raining. And suddenly his legs gave at the knees as if the joints had softened. He tried to get up. But he was swallowed by the earth. The ground was like a morass. He looked down. The ground was solid. It was his legs. They were of rubber. Now he heard his pursuers closer. They came directly toward him. He dragged himself up but he sank down again on his rubber knees. He dragged his legs, he waded on, laboriously, and he heard the crackling coming closer and closer, then all of a sudden a patch of blue sky appeared through the branches, a glade opened, he knew he was lost if he could not run swiftly across it, he dragged along and, turning around, he saw behind him a face, craftily smiling, Haake's face, he sank and sank down, defenseless, helpless, he was suffocating, he tore at his sinking chest with his hands, he groaned—

Had he groaned? Where was he? He felt his hands at his throat. His hands were wet. His throat was wet. His chest was wet, his face was wet. He opened his eyes. He was not yet fully aware of where he was, in the swamp amid the pines or somewhere else. As yet he was altogether unaware of Paris. A white moon hung on a cross above an unknown world. A pale light hung behind a dark cross like a martyred halo. A white dead light cried noiselessly on a pallid iron-colored sky. The full moon stood behind the wooden cross in the window of a room in the Hôtel International in Paris. Ravic sat up. What had this been? A railway train full of blood, dripping blood, madly racing through a summer evening along bloody rails—the hundred times repeated dream of being in Germany again, to be surrounded, persecuted, hunted by the hangmen of a bloody regime which had legalized murder; how often had he gone through it! He stared into the moon, the white vampire sucking the colors of the world with its borrowed light. Those dreams, filled with the horror of the concentration camps, full of the torpid faces of slain friends, full of the tearless, petrified pain of those surviving, full of disconsolate farewell and of loneliness that was beyond lamentation—during the day one succeeded in erecting the barrier, the rampart that was higher than one's eyes—one had slowly built it during long laborious years, desires strangled with cynicism, memories buried with callousness and trampled down, one had stript everything from oneself including one's name, cemented over one's feelings—and when in spite of it at times the livid face of one's past emerged in an unguarded hour, sweet, ghostlike and calling, one had drowned it by drinking to the point of insensibility. During the day— but nights one was still at its mercy, the brakes of discipline were loosed and the cart began to slip, behind the horizon of consciousness it rose again, it broke out of graves, the frozen cramp was loosened, the shadows came back, one's blood boiled, one's sores ran, and the black storm swept across all bulwarks and barricades! To forget—that was easy as long as the lanterns of willpower illuminated the world—but when they faded and the noise of the worms became audible, when a destroyed world emerged out of the floods like a sunken Vineta and lived again—that was something else. One could get drunk, dull, and leaden, night after night, to overcome all that—one could turn the nights into days and the days into night—during the day one dreamed differently from nights, not in such forlornness, cut off from everything. Hadn't he done it? How often had he returned to the hotel when the first gray of the morning was creeping through the streets? Or had he not waited in the Catacombs with anyone willing to drink with him until Morosow came, from the Scheherazade, who went on drinking with him under the artificial palm where only the clock in that windowless room showed how far the light had waxed outside? Getting drunk in a U-boat, that's what it was. It was easy to shake your head and declare that one should be sensible. But hell, it wasn't so easy! Life was life, it was worth nothing and everything; one could throw it away, that was easy, too. But did one not also throw away one's revenge with it and then did one not throw away as well the thing that sneered at, spat on, daily and hourly ridiculed, was, nevertheless, roughly called belief in humaneness and humanity? An empty life—one didn't throw that away like an empty cartridge! It was still good enough to fight with when the time came for it and when it was needed. Not for personal reasons, not even for revenge, however blood-deep revenge might be, not out of egotism, nor for altruistic reasons, however important it might be for one turn of the wheel to help push this world forward out of blood and debris—for no other reason, finally, than to fight, merely to fight, and to wait for one's chance to fight as long as one still breathed. But the waiting was corrosive and maybe it was hopeless, and to it was added the secret fear that if the time finally came one would be too crushed by then, too eaten up, too inert from waiting, too tired in one's cells still to be able to march along with the others! Wasn't that the reason one trampled into oblivion everything that could feed on the nerves, extinguished it, efficiently and callously, with sarcasm, with irony, even with counter-sentimentality, with the escape into another human being, into an alien ego? Until that was done the brutal helplessness would come back again while one was at the mercy of sleep and ghosts. . . .

The round moon crept under the crossbar of the window. It was no longer a crucified halo—it was a fat, obscene *voyeur* staring into chambers and beds. Ravic was now wide awake. This had been a comparatively harmless dream. He had known others. But it was a long time since he had dreamed at all. He pondered—it was almost the whole time since he had ceased sleeping alone.

He groped beside the bed. The bottle was not there. It had not stood there for quite a while. It stood on the table in the corner of the room. He hesitated a moment. It was not necessary to drink. He knew that. It was also not necessary to refrain from drinking. He got up and walked, barefooted, to the table. He found a glass, uncorked the bottle and drank. It was the remainder of the old calvados. He held the glass up to the window. The moon turned it into an opal. Brandy should not stand in the light, he thought. Neither in the sun, nor in the moon. Wounded soldiers who had lain outside through the night under a full moon were weaker than after other nights. He shook his head and emptied his glass. Then he poured himself another. Glancing up he noticed that Joan had opened her eyes and was looking at him. He stopped. He did not know whether she was awake and really saw him.

"Ravic," she said.

"Yes—"

She shivered as if she had only just awakened. "Ravic," she said in an altered voice. "Ravic—what are you doing there?"

"I'm taking a drink."

"But why—" She straightened up. "What's the matter?" she said dazedly. "What has happened?"

"Nothing."

She smoothed back her hair. "My God," she said, "how frightened I was!"

"I didn't intend that. I thought you would go on sleeping."

"Suddenly you were standing there—in the corner—quite changed."

"I'm sorry, Joan. I didn't think you would wake up."

"I felt that you were gone. It was cold. Like a wind. A cold fright. And then suddenly you were standing there. Has anything happened?"

"No, nothing. Nothing at all, Joan. I woke up and wanted a drink."

"Let me have a sip."

Ravic filled the glass and walked over to the bed. "Now you look like a child," he said.

She took the glass with both hands and drank. She drank slowly and looked over the rim of the glass at him. "What made you wake up?" she asked.

"I don't know. I think it was the moon."

"I hate the moon."

"You will not hate it in Antibes."

She lowered the glass. "Are we really going?"

"Yes, we'll go."

"Away from this mist and rain?"

"Yes—away from this damned mist and rain!"

"Give me another glass."

"Don't you want to sleep?"

"No. It's a pity to sleep. One misses too much life by sleeping. Give me a glass. Is it the good one? Didn't we want to take it along?"

"One shouldn't take anything along."

She looked at him. "Never?"

"Never."

Ravic went to the window and drew the curtains. They closed only half way. The moonlight came through the opening in a shaft of light and divided the room into two halves of diffused darkness. "Why don't you come to bed?" Joan asked.

Ravic stood by the sofa on the other side of the moonlight. He saw Joan indistinctly, sitting in bed. Her hair hung darkly bright over the nape of her neck. She was naked. Between him and her flowed the cold light as though between two dark shores, flowing nowhere, flowing into itself alone. Into the square of the room, filled with the warm smell of sleep, it flowed from an endless way through the black airless ether, a broken light, rebounding from a remote dead star and magically transformed out of warm sun gleams into leaden cold rivers—it flowed and flowed and yet stood still and never filled the room.

"Why don't you come?" Joan asked.

Ravic walked across the room, through the dark and the light and again through the dark—it was only a few steps, but it seemed far to him.

"Did you bring the bottle with you?"

"Yes."

"Do you want the glass? How late is it?"

Ravic looked at the phosphorescent numbers on the dial of his little watch. "About five o'clock."

"Five. It could just as well be three. Or seven. At night time stands still. Only the clocks move."

"Yes. And nevertheless everything happens at night. Or because of it."

"What?"

"That which later becomes visible during the day."

"Don't frighten me. You mean it happens beforehand while one sleeps."

"Yes."

She took the glass from his hand and drank. She was very beautiful and he felt he loved her. She was not beautiful as a statue or a picture is beautiful; she was beautiful as a meadow across which the wind blows. It was life that pulsed in her and that had formed her into what she was, formed her mysteriously through the meeting of two cells, out of nothingness in a womb. It was the same incomprehensible enigma that in one tiny seed was contained the entire tree, petrified, microscopic, but there, predestined already, crown and fruit and the showering blossoms of all April mornings—and that out of a night of love and the meeting of a bit of slime there came a face, shoulders, and eyes, just these eyes and these shoulders, and that they had been somewhere, among millions of people somewhere in the world, and then one stood on a November night on the Pont de l'Alma in Paris, and they came toward one—

"Why at night?" Joan asked.

"Because—come close to me, beloved, given back to me from the abyss of sleep, returned from the moon meadows of chance—because night and sleep are betrayers. Do you remember how we fell asleep tonight, one close to the other, we were so close to each other, as close as humans can be. Our foreheads, our skins, our thoughts, our breath touched each other, mixed—and then sleep gradually began to seep between us, gray, colorless, first a few spots only, then more, it came upon our thoughts like a scab, into our blood, it dropped and dropped the blindness of unconsciousness into us—and then suddenly each of us was alone, we drifted lonely somewhere along dark canals, delivered to unknown powers and every shapeless menace. When I awoke I saw you. You slept. You were still far away. You had entirely slipped away from me. You no longer knew anything of me. You were somewhere I could never follow you." He kissed her hair. "How can love be perfect when I every night lose you in sleep."

"I lay close to you. At your side. In your arms."

"You were in an unknown land. You were at my side, but you were farther away than if you had been on Sirius. When you are away during the day, it doesn't matter—I am aware of everything during the day. But who is aware of anything during the night?"

"I was with you."

"You were not with me. You just lay at my side. Whoever knows how he'll come back from that land where one is without controls? Transformed without knowing it."

"You too."

"Yes, I too." Ravic said. "And now give me the glass again. While I talk nonsense, you're drinking."

She handed him the glass. "It's good you woke up, Ravic. Blessed be the moon. Without it we would have slept and known nothing of each other. Or, in one of us, the seed of leave-taking might have been sown while we were defenseless. And, gradually and invisibly, it would grow and grow until it came to light one day."

She laughed softly. Ravic looked at her. "You don't take it very seriously, do you?"

"No. And you?"

"No. But there is something to it. That's why we don't take it seriously. Therein man is great."

She laughed again. "I'm not afraid of it. I trust our bodies.

They know better what they want than the thoughts that haunt our brains at night.''

Ravic emptied his glass. "All right," he said. "And quite right too.''

"Don't let's go to sleep any more tonight.''

Ravic held the bottle against the silver shaft of the moonlight. It was still one third full. "Not much left," he said. "But we can try.''

He put it on the table by the bed. Then he turned around and looked at Joan. "You look like all desires of a man and one more of which he was not aware.''

"Good," she said. "We should wake up every night, Ravic. At night you're different from what you are during the day.''

"Better?''

"Different. Nights you're surprising. You are always coming from somewhere, somewhere about which one knows nothing.''

"Not during the day?''

"Not always. Sometimes.''

"Lovely confidences," Ravic said. "You wouldn't have told me that a few weeks ago.''

"No. Then I knew you less well.''

He glanced up. There was not a shadow of ambiguity in her face. She simply meant it this way and found it quite natural. She neither wanted to hurt him, nor to say anything important. "That's going to be just fine," he said.

"Why?''

"In a few more weeks you'll know me even better and I'll be still less surprising to you.''

"Just like me," Joan said and laughed.

"Not you.''

"Why not?''

"That has its reason in fifty thousand years of biology. Love makes the women keen-sighted and confuses the man.''

"Do you love me?''

"Yes.''

"You don't say it often enough." She stretched herself. Like a satisfied cat, Ravic thought. Like a satisfied cat sure of its victim.

"Sometimes I could throw you out of the window," he said.

"Why don't you do it?''

He looked at her. "Could you do it?" she asked.

He did not answer. She lay back on the pillow. "Destroy omeone because one loves him? Kill him because one loves im too much?"

Ravic reached for the bottle. "My God," he said. "What ave I done to deserve this? To awake at night and be forced o listen to something like this?"

"Isn't it true?"

"Yes. For third-rate poets and women to whom it doesn't appen."

"For those who do it, too."

"All right."

"Could you do it?"

"Joan," Ravic said. "Stop this servant-girl chatter. I'm ot the man for such speculations. I've already killed too any people. As an amateur and as a professional. As a oldier and as a surgeon. That gives one contempt, indifference, nd respect for life. One does not erase much by killing. Who as killed often would not kill out of love. One ridicules and iminishes death by it. And death is never small, or ridiculous. nd it does not concern women; it is a matter for men." He emained silent for a while. "What are we talking about?" he aid then and bent over her. "Aren't you my unrooted appiness? My happiness in the clouds, my searchlight appiness? Come, let me kiss you. Life was never so pre- ious as today—when it matters so little."

Chapter 16

THE LIGHT. Ever anew it was the light. It came flying from th
horizon like white foam between the deep blue of the ocea
and the lighter blue of the sky, it came flying, breathless an
deepest breath at the same time, radiance and reflection i
one, the simple, primordial happiness of being so bright, s
gleaming, of floating thus without substance. . . .

How it stands behind her head, Ravic thought. Like a
aureole without color! Space without perspective! How
flows over her shoulders! Milk from Canaan, silk spun fro
beams! No one can be naked in this light. The skin catche
and radiates it, like the rocks and the sea out there, light-foam
most transparent confusion, thinnest dress of brightest mist.

"How long have we been here now?" Joan asked.

"Eight days."

"It is like eight years. Don't you think?"

"No." Ravic said. "It is like eight hours. Eight hours an
three thousand years. Here where you stand, a young Etrusca
woman stood in just the same way three thousand year
ago—and the wind came in just this way from Africa an
chased the light across the ocean."

Joan crouched down beside him on the rock. "When do w
have to go back to Paris?"

"We'll find out tonight in the Casino."

"Have we been winning?"

"Not enough."

"You play as if you were used to playing. Maybe you are
I really don't know anything about you. Why did the croupie
greet you like a rich munitions maker?"

"He mistook me for a munitions maker."

"That's not true. You recognized him, too."

"It was politer to pretend so."

"When were you last here?"

186

"I don't know. Once many years ago. How tanned you are! You should always be as brown as that."

"Then I would have to live here all the time."

"Would you like to?"

"Not all the time. But I would like to live always the way we live here." She flung her hair back over her shoulders. "I'm sure you find that very superficial, don't you?"

"No," Ravic said.

She smiled and turned to him. "I know it's superficial but, my God, we have had too little superficiality in our wretched lives! We've had enough wars, hunger and upheavals and revolutions and inflations—but never a little security and lightness and quiet and time. And now you say there's another war coming. Really, it was easier for our parents, Ravic."

"Yes."

"We have only this one short life, and it passes—" She put her hands on the warm rock. "I am not worth much, Ravic. I am not anxious to live in an historical age. I want to be happy and I wish things would not be so burdensome and difficult. That's all."

"Who wouldn't wish that, Joan?"

"You too?"

"Of course."

That blue, Ravic thought. That almost colorless blue of the horizon, where the sky plunges into the sea, and then this storm deepening along sea and zenith, up to these eyes which are bluer here than they ever were in Paris!

"I wish we could," Joan said.

"But we do it—for the moment."

"Yes, for the moment, for a few days; but then we'll be going back to Paris again; to that night club in which nothing changes; to that life in a dirty hotel—"

"You exaggerate. Your hotel isn't dirty. Mine is pretty dirty—except my room."

She rested her elbows on her knees. The wind blew through her hair. "Morosow says you were a wonderful doctor. It's a pity things are the way they are with you. Otherwise you could earn a lot of money. Particularly as a surgeon. Professor Durant—"

"How do you happen to hit on him?"

"Sometimes he comes to the Scheherazade. René, the

headwaiter, says he doesn't move a finger for less than ten thousand francs."

"René is well informed."

"And sometimes he performs two or three operations in one day. He has a wonderful house, a Packard—"

Strange, Ravic thought. Her face doesn't change. It is if anything even more captivating than before while she babbles this millenium-old woman's nonsense. She looks like a sea-eyed Amazon while, with procreative instinct, she preaches bankers' ideals. But isn't she right? Isn't so much beauty always right? And hasn't she every excuse in the world?

He saw the motorboat approach in a wave of foam. He did not move; he knew why it was coming. "There come your friends," he said.

"Where?" Joan had already seen the boat. "Why my friends?" she asked. "They are really more your friends. They've known you longer than me."

"Ten minutes longer—"

"Anyway, longer."

Ravic laughed. "All right, Joan."

"I don't have to go. That's quite simple. I won't go."

"Of course not."

Ravic stretched himself out on the rock and closed his eyes. The sun at once became a warm golden blanket. He knew what would follow.

"We are not very polite," Joan said after a while.

"Lovers are never polite."

"They have both come because of us. To call for us. If you don't want to go for a ride, the least you can do is to go down and tell them so."

"All right." Ravic half opened his eyes. "Let's simplify it. You go down and tell them I have to work, and go with them. Just as you did yesterday."

"To work—that sounds odd. Who does any work here? Why don't you come with us? They like you very much. They were disappointed yesterday when you didn't come."

"Oh, God!" Ravic opened his eyes fully. "Why is it that all women love these idiotic conversations? You would like to go for a ride, I have no boat, life is short, we are only here for a few days, why should I behave magnanimously for you now and persuade you to do what you will do anyway, just to make you feel better?"

"You don't have to persuade me. I can do it by myself."

She looked at him. Her eyes were of the same radiant intensity; only her mouth was drawn down for a second—it was an expression flitting across her face so quickly that Ravic could believe he was mistaken. But he knew he was not mistaken. The ocean beat resoundingly against the rocks of the jetty. It spirited high and the wind carried off a spray of glistening drops. Ravic felt it on his skin like a brief shiver. "That was your wave," Joan said. "Your wave of the story you told me in Paris."

"I see—have you kept it in mind?"

"Yes. But you aren't a rock. You are a block of concrete."

She walked down to the dock and the whole sky rested on her beautiful shoulders. It was as if she carried it. She had her excuse. She would sit in the white boat, her hair would fly in the wind—and I am an idiot for not going with them, Ravic thought. But I am not yet suited for that role. This too is foolish arrogance of forgotten days, a quixotism—but what else is left? Blooming fig trees in moonlight nights. Seneca's and Socrates' philosophy, Schumann's violin concerto, and foreknowledge of loss gained earlier than by others.

He heard Joan's voice from below. Then he heard the low thunder of the motor. He did not sit up. She would take her place in the stern. There was an island with a cloister somewhere in the sea. Sometimes the cocks crowed from over there. How red the sun shone through one's eyelids! The soft meadows of youth red with flowers of the expectant blood. The old lullaby of the sea. The bells of Vineta. The magic happiness of nonthinking. He quickly fell asleep.

In the afternoon he went to fetch the car from the garage. It was a Talbot which Morosow had rented for him in Paris. He had come down in it with Joan.

He drove along the coast. The day was very clear and almost too bright. He drove across the middle Corniche to Nice and Monte Carlo, and then to Villefranche. He loved the old small harbor and sat for a while in front of one of the bistros on the quay. He strolled about the garden in front of the Casino in Monte Carlo and the suicide cemetery high above the sea; he looked for a grave and stood before it for a long time and smiled. He drove through the narrow streets of Old Nice and across the new part of the city, through the squares with the monuments; then he drove back to Cannes and beyond Cannes up to where the rocks were red and the fishing villages had Biblical names.

He forgot Joan. He forgot himself. He simply opened up to this clear day, to the triad of sun, sea, and land which made a coast blossom while the mountain roads above it were still full of snow. Rain hung over France, the storm roared over Europe—but this narrow coast seemed not yet to know about all that. It seemed to have been forgotten; life had a different pulse beat here; and while the land behind it grew gray with the mist of misery, of foreboding and danger, the sun shone here and it was serene and in its radiance gathered the last foam of a dying world.

A brief dance of moths and gnats around the last light—meaningless like every dance of gnats; foolish as the light music coming from the cafés—a world having become superfluous as butterflies in October, frost already in their little summer hearts; thus it danced, chattered, flirted, loved, betrayed, and deluded its senses for yet a little before the scythes and the big winds came.

Ravic turned the car in St.-Raphaël. The small square harbor was full of sailboats and motorboats. The cafés on the quay had set up garish umbrellas. Tanned women were sitting at the tables. How it all came back again, Ravic thought—the pleasant, easy-going way of life. The gay temptation, the release, the game—how it came back, no matter from how long ago. Once he too had experienced this butterfly existence and had thought it would suffice. The car shot out of the turn along the street into the glowing sunset.

He returned to the hotel and found a message from Joan. She had called and left word she wouldn't be back for dinner. He went down to the Eden Roc. There were few people for dinner. Most of the others were in Juan-les-Pins and in Cannes. He sat by the railing of the terrace which was built on the rock like a ship's deck. Below the surf foamed. The waves emerged from the sunset, dark red and greenish blue, changed to a lighter golden-red and orange, and then took the dusk on their slender backs and scattered it into twilight-colored foam.

Ravic sat on the terrace for a long time. He felt cool and deeply alone. He saw what would happen clearly and without emotion. He knew that he could still prevent it for a while; tricks and clever moves were possible. He knew them and would not use them. This had already gone too far for that. Tricks were something for small affairs. There was only one thing left: to face it. To face it honestly, without self-deception and without dodging.

Ravic lifted the glass of clear light Provençal wine against the light. A cool night, a sea-ringed terrace, the sky filled with the laughter of the sun's farewell and with the bells of faraway stars—and, cool within me, he thought, a searchlight which penetrates the silent months of the future and sweeps over them and leaves them in the dark again, and I am aware of it, painlessly as yet, but I am also aware that it won't remain painless, and once again my life is like a glass in my hand, transparent, filled with alien wine which can't be kept because it would become flat, would become the stale vinegar of dead passion.

It would not last. There was much too much of a beginning in that other life for it to last. Innocently and thoughtlessly, like a plant toward light, it turned toward the temptation and the variegated multifariousness of a lighter life. It wanted future—and all he had to offer was a bit of shabby present. Nothing had happened yet. But that wasn't necessary. Things were always decided a long time in advance. Usually one didn't notice and took the spectacular ending for the decision which, long months before, had come in silence.

Ravic emptied his glass. The light wine seemed to taste different than before. He refilled the glass and drank again. The wine once more had its old light flaky taste.

He got up and drove to Cannes, to the Casino.

He played calmly and for small stakes. He still felt the coolness within him and knew he could win as long as it lasted. He played the last Twelve, the Twenty-seven square and Twenty-seven. After an hour he had won three thousand francs. He doubled his stakes for the square and played Four as well.

He noticed Joan when she entered. She had changed her dress and so she must have returned immediately after he had left the hotel. She was with the two men who had called for her in the motorboat. He knew them as Le Clerq, a Belgian, and Nugent, an American. Joan looked very beautiful. She wore a white evening gown with large gray flowers. He had bought it for her the day before their departure. She had seen it and rushed toward it. "How do you know so much about evening gowns?" she had asked. "It is much better than mine." And after a second glance, "Also more expensive."

Bird, he thought, still on my branches but with wings ready for flight.

The croupier pushed some chips toward him. The square had won. He withdrew the winnings and left the stake. Joan went to the baccarat tables. He did not know whether she had seen him. Some people who were not playing glanced after her. She always walked as if she were walking against a light wind and as if she had no goal. She turned her head and said something to Nugent—and suddenly Ravic felt the urge in his hands to push away the chips, to push himself away from this green table, to get up, to take Joan away, quickly, past all the people, doors, away, to an island, perhaps to that island on the horizon off Antibes away from all this to isolate her and keep her. . . .

He bet again. The Seven had come up. Islands did not isolate. And the restlessness of the heart could not be confined; one lost easiest what one held in one's arms—never what one left. The ball slowly stopped rolling. The Twelve. He bet again.

When he glanced up he was looking straight into Joan's eyes. She stood at the other side of the table and was looking at him. He nodded to her and smiled. She stared at him. He pointed at the wheel and shrugged his shoulders. The Nineteen came up.

He placed his bets and looked up again. Joan was not there any more. He forced himself to remain sitting. He took a cigarette out of the package that lay beside him. One of the attendants gave him a light. He was a fat, bald-headed man, in uniform. "Times have changed," he said.

"Yes," Ravic said. He did not know the man.

"It was different in twenty-nine."

"Yes—"

Ravic no longer knew whether he had been in Cannes in 1929 or whether the man was just talking. He saw that the Four had come up without his having noticed it and he tried to concentrate better. But suddenly it seemed stupid to him to be gambling here with a few francs in order to be able to stay a few days more. To what purpose? Why had he come here at all? It was confounded weakness, nothing else. That fed on one, slowly, silently, and one noticed it only when one wanted to exert oneself to the utmost and broke. Morosow was right. The best way to lose a woman was to show her a kind of life that one could offer her for only a few days. She would try to regain it—but with someone else who was capable of making it permanent. I'll tell her that we have to break up, he thought. I'll part from her in Paris before it is too late.

He considered going on playing at another table. But suddenly he felt no desire to. One should not do something on a small scale that one had done on a large scale. He looked around. Joan was not to be seen. He went into the bar and drank cognac. Then he went to the parking place to get his car and drive around for an hour.

As he was starting the car, he saw Joan coming. He got out. She came toward him quickly. "Were you going to drive home without me?" she asked.

"I was going to drive through the mountains for an hour and then come back."

"You are lying! You didn't intend to come back! You were going to leave me behind with those idiots."

"Joan," Ravic said. "Soon you will claim it's my fault you are with those idiots."

"It is your fault! I went in the boat with them because I was angry! Why weren't you in the hotel when I returned?"

"You had a dinner appointment with your idiots."

She was taken aback for a second. "I only made it because you weren't there when I came back."

"All right, Joan," Ravic said. "Let's not go on talking about it. Did you enjoy it?"

"No."

She stood before him, breathless, agitated, impetuous, in the blue darkness of the soft night, the moon was in her hair and her lips were of such a deep red in her pale face that they were almost black; it was February, 1939, and in Paris the inevitable would begin, slowly, crawlingly, with all the little lies, humiliations and disputes; he wanted to leave her before this happened, and yet she was here and there weren't many more days left.

"Where were you going to drive?" she asked.

"Nowhere in particular. Just drive."

"I'll ride with you."

"But what will your idiots say?"

"Nothing. I have said goodbye to them already. I told them you were waiting for me."

"Not bad," Ravic said. "You are a child with deliberation. Wait till I put the top up."

"Leave it down! My coat will keep me warm enough. Let's drive slowly. Past all the cafés where the people who have nothing to do but be happy, sit and have no arguments."

She slid onto the seat beside him and kissed him. "This is the first time I've been on the Riviera, Ravic," she said. "Don't be hard on me! This is the first time I've really been with you and the nights aren't cold any more and I am happy."

He drove the car out of the heavy traffic to the road past the Hôtel Carlton and then in the direction of Juan-les-Pins. "The first time," she repeated. "The first time, Ravic, and I know everything you could answer, and it has nothing to do with it." She leaned close to him and put her head on his shoulder. "Forget what happened today! Don't think about it. You are a wonderful driver, Ravic, do you know that? What you did just now was beautiful. The idiots were saying the same thing. Yesterday they saw what you could do with a car. You are uncanny. You have no past. One doesn't know anything about you. I know a hundred times more about the life of those idiots by now than about yours. Do you think that I could get some calvados somewhere? I need some after all the excitement tonight. It is difficult to live with you."

The car swept over the road like a low-flying bird. "Too fast?" Ravic asked.

"No! Drive faster! So that it blows through us like wind through a tree. How the night rushes past! I am penetrated through and through by love. One can look through me because of my love. I love you so much that my heart spreads out like a woman in a cornfield before a man who looks at her. My heart wants to lie down on the ground. In a meadow. It wants to lie and to fly. It is mad. It loves you when you drive a car. Let's never go back to Paris. Let's steal a trunk full of jewelry or rob a bank and take this car and never come back."

Ravic stopped in front of a little bar. The hum of the motor died and softly from afar came suddenly the deep breathing of the sea. "Come," he said. "We'll get your calvados here. How much have you had already?"

"Too much. Because of you. Besides, all of a sudden I couldn't listen to the babbling of those idiots any longer."

"Then why didn't you come to me?"

"I have come to you."

"Yes. When you thought I would leave. Have you had anything to eat?"

"Not much. I'm hungry. Did you win?"

"Yes."

"Then let's drive to the most expensive restaurant and eat caviar and drink champagne and let's be as our parents were before all these wars, carefree and sentimental and without fear, uninhibited and full of bad taste, with tears, the moon, oleanders, violins, the ocean, and love. And I want to believe that we'll have children and a garden and a house and you'll have a passport and a future, and I have given up a great career for your sake and we still love each other after twenty years and are jealous and you still think me beautiful and I cannot sleep when you aren't home for a night, and . . ."

He saw the tears streaming down her face. She smiled. "That is all part of it, beloved—all part of that bad taste. . . ."

"Come," he said, "we'll drive to the Château Madrid. That's in the mountains and they have Russian gypsies there and you shall have anything you want."

It was early in the morning. The sea below was gray and without waves. The sky had neither clouds nor colors. Only on the horizon a small streak of silver emerged from the water. It was so still that they heard each other breathing. They were the last guests up there. The gypsies had driven past them in an old Ford down the serpentine road. The waiter in a Citroën. The cook, to get supplies, in a six-passenger 1929 Delahaye.

"Daybreak," Ravic said. "Now the night is somewhere on the other side of the earth. There will be aeroplanes some time with which one will be able to overtake it. They will go as fast as the earth turns. Then if you tell me again at four o'clock in the morning that you love me we can let it be four o'clock forever; we will simply fly around the earth with time and the hours will stand still."

Joan leaned against him. "I can't help it. It is beautiful. It is heartbreakingly beautiful. You may laugh—"

"It is beautiful, Joan."

She looked at him. "Where is the plane of which you spoke? We'll be old, beloved, when your plane is invented. And I don't want to get old. Do you?"

"Yes."

"Really?"

"As old as possible."

"Why?"

"I want to see what becomes of this planet."

"I don't want to get old."

"You won't get old. Life will pass over your face, that will be all, and it will become more beautiful. One is old only when one no longer feels."

"No. When one no longer loves."

Ravic did not answer. To leave you, he thought. To leave you! What was I thinking a few hours ago in Cannes?

She stirred in his arms. "Now the party is over and I am going home with you and we are going to sleep together. How beautiful it all is! How beautiful it is when one lives completely and not with just a part of oneself. When one is full to the rim and calm because there is nothing more to get in. Come, let's drive home. To our borrowed home, to that white hotel that looks like a country house."

The car slid down the serpentine road almost without aid of the motor. The day was slowly becoming brighter. The earth smelled of dew. Ravic turned off the headlights. When they were passing the Corniche they met vans with vegetables and flowers. They were on the road to Nice. Later they passed a company of spahis. They heard the trotting of the horses through the droning of the motor. It sounded clear and almost artificial on the macadam road. The riders' faces were dark under their burnooses.

Ravic looked at Joan. She smiled at him. Her face was pale and tired and more fragile than before. In its soft fatigue it seemed to him more beautiful than ever on this magic, dark, still morning whose yesterday was sunk in the distance and which had not as yet any hour; which still floated timelessly— full of quietude, without fear or question.

The bay of Antibes came toward them in a great circle. The dawn was steadily growing lighter. Iron-gray shadows of four men-of-war, three destroyers and a cruiser, stood against the brightening day. They must have come into the harbor during the night. Low and menacing and silent they stood against the receding sky. Ravic looked down at Joan. She had fallen asleep on his shoulder.

Chapter 17

RAVIC was going to the hospital. He had been back from the Riviera for a week. Suddenly he stopped. What he saw was like something out of a child's toy box. The new building shone in the sun as if it had been constructed from a model kit; the scaffolding stood out against the bright sky like filigree—and when a beam with a figure on it began to topple, it looked as if a matchstick with a fly on it were tumbling down. It fell and fell and seemed to fall endlessly— the figure freed itself and now it was like a tiny doll that stretched out its arms and sailed clumsily through space. It was as if the world were frozen and still as death for a moment. Nothing stirred, no breeze, no breath, no sound— only the little figure and the rigid beam fell and fell—

Then suddenly everything was noise and movement. Ravic realized that he had been holding his breath. He ran.

The victim lay on the pavement. A second ago the street had been almost empty. Now it was swarming with people. They came from all directions as if an alarm had sounded. Ravic forced his way through the crowd. He noticed that two workers were attempting to life the victim. "Don't lift him! Leave him where he is!" he shouted.

The people around and in front of him made way. The two workers held the victim half suspended. "Let him down slowly! Careful! Slowly!"

"What are you?" one of the workers asked. "A doctor!"

"Yes."

"All right."

The workers laid the victim on the pavement. Ravic knelt beside him and examined him. He carefully opened the sweaty blouse and felt the body. Then he rose. "What?" asked the worker who had spoken to him before. "Unconscious, isn't he?"

Ravic shook his head. "What?" the worker asked.

"Dead," Ravic said.

"Dead?"

"Yes."

"But—" the man said incredulously, "we had just been eating lunch together."

"Is there a doctor here?" someone asked behind the ring of gaping people."

"What's the matter?" Ravic said.

"Is there a doctor here? Quick!"

"What's the matter?"

"That woman—"

"What woman?"

"The beam hit her. She's bleeding."

Ravic forced his way out through the crowd. A short woman with a large blue apron lay on a heap of sand beside a lime trough. Her face was wrinkled, very pale, and her eyes were as motionless as lumps of coal. Blood spurted like a little fountain from below her neck. It spurted sideways in a throbbing, oblique ray and gave a strange impression of disorder. Under her head a dark pool was quickly seeping into the sand.

Ravic pressed his fingers on the artery. He pulled out of his pocket a bandage and the small first-aid kit he always kept with him. "Hold this!" he said to the man next to him.

Four hands grasped for the bag simultaneously. It fell to the sand and opened. He pulled out the scissors and a stick and tore open the bandage.

The woman did not say anything. Not even her eyes moved. She was rigid and every muscle of her body was tense. "Everything will be all right."

The beam had struck her shoulder and neck. The shoulder was crushed; her collarbone was broken and the joint smashed. It would remain stiff. "It is your left arm," Ravic said and carefully examined the neck. The skin was lacerated, but everything else was uninjured. The foot was twisted; he tapped the bone and the leg. Gray stockings, well mended but whole, tied under the knee with a black ribbon—with what detail one always saw all this! Black laced boots, mended the laces tied with a double knot, the shoes repaired at the toe.

"Has anyone telephoned for an ambulance?" he asked.

Nobody answered. "I think the policeman has," someone said after a while.

Ravic raised his head. "Policeman? Where is he?"

"Over there—with the other—"

Ravic got up. "Everything has been taken care of then."

He was about to walk away. At this moment the policeman pushed through the crowd. He was a young man with a notebook in his hand. He excitedly licked his short, blunt pencil.

"One moment," he said, and started to write.

"Everything has been taken care of here," Ravic said.

"One moment, sir!"

"I'm in a hurry. I have an urgent case."

"One moment, sir. Are you the physician?"

"I've tied off the artery, that's all. Now all that's needed is to wait for the ambulance."

"One moment, doctor! I must put down your name. You are a witness."

"I didn't see the accident. I happened to come by afterwards."

"Nevertheless, I must put down everything. This is a serious accident, doctor!"

"I can see that," Ravic said.

The policeman tried to learn the woman's name. The woman could not answer. She only stared at him without seeing him. The policeman bent over her zealously. Ravic looked around. The crowd fenced him in like a wall. He could not get through.

"Listen," he said to the policeman. "I'm in a great hurry—"

"Very well, doctor. Don't make it more difficult. I must put everything down in order. The fact that you are a witness is important. The woman may die."

"She won't die."

"No one can tell about that. And then there is the question of compensation."

"Did you call for an ambulance?"

"My colleague is attending to that. Don't bother me now or it will take that much longer."

"The woman is half dead and you want to disappear," one of the workmen said reproachfully to Ravic.

"She'd be dead by now if I hadn't been here."

"Well then," the workman said without obvious logic. "You've got to stay."

The shutter of a camera clicked. A man wearing a hat

199

turned up in front, smiled. "Will you just go through that again as if you were applying the bandage?" he asked Ravic.

"No."

"It's for the press," the man said. "Your picture will be in the paper with your address and a caption saying you saved the woman's life. Good publicity. Please, over here, this way—the light is better here."

"Go to hell," Ravic said. "The woman urgently needs an ambulance. The bandage can't remain like that for long. See that an ambulance is called."

"One thing after the other, doctor!" the policeman declared. "First I must finish the report."

"Has the deceased told you his name yet?" asked a half-grown youth.

"Ta gueule!" The policeman spat in front of the boy's feet.

"Take another picture from here," someone said to the photographer.

"Why?"

"So that it will show that the women was on the closed-off part of the sidewalk. See that—" He pointed at a board that was standing sidewise, with the inscription: *Attention! Danger!* "Take the picture so that one can see it. We need it. Compensation is out of the question here."

"I'm a press photographer," the man with the hat declared brushing the suggestion aside. "I only photograph what I consider interesting."

"But this is interesting! What is more interesting? With the board in the background!"

"A board is not interesting. Action is interesting."

"Then put it down in your report." The man tapped the policeman on the shoulder.

"Who are you?" he asked angrily.

"I am the representative of the construction company."

"All right," the policeman said. "You stay here, too. What's your name? You must know that!" he asked the woman.

The woman moved her lips. Her eyelids began to flutter. Like butterflies, like deathly tired gray moths, Ravic thought—and at the same moment: Idiot that I am! I must try to get away!

"Damn it," the policeman said. "Maybe she's gone crazy. That makes more work! And my office hours end at three."

"Marcel," the woman said.

"What? Just a moment! What?" The policeman bent down again. The woman was silent. "What?" The policeman waited. "Once more. Say it once more!"

The woman remained silent. "You with your damned chatter," the policeman said to the representative of the construction company. "How can a man get his report together this way?"

At that moment the shutter clicked. "Thank you!" the photographer said. "Full of action."

"Have you got our sign in it?" the representative of the construction company asked without waiting for the policeman. "I'll order half a dozen immediately."

"No," the photographer declared. "I'm a Socialist. Just pay the insurance, you miserable watchdog of the millionaires."

A siren shrieked. The ambulance. This is the moment, Ravic thought. He cautiously took a step. But the policeman held him back. "You must come with us to headquarters, doctor. I'm sorry, but we must have a record of everything."

The other policeman stood beside him now. There was nothing to be done. Let's hope it will work out all right, Ravic thought, and went with them.

The official on duty at police headquarters had listened quietly to the gendarme and policeman who had written the report. Now he turned to Ravic. "You are not a Frenchman," he said. He didn't ask; he stated it as a fact.

"No," Ravic said.

"What are you?"

"A Czech."

"How is it that you are a doctor here? As a foreigner you can't practice if you aren't naturalized."

Ravic smiled. "I don't practice here. I'm here as a tourist. For pleasure."

"Have you your passport with you?"

"Is that necessary, Fernand?" another official asked. "The gentleman has helped the woman and we have his address. That should be enough. There are still other witnesses."

"I'm interested. Have you your passport with you? Or your *carte d'identité?*"

"Of course not," Ravic said. "Who keeps his passport with him all the time?"

"Where is it?"

"At the consulate. I took it there a week ago. It had to be extended."

Ravic knew that if he said his passport was at his hotel he might be sent there with a policeman and the bluff would be discovered at once. Besides, to be on the safe side, he had given a false address. He had a chance at the consulate.

"At which consulate?" Fernand asked.

"The Czech."

"We can call up and ask them." Fernand looked at Ravic.

"Of course."

Fernand waited awhile. "All right," he said then. "We'll just ask."

He rose and went into one of the adjoining rooms. The other official was very embarrassed. "Pardon us, doctor," he said to Ravic. "Of course, it isn't necessary at all. It will be cleared up immediately. We are obliged to you for your help."

Cleared up, Ravic thought. He looked about calmly while he took out a cigarette. The gendarme stood by the door. That was mere chance. No one really suspected him as yet. He might push him aside, but there were still the man from the construction company and the two workmen. He gave it up. It would be too hard to break through; a few more policemen would be standing outside the door.

Fernand returned. "There is no passport with your name at the consulate."

"Maybe there is," Ravic said.

"How is that possible?"

"An official at the telephone doesn't necessarily know everything. There are half a dozen people who deal with these matters."

"This one knew."

Ravic did not reply. "You are not a Czech," Fernand replied.

"Listen, Fernand—" the other official began.

"You haven't a Czech accent," Fernand said.

"Maybe not."

"You are a German," Fernand declared triumphantly. "And you have no passport."

"No," Ravic replied. "I am a Moroccan and have all the French passports in the world."

"Sir!" Fernand shouted. "How dare you! You're insulting the French Colonial Empire!"

"*Merde*," one of the workmen said. The representative of the construction company made a face as if he wanted to salute.

"Fernand, now don't—"

"You're lying! You're not a Czech. Have you a passport or not? Answer!"

The rat in man, Ravic thought. The rat in man which one can never drown. What does it matter to this idiot whether I have a passport or not? But the rat smells something and here it comes creeping out of its hole.

"Answer!" Fernand barked at him.

A piece of paper! To have it or not to have it. This creature would beg my pardon and bow if I had that scrap of paper. It would not make any differece if I had murdered a family or robbed a bank—this man would salute me. But even Christ without a passport—nowadays he would perish in a prison. Anyhow, he would be slain long before his thirty-third year.

"You'll stay here until this is cleared up," Fernand said. "I'll see to that."

"All right," Ravic said.

Fernand stamped out of the room. The second official rummaged among his papers. "Sir," he said presently, "I am sorry. He is crazy on this subject."

"Never mind."

"Are we through?" one of the workmen asked.

"Yes."

"All right." He turned to Ravic. "When the world revolution comes, you won't need a passport."

"You must understand, sir," the official said. "Fernand's father was killed in the World War. That's why he hates the Germans and does such things." He looked at Ravic for a moment in embarrassment. He seemed to surmise what was wrong. "I am awfully sorry, sir. If it was up to me . . ."

"Never mind," Ravic looked around. "May I use the telephone before this Fernand returns?"

"Of course. There on the table. Do it quickly."

Ravic telephoned Morosow. He told him in German what had happened. He was to let Veber know.

"Joan too?" Morosow asked.

Ravic hesitated. "No. Not yet. Tell her I have been detained, but everything will be all right again in two or three days. Take care of her."

"All right," Morosow replied, not over-enthusiastically. "All right, Wozzek."

When Fernand returned, Ravic put the receiver down. "What were you talking just now?" he asked with a grin. "Czech?"

"Esperanto."

Veber came next morning. "A damned hole," he said as he looked around.

"French prisons are still real prisons," Ravic replied. "Not tainted with the humbling of humanitarianism. Good stinking eighteenth century."

"Disgusting," Veber said. "Disgusting that you got into it."

"One shouldn't do any good deeds. One has to suffer for them immediately. I should have let the woman bleed to death. We live in an iron age, Veber."

"In a cast-iron one. Did our friends find out that you are here illegally?"

"Naturally."

"The address too?"

"Of course not. I would never expose the old International. The hotelkeeper would be punished because she harbors unregistered guests. And a raid would ensue during which a dozen refugees would be caught. I gave the Hôtel Lancaster as my address this time. An expensive, fine little hotel. I stayed there once during my former life."

"And your new name is Wozzek?"

"Vladimir Wozzek." Ravic grinned. "My fourth."

"Hell," Veber said. "What can be done, Ravic?"

"Not much. The main thing is that our friends mustn't find out that I've been here a few times before. Otherwise it will mean six months in prison."

"Damn it!"

"Yes, the world becomes more humane day by day. Live dangerously, Nietzsche said. The refugees do—against their will."

"And if they don't find out?"

"Two weeks, I guess. And the usual deportation."

"And then?"

"Then I'll return."

"Until you are caught again?"

"Exactly. It has taken a long while this time. Two years. A lifetime."

"We must do something. It can't go on like this."

"It can. What can you do?"

Veber thought about it. "Durant!" he then said suddenly. "Naturally! Durant knows a lot of people and is influential—" He interrupted himself. "My God, you yourself performed an operation on one of the principal big-wigs! That man with the gall bladder!"

"Not I. Durant—"

Veber laughed. "Naturally he can't tell that to the old gentleman. But he'll be able to do something. I'll wring his heart."

"You'll achieve very little. I cost him two thousand francs some time ago. His type doesn't forget that sort of thing easily."

"He will," Veber said, rather amused. "The thing is he'll be afraid you might tell about those ghosted operations. You have performed dozens for him. Besides he needs you badly."

"He can easily find someone else. Binot or some refugee surgeon. There are plenty of them."

Veber smoothed his mustache. "Not with your hand. We'll try it anyway. I'll do it this very day. Can I get anything for you here? How is the food?"

"Ghastly. But I can make them bring in something."

"Cigarettes?"

"Enough. You can't help me with what I really need—a bath."

Ravic lived there for two weeks with a Jewish plumber, a half-Jewish writer, and a Pole. The plumber was homesick for Berlin; the writer hated it; nothing mattered to the Pole. Ravic provided the cigarettes. The writer told Jewish jokes. The plumber was indispensable as an expert in combatting the stench.

After two weeks, Ravic was summoned. First he was brought before an inspector who only asked him whether he had any money.

"Yes."

"All right. Then you can take a taxi."

An official went with him. The street was light and sunny. It was good to be outside again. An old man was selling balloons at the entrance. Ravic could not imagine why he was selling them in front of the prison. The official hailed a taxi. "Where are we going?" Ravic asked.

"To the chief."

Ravic did not know which chief it was. It didn't make much difference to him either as long as it wasn't the chief of a German concentration camp. There was only one real horror in the world: to be completely and helplessly at the mercy of brutal terrorism. The present incident was harmless.

The taxi had a radio. Ravic turned it on. He got the vegetable market reports; then the political news. The official yawned. Ravic dialed another station. Music. A hit. The official perked up. "Charles Trenet," he said. "Ménilmontant. Real class!"

The taxi stopped. Ravic paid. He was conducted into a waiting room that smelled of expectation, sweat and dust, like all the waiting rooms in the world.

He sat for half an hour and read an old issue of *La Vie Parisienne* left behind by a visitor. It was like classic literature after two weeks without books. Then he was taken before the chief.

It took some time before he recognized the short, fat man. Usually he was not concerned with faces when he operated. They were as unimportant to him as so many numbers. He was interested in the sick places only. But he had looked at his face with curiosity. There he sat, healthy, his potbelly filled again, minus gall bladder: Leval. Ravic had forgotten by this time that Veber had intended to seek Durant's aid and he had not expected to be presented to Leval himself.

Leval looked him up and down. Thereby giving himself time. "Of course your name is not Wozzek," he grumbled.

"No."

"What is your name?"

"Neumann." Ravic had arranged this with Veber, who had explained it to Durant. Wozzek was too improbable.

"You are a German, aren't you?"

"Yes."

"Refugee?"

"Yes."

"One never can tell. You don't look it."

"Not all refugees are Jews," Ravic explained.

"Why were you lying? About your name."

Ravic shrugged his shoulders. "What else can we do? We lie as little as possible. We have to—do you think it's fun for us?"

Leval swelled up. "Do you think it is fun for us to be bothered with you?"

Gray, Ravic thought. His head had been whitish gray, the lacrimal sacs dirty-blue, the mouth had gaped half open. At that time he hadn't talked; then he had been a heap of flabby flesh with a rotting gall bladder in it.

"Where do you live? The address was wrong, too."

"I have lived everywhere. Sometimes here, sometimes there."

"For how long?"

"For three weeks. Three weeks ago I came from Switzerland. I was put across the border. You know that from a legal point of view we haven't the right to live anywhere without papers—and that most of us haven't yet been able to make up our minds to commit suicide. That's the reason we bother you."

"You should have remained in Germany," Leval grumbled. "It isn't quite so bad there. People exaggerate."

A slightly different incision, Ravic thought, and you wouldn't be here to talk this nonsense. The worms would have crossed your borderline without papers—or you would be a handful of dust in an undistinguished urn.

"Where did you live here?" Leval asked.

That's what you would like to know to catch the others too, Ravic thought. "In first-rate hotels," he said. "Under various names. Always for only a few days."

"That's not true."

"Why do you ask me if you know better?" said Ravic, who was slowly getting fed up.

Leval struck the table angrily with the flat of his hand. "Don't be impudent!" Immediately afterwards he examined his hand.

"You hit the scissors," Ravic said,

Leval put his hand into his pocket. "Don't you think you're rather impertinent?" he asked suddenly with the calm of a man who can afford to control himself because the other person is dependent on him.

"Impertinent?" Ravic looked at him, astonished. "You call that impertinence? We are neither in school nor in a reformatory for repentant criminals. I'm acting in self-defense—would you like me to feel like a criminal begging for a mild sentence? Only because I'm not a Nazi and therefore have no papers? The fact that we still don't consider ourselves criminals, although we have had experience of all kinds of prison, police, humiliations, only because we want to remain alive—that's the only thing that keeps us upright, don't you understand? God knows this is something other than impertinence.

Leval did not answer. "Have you practiced here?" he asked.

"No."

The scar must be smaller by now, Ravic thought. I sewed it nicely at that time. It was quite a job with all that fat. Meanwhile he's been stuffing himself again. Stuffing and drinking.

"That's where the greatest danger is," Leval explained. "Without examinations, without control, you hang around here. Who knows for how long! Don't think that I believe you about those three weeks. Who knows what you had your hand in, in how many shady affairs!"

In your paunch with its hardened arteries, its swollen liver, and its fermenting gall bladder, Ravic thought. And if I hadn't had my hand in it, your friend, Durant, would probably have killed you in a humane and idiotic way and would have become even more famous as a surgeon because of it and would have raised his fees.

"This is where the greatest danger lies," Leval repeated. "You are not permitted to practice. So you will accept anything that comes your way, that's obvious. I was talking about it with one of our authorities. He's of entirely the same opinion. If you really know anything about medical science, his name should be familiar to you—"

No, Ravic thought, that's impossible. He won't say Durant now. Life can't crack such jokes!

"Professor Durant," Leval said with dignity. "He explained it to me. Menials, students who have not yet completed their studies, masseurs, assistants, here all these claim to have been great medical men in Germany. Who can check on that? Illegal operations, abortions, collaboration with midwives, quackery, and heaven knows what else. We can't be severe enough!"

Durant, Ravic thought. That's his revenge for the two thousand francs. But who'll do his operations now? Binot, surely. Very likely they have got together again.

He noticed that he was no longer listening. He did not become attentive again until Veber's name was mentioned.

"A certain Doctor Veber has spoken in your behalf. Do you know him?"

"Slightly."

"He was here." Leval gazed straight ahead for a moment. Then he sneezed loudly, got his handkerchief out and blew his nose circumstantially, contemplated what he had blown out, folded his handkerchief together and put it into his pocket again. "I can't do anything for you. We must be severe. You'll be deported."

"I know that."

"Have you been in France before?"

"No."

"Six months' imprisonment if you return. You know that?"

"Yes."

"I'll see to it that you are deported as soon as possible. That's all I can do. Have you any money?"

"Yes."

"All right. Then you will have to pay for the trip of your escort and yourself to the border." He nodded. "You may go now."

"Any special hour when we have to be back?" Ravic asked the official who was escorting him.

"Not exactly. It depends. Why?"

"I'd like to drink an apéritif."

The official looked at him. "I won't run away," Ravic said. He drew a twenty-franc bill out of his pocket and toyed with it.

"All right. A few minutes can't make any difference."

They had the taxi stop at the next bistro. There were a few tables already standing outside. It was cool, but the sun was shining. "What will you have?" Ravic asked.

"Amèr Picon. Nothing else at this hour of the day."

"Give me a fine. Without water."

Ravic sat there calmly and breathed deeply. Air—what could that be! The branches of the trees on the sidewalk had brown shining buds. There was a smell of fresh bread and new wine. The waiter brought the glasses. "Where is the telephone?" Ravic asked.

"Inside—to your right, next to the toilets."

"But—" the official said.

Ravic put the twenty-franc bill into his hand. "You can

probably imagine to whom I'm going to telephone. I won't disappear. You can come with me. Come along."

The official didn't hesitate for long. "All right," he said and got up. "A human being is a human being, after all."

"Joan—"

"Ravic! My God! where are you? Have they let you out? Tell me where you are!"

"In a bistro—"

"Stop it! Tell me where you really are!"

"I'm really in a bistro."

"Where? Are you no longer in prison? Where have you been all this time? This Morosow—"

"He told you exactly what went wrong with me."

"He hasn't even told me where they took you. I would have come right away—"

"That's why he didn't tell you, Joan. Better so."

"Why do you telephone from a bistro? Why don't you come here?"

"I can't come. I've only a few minutes. I had to persuade the official to stop here for a moment. Joan, I'll be sent to Switzerland in the next few days, and—" Ravic glanced out the window. The official was leaning on the counter and talking. "And I'll be back at once." He waited. "Joan."

"I'll come. I'll come at once. Where are you?"

"You can't come. I'm half an hour's distance from you. I've only a few minutes left."

"Hold the official off! Give him money! I can bring money with me!"

"Joan," Ravic said. "It won't work. I must stop now."

He heard her breathe. "You don't want to see me?" she then asked.

It was difficult. I shouldn't have telephoned, he thought. How can one explain anything without being able to look at the other person. "I'd like nothing better than to see you, Joan."

"Then come! That man can come with you!"

"It's impossible. I must stop now. Tell me quickly what you're doing now."

"What? How do you mean that?"

"What are you wearing? Where are you?"

"In my room. In bed. I was up late last night. I can put something on in a minute and come right away."

Late last night. Of course. All that went right on also while one was imprisoned. One forgot about it. In bed, half asleep, her hair tumbled on the pillows, stockings scattered on chairs, lingerie, an evening gown—things began to reel; the window of the hot telephone booth, half misted by his breath; the infinitely remote head of the official that swam in it as though in an aquarium—he pulled himself together. "I must stop now, Joan."

He heard her disconcerted voice. "But that's impossible! You can't simply go away like this and I don't know anything, either where you are going or what—" Propped up, the pillows pushed aside, the telephone like a weapon and an enemy in her hand, the shoulders, the eyes, deep and dark with excitement . . .

"I'm not going to war. I'm merely traveling to Switzerland. I'll be back soon. Imagine I am a businessman who is going to sell a carload of machine guns to the League of Nations."

"When you come back, then it will be the same all over again. I won't be able to live from fear."

"Say the last sentence once more."

"It's true." Her voice became angry. "I'm the last one to be told anything. Veber can visit you, not I! You've called up Morosow, not me! And now you're going—"

"My God," Ravic said. "We won't quarrel, Joan."

"I'm not quarreling. I'm merely saying what's wrong."

"All right. I must stop now. Adieu, Joan."

"Ravic!" she called. "Ravic!"

"Yes—"

"Come back again! Come back again! I'm lost without you!"

"I'll come back."

"Yes—yes—"

"Adieu, Joan. I'll be back soon."

He stood in the hot steaming booth for a moment. Then he noticed that his hand had not let go of the receiver. He opened the door. The official looked up. He smiled good-naturedly. "Through?"

"Yes."

They went back outside to their table. Ravic emptied his glass. I shouldn't have telephoned, he thought. I was calm before. Now I am confused. I should have known that a telephone conversation could bring nothing else. Not for me, or for Joan. He felt the temptation to go back, to call up again and tell her everything he really wanted to tell her. To explain to her why he couldn't see her. That he didn't want her to see him as he was, dirty, under guard. But he would come out and it would be the same all over again.

"I think we've got to move on," the official said.

"Yes—"

Ravic called the waiter. "Give me two small bottles of cognac, all the newspapers and a dozen packages of Caporals. And the check." He looked at the official. "Permissible, isn't it?"

"A man is a man," the official said.

The waiter brought the bottles and cigarettes. "Open the bottles," Ravic said, while he carefully distributed the cigarettes in his pockets. He corked the bottles again in such a way that he could easily open them without a cork screw and put them into the inside pocket of his coat.

"You're good at that," the official said.

"Practice. Sorry to say. As a boy I would never have thought I might have to play Indian again in my old age."

The Pole and the writer were enthusiastic about the cognac. The plumber did not drink strong liquor. He was a beer drinker and explained in detail how much better the beer had been in Berlin. Ravic lay on his plank and read the papers. The Pole did not read; he didn't understand French. He smoked and was happy. At night the plumber began to cry. Ravic was awake. He listened to the suppressed sobbing and stared at the small window behind which glimmered a pale sky. He could not sleep. Nor could he later on when the plumber was calm. Too well lived, he thought. Too many things already to hurt when one didn't have them any more.

Chapter 18

RAVIC WAS on his way from the station. He was tired and dirty. Thirteen hours in a hot train with people who ate garlic, with hunters and their dogs, with women who held cages containing chickens and pigeons on their laps. And before that almost three months at the frontier—

He walked along the Champs Elysées. There was a twinkling in the dusk. Ravis looked up. The twinkling seemed to come from pyramids of mirrors standing around the Rond Point and reflecting back and forth the last gray light of May.

He stopped and looked more sharply. There actually were pyramids of mirrors. They were everywhere, behind the tulip beds in ghostlike repetition. "What's that?" he asked a gardener who was leveling a bed of newly turned dirt.

"Mirrors," the gardener answered, without looking up.

"I can see that. The last time I was here they weren't around."

"Haven't you been here for some time?"

"Three months."

"Ah, three months. This was done in the last two weeks. For the King of England. Coming for a visit. So he can see his face mirrored here."

"Terrible," Ravic said.

"Of course," the gardener replied without surprise.

Ravic walked on. Three months—three years—three days; what was time? Nothing and everything. The fact that the chestnut trees were in bloom now—and before they hadn't yet had any leaves—that Germany had broken her treaties again and occupied the whole of Czechoslovakia—that in Geneva, the refugee Josef Blumenthal had shot himself in a fit of hysterical laughter in front of the Palace of the League of Nations—that somewhere in his own chest there was the aching remnant of the pneumonia he had survived in Belfort under the name of Guenther—and that now, on an evening soft as a woman's breast, he was back again; all this held almost no surprise for him. One took it as one took many things, with fatalistic calm, which was the only weapon of helplessness. The sky was the same everywhere, always the same, above murder and hatred and sacrifice and love—the trees blossomed anew, unsuspectingly, every year—the plum-blue dusk changed and came and went, unconcerned with passports, betrayal, despair, and hope. It was good to be in Paris again. It was good to walk, to walk slowly, without thinking, along this street in the silver-gray light; it was good to have this hour, still full of respite, full of a mild inter-change at the boundary where a distant grief and the tender recurrent happiness of simply being alive melted into each other like horizons—this first hour of arrival before one was again pierced by knives and arrows—this strange animal feeling, this breath reaching far and coming from afar, this breeze, without emotion yet, along the streets of the heart, past the dull fires of facts, past the nail-studded cross of bygone days and past the barbed hooks of the future, this caesura, the silence within oscillation, the moment of pause, most open and most secret form of being, the unemphatic beat of eternity in the very transitoriness of the world—

Morosow sat in the Palm Room of the International. He was drinking a bottle of Vouvray. "Hello, Boris old fellow," Ravic said. "I seem to have returned at the right moment. Is that Vouvray?"

"Still the same. Thirty-four this time. Slightly sweeter and stronger. Good that you're back again. It was three months, wasn't it?"

"Yes. Longer than usual."

Morosow rang an old-fashioned table bell. It pealed like a sacristan's bell in a village church. The Catacombs had only electric lights, no electric bells. It didn't pay; the refugees rarely dared to ring. "What's your name now?" Morosow asked.

"Still Ravic. I didn't mention this name at the police station. I called myself Wozzek, Neumann, and Guenther. A caprice. I didn't want to give up Ravic. I like it as a name."

"They didn't find out that you were living here, did they?"

"Of course not."

"Obviously. Otherwise there would have been a raid. So you can stay here again. Your room is vacant."

"Does the old lady know what happened?"

"No. Nobody. I told them you went to Rouen. Your things are at my place."

The girl came in with a tray. "Clarisse, bring a glass for Mr. Ravic," Morosow said.

"Ah, Mr. Ravic!" The girl showed her yellow teeth. "Back again? You stayed away more than six months, monsieur."

"Three months, Clarisse."

"Impossible. I thought it was six months."

The girl shuffled off. Immediately afterwards the slovenly waiter of the Catacombs came with a wine glass in his hand. He had no tray; he had been in this place for a long time and could afford to be informal. His face indicated what would follow and Morosow anticipated it. "All right, Jean. Tell me how long Mr. Ravic has been away. Do you know exactly?"

"But Mr. Morosow! Naturally I know to the very day! It's exactly—" He paused for effect, smiled, and said: "Exactly four and a half weeks!"

"Correct," Ravic said before Morosow could answer.

"Correct," Morosow replied too.

"Naturally. I'm never mistaken." Jean disappeared.

"I didn't want to disappoint him, Boris."

"Neither did I. I only wanted to demonstrate to you the feebleness of time once it becomes the past. That's comforting, frightening, or a matter of indifference. I lost sight of First Lieutenant Bielski of the Neobrashensk Guard Regiment in 1917 in Moscow. We were friends. He went north across Finland. I made my way across Manchuria and Japan. When we met again here eight years later, I thought I had seen him last in 1919 in Harbin; he thought it had been in 1921 in Helsinki. A difference of two years—and a few thousand miles." Morosow took the bottle and filled the glasses. "You see, at least they recognized you again. That in itself gives one some feeling of being home, doesn't it?"

Ravic drank. The wine was cool and light. "In the meantime I've been close to the border," he said. "Very close, below Basel. One side of the road belonged to Switzerland, the other was German. I stood on the Swiss side and ate cherries. I could spit the pits into Germany."

"Did that give you a feeling of being at home?"

"No. I never felt farther away."

Morosow grinned. "I can understand that. How was it on the way?"

"As usual. It's getting more difficult, that's all. They watch the frontiers more closely. Once they caught me in Switzerland, once in France."

"Why did you never drop us a line?"

"I didn't know how far the police might go here. Sometimes they have fits of energy. It's better not to jeopardize anyone. After all, our alibis aren't really so very good. Old front-line rule: lie still and disappear. Did you expect anything else?"

"Not I."

Ravic looked at him. "Letters," he said then. "What are letters? Letters never help."

"No."

Ravic took a package of cigarettes out of his pocket. "Strange, how everything turns out when one is away."

"Don't fool yourself," Morosow replied.

"I'm not."

"When one stays away it's good. When one returns, it's different. Then it starts again."

"Perhaps. Perhaps not."

"You're pretty cryptic. It's a good thing you take it that way. Do you want to play a game of chess? The professor died. He was my only worthy opponent. Levy went to Brazil. Job as a waiter. Life moves damned fast nowadays. One shouldn't get used to anything."

"One shouldn't."

Morosow looked at Ravic attentively. "I didn't mean it that way."

"Neither did I. But couldn't we leave this musty palm grave? I haven't been here for three months; nevertheless, it stinks just as it always did—of the kitchen, dust, and fear. When do you have to go?"

"Not at all today. It's my day off."

"Right." Ravic smiled briefly. "The evening of elegance, of old Russia, and of the large glasses."

"Do you want to come with me?"

"No. Not tonight. I'm tired. I've hardly slept at all the last few nights. Not very quietly anyhow. Let's wander around for an hour and sit somewhere. I haven't done that in a long time."

"Vouvray?" Morosow asked. They were sitting in front of the Café Colisée. "It's early evening, old fellow. The hour for vodka."

216

"Yes. Nevertheless, Vourvray."

"I'm getting worried. At least a fine?"

Ravic shook his head. "When one arrives somewhere one should drink oneself stiff the first night, brother," Morosow declared. "It's unnecessary heroism to stare soberly into the dreary faces of the shadows of the past."

"I'm not staring, Boris. I am enjoying life cautiously."

Ravic saw that Morosow didn't believe him. He made no attempt to convince him. He sat calmly at the table, in the first row on the street, drank his wine and watched the strolling evening crowds. As long as he had been away from Paris, everything had been sharp and clear. Now it was misty, pale, and colorful, pleasantly flowing, but as things appear to someone who has descended a mountain too quickly and who can only hear the noise down in the valley as if through cotton-wool.

"Did you go anywhere else before you came to the hotel?" Morosow asked.

"No."

"Veber asked for you several times."

"I'll call him up."

"I don't like the way you behave. Tell me what's wrong."

"Nothing in particular. The border at Geneva was too well guarded. I tried it there first. Then at Basel. Difficult there too. Finally I got across. Caught a cold. Rain and snow at night in the open fields. Couldn't do much about it. It turned into pneumonia. A doctor in Belfort got me into a hospital. He smuggled me in and out. Kept me in his house ten days after that. I've got to send the money back to him."

"Are you all right again?"

"Pretty much."

"That's why you aren't drinking any hard liquor?"

Ravic smiled. "Why are we talking around the point? I'm a little tired and want to get used to things again. That's really so. Strange, how much you think when you're on the road. And how little when you arrive."

Morosow waved this aside. "Ravic," he said in a fatherly tone, "you are talking to your father Boris, a connoisseur of the human heart. Don't make detours and ask me quickly so that we can get it behind us."

"All right. Where is Joan?"

"I don't know. I haven't heard anything about her for several weeks now. Haven't seen her either."

217

"And before that?"

"Before that she inquired about you for some time. Then not any more."

"She is no longer at the Scheherazade?"

"No. She left about six weeks ago. She came there two or three times later. But not after that."

"Isn't she in Paris now?"

"I don't think so. At least it would seem not. Otherwise she would have come again to the Scheherazade from time to time."

"Do you know what she's doing?"

"Something in the movies, I think. At least that's what she told the hat-check girl. You know how it is. One of those damned pretenses."

"Pretenses?"

"Yes, pretenses," Morosow said angrily. "What else, Ravic? Did you expect anything else?"

"Yes."

Morosow remained silent. "To expect and to know are two different things," Ravic said.

"Only for God damned romantics. Now drink something sensible—not this lemonade. Some decent calvados—"

"Certainly not calvados. Cognac, if it will make you feel any better. Or even calvados, for all I care."

"At last," Morosow said.

The window. The blue silhouette of the roofs. The faded red sofa. The bed. Ravic knew that he had to bear it. He sat on the sofa and smoked. Morosow had brought him his belongings and told him where he could find him if he wanted to.

He had thrown away his old suit. He had taken a bath, hot and cold, a long bath with much soap. He had washed away the three months and rubbed it from his skin. He had put on clean underwear and another suit; he had shaved; most of all he would have liked to go to a Turkish bath if it had not been too late. He had done all this and felt fine doing it. He would have liked to do even more, because suddenly now while sitting by the window, the emptiness began crawling out of the corners.

He filled a glass with calvados. Among his belongings had been an opened bottle with a little left in it. He recalled the night when he had been drinking it with Joan, but it evoked little feeling. It had been too long ago. He merely noticed that it was very good old calvados.

The moon rose slowly above the roofs. The dirty yard opposite became a palace of shadows and silver. Everything could be turned from dirt into silver, with a little imagination. The fragrance of flowers came through the window. The sharp smell of carnations at night. Ravic leaned over the sill and looked down. A wooden box with flowers stood below him on the sill. They belonged to the refugee Wiesenhoff if he was still living there. Ravic had pumped out his stomach once. It had been at Christmas, a year ago.

The bottle was empty. He threw it onto the bed. There it lay like a black embryo. He rose. Why was he staring at the bed? When one had no woman, one had to get one. That was easy in Paris.

He went through the narrow streets to the Etoile. The warm life of the city at night vibrated from the Champs Elysées. He walked back, faster, then gradually more slowly till he arrived at the Hôtel de Milan.

"How is everything?" he asked the porter.

"Ah, monsieur!" The porter got up. "Monsieur hasn't been here for a long time."

"Yes, not for quite a while. I wasn't in Paris."

The porter took stock of him with his small lively eyes. "Madame isn't here any longer."

"I know. Not for quite some time."

The porter was a good porter. He knew what was wanted of him without being asked. "Four weeks now," he said. "Four weeks ago she moved out."

Ravic took a cigarette out of his package. "Is Madame no longer in Paris?" the porter asked.

"She is in Cannes."

"Cannes!" The porter rubbed his large hand across his face. "You won't believe it, sir, that I was a porter at the Hôtel Ruhl in Nice eighteen years ago, would you?"

"I do."

"Those days! Those tips! That wonderful time after the war. Nowadays—"

Ravic was a good guest. He understood hotel employees without need of too broad a hint. He drew a five-franc bill out of his pocket and put it on the table.

"Thank you, sir! Have a good time! You look younger, sir!"

"I feel it, too. Good night."

Ravic stood on the street. Why had he gone to that hotel? All that was lacking now was to go to the Scheherazade and get drunk.

He gazed at the star-filled sky. He should be glad it had turned out this way. He had been saved a lot of unnecessary recrimination. He had known it and Joan had known it, too. In the long run, at least. She had done what was the only right thing to do. No explanations. Explanations were second-rate. Where feelings were concerned, there were no explanations. Only actions. Thank God the wagon grease of morals had no part in it. Thank God that Joan knew nothing about that. She had acted, and it was done with. No tugging back and forth. He had acted, too. Why was he loitering here now? It must be the air. This soft fabric woven out of May and evening and Paris. And the night, of course. At night one was always different than by day.

He went back to the hotel. "May I use your telephone?"

"Certainly, sir. But we have no booth. Only this instrument."

"That's good enough."

Ravic looked at his watch. Veber might be at the hospital. It was the time for the last nightly round. "Is Doctor Veber in?" he asked the nurse. He did not recognize her voice. It must be a new one.

"You can't talk to Doctor Veber now."

"Is he in?"

"He's in. But you can't talk to him now."

"Listen," Ravic said. "Go and tell him that Ravic is on the phone. Go immediately. It's important. I'll wait."

"All right," the nurse said hesitatingly. "I'll ask him, but he won't come."

"We'll see about that. Ask him. Ravic."

A moment later Veber was at the telephone. "Ravic! Where are you?"

"In Paris. Arrived today. Do you still have to operate?"

"Yes. In twenty minutes. An urgent appendectomy. Could we meet afterwards?"

"I can come over."

"Wonderful. When?"

"At once."

"All right. Then I'll wait for you."

*   *   *

"Here is some good liquor," Veber said. "Here are newspapers and medical journals. Make yourself comfortable."

"A drink. And a gown and gloves."

Veber looked at Ravic. "Simple case of appendicitis. Below your dignity. I can get through with it quickly with Morel's help. Called him already. I'm sure you're tired."

"Veber, do me a favor and let me perform the operation. I'm not tired and I'm all right."

Veber laughed. "You're certainly in a hurry to get back to work! All right, just as you like. I'll call off Morel then. In fact, I understand."

Ravic washed and put on the gown and gloves. The operating room. He inhaled the smell of the ether deeply. Eugénie stood by the head of the table, administering the anesthetic. A second, very beautiful young nurse was putting the instruments in order. "Good evening, Eugénie," Ravic said.

She almost let the dropper fall. "Good evening, Doctor Ravic," she replied.

Veber smiled. It was the first time she had addressed Ravic this way. Ravic bent over the patient. The strong operating lights blazed white and intense. They shut the world out. They shut off thought. They were objective and cold and merciless and good. Ravic took the knife which the beautiful nurse handed him. The steel felt cool through the thin gloves. It was good to feel it. It was good to get away from wavering uncertainty to clear preciseness. He made the incision. Narrow and red, the line of blood followed the knife. Suddenly everything was simple. For the first time since he had been back he felt like himself again. The soundless humming of the light. At home, he thought. At last!

Chapter 19

"She is here." Morosow said.

"Who?"

Morosow smoothed his uniform. "Don't act as if you didn't know whom I mean. You mustn't annoy your father Boris in a public thoroughfare. Do you think I can't guess why you have been at the Scheherazade three times in two weeks? Once accompanied by a miracle of blue eyes and black hair, but twice alone? Man is weak—otherwise where would his charm be?"

"Go to hell," Ravic said. "Don't humiliate me, just when I need all my strength, you gossipy doorkeeper."

"Would you rather I hadn't told you?"

"Of course."

Morosow stepped aside and let two Americans in. "Then go away and come back again some other evening," he said.

"Is she here alone?"

"We don't even admit reigning princesses unattended. You ought to know that. Sigmund Freud would have liked your question."

"What do you know about Sigmund Freud? You are tight and I'll complain about you to your manager, Captain Tschedschenedse."

"Captain Tschedschenedse was lieutenant in the same regiment in which I was a lieutenant colonel, my boy. He still remembers that. Just try."

"All right. Let me by."

"Ravic!" Morosow put his heavy hands on his shoulders. "Don't be a fool! Go, telephone the miracle with the blue eyes and come back with her, if you feel you must. That's the simple advice of an experienced old man. Extremely cheap, but none the less effective."

"No, Boris." Ravic looked at him. "Tricks have no place here. I'll have none of them."

"Then go home," Morosow said.

"To the musty Palm Room? Or to my hole?"

Morosow left Ravic and strode ahead of a couple that wanted a taxi. Ravic waited until he returned. "You're more sensible than I thought," Morosow said. "Otherwise you'd be inside already."

He pushed back his cap with the gold braid. Before he could go on, an intoxicated young man in a white tuxedo appeared in the door. "Colonel! A racing car!"

Morosow called the next taxi in the row and helped the wavering man in. "You don't laugh," the drunk said. "But colonel was a good joke, or wasn't it?"

"Very good. Racing car was perhaps even better."

"I've thought it over," Morosow said when he came back. "Go in. I'd do it, too. It will have to happen sometime anyway; why not now? Finish it one way or another. When we're no longer childish we are getting old."

"I've thought it over, too. I'm going somewhere else."

Morosow looked at Ravic in amusement. "All right," he said finally. "Then I'll see you again in half an hour."

"Maybe not."

"Then in an hour."

Two hours later Ravic was sitting in the Cloche d'Or. The place was still rather empty. Whores sat at the long bar, like parrots on a perch, chattering. Near them several peddlers of fake cocaine stood around waiting for tourists. In the room upstairs, a few couples sat and ate onion soup. In a corner, on a sofa, two Lesbians whispered together drinking sherry brandy. One of them in a tailored suit with a tie was wearing a monocle and the other was a red-haired buxom person, in a very low-cut sparkling evening gown.

How idiotic, Ravic thought. Why didn't I go to the Scheherazade? What am I afraid of? And why do I run away? It has grown, I know. These three months have not destroyed it—they have made it stronger. There's no point in going on deluding myself. It was almost the only thing that stayed with me in all that creeping across frontiers, waiting in hidden rooms, in all that dripping loneliness of alien starless nights. Absence has strengthened it more than she herself could ever have, and now—

A stifled scream woke him out of his brooding. A few women had come in meanwhile. One of them who looked

223

like a very light Negress, rather drunk, a flowered hat pushed to the back of her head, threw away a table knife and walked slowly down the stairs, shouting threats in the direction of the corner where the Lesbians were. No one stopped her. A waiter came upstairs. Another woman stood there and blocked his way. "Nothing has happened," she said. "Nothing has happened."

The waiter shrugged his shoulders and turned back. Ravic saw the red-haired woman in the corner getting up. At the same time, the woman who had kept the waiter off went quickly downstairs to the bar. The redhead stood still, her hand at her full bosom. She carefully opened two fingers of her hand and looked down. Her gown was slashed a few inches and underneath one saw the open wound. One did not see any skin; only the open wound in the green iridescent evening gown. The red-haired woman stared at it as though she could not believe it.

Ravic made an involuntary movement. Then he let himself sink back. One deportation was enough. He saw the woman in the tailored suit pulling the redhead back onto the sofa. At the same moment the second woman came back upstairs from the bar with a glass of brandy. The woman in the tailored suit knelt on the banquette, with one hand she kept the redhead's mouth closed as she quickly pulled her hand away from the wound. The other woman poured the brandy into it. A primitive form of disinfectant, Ravic thought. The redhead moaned, moved convulsively, but the other one held her in a grip of steel. Two other women hid the table from the remaining guests. Hardly anyone saw the occurrence. A minute later a number of Lesbians and homosexuals crowded into the place as if summoned by magic. They surrounded the table in the corner, two lifted the redhead, held her up, the others, laughing and chattering, shielded the group, and they all left the place as if nothing had happened. Most of the guests were hardly aware of the disturbance.

"Good, wasn't it?" someone asked Ravic from behind. It was the waiter.

Ravic nodded. "What was it about?"

"Jealousy. These perverts are an excitable lot."

"Where did all the others come from so quickly? That seemed sheer telepathy."

"They smell it, sir," the waiter said.

"Very likely one of them telephoned. But it went fast."

"They smell it. And they stick to each other like death and the devil. They don't give each other away. No police—that's all they want. They settle it among themselves." The waiter picked up Ravic's glass from the table. "Another? What was it?"

"Calvados."

"All right. Another calvados."

He shuffled away. Ravic looked up and saw Joan sitting a few tables from him. She had come in while he was talking to the waiter. He hadn't seen her enter. She was sitting with two men. At the same moment she noticed him. She turned pale under her tan. She sat still a few seconds, without taking her eyes from him. Then, with a brusque movement, she pushed her table aside, got up, and came toward him. As she walked her face changed. It relaxed and became soft; only her eyes remained steady and transparent as crystals. To Ravic they appeared brighter than ever. They were of an almost furious intensity.

"You are back?" she said breathlessly in a low voice.

She stood close to him. For a moment she made a move as if she were about to put her arms around him. But she did not do it. Nor did she shake hands with him. "You are back?" she repeated.

Ravic did not answer.

"How long have you been back?" she asked in the same low tone as before.

"For two weeks."

"For two—and I didn't—you didn't even—"

"No one knew where you were. Neither at your hotel nor the Scheherazade."

"The Scheherazade—but I was—" She interrupted herself. "Why did you never write?"

"I could not."

"You are lying."

"All right. I didn't want to. I didn't know whether I would come back again."

"You are lying again. That's no reason."

"It is. I could come back or not come back. Don't you understand?"

"No. But I do understand that you have been here for two weeks and you haven't done the least thing to—"

"Joan," Ravic said calmly. "You didn't get those brown shoulders in Paris."

The waiter passed by, sniffing. He cast a look at Joan and Ravic. He was still full of the scene that had occurred earlier. As if by chance he removed the two knives and forks together with a plate from the red and white checked tablecloth. Ravic noticed it. "Everything is all right," he said.

"What is all right?" Joan asked.

"Nothing. Something happened here a while ago."

She stared at him. "Are you waiting here for a woman?"

"My God, no. Some people had a scene. One of them was bleeding. This time I did not interfere."

"Interfere?" Suddenly she understood. Her expression changed. "What are you doing here? They will arrest you again. Now I know all about it. Half a year's imprisonment next time. You must go away! I didn't know you were in Paris. I thought you would never come back again."

Ravic did not answer.

"I thought you would never come back again," she repeated.

Ravic looked at her. "Joan—"

"No! Not a thing is true! Nothing is true! Nothing!"

"Joan," Ravic said warily. "Go back to your table."

Suddenly her eyes were moist. "Go back to your table," he said.

"It's your fault!" she burst out. "Yours! Yours alone!"

Abruptly she turned around and went back. Ravic pushed his table to one side and sat down. He looked at the glass of calvados and made a move as if to drink it. He didn't. He had been calm while speaking to Joan. Now, suddenly, he felt the excitement. Strange, he thought, the chest muscles vibrate under the skin. Why just those? He lifted the glass and observed his hand. It was steady. He emptied half the glass. While he was drinking he could feel Joan's look. He did not glance her way again. The waiter passed by. "Cigarettes," Ravic said. "Caporals."

He lighted a cigarette and drained the remaining half of his glass. He could feel Joan's look again. What does she expect? he thought. That I will get drunk from misery right here in front of her? He called the waiter and paid. The moment he got up Joan began talking vivaciously to one of her companions. She did not look up as he passed her table. Her face was hard and entirely expressionless and her smile was forced.

Ravic wandered through the streets and found himself unexpectedly in front of the Scheherazade again. Morosow's face lit up. "Well done, soldier! I almost gave you up for lost. One is always pleased when a prophecy comes true."

"Don't be pleased too soon."

"Don't you be either. You've come too late."

"I know that. I have already run into her."

"What?"

"In the Cloche d'Or."

"What the—" Morosow said, taken aback. "Mother Life has always new tricks up her sleeve."

"When will you be through here, Boris?"

"In a few minutes. Everyone has gone. I have to change. Come in meanwhile. Have a drink of vodka on the house."

"No. I'll wait here."

Morosow looked at him. "How are you feeling?"

"I feel like vomiting."

"Did you expect anything else?"

"Yes. One always expects something else. Go and change."

Ravic leaned against the wall. Beside him the old flower woman packed up her roses. She did not offer him any. It was a foolish thought, but he would have liked her to ask him. Now it was as if she did not think he would need any. He looked along the rows of houses. A few windows were still lit up. Taxis passed slowly. What did he expect? He didn't exactly know. What he had not expected was that Joan would take the initiative. But why not? How much in the right anyone was already the minute he attacked!

The waiters left. During the night they had been Caucasians and Circassians in red coats and high boots. Now they were tired civilians. They slunk home in everyday clothes which looked strange on them. The last was Morosow. "Where to?" he asked.

"I've been everywhere today."

"Then let's go to the hotel and play chess."

"What?"

"Chess. A game with wooden figures which simultaneously diverts you and makes you concentrate."

"Good," Ravic said. "Why not?"

He woke up and knew at once that Joan was in the room. It was still dark and he could not see her, but he knew she was there. The room was different, the window was different, the air was different, and even he was different. "Stop this nonsense!" he said. "Turn on the light and come here."

She did not move. He did not even hear her breathe. "Joan," he said. "We are not going to play hide-and-seek."

"I'm not playing hide-and-seek."

"Then come here."

"Did you know that I would come?"

"No."

"Your door was open."

"My door is almost always open."

She remained silent for a moment. "I thought you wouldn't be here yet," she said then. "I only wanted—I thought you would be sitting somewhere and drinking."

"I thought so, too. I was playing chess instead."

"What?"

"Chess. With Morosow. Downstairs in the hole that looks like a dry aquarium."

"Chess!" She came out of her corner. "Chess! But that's—! Someone who can play chess when—"

"I wouldn't have thought it myself. But it worked. In fact it worked well. I was able to win a game."

"You're the coldest, most unfeeling—"

"Joan," Ravic said. "No scenes. I'm in favor of good scenes. But not today!"

"I'm not making a scene. I am terribly unhappy."

"All right. Then we'd better skip all that. Scenes are justifiable when one is moderately unhappy. I knew a man who locked himself in his room and solved chess problems from the minute his wife died until she was buried. People thought him unfeeling, but I know that he loved his wife more than anything in the world. He simply couldn't act otherwise. Day and night he solved chess problems so he wouldn't think about it."

Joan was now standing in the middle of the room. "Is that why you did it?"

"No. I told you that was another man. I was sleeping when you came."

"Yes, you were asleep! You can sleep!"

Ravic propped himself up. "I knew another man. Joan, who had lost his wife, too. He went to bed and slept for two days. His wife's mother was beside herself because he did that. She didn't know that one can do many incongruous things and be disconsolate at the same time. It is strange what etiquette has been built up just for unhappiness! If you had found me blind drunk, everything would have been in good

228

taste. The fact that I played chess and went to sleep is proof that I am crude and unfeeling. Simple, isn't it?''

A sound of crashing and shattering. Joan had seized a vase and thrown it to the floor. "Fine," Ravic said. "I couldn't stand that thing anyway. Just be careful you don't get splinters in your feet."

She kicked the pieces aside. "Ravic," she said. "Why are you doing this?''

"Yes," he replied. "Why? To give myself courage, Joan. Don't you see that?''

She turned her face toward him quickly. "It looks that way. But with you one never knows what's going on.''

She carefully stepped over the scattered pieces and sat down on his bed. He could see her face distinctly now in the early dawn. He was surprised that it was not tired. It was young and clear and intense. She wore a light coat which he had not seen before and a different dress from the one she had worn in the Cloche d'Or.

"I thought you'd never come back again, Ravic," she said.

"It took a long time. I couldn't have come any sooner."

"Why didn't you write to me?''

"Would it have helped?''

She looked aside. "It would have been better."

"It would have been better if I hadn't come back. But there is no longer any other country or any other city for me. Switzerland is too small; everywhere else are the Fascists.''

"But here—won't the police—''

"The police have just as little chance of catching me as before. That was an unfortunate accident. We don't need to think about it any more.''

Ravic reached for a pack of cigarettes. They lay on the table beside his bed. It was a comfortable table of medium size with books, cigarettes, and a few other things on it. Ravic hated the night tables and consoles with imitation marble tops that usually stand beside beds.

"Let me have a cigarette, too," Joan said.

"Do you want something to drink?'' he asked.

"Yes. Lie there. I'll get it.''

She fetched the bottle and filled two glasses. She gave him one, took the other, and emptied it. While she was drinking, her coat slipped from her shoulders. Now in the brightening dawn Ravic recognized the dress she wore. It was the one he had given her as a present for Antibes. Why had she put it on? It was the only dress he had ever given her. He had never thought about things like that. He had never wanted to think about things like that either.

"When I saw you, Ravic—suddenly—" she said. "I couldn't think at all. Not at all. And when you left—I thought I'd never see you again. I didn't think so immediately. First I waited for you to come back to the Cloche d'Or. I thought you must come back. Why didn't you?"

"Why should I have come back?"

"I'd have gone with you."

Ravic knew that was not true. But he did not want to think about it now. Suddenly he did not want to think about anything. There Joan sat at his side, that was enough for the moment. He had not thought it would be enough. He didn't know why she had come or what she really wanted—but suddenly, in a strange and deep and disquieting way, it was enough that she was there. What is it? he thought. Has it already gone that far? Beyond all control? To the point where darkness begins, the uproar of the blood, the compulsion of the imagination and the menace?

"I thought you wanted to leave me," Joan said. "You did want to. Tell the truth!"

Ravic was silent.

She looked at him. "I knew it! I knew it!" she repeated with deep conviction.

"Give me another glass of calvados."

"Is it calvados?"

"Yes. Didn't you notice?"

"No." She poured it. She rested her arm against his chest while she held the bottle. He felt her touch go through his ribs. She took her glass and drank. "Yes, it is calvados." Then she looked at him again. "It's good that I came. I knew it. It's good that I came!"

It was growing lighter outside. The shutters began a low creaking. The morning wind rose. "Is it good that I've come?" she asked.

"I don't know, Joan."

She bent over him. "You know. You must know."

Her face was so close to his that her hair fell over his shoulders. He looked at it. It was a landscape that he knew and did not know, very strange and very familiar, always the same and never the same. He saw that the skin on her forehead was peeling, he saw that the red of her lipstick was caked on her upper lip, he saw that she wasn't made up quite properly—he saw all that in the face which was now so close above his that in this moment it blotted out all the rest of the world for him—he saw it and he knew that it was only his fantasy which made it mysterious, he knew that there were more beautiful faces, better faces, purer faces—but he knew too that this face, like no other, had power over him. And he himself had given it this power.

"Yes," he said. "It is good. One way or another."

"I couldn't have endured it, Ravic."

"What?"

"For you to have stayed away. For good."

"Didn't you say you thought I would never come back?"

"That's not the same. It would have been different if you had been living in another country. We would only have separated. I could have come to you, sometime. Or I'd always have been able to believe that. But here, in the same city—don't you understand?"

"I do."

She straightened up and smoothed her hair. "You can't leave me alone. You are responsible for me."

"Are you alone?"

"You are responsible for me," she said and smiled.

He hated her for a second—for her smile and for the way she said it.

"Don't talk nonsense, Joan."

"I'm not. You are. From that time on. Without you—"

"All right. I am responsible for the occupation of Czechoslovakia too. And now stop it. It's getting light. Soon you must go."

"What?" She stared at him. "You don't want me to stay here?"

"No."

"So—" she said in a low voice, suddenly very angry. "You don't love me any more."

"Good Heavens!" Ravic said. "That too! What idiots have you been with the last few months?"

"They weren't idiots. What else could I have done? Sit in the Hôtel de Milan and stare at the walls and go mad?"

Ravic half straightened up. "No confessions!" he said. "I do not want any confessions! I merely wanted to raise the level of our conversation a bit."

She looked at him. Her mouth and her eyes were flat. "Why do you always criticize me? Other people don't criticize me. With you every little thing immediately becomes a problem."

"All right." Ravic took a big gulp hastily and let himself sink back.

"It is true!" she said. "One never knows what to make of you. You force me to say things I never intended to say. And then you attack me."

Ravic breathed deeply. What was it that he had just before been thinking about? Darkness of love, power of imagination—how fast that could be changed! They did it themselves, incessantly, themselves. They were the most avid destroyers of dreams. But was it their fault? Was it really their fault? Beautiful forlorn driven creatures—a huge magnet somewhere deep in the earth, and above it the multitudinous figures who thought they had their own wills and their own fates—was it their fault? Wasn't he himself one of them? Did he not cling suspiciously to a bit of tiresome caution and cheap sarcasm—at bottom already knowing what would inevitably happen.

Joan was huddled at the foot of the bed. She looked like a beautiful angry scrubwoman and at the same time like something that had flown down from the moon and did not know where it was.

The dawn had turned into the first red of morning and shone on them. The early day blew its pure breath from afar, across all the dirty backyards and the smoky roofs into the window, and there was still the breath of wood and plains in it.

"Joan," Ravic said. "Why have you come?"

"Why do you ask?"

"Yes—why do I ask?"

"Why do you always ask? I am here. Isn't that enough?"

"Yes, Joan. You are right. It is enough."

She raised her head. "At last! But first you have to take away all the joy!"

Joy, Ravic thought. She calls that joy! To be driven by multiple dark propellers, in a gust of breathless desire for repossession—joy? Outside there is a moment of joy, the dew at the window, the ten minutes of silence before the day stretches out its claws. But what the devil was all this about? Wasn't she right? Wasn't she right as the dew and the sparrows and the wind and the blood were right? Why did he ask?

What did he want to know? She was here, she had flown here, unthinkingly, a night butterfly, a privet hawk moth, a peacock butterfly, quickly—and now he was lying counting the eyes and small cuts in its wings and staring at the slightly faded blending of its colors. Why all this pretense? And why this hide-and-seek? She has come and I am thus stupidly superior only because she has come, he thought. If she had not come I should be lying here and brooding and heroically trying to deceive myself and wishing secretly that she would come.

He flung the blankets aside, swung his feet over the edge of the bed, and stepped into his slippers. "What are you going to do?" Joan asked, surprised. "Are you going to throw me out?"

"No. I'm going to kiss you. I should have done it long before! I'm an idiot, Joan. I have been talking nonsense. It's wonderful that you have come!"

A radiance lit up her eyes. "You needn't get up to kiss me," she said.

The red of morning stood high behind the houses. The sky above was a faint blue. A few clouds floated there like sleeping flamingos. "Look at that, Joan! What a day! Do you remember how it used to rain?"

"Yes. It was always raining, darling. It was gray and it rained."

"It was still raining when I left. You were desperate about all that rain. And now—"

"Yes," she said. "And now—"

She was lying close beside him. "Now we have everything," he said. "Everything. Even a garden. The carnations on the window sill of the refugee Wiesenhoff. And the birds down there in the chestnut tree."

He saw that she was crying.

"Why don't you ask me, Ravic?" she said.

"I've asked too much already. Didn't you say so yourself?"

"That's different."

"There isn't anything to ask."

"About what happened in between."

"Nothing happened."

She shook her head.

"My God, what do you think I am, Joan?" he said. "Look at that outside. The red and gold and blue. Ask it whether it

233

rained yesterday. Whether there was a war in China or Spain. Whether a thousand men are dying or a thousand men are being born at this moment. It exists, it raises, that's all there is to it. And you want me to ask you? Your shoulders are bronze in this light, and I am to question you? Your eyes in this red glow are like the sea of the Greeks, violet and wine-colored, and I am to inquire about something that is done with? You've come back and I am to be a fool and rummage about among the withered leaves of the past? What do you take me for, Joan?''

Her tears had ceased. ''I haven't heard that for a long time,'' she said.

''Then you have been among blockheads. Women should be adored or abandoned. Nothing in between.''

She slept clinging to him as if she didn't ever want to let him go. She slept deeply and he felt her regular light breath on his chest. He lay awake for a while. The noises of the morning began in the hotel. Water gurgled, doors were slammed, and below old Aaron Goldberg went through his morning routine of coughing at the open window. He felt Joan's shoulders on his arm, he felt her warm slumbering skin, and turning his head he could see her completely relaxed face given up to sleep, a face that was as pure as innocence itself. Adore or abandon, he thought. Big words. Who could do that! But who really wanted to?

Chapter 20

HE AWOKE. Joan was no longer lying beside him. He heard the water in the bathroom running and sat up. He was immediately fully awake. This was something he had learned again in the last few months. Whoever wakes instantly may sometimes still escape. He looked at his watch. It was ten o'clock in the morning. Joan's evening gown was lying on the floor together with her coat. Her brocade shoes stood by the window. One of them had fallen on its side.

"Joan," he called. "What are you doing taking a shower in the middle of the night?"

She opened the door. "I didn't want to wake you up."

"That makes no difference. I can always sleep. But why are you up at this hour?"

She had put on a bathing cap and was dripping with water. Her gleaming shoulders were a light brown. She looked like an Amazon with a close-fitting helmet. "I'm not a night owl any more, Ravic, I'm no longer at the Scheherazade."

"I know that."

"From whom?"

"Morosow."

She looked at him searchingly for a second. "Morosow," she said. "That old babbler. What else did he tell you?"

"Nothing. Is there anything more to tell?"

"Nothing that a night doorman could tell. They are like hat-check girls. Professional gossipers."

"Leave Morosow alone. Night doormen and doctors are professional pessimists. They get their living from the shadow side of life. But they don't gossip. They are obliged to be discreet."

"The shadow side of life," Joan said. "Who wants that?"

"No one. But most people live in it. Besides Morosow helped you get your job at the Scheherazade."

"I can't be eternally and tearfully grateful to him for that. I was no disappointment. I was worth my money, otherwise they wouldn't have kept me. Besides he did it for you. Not for me."

Ravic reached for a cigarette. "What have you really got against him?"

"Nothing. I don't like him. He has a way of looking at you. I wouldn't trust him. You shouldn't either."

"What?"

"You shouldn't trust him. You know, all doormen in France are stool pigeons for the police."

"Anything else?" Ravic asked calmly.

"Of course you don't believe me. Everyone in the Scheherazade knew it. Who knows whether—"

"Joan!" Ravic flung back the blanket and got up. "Don't talk nonsense. What's wrong with you?"

"Nothing. What should be wrong with me? I can't stand him, that's all. He has a bad influence. And you are constantly with him."

"I see," Ravic said. "That's why."

Suddenly she laughed. "Yes, that's why."

Ravic felt that this was not the only reason. There was something else besides. "What do you want for breakfast?" he asked.

"Are you angry?" she asked in return.

"No."

She came out of the bathroom and put her arms around his neck. He felt her wet skin through the thin fabric of his pajamas. He felt her body and he felt his blood. "Are you angry because I am jealous of your friends?" she asked.

He shook his head. A helmet, an Amazon. A Naiad, come up out of the ocean, the scent of water and youth still on her smooth skin.

"Let me go," he said.

She did not answer. The line from the high cheekbones to the chin. The mouth. The too heavy eyelids. The breasts pressing his bare skin under the open pajama jacket. "Let me go or—"

"Or what?" she asked.

A bee was buzzing outside the window. Ravic followed it with his eyes. Very likely it had been attracted by the carnations of the refugee Wiesenhoff and now was looking for other flowers. It flew inside and alighted on an unwashed calvados glass which stood on the window sill.

"Did you miss me?" Joan asked.

"Yes."

"Much?"

"Yes."

The bee flew up. It circled around the glass several times. Then it buzzed through the window back to the sun and the refugee Wiesenhoff's carnations.

Ravic was lying at Joan's side. Summer, he thought. Summer, meadows in the morning, hair full of the scent of hay and skin like clover—the grateful blood silently flowing like a rivulet and desirelessly flooding the sandy places, a smooth surface in which a smiling face was reflected. For a bright moment nothing was dry and dead any longer. Birches and poplars, quiet and a soft murmur that came like an echo from far, lost heavens and beat in one's veins.

"I'd like to stay here," Joan said leaning against his shoulder.

"Stay here. Let us sleep. We haven't slept much."

"I can't. I must go."

"You can't go anywhere in your evening gown at this time."

"I brought another dress with me."

"Where?"

"I had it under my coat. Shoes, too. It must be among my things. I have everything with me."

She did not say where she had to go. Nor why. And Ravic did not ask.

The bee reappeared. It was no longer buzzing around aimlessly. It flew straight toward the glass and sat on its rim. It seemed to know something about calvados. Or about fruit sugar.

"Were you so sure you would stay here?"

"Yes," Joan said without moving.

Rolande brought a tray with bottles and glasses. "Nothing to drink," Ravic said.

"Don't you want some vodka? It is Subrovka."

"Not today. You may give me some coffee. Strong coffee."

"All right."

He put the microscope aside. Then he lit a cigarette and went to the window. The plane trees had put on their fresh full foliage. The last time he was here they had still been bare.

Rolande brought the coffee. "You have more girls now than before," Ravic said.

"Twenty more."

"Is business so good? Now in June?"

Rolande sat down with him. "We don't understand either why business is so good. The people seem to have gone crazy. It starts even in the afternoon. But then in the evening—"

"Maybe it's the weather."

"It isn't the weather. I know how it is in May and June. But this is some kind of madness. You wouldn't believe how well the bar is doing. Can you imagine Frenchmen ordering champagne?"

"No."

"Foreigners, certainly. We carry it for them. But Frenchmen! Even Parisians! Champagne! And they pay for it too! Instead of Dubonnet or Pernod or beer or a fine. Can you believe it?"

"Only when I see it."

Rolande poured the coffee for him. "And the activity!" she said. "It deafens you. You'll see for yourself when you come down. Even at this time of day! No longer just the cautious experts waiting for your visits. A whole crowd are sitting there already! What has got into these people, Ravic?"

Ravic shrugged his shoulders. "There is a story of an ocean liner sinking—"

"But nothing is sinking with us! Business is wonderful."

The door was opened. Ninette, twenty-one years old, slim as a boy in her short pink silk panties, entered. She had the face of a saint and was one of the best whores in the place. At the moment she carried a tray with bread, butter, and two pots of jam. "Madame learned that the doctor was drinking coffee," she declared in a hoarse bass. "She sends you some jam to taste. Home-made." Suddenly Ninette grinned. The angelic countenance broke into a gamin's grimace. She shoved the tray onto the table and skipped out of the room.

"There you see," Rolande sighed. "They get fresh the minute they know we need them."

"Quite right," Ravic said. "When else should they be fresh? What does this jam mean?"

"Madame's pride. She made it herself. On her estate on the Riviera. It is really good. Will you try it?"

"I hate jam. Particularly when made by millionaires."

Rolande unscrewed the glass top, took out several spoonfuls of jam, smeared them on a sheet of thick paper, put a piece of butter and a few pieces of toast with it, wrapped it all up tightly and handed it to Ravic. "Throw it away afterwards," she said. "Do it as a favor to her. She checks on whether you have eaten or not. The last pride of an aging and disillusioned woman. Do it out of politeness."

"All right." Ravic got up and opened the door. He heard voices from downstairs, music, laughter, and shouting. "Quite a pandemonium," he said. "Are those all Frenchmen?"

"Not those. They are mostly foreigners."

"Americans?"

"No, that's the strange thing. They are mostly Germans. We have never had so many Germans here before."

"That's not strange."

"Most of them speak French very well. Not at all the way the Germans used to speak a few years ago."

"I thought so. Aren't there a good many poilus here too? Recruits and colonial soldiers?"

"They are always around."

Ravic nodded. "And the Germans spend a lot of money, don't they?"

Rolande laughed. "They do. They treat everyone who wants to drink with them."

"Especially soldiers, I imagine. And Germany has a currency embargo and has closed the frontiers. One can get out only by permission of the authorities. And one can't take more than ten marks with him. Odd, these merry Germans with plenty of money and speaking French so well, eh?"

Rolande shrugged her shoulders. "For all I care—as long as their money is good—"

It was after eight when he got home. "Has anyone called me up?" he asked the porter.

"No."

"Nor in the afternoon?"

"No. Not the whole day."

"Has anyone been here inquiring for me?"

The porter shook his head. "Nobody."

Ravic went upstairs. On the first floor he heard the Goldberg couple quarreling. On the second floor a child was crying. It was the French citizen Lucien Silbermann, one year and two months old. He was an object of veneration and high hope to his parents, the coffee dealer Siegfred Silbermann and his wife Nelly, *née* Levi, from Frankfort on the Main. He was born in France and they hoped to get French passports two years earlier because of him. As a result Lucién had developed into a family tyrant with the intelligence of the one-year-old. A phonograph was playing on the third floor. It belonged to the refugee Wohlmeier, formerly of the Oranienburg concentration camp, who played German folk songs on it. The corridor smelled of cabbage and dusk.

Ravic went into his room to read. He had once bought several volumes of world history and now he took them out. It was not particularly cheerful to read them. The only thing one gained by it was a strange depressing satisfaction that what was happening today was not new. Everything had happened before dozens of times. The lies, the breaches of faith, the murders, the St. Bartholomew massacres, the corruption through the lust for power, the unbroken chain of wars—the history of mankind was written in blood and tears, and among the thousands of bloodstained statues of the past, only a few wore the silver halo of kindness. The demagogues, the cheats, the parricides, the murderers, the egoists inebriated with power, the fanatic prophets who preached love with the sword, it was the same time and again—and time and again patient peoples allowed themselves to be driven against one another in a senseless slaughter for kaisers, kings, religions, and madmen—there was no end to it.

He put the books aside again. Voices came through the open window from below. He recognized them—they were Wiesenhoff's and Mrs. Goldberg's. "Not now," Ruth Goldberg said. "He'll be back soon. In an hour at the latest."

"An hour is an hour."

"He may possibly come sooner."

"Where did he go?"

"To the American Embassy. He does it every night. Stands outside and looks at it. Nothing else. Then he comes back."

Wiesenhoff said something that Ravic could not understand. "Naturally," Ruth Goldberg replied in a quarrelsome tone. "Who isn't crazy? That he is old I know too."

"Don't do that," she said after a while. "I'm not interested. Not in the mood."

Wiesenhoff made some reply.

"It's easy for you to talk," she said. "He has the money. I haven't a centime. And you—"

Ravic got up. He looked at the telephone and hesitated. It was almost ten o'clock. He had not heard from Joan since she had left him that morning. He had not asked her if she would come in the evening. He had been sure she would. Now he wasn't sure any longer.

"For you it's simple. You only want to have your pleasure— nothing else," Mrs. Goldberg said.

Ravic went to look for Morosow. His room was locked. He walked downstairs to the Catacombs. "In case anyone calls, I'll be downstairs," he said to the concierge.

Morosow was there. He was playing chess with a red-headed man. A few women were still sitting in the corners. They were knitting or reading with sorrowful faces.

Ravic watched the game for a while. The red-headed man was good at it. He played quickly and with complete indifference, and Morosow was losing. "See what's happening to me," he said.

Ravic shrugged his shoulders. The red-headed man looked up. "This is Mr. Finkenstein," Morosow said. "Just out of Germany."

Ravic nodded. "How is it there now?" he asked without interest just in order to say something.

The red-headed man moved his shoulders and did not say anything. Nor had Ravic expected him to. That had happened during the first years only: the hasty questions, the expectation, the feverish waiting for news of a collapse. Everyone knew by now that only war could bring it about. And everyone with any wit knew as well that a government which solves its unemployment problems by building an armament industry has only two possibilities: war or a domestic catastrophe. Therefore war.

"Check and mate," Finkenstein said without enthusiasm and got up. He looked at Ravic. "What can one do to get some sleep? I can't sleep here. I fall asleep and wake up again right away."

"Drink," Morosow said. "Burgundy. Much Burgundy or beer."

"I don't drink. I've walked through the streets for hours until I thought I was dead tired. It doesn't help. I can't sleep."

"I'll give you a few tablets," Ravic said. "Come up with me."

"Come back, Ravic," Morosow called after him. "Don't leave me here alone, brother!"

A few women glanced up. Then they continued to knit and to read as if their lives depended on it. Ravic went with Finkenstein to his room. When he opened the door the night air streamed through the window toward him like a dark cool wave. He breathed deeply and, turning on the light, he looked around the room quickly. No one was there. He gave Finkenstein several sleeping tablets.

"Thank you," Finkenstein said without moving a muscle on his face and left like a shadow.

Suddenly Ravic knew that Joan would not come. He also knew that he had foreseen it that morning. He only had not wanted to believe it. He turned around as though someone had said something behind him. All of a sudden everything was quite clear and simple. She had gained what she wanted, and now she was taking her time. What else had he expected? That she would throw away everything because of him? That she would return as she had done before? What foolishness! Of course there was someone else, and not only someone else but also another life that she did not want to give up!

He went downstairs. He felt rather miserable. "Has anyone called?" he asked.

The night concierge, who had just arrived, shook his head. His mouth was full of garlic sausage.

"I expect a call. Meanwhile I'll be downstairs."

He went back to Morosow.

They played a game of chess. Morosow won and looked around contentedly. Meanwhile the women had silently disappeared. He rang the sacristan bell. "Clarisse! A carafe of rosé.

"That Finkenstein plays like a sewing machine," he declared. "It's nauseating! A mathematician. I hate perfection. It's not human." He looked at Ravic. "Why are you here on such an evening?"

"I'm waiting for a call."

"Are you engaged again in killing someone in a scientific manner?"

"I removed a man's stomach yesterday."

Morosow filled their glasses. "Here you are sitting and drinking," he said reproachfully, "and over there your victim is lying in delirium. There's something inhuman in that too. At least you should have a stomach-ache."

"Correct," Ravic replied. "Therein lies the misery of the world, Boris. We never feel what we do to others. But why do you want to start your reform with the doctors? Politicians and generals would be better. Then we would have world peace."

Morosow leaned back and studied Ravic. "One should never know doctors personally," he declared. "It takes away some of our confidence in them. I have been drunk with you—how could I have you operate on me? I might be sure that you were a better surgeon than someone else I didn't know—nevertheless I'd take the other. Confidence in the unknown—a deep-rooted human quality, old fellow! Doctors should live in hospitals and never be let out into the world of the uninitiated. Your predecessors, the witches and medicine men, knew that. When I'm operated on I wish to believe in superhuman power."

"I wouldn't operate on you either, Boris."

"Why not?"

"No doctor likes to operate on his brother."

"I won't do you the favor anyhow. I'll die of apoplexy during my sleep. I work toward it cheerfully." Morosow stared at Ravic like a happy child. Then he got up. "I've got to go. To open doors in that center of culture, Montmartre. Actually, what does man live for?"

"To think about it. Any other question?"

"Yes. Why does he die just when he has done that and has become a bit more sensible?"

"Some people die without having become more sensible."

"Don't evade my question. And don't start talking about the transmigration of souls."

"I'll ask you something else first. Lions kill antelopes; spiders flies; foxes chickens; which is the only race in the world that wars on itself uninterruptedly, fighting and killing one another?"

"Those are questions for children. The crown of creation, of course, the human being—who invented the words love, kindness, and mercy."

"Good. And who is the only being in Nature that is capable of committing suicide and does it?"

"Again the human being—who invented eternity, God, and resurrection."

"Excellent," Ravic said. "You see of how many contradictions we consist. And you want to know why we die?"

Morosow looked up with surprise. Then he took a big gulp. "You sophist," he declared. "You dodger."

Ravic looked at him. Joan, something thought inside him. If she would only come in now, through that dirty glass door over there! "The mistake was, Boris," he said, "that we began to think. If we had stuck to the bliss of ruttishness and feeding, all this would not have happened. Someone experiments with us—but he doesn't seem to have found the solution as yet. We won't complain. Experimental animals too should have professional pride."

"The slaughterers say so. Never the oxen. The scientists say so. Never the guinea pigs. The doctors say so. Never the white mice."

"Correct—" If she would come in with her swaying stride which always gave her the appearance of walking against a gentle wind. "Long live the law of sufficient reason! Come, Boris, let's drink a glass to beauty—the gracious eternity of the instant! Do you know what else the human being alone can do? Laugh and cry."

"And get drunk. On brandy, wine, philosophy and women and hope and despair. Do you know what he too alone knows? That he must die. As antitoxin he was given imagination. The stone is real. The plant too. The animal as well. They are fitted for their purpose. They don't know they have to die. Man knows it. Ascend, soul! Fly! Don't sob, you legal murderer! Haven't we just sung the song of songs of mankind?"

Morosow shook the gray palm so that its dust flew up. "Brave symbol of a touching southern hope, dream plant of a French landlady, farewell! And you too, man without a home, creeping plant without ground, pickpocket of death, farewell! Be proud that you are a romantic!"

He grinned at Ravic.

Ravic did not return the grin. He looked at the door. It was opening. The night concierge came in. He approached their table. The telephone, Ravic thought. Finally! After all! He did not get up. He waited. He felt his arms tightening.

"Your cigarettes, Mr. Morosow," the concierge said. "The boy has just brought them."

"Thanks." Morosow put the box with the Russian cigarettes into his pocket. "So long, Ravic. Will I see you later?"

"Maybe. So long, Boris."

The man without a stomach stared at Ravic. He felt sick but could not vomit. He no longer had anything to vomit with. He was like a man without legs whose feet ached.

He was very restless. Ravic gave him an injection. This man had little chance of staying alive. His heart was not too good and one of his lungs was full of healed-up caverns. During his thirty-five years of life he had not had much health. For years a stomach ulcer, an arrested tuberculosis, and now a carcinoma. His hospital report showed that he had been married for four years; his wife had died in childbed; the child died three years later of tuberculosis. No relatives. Now he was lying here and staring at him and he did not want to die and was patient and brave and did not know that he would have to be fed through the colon and that he could no longer enjoy one of the few pleasures of his existence, pickles and boiled beef. There he lay, smelling and cut to pieces, and he possessed something that made his eyes move and that was called a soul. Be proud that you are a romantic! The song of songs of mankind!

Ravic hung up the tablet with the fever chart and the pulse. The nurse rose and waited. Lying beside her on the chair she had a red sweater which she had started to knit. The knitting needles were stuck in it and the yarn was lying on the floor. The thin thread of wool which hung down was like a thin thread of blood, as if the sweater were bleeding.

That man is lying there, Ravic thought, and even with the injection he will go through a terrible night with pain, immobility, shortness of breath, and nightmares—and I am waiting for a woman and I think it will be a difficult night for me if she doesn't come. I know how ridiculous it is in comparison with this dying man, in comparison with Baston Perrier in the next room, whose arm was crushed, in comparison with thousands of others, in comparison with all that is happening tonight in the world—and nevertheless it does not help. It doesn't help, it is of no avail, it does not change anything, it remains the same. What had Morosow said? Why don't you have a stomach-ache? Yes, why not?

"Call me in case anything happens," he said to the nurse. It was the same one who had received the record-player from Kate Hegstroem.

"The gentleman is very resigned," she said.

"What is he?" Ravic asked, astonished.

"Very resigned. A good patient."

Ravic looked around. There was nothing the nurse could expect as a present. Very resigned—what expressions nurses used at times! This poor devil was fighting with all the armies of his blood corpuscles and his nerve cells against death—he was not a bit resigned.

He went back to the hotel. He met Goldberg in front of the door. An old man with a gray beard and a thick gold watch chain across his vest. "Nice evening," Goldberg said.

"Yes." Ravic thought of the woman in Wiesenhoff's room. "Don't you want to go for a walk?" he asked.

"I have. To the Concorde and back."

To the Concorde. There stood the American Embassy, white under the stars, silent and empty, a Noah's Ark in which there were stamps for visas, unattainable. Goldberg had stood before it, outside by the Crillon, and had stared at the entrance and the dark windows as if at a Rembrandt or the Koh-i-noor diamond.

"Don't you want to walk around a bit more? We could go to the Arc and back," Ravic said and thought: If I save those two up there, then Joan will be in my room. Or she will come in meanwhile.

Goldberg shook his head. "I must go upstairs. I'm sure my wife is waiting for me. I've been away for more than two hours."

Ravic looked at his watch. It was almost half past twelve. There was no need to save anybody. Mrs. Goldberg would have been back in her room some time ago. He watched Goldberg slowly climbing up the stairs. Then he went to the concierge. "Has anyone called me up?"

"No."

His room was brightly lit. He remembered leaving it that way. The bed gleamed as if snow had surprisingly fallen. He took the slip he had put on the table before he left and on which he had written that he would be back in half an hour, and tore it to pieces. He looked for something to drink. There was nothing. He went downstairs again. The concierge had no calvados. He only had cognac. Ravic took with him a bottle of Hennessy and a bottle of Vouvray. He talked to the concierge for some time and the latter proved to him that

Loulou II would have the best chance in the next race for two-year-olds at Saint-Cloud. The Spaniard Alvarez passed by. Ravic noticed that he still limped a bit. He bought a newspaper and went back to his room. How long such an evening could be! Who does not believe in miracles where love is concerned is lost, the lawyer Arensen had said in Berlin in 1933. Two weeks later he was sent to a concentration camp because his beloved had denounced him. Ravic opened the bottle of Vouvray and got a volume of Plato from the table. A few minutes later he put it aside and sat down by the window.

He stared at the telephone. That damned, black instrument. He could not call up Joan. He did not know her new number. He did not even know where she was living. He had not asked her and she had told him nothing. Probably she had purposely not said anything. So she would still have an excuse.

He drank a glass of the light wine. Foolish, he thought. I am waiting for a woman who was here this very morning. For three and a half months I didn't see her and I did not miss her as much as now when she has been away for a day. It would have been simpler if I had never seen her again. I was adjusted to it. Now . . .

He rose. It wasn't that either. It was the uncertainty that fed on him. It was mistrust that had stolen into him increasingly hour by hour.

He went to the door. He knew it was not locked; but he made sure of it once more. He began to read the paper; but he read it as if through a veil. Disturbances in Poland. The inevitable clash. The claim to the Corridor, the treaty of England and France with Poland. The approaching war. He let the paper drop and turned off the light. He lay in the dark and waited. He could not sleep. He switched the light on again. The bottle of Hennessy stood on the table. He did not open it. He got up and again sat down by the window. The night was cool and high and starlit. A few cats screeched in the yards. A man in shorts stood on the balcony opposite and scratched himself. He yawned aloud and retired to his lighted room. Ravic looked at the bed. He knew he would not be able to sleep. There was no point in reading either. He hardly remembered what he had read before. To leave—that would be best. But where to go? It made no difference. He did not want to leave either. He wanted to know something. Damn it—he held the bottle of cognac in his hand and put it back. Then he looked in his pocket for a few sleeping tablets. The same kind he had given the red-headed Finkenstein. He was sleeping now. Ravic swallowed them. It was doubtful whether he himself would sleep. He took one more. If Joan came he would wake up.

She did not come. Nor did she come next night.

Chapter 21

EUGÉNIE came into the room in which the man without a stomach was lying. "Telephone, Mr. Ravic."

"Who is it?"

"I don't know. I didn't ask. The switchboard girl told me outside."

Ravic did not at once recognize Joan's voice. It sounded blurred and very far away. "Joan," he said, "where are you?"

It sounded as if she were away from Paris. He almost expected her to mention some place on the Riviera. She had never called him at the hospital before. "I am in my apartment," she said.

"Here in Paris?"

"Of course. Where else?"

"Are you sick?"

"No. Why?"

"Because you called me at the hospital."

"I called your hotel. You had left. That's why I called the hospital."

"Is something wrong?"

"No. What should be wrong? I wanted to know how you are."

Her voice was clearer now. Ravic got out a cigarette and a book of matches. He squeezed the upper part beneath his elbow, tore off a match, and lighted it.

"It's the hospital, Joan," he said. "One always expects to hear of accidents and sickness here."

"I'm not sick. I'm in bed. But I'm not sick."

"Fine." Ravic pushed the matches back and forth on the white oilcloth of the table. He was waiting for what would come next.

Joan too was waiting. He heard her breathe. She wanted him to start. That would make it easier for her.

"Joan," he said, "I can't stay at the phone long now. I left someone with an open bandage and I must go back."

She was silent for a moment. "Why haven't I heard from you?" she said then.

"You couldn't hear from me because I haven't your telephone number, nor do I know where you are living now."

"But I told you."

"No, Joan."

"But I did. I told you." She was on safe ground now. "Certainly, I know. You must have forgotten."

"All right. I forgot. Tell me once more. I have a pencil."

She gave him her address and telephone number. "I'm sure I told you, Ravic, quite sure."

"All right, Joan. I must go back now. Will you have dinner with me tonight?"

She was silent for a moment. "Why don't you come to see me?" she said.

"All right. I can do that too. Tonight. At eight?"

"Why don't you come now?"

"Now I have to work."

"For how long?"

"About an hour more."

"Come then!"

You have no time in the evening, he thought and asked, "Why not tonight?"

"But Ravic," she said, "sometimes you don't know the simplest things. Because I would like you to come now. I don't want to wait until tonight. Otherwise why would I call up the hospital at this time of day?"

"All right. I'll come as soon as I am through here."

He reflectively folded up the slip of paper and went back.

It was a building at the corner of the Rue Pascal. Joan lived on the top floor. She opened the door. "Come," she said. "It's good to have you here! Come in!"

She wore a simple black dressing gown that was cut like a man's. One of the traits that Ravic liked in her was that she never wore fluffy tulle or silk dresses. Her face was paler than usual and slightly agitated. "Come," she said. "I've been waiting for you. You shall see how I live."

She walked ahead of him. Ravic smiled. She was smart. She took care of all questions in advance. He looked at her beautiful straight shoulders. The light fell on her hair. For a breathless instant, he loved her very much.

She led him into a large room. It was a studio now filled with the light of midafternoon. A high, wide window opened onto the gardens between the Avenue Raphaël and the Avenue Proudhon. To the right one could look up to the Porte de la Muette. Behind it, gold and green, shimmered a part of the Bois.

The room was furnished in semimodern taste. A large couch with a cover that was too blue; a few chairs which looked more comfortable than they were; tables which were too low; a rubber plant, an American victrola, and one of Joan's suitcases in the corner. There was nothing disquieting, but in spite of that Ravic did not think much of it. Either very good or completely bad—halfway things meant nothing to him. And he could not stand rubber plants.

He noticed that Joan was watching him. She was not quite sure of how he would take it, but she had been sure enough to risk it.

"Nice," he said, "large and nice."

He lifted the victrola top. It was a trunk-shaped apparatus with an automatic record-changer. A great many records were lying on a table beside it. Joan took some of them and put them on. "Do you know how it works?"

He knew. "No," he said.

She turned a knob. "It's wonderful. It plays for hours. One doesn't have to get up to change the records or to turn anything. One can lie there and listen and watch it getting darker outside and dream."

The victrola was excellent. Ravic recognized the make and knew it had cost about twenty thousand francs. It filled the room with soft airy music, with the sentimental songs of Paris. *"J'attendrai—"*

Joan leaned forward and listened. "Do you like it?" she asked.

Ravic nodded. He was not looking at the victrola. He was looking at Joan. He was looking at her face, which was enchanted and absorbed in the music. How easy that was with her, and how he had loved her for this easiness which he did not possess! Finished, he thought, without pain, with the feeling of someone who leaves Italy to return to the foggy north.

She straightened up, and smiled. "Come—you have not yet seen the bedroom."

"Do I have to see it?"

She looked at him searchingly for a second. "Don't you want to see it? Why not?"

"Yes, why not?" he said. "Of course."

She touched his face and kissed him, and he knew why. "Come," she said and took his arm.

The bedroom was furnished in the French manner. A large imitation antique bed in Louis XVI style; a kidney-shaped dressing table of the same sort; an imitation baroque mirror; a modern Aubusson rug; stools, chairs, all in the style of a second-rate movie set. Among them a very fine painted Florentine chest of the sixteenth century which did not fit in at all and gave the impression of a princess among the *nouveaux riches*. It had been carelessly pushed into a corner. A hat with violets and a pair of silver shoes lay on its precious cover.

The bed was open and not made. Ravic could see where Joan had been lying. A number of perfume bottles were standing on the dresser. One of the closets was opened. There were a great many dresses hanging inside. More than she had had before. Joan had not let go of Ravic's arm. She leaned against him. "Do you like it?"

"Fine. It suits you very well."

She nodded. He could feel her arm and her breast and without thinking he drew her closer. She let it happen and yielded. Her shoulder touched his shoulder. Her face was calm now; there was nothing left in it of the slight agitation it had showed at the beginning. It was sure and clear and it seemed to Ravic as if there were more than suppressed satisfaction in it, an almost invisible, very remote shadow of triumph.

Strange, that baseness is most becoming to them, he thought. She wants to turn me into a sort of second-rate gigolo and with naïve shamelessness she even shows me the place her lover has furnished for her—and at the same time she looks just like the Nike of Samothrace.

"It's a pity you can't have something like this," she said. "An apartment. One feels quite different. Different than when one is in those dreary hotel rooms."

"You are right. It was nice to have had a look at all this. I'll go now, Joan—"

"Go? Already? But you've just come!"

He took her hands. "I'll go, Joan. For good. You are living with somebody else. And I don't share women I love with other men."

She tore her hands away from him. "What? What are you saying? I— Who told you this? What a story—" She stared at him. "I can imagine Morosow of course, that—"

"Not Morosow. No one had to tell me anything. It speaks for itself."

Her face was suddenly pale with rage. She had been so sure, and now it had come. "I know! Because I have this apartment and don't work at the Scheherazade any longer! Naturally there must be someone keeping me. Naturally! It couldn't be otherwise!"

"I didn't say that someone was keeping you."

"It's the same thing! I understand! First you get me into that miserable night club, then you leave me alone, and then when someone talks to me or cares about me, then it's immediately certain that someone is keeping me! That sort of doorman has nothing but his dirty imagination. That a person can be somebody and work and make something of herself doesn't penetrate his tip-taking soul! And you, you of all people, believe it! You should be ashamed of yourself!"

Ravic turned around, grabbed her by the arm, lifted her and threw her over the footboard onto the bed. "There," he said, "and now stop your nonsense!"

She was so surprised that she remained where she was. "Aren't you going to beat me too?" she asked then.

"No. I just wanted to stop that babbling."

"It wouldn't surprise me," she said in a low and constrained voice. "It wouldn't surprise me!"

She lay there silently. Her face was empty and white, her mouth was pale, her eyes had a lifeless glitter like glass. Her breast was half exposed, and one naked leg hung over the edge of the bed. "I call you up," she said, "unsuspecting, I look forward to being with you—and then this happens! This!" she repeated contemptuously. "And I thought you were different!"

Ravic was standing at the bedroom door. He saw the room with its imitation furniture, he saw Joan lying on her bed, and he saw how well everything fitted together. He felt angry with himself for having said anything at all. He should have gone without saying anything, and been done with it. But then she would have come to him and it would have been the same thing.

"You," she repeated. "You were the last I would have expected this from. I thought you were different."

He did not answer. Everything was so cheap it was almost unbearable. Suddenly he could not comprehend any longer why he had thought for three days that if she did not come he would never sleep again. What did all this concern him still? He took a cigarette out of his pocket and lighted it. His mouth was dry. He heard the victrola still playing. It was repeating the record it had played at the beginning—*J'attendrai*. He went into the other room and turned it off.

She was lying there motionless when he returned. It looked as if she hadn't moved. But the dressing gown was wider open than before. "Joan," he said, "the less we talk about it, the better—"

"I didn't begin."

He felt like flinging a bottle of perfume at her head. "I know," he said. "I began and now I am ending."

He turned and left. But before he had reached the door of the studio she was standing before him. She slammed the door and stood before it, her arms and hands pressed against the wood. "So!" she said. "You'll break it off! You'll break it off and go! As simple as that! But I've still got a lot to say! You yourself saw me in the Cloche d'Or, you saw who I was with and when I came to you that night, then nothing mattered to you at all, you slept with me and in the morning it still did not matter to you, you had not had enough and slept with me again, and I loved you and you were wonderful and you didn't want to know about anything and I loved you for it as I never had before, I knew you had to be like that and not different, I cried while you slept and I kissed you and I was happy and went home and worshiped you—and now! Now you come and reproach me for what you waved aside with such a grand gesture and forgot on that night when you wanted to sleep with me! Now you bring it up and throw it in my face, now you stand here like an injured guardian of virtue and you make a scene just like a jealous husband! What do you want of me, anyway? What rights have you?"

"None," Ravic said.

"So! It's a good thing that you at least admit that. Why then did you come to me today to throw this in my face? Why didn't you do it when I came to you that night? Naturally, then—"

"Joan," Ravic said.

She was silent. Her breath came fast and she stared at him.

"Joan," he said. "That night when you came to me I

thought you were returning to me. I did not want to know anything of what had happened. You came back. That was enough. It was a mistake. You have not come back.''

"I haven't come back? What then? Was it a spirit that came to you?"

"You came to me. But you did not come back."

"That's too complicated for me. I'd like to know what difference there is?"

"You know. I didn't know then. Today I know. You are living with someone else."

"So, I'm living with someone else! There it is again! When I have a few friends I'm living with someone! Maybe I should lock myself in, the whole day, and talk to nobody so that nobody could say that I'm living with someone?"

"Joan," Ravic said. "Don't be ridiculous!"

"Ridiculous? Who is ridiculous? You're the ridiculous one!"

"Have it your way. Must I use force to get you away from that door?"

She did not move. "If I was with someone what business is it of yours? You said yourself you didn't want to know."

"All right. I really did not want to know. I thought it was over. What had been did not concern me. It was a mistake. I should have known better. It is possible that I wished to deceive myself. Weakness. But that doesn't change anything."

"Why doesn't it change anything? When you admit that you're wrong—"

"This isn't a question of right or wrong. Not only were you living with someone. You still are. And you intend to stay with him. I didn't know this at that time."

"Don't lie!" she interrupted him with sudden calm. "You knew it all along. At that time too."

She looked straight into his face. "All right," he said. "Let's say I knew it. But I did not want to know it. I knew it and did not believe it. You can't understand that. Things like that don't happen to a woman. Besides it has nothing to do with it."

Her face was suddenly clouded by a wild and desperate fear. "After all, I can't just throw out someone who hasn't done me any harm—only because you suddenly turn up again! Don't you understand?"

"Yes," Ravic said.

She stood there like a cat, driven into a corner, that wants to jump and from under whose feet the ground has been pulled away. "You do?" she asked in surprise. The tension left her eyes. She let her shoulders droop. "Then why do you torture me if you do understand," she said wearily.

"Come away from the door." Ravic sat down in one of the chairs, which were more uncomfortable than they looked. Joan hesitated. "Come," he said. "I won't run away now."

She came to him reluctantly and let herself drop onto the couch. She acted as if she were tired, but Ravic could see she was not. "Give me something to drink," she said.

He saw that she was playing for time. It made no difference to him. "Where are the bottles?" he asked.

"There in the cabinet."

Ravic opened the low cabinet. There were a few bottles in it. Most of them were white crème de menthe. He eyed them with distaste and pushed them aside. In another corner he found a half-filled bottle of Martell and a bottle of calvados. The bottle of calvados was unopened. He passed it over and took the cognac. "Do you drink peppermint brandy now?" he asked over his shoulder.

"No," she replied from the couch.

"All right. Then I'll bring the cognac."

"There is some calvados," she said. "Open the calvados."

"The cognac will do."

"Do open the calvados."

"Some other time."

"I don't want cognac. I want calvados. Please, open the bottle."

Ravic looked into the cabinet once more. To his right, there was the white peppermint for the other man—and to the left, the calvados for him. Everything was so neat and housewifely, it was almost touching. He took the bottle of calvados and opened it. After all, why not? A nice bit of symbolism, their favorite drink sentimentally degraded in an absurd farewell scene. He picked up two glasses and went back to the table. Joan watched him while he poured the apple brandy.

The afternoon was spacious and golden outside the window. The light was more colorful now and the sky had grown lighter. Ravic looked at his watch. It was just after three. He looked at the second hand; he thought his watch had stopped. But the second hand, like a little golden beak, continued to tick off the points of the circle. It was a fact—he had been here only half an hour. Crème de menthe, he thought. What a taste!

Joan huddled on the blue couch. "Ravic," she said in a soft voice, tired and wary. "Was that another of your tricks or is it true that you understand?"

"It's not a trick. It's true!"

"You understand?"

"Yes."

"I knew it." She smiled at him. "I knew it, Ravic."

"It is quite easy to understand."

She nodded. "I need time. I can't do it immediately. He hasn't done me any harm. I did not know whether you would ever come back! I can't tell him right away."

Ravic gulped down his calvados. "Why do we need details?"

"You must know. You must understand. It is—I need time. He would—I don't know what he would do. He loves me. And he needs me. And all this is not his fault."

"Of course not. Take all the time in the world, Joan."

"No. Only a short while. Not right away." She leaned against the pillow of the couch. "And this apartment, Ravic—it isn't the way you perhaps think. I earn money myself. More than before. He helped me. He's an actor. I have small parts in movies. He brought me in."

"I thought so."

She did not pay attention. "I'm not very talented," she said. "I don't deceive myself. But I wanted to get away from those night clubs. One can't get ahead there. Here you can. Even without talent. I want to become independent. You may find all this ridiculous—"

"No," Ravic said. "It is sensible."

She looked at him. "Didn't you come to Paris with that intention in the beginning?" he asked.

"Yes."

There she sits, he thought, a gently reproachful innocent who has been badly treated by life and by me. She is calm, the first storm has been weathered, and she will forgive me, and if I don't go soon she'll tell me the story of the last few months in all its details, this steel orchid whom I came here to break with and who has been so adroit I am almost forced to grant she is right.

"Fine, Joan," he said. "Now you are this far. You'll get ahead."

She bent forward. "Do you think so?"

"Certainly."

"Really, Ravic?"

He got up. Another three minutes and he would be involved in shoptalk about the movies. One must never get into discussions with them, he thought. One always ends up the loser. Logic is like wax in their hands. One should act, and make an end of it.

"I didn't mean it that way," he said. "There you'd better ask your expert."

"Are you going already?" she asked.

"I have to."

"Why don't you stay?"

"I must go back to the hospital."

She took his hand and looked up at him. "You said before you came that you were through at the hospital."

He debated whether to tell her he would not come back. But this was enough for today. It was enough for her and for him. Just the same she had prevented that. But it would come. "Stay here, Ravic," she said.

"I can't."

She got up and leaned close against him. That too, he thought. The old cliché. Cheap and well tested. She doesn't omit anything. But who expects a cat to eat grass? He freed himself. "I must go back. There is a dying man at the hospital."

"Doctors always have good reasons," she said slowly and looked at him.

"Like women, Joan. We supervise death and you supervise love. Therein are all the reasons and all the rights in the world."

She did not answer.

"We have strong stomachs too," Ravic said. "We need them. We could not do our work otherwise. Where others faint we begin to get interested. Adieu, Joan."

"You'll come again, Ravic?"

"Don't think about it. Take your time. You'll find out for yourself."

He walked quickly to the door and did not turn around. She did not follow him. But he knew that she was looking after him. He felt strangely numb—as if he were walking under water.

Chapter 22

THE SCREAM came from the window of the Goldberg family. Ravic listened for a moment. It seemed to him hardly possible that old man Goldberg had flung something at his wife or beaten her. Nor did he hear anything any more. Only the sound of running, then a short excited conversation in the room of the refugee Wiesenhoff and the slamming of doors.

Immediately afterwards there was a knock at his door and the proprietress rushed in. "Quick—quick—Monsieur Goldberg—"

"What?"

"He's hanged himself. In the window. Quick—"

Ravic threw down his book. "Are the police here?"

"Of course not. Otherwise I wouldn't have called you. She has just found him."

Ravic ran downstairs with her. "Have they cut him down?"

"Not yet. They are holding him—"

In the twilit room a dark group was standing by the window. Ruth Goldberg, the refugee Wiesenhoff, and someone else. Ravic turned the light on. Wiesenhoff and Ruth Goldberg held old Goldberg in their arms like a puppet and the third man was nervously trying to loosen the knot of a tie that was fastened to the window bolt.

"Cut him down—"

"We haven't a knife," Ruth Goldberg shouted.

Ravic got a pair of scissors out of his bag and began to cut. This tie was made of smooth thick heavy silk and it took a few seconds before it was severed. As he worked Ravic had Goldberg's face close in front of him. The protruding eyes, the open mouth, the thin gray beard, the thick tongue, the dark-green tie with white dots cutting deep into the scrawny, swollen throat—the body oscillated in Wiesenhoff's and Ruth Goldberg's arms as if it were swaying back and forth in a frightful, frozen laughter.

Ruth Goldberg's face was red and flooded with tears; beside her Wiesenhoff sweated under the burden of the body which was heavier than ever in life. Two wet horrified sobbing faces and above them, silently grinning into the beyond, the gently rolling head which, as Ravic cut the tie, fell against Ruth Goldberg so that she started back screaming, dropped her arms, and the body slid sidewise with sprawling arms and seemed to follow her in a grotesque clownlike movement.

Ravic caught the body and put it on the floor with Wiesenhoff's help. He loosened the noose and began his examination.

"To the movies," Ruth Goldberg jabbered. "He sent me to the movies. 'Ruthy,' he said, 'you get so little entertainment, why don't you go to the Théâtre Courcelles, there is a Garbo picture on, *Queen Christine*, why don't you go and see it? Take a good seat, take a fauteuil or a loge, go and see it, two hours away from misery is something after all.' He said it calmly and kindly and patted my cheeks. 'And afterwards go and have a chocolate and vanilla ice-cream in front of the café on the Parc Monceau, have a good time for once, Ruthy,' he said and I went and when I came back, there—"

Ravic got up. Ruth Goldberg stopped talking. "He must have done it right after you left," he said.

She pressed her fists against her mouth. "Is he—"

"We can still try. First artificial respiration. Do you know anything about it?" Ravic asked Wiesenhoff.

"No. Not too much. Something."

"Look here."

Ravic took Goldberg's arms, drew them backward to the floor, then forward pressing them against his chest, and backward and forward again. There was a rattling in Goldberg's throat. "He's alive!" the woman screamed.

"No. That's the compressed windpipe."

Ravic demonstrated the movement a few more times. "So. Try it now," he said to Wiesenhoff.

Reluctantly Wiesenhoff knelt behind Goldberg. "Go ahead," Ravic said impatiently. "Hold him by the wrists. Or better yet by the forearms."

Wiesenhoff was sweating. "Harder," Ravic said. "Press all the air out of his lungs."

He turned toward the proprietress. Meanwhile more people had come into the room. He motioned to the proprietress to

eave. "He's dead," he said in the corridor. "What's going
on inside is nonsense. A ritual that has to be gone through,
nothing else. It would be a miracle if anything helped now."

"What shall we do?"

"The usual thing."

"Ambulance? First aid? That means the police ten minutes
later."

"You have to call the police anyhow. Did the Goldbergs
have papers?"

"Yes. Valid ones. Passports and *cartes d'identité*."

"Wiesenhoff?"

"Permit to stay. Extended visa."

"Then they are all right. Tell both of them not to mention
that I was there. She came home, found him, screamed.
Wiesenhoff cut him down and tried artificial respiration until
the ambulance came. Can you do that?"

The proprietress looked at him with her birdlike eyes. "Of
course. I'll be there anyhow when the police come. I'll take
good care."

"Fine."

They went back. Wiesenhoff was bending over Goldberg
and working. For a moment it seemed as if both were doing
gymnastics on the floor. The proprietress remained standing
at the door. *"Mesdames et messieurs,"* she said. "I must call
the ambulance and the police. I'll call the ambulance first.
The orderly or doctor who comes with it will have to inform
the police immediately. They will be here in half an hour at
the latest. Any of you who hasn't papers had better pack his
things right away, at least those lying around, carry them to
the Catacombs and stay down there. It's possible that the
police will search the rooms or ask for witnesses."

The room emptied immediately. The proprietress nodded to
Ravic that she would instruct Ruth Goldberg and Wiesenhoff.
He picked up his bag and the scissors lying on the floor by the
cut tie. The tie lay there with the store label showing—"S.
Foerder, Berlin." It was a tie that had cost at least ten marks.
From Goldberg's prosperous days. Ravic knew the firm. He
had made purchases there himself.

He quickly put his belongings into a couple of suitcases
and took them into Morosow's room. It was a precaution
only. Very likely the police would not bother about anything.
But it was better—the memory of Fernand still smarted in
Ravic's mind. He went down to the Catacombs.

261

A number of people were running about excitedly. They were the refugees without papers. The illegal brigade. Clarisse, the waitress, and Jean, the waiter, were directing the placing of the suitcases in a vaultlike room adjoining the Catacombs. The Catacombs themselves were in readiness for supper. The tables were set, bread baskets stood here and there, and a smell of fat and fish came from the kitchen.

"Take your time," Jean said to the nervous refugees. "The police are not so prompt."

The refugees were taking no chances. They were not used to luck. They bustled hastily into the cellar with their few belongings. The Spaniard Alvarez was among them. The proprietress had sent word through the entire hotel that the police were coming. Alvarez smiled at Ravic almost apologetically. Racic did not know why.

A thin man placidly approached him. It was Ernst Seidenbaum, Doctor of Philology and Philosophy. "Maneuvers," he said to Ravic. "Dress rehearsal. Will you stay in the Catacombs?"

"No."

Seidenbaum, a veteran of the last six years, shrugged his shoulders. "I'll stay. I'm not in the mood to run away. I don't think they'll do more than take down the evidence in the case. Who is interested in an old dead German Jew?"

"Not in him. But in live illegal refugees."

Seidenbaum adjusted his pince-nez. "It makes no difference to me. Do you know what I did during the last raid? At that time a sergeant even came down into the Catacombs. More than two years ago. I put on one of Jean's white jackets and served at table. Brandy for the police."

"Good idea."

Seidenbaum nodded. "A time comes for everyone when he has had enough of running away." He calmly strolled into the kitchen to find out what there would be for supper.

Ravic went through the back door of the Catacombs across the yard. A cat ran by, brushed against his feet. The others walked in front of him. They quickly dispersed on the street. Alvarez was limping a little. Maybe that could be remedied by an operation, Ravic thought absent-mindedly.

He was sitting on the Place des Ternes and suddenly he had the feeling that Joan would come this night. He could not say why; he simply knew it suddenly.

He paid for his supper and walked slowly back to the hotel. : was warm and in the narrow streets the signs of the hotels -hich rent rooms by the hour blazed red in the early night. lits of light gleamed from behind curtained windows. A roup of sailors were following several whores. They were oung and loud and hot with wine and summer; they disapeared into one of the hotels. The music of a harmonica was oming from somewhere. A thought like a rocket shot up in avic, unfolded, spread above him, and plucked a magic andscape out of the dark: Joan waiting for him at the hotel to ell him that she had put everything behind her and was oming back—

He stood still. What's the matter with me? he thought. Vhy am I standing here and why do my hands touch the air s if it were the nape of a neck and a wave of hair? Too late.)ne can't summon anything back. No one comes back. Just s the once-lived hour never returns.

He walked on to the hotel, across the yard to the back door f the Catacombs. At the door, he noticed a number of people itting inside. Seidenbaum was among them. Not as a waiter, s a guest. The danger seemed to be over. He entered.

Morosow was in his room. "I was just going to leave," he aid. "I thought you were off to Switzerland again when I aw your suitcases."

"Is everything all right?"

"Yes. The police aren't coming back. They have released he corpse. A simple case. The body is upstairs; they are aying it out now."

"Good. Then I can move back into my room."

Morosow laughed. "That Seidenbaum!" he said. "He was here the whole time. With a brief case, containing some apers or other and his pince-nez. He presented himself as a awyer and representative of the insurance company. He was ather rough with the police. He saved old man Goldberg's assport. Claimed he would need it; the police were entitled o his *carte d'identité* only. He got away with it. Has he any apers himself?"

"Not a scrap."

"Fine," Morosow declared. "The passport is worth its weight in gold. It's valid for another year. Someone can live on it. Not in Paris, exactly, unless he's as daring as Seidenbaum. The photograph can easily be changed. There are inexpensive experts who will change the date of birth in case the new Aaron Goldberg should be younger. A modern kind of transmigration of souls—a passport valid for several lives."

"Then Seidenbaum will be called Goldberg from now on?"

"Not Seidenbaum. He rejected it. It is beneath his dignity. He is the Don Quixote among the world citizens of the underground. He's too fatalistic and too curious about what will happen to men of his type to want it falsified by a borrowed passport. How about you?"

Ravic shook his head. "Not for me. I'm on Seidenbaum's side."

He took his suitcases and walked upstairs. In the corridor where the Goldbergs lived he was passed by an old Jew in a black caftan, with a beard and sidelocks, who had the face of a Biblical patriarch. The old man walked soundlessly as if on rubber soles, and he seemed to float through the dimly lit corridor, vague and wan. He opened Goldberg's door. For a moment a reddish light as though from candles emanated from inside and Ravic heard a strange, half-suppressed, half-wild, monotonous wailing that was almost melodious. Professional women mourners, he thought. Could something like that still exist? Or was it only Ruth Goldberg?

He opened his door and saw Joan sitting by the window. She jumped up. "There you are! What has happened? Why do you have your suitcases with you? Do you have to leave again?"

Ravic put the suitcases beside the bed. "Nothing is the matter. It was only a precaution. Someone died. The police had to come. Everything is all right again."

"I called you up. Someone at the telephone said you did not live here any longer."

"That was our landlady. Cautious and smart as always."

"I rushed here. The room was open. And empty. Your things weren't here. I thought—Ravic!" Her voice trembled.

Ravic smiled with an effort. "You see—I am an unreliable creature. Nothing to build on."

There was a knock at the door. Morosow came in, a couple of bottles in his hand. "Ravic, you forgot your ammunition—"

He noticed Joan standing in the dark and acted as though he did not see her. Ravic did not know whether he had recognized her at all. He handed the bottles to Ravic and left without coming in.

Ravic put the calvados and Vouvray on the table. Through the open window he heard the voice he had heard in the corridor. The wailing for the dead. It grew louder, ebbed away, and began again. Very likely the windows at Goldberg's were standing open in the warm night, in which old Aaron's rigid body was now slowly beginning to disintegrate in the room with the mahogany furniture.

"Ravic," Joan said. "I'm sad. I don't know why. I have been all day. Let me stay here."

He did not answer immediately. He felt taken by surprise. He had expected it otherwise. Not so direct.

"How long?" he asked.

"Until tomorrow."

"That's not long enough."

She sat down on the bed. "Can't we forget that for once."

"No, Joan."

"I don't want anything. I merely want to sleep at your side. Or let me sleep on the sofa."

"It won't do. Besides, I have to leave. For the hospital."

"That doesn't matter. I'll wait for you. I've done that often enough."

He did not answer. He was surprised that he was so calm. The warmth and excitement he had felt on the street had disappeared.

"And you don't have to go to the hospital," Joan said.

He remained silent for a moment. He knew if he slept with her he was lost. It was like signing a check for which there were no funds. She would come again and again and stand on what she had gained as on her rights, and she would ask for a little more every time without yielding anything herself until he was completely in her hands and she would finally become bored and leave him then, a victim of his own weakness and his shattered desires, weak and thoroughly corrupt. She did not intend it; she was not even aware of it; but it would happen that way. It was simple to think that one night would make no difference; but every time one lost part of one's resistance and part of what should never be corrupted in life. Sins against the Holy Ghost, the Catholic catechism called that, with strange and cautionary dread, and added darkly in contradiction to its entire dogma that they would not be forgiven in this life or in the life to come.

"It is true," Ravic said. "I do not have to go to the hospital. But I don't want you to stay here."

He expected an outbreak. But she only said calmly, "Why not?"

Should he try to explain it to her? Was he able to do it at all? "You no longer belong here," he said.

"I do belong here."

"No."

"Why not?"

How smart she is! he thought. Simply by questioning him she forced explanations. And who explained was already on the defensive.

"You know," he said. "Don't ask so foolishly."

"You no longer want me?"

"No," he replied and added against his will, "Not this way."

The monotonous wailing came through the window from Goldberg's room. The lamentation for the dead. The grief of the shepherds of Lebanon in a Parisian side-street.

"Ravic," Joan said. "You must help me."

"I can help you best by leaving you alone. And you me."

She paid no attention. "You've got to help me. I could tell you lies, but I don't want to any more. Yes, there is someone. But it is different than with you. If it were the same, I wouldn't be here."

Ravic took a cigarette out of his pocket. He felt the dry paper. There it was now. Now he knew. It was like a cool knife that did not hurt. Certainly never hurts. Only the before and after.

"It is never the same," he said. "And it is always the same."

What cheap stuff I talk, he thought. Newspaper paradoxes. How shabby the truth can become when one articulates it.

Joan straightened up. "Ravic," she said. "You know it is not true, that one can love only one person. There are those who can only do that. They are happy. And there are others who are thrown into confusion. You know that."

He lit his cigarette. Without glancing at her he knew what Joan looked like now. Pale, her eyes dark, silent, concentrated, almost beseeching, frail—and never to be overcome. That was how she had looked in her apartment that afternoon—like an angel of the annunciation, full of faith and radiant conviction, an angel pretending to save, while she attempted to crucify one slowly so that one would not escape her.

"Yes," he said. "It is one of our excuses."

"It is no excuse. One is not happy doing it. One is pitched into it and can't help it. It is something sinister, a maze of things, a spasm—something you have got to go through. You can't run away. It comes after you. It catches up with you. You don't want it. But it is stronger."

"Why do you think about it? Follow it if it is stronger."

"That's what I am doing. I know there is nothing else I can do. But—" Her voice changed. "Ravic, I must not lose you. I don't know what it is, but I can't lose you."

Ravic smoked and did not taste the smoke. You don't want to lose me, he thought. Nor the other man either. That's it. That you are able to do such a thing! That's why I must get away from you. It isn't the one man—that could be quickly forgotten. You had every excuse for it. But that it has got hold of you so that you can't get away, that's the thing. You will get away. But it will happen again. It will happen time and again. It is in you. I too could do that earlier. I can't do it with you. That's why I must get away from you. Now I may still be able to do it. Next time—

"You think it is an extraordinary situation," he said. "It is the commonest in the world. The husband and the lover."

"That's not true."

"It is. It has many variations. Yours is one of them."

"How can you say anything like that!" She jumped up. "You are anything but that and you never were and you'll never be. The other one is much more—" She interrupted herself. "No, it isn't that way either. I can't explain it."

"Let's say security and adventure. It sounds better. It is the same. You want to have the one and don't want to let go the other."

She shook her head. "Ravic," she said, out of the dark, in a voice that moved his heart. "One can use good words for it and bad ones. It doesn't change anything. I love you and I'll love you until the end of my life. That I know and that is clear to me. You are the horizon and all my thoughts end in you. Whatever happens is still always within you. It is no deceit. It takes nothing from you. That's why I come to you again and again and that's why I can't regret it and why I can't feel guilty."

"There is no guilt in feelings ever, Joan. What made you think of such a thing?"

"I have thought it over. I have thought so much about it, Ravic. About you and about myself. You never wholly wanted me. Perhaps you don't realize it yourself. There was always something that was closed off from me. I could never get completely into you. I wanted to! How much I wanted to! It was always as if you might go away any minute. I never felt sure. The fact that the police sent you away, that you had to leave—it might just as well have happened in another way— that you would have gone one day, on your own, that you would simply not have been here any more, off somewhere—"

Ravic stared at the face in the uncertain dark before him. There was something right in what she said.

"It was always that way," she continued. "Always. And then someone came who wanted me, nothing but me, wholly and forever, without any complications. I laughed, I did not want it, I played with it, it seemed so harmless, so easy to push aside again—and then suddenly it became more, a compulsion, also there was something within me that wanted too, I resisted but it did not help, I did not belong there and not everything within me wanted it, a part of me only, but it pushed me, it was like a slow landslide which one laughs at in the beginning and suddenly there is nothing left to hold onto and you can't resist any longer. But I don't belong there, Ravic. I belong to you."

He threw his cigarette out the window. It flew like a glowworm down into the yard. "What has happened has happened, Joan," he said. "We can't change it now."

"I don't want to change anything. It will pass. I belong to you. Why do I come back again? Why do I stand before your door? Why do I wait for you here and you throw me out and I will come again? I know you won't believe it and you think I have other reasons. What reasons, then? If this other thing satisfied me, I would not have come back. I'd have forgotten you. You say what I look for with you is security. That's not true. It is love."

Words, Ravic thought. Sweet words. Gentle deceptive balm. Help, love, to belong together, to come back again—words, sweet words. Nothing but words. How many words existed for this simple, wild, cruel attraction of two bodies? What a rainbow of imagination, lies, sentiment, and self-deception enclosed it! There he stood on this farewell night, there he stood, calm, in the dark, and he let this rain of sweet words trickle over him, words that meant nothing but farewell, farewell, farewell. When one talked about it, it was already lost. The God of Love had a bloodstained forehead. He did not know anything about words.

"You must go now, Joan."

She got up. "I want to stay here. Let me stay here. Only tonight."

He shook his head. "What do you take me for? I'm not an automaton."

She leaned against him. He felt her trembling.

"It doesn't matter. Let me stay here."

He pushed her gently away. "You shouldn't start with me just to deceive the other man. He'll have to suffer enough without that."

"I can't go home alone now."

"You won't have to be alone for long."

"I will, I am alone. For days now. He's away. He isn't in Paris."

"So—" Ravic replied calmly. He looked at her. "Well, at least you are candid. One knows where one stands with you."

"That's not why I came."

"Of course not."

"There was no need for me to tell you."

"Right."

"Ravic, I don't want to go home alone."

"Then I'll take you home."

She slowly took one step backward. "You don't love me any more—" she said softly and almost threateningly.

"Did you come to find that out?"

"Yes—that too. Not only that—but that was part of it."

"My God, Joan," Ravic replied impatiently. "Then you have just heard one of the most candid confessions of love."

She did not answer. She looked at him. "Do you think that otherwise I would mind keeping you here, no matter who you're living with?" he said.

Slowly she began to smile. It wasn't really a smile—it was a radiance from within as if someone had lit a lamp in her and the glow was gradually mounting to her eyes. "Thank you, Ravic," she said. And after a while warily, still looking at him, "You won't leave me?"

"Why do you ask?"

"You'll wait? You won't leave me?"

"I think there is not much danger. To judge by my experience with you."

"Thank you." She was changed. How quickly she consoles herself, he thought. But why shouldn't she? She thought she had gained what she wanted even without staying there. She kissed him. "I knew you would be this way, Ravic. You had to be this way. Now I'll go. Don't take me home. Now I can go alone."

She stood by the door. "Don't come again," he said. "And don't think about anything. You won't perish."

"No. Good night, Ravic."

"Good night, Joan."

He went to the wall and turned on the light. You have to be this way—he shook himself slightly. They are made of clay and gold, he thought. Of lies and infatuation. Of deception and shameless truth. He sat down by the window. From below still came the low, monotonous wailing. A woman who had deceived her husband and was bewailing him because he was dead. But perhaps only because her religion prescribed it. Ravic wondered that he was not more unhappy.

Chapter 23

"YES, I'M BACK, Ravic," Kate Hegstroem said.

She was sitting in her room in the Hôtel Lancaster. She had become thinner. The flesh under her skin appeared sunken, as if it had been hollowed out from inside with fine instruments. Her features stood out more sharply and her skin was like silk that would tear easily.

"I thought you were still in Florence—or in Cannes—or America by now."

"I was in Florence the whole time. In Fiesole. Until I couldn't stand it any more. Do you remember how I tried to persuade you to come with me? Books, a fireplace, evenings, peace? The books were there—the fireplace too—but the peace! Ravic, even the town of Francis of Assisi has become loud. Loud and disquieting like everything else there. Where he preached love to the birds, there are now files of men in uniform marching hither and yon, growing drunk on boasts, big words, and groundless hate."

"But it was always that way, Kate."

"Not this way. A few years ago my major-domo was still a friendly man in Manchester trousers and bast shoes. Now he is a hero in high boots and black shirt, complete with daggers, and he delivers speeches saying that the Mediterranean Sea must become Italian, that England must be destroyed, and that Nice, Corsica, and Savoy must be returned to Italy. Ravic, this amiable nation that hasn't won a war for ages has gone mad since she was allowed to win in Ethiopia and Spain. Friends of mine who were reasonable even a few years ago seriously believe today that they can conquer England within three months. The country is boiling. What's going on? I fled from the brutality of brown shirts in Vienna; now I have left Italy because of the madness of black ones; some-where else there are said to be green ones, in America silver ones, of course—is the world in the midst of a shirt delirium?"

"Apparently. But that will change soon. The single color will be red."

"Red?"

"Yes. Red like blood."

Kate Hegstroem looked down into the yard. The late afternoon light filtered soft and green through the foliage of the chestnut trees. "One can't believe it," she said. "Two wars within twenty years—that's too much. We are still too tired from the first."

"Only the victors. Not the vanquished. To be victorious makes one careless."

"Yes, maybe." She looked at him. "Then there isn't much time left, is there?"

"Not too much now, I'm afraid."

"Do you think there will be enough for me?"

"Why not?" Ravic glanced up. She did not avoid his eyes. "Did you see Fiola?" he asked.

"Yes, once or twice. He was one of the few who had not yet been infected with the black pest."

Ravic did not answer. He waited.

Kate Hegstroem took a string of pearls from the table and let them glide through her hands. Between her long thin fingers they were like a costly rosary. "I almost feel like the Wandering Jew," she said. "In search of a little peace. But I seem to have set out at the wrong time. It is no longer anywhere. Only here—here there is still a remnant of it."

Ravic looked at the pearls. They were formed by shapeless gray mollusks irritated by a foreign substance, a grain of sand between their shells. Such softly gleaming beauty arose from an accidental irritation. One should make a note of that, he thought. "Didn't you intend to go to America, Kate? Anyone who can leave Europe should do so. It is too late for anything else."

"Do you want to send me away?"

"No. But didn't you say last time that you intended to settle your affairs and return to America?"

"Yes. But now I no longer want to. Not yet. I'll stay on here for some time."

"Paris is hot and unpleasant in summer."

She put her pearls aside. "Not if it is the last summer, Ravic."

"The last?"

"Yes. The last before I go back."

Ravic was silent. How much does she know? he wondered. What has Fiola told her?

"What's been going on at the Scheherazade?" she asked.

"I haven't been there for a long time. Morosow says it is overcrowded every night. As all other places are."

"In summer?"

"Yes, in summer when most of them used to be closed. Are you surprised at that?"

"No. Everyone is grasping whatever he can before the end."

"Yes," Ravic said.

"Will you take me there some time?"

"Of course, Kate. Whenever you like. I thought you didn't want to go there again."

"I thought so, too. I've changed my mind. I too intend to grasp whatever I still can."

He looked at her. "All right, Kate," he said then. "Whenever you like."

He got up. She went to the door with him. She leaned against the doorframe, slender, with her dry, silken skin that looked as though it would rustle if one touched it. Her eyes were very clear and larger than before. She gave him her hand. It was hot and dry. "Why didn't you tell me what was wrong with me?" she asked lightly as if she were asking about the weather.

He stared at her and did not answer.

"I could have stood it," she said and the ghost of an ironical smile with no reproach in it flitted across her face. "Adieu, Ravic!"

The man without the stomach was dead. He had moaned for three days and by that time morphine was of little help. Ravic and Veber had known that he would die. They could have spared him these three last days. They had not done it because there was a religion that preached love of one's neighbor and prohibited the shortening of his sufferings. And there was a law to back it up.

"Did you send a wire to his family?" Ravic asked.

"He has none," Veber said.

"Or to any other of his connections?"

"There is nobody."

"Nobody?"

"Nobody. The concierge from his apartment house was

here. He never received any letters, except catalogues from mail order houses and pamphlets about alcoholism, tuberculosis, venereal disease, and the like. He never had visitors. He had paid in advance for the operation and four weeks of hospitalization. Two weeks of hospitalization too much. The concierge claims he promised her everything he possessed because she had taken care of him. She demanded a refund for the two weeks. She had been like a mother to him. You should have seen that mother. She said she had been put to all kinds of expenses for him. She had paid out the money for his rent. I told her that he had paid here in advance; there was no good reason why he shouldn't have done it for his apartment as well. Besides, all that was a matter for the police. Whereupon she cursed me.''

"Money," Ravic said. "How inventive it makes one!"

Veber laughed. "We'll inform the authorities. They can take care of it. And the funeral as well."

Ravic cast one more look at the man without relatives and stomach. There he lay and his face was changing during this hour as it had never changed during the thirty-five years of his life. Out of the frozen spasm of his last breath was gradually emerging the stark face of death. The accidental in it was melting away, the marks of dying were being washed out, and from this twisted ordinary face was being formed, austere and silent, the eternal mask. Ravic went on. He met the night nurse in the corridor. She had just arrived. "The man in twelve is dead," he said. "He died half an hour ago. You don't have to sit up any more." And when he saw her face, "Did he leave you anything?"

She hesitated. "No. He was a very cool person. And he hardly spoke at all in the last days."

"No, he didn't."

The nurse looked at Ravic in a housewifely manner. "He had a wonderful dressing case. All silver. In fact, rather too dainty for a man. More for a lady."

"Didn't you tell him?"

"We did speak about it once. Tuesday night; at that time he was calmer. But he said that silver was all right for a man too. And the brushes were so good. They were no longer to be had nowadays. Otherwise he spoke little."

"The silver will go to the authorities now. He had no relatives."

The nurse nodded understandingly. "It's a pity! It'll get

black. And brushes deteriorate if they aren't new and don't get used. They should be washed first.''

"Yes, it's a pity,'' Ravic said. "It would have been better if you had got them. Then, at least, someone would have enjoyed them.''

The nurse smiled gratefully. "It doesn't matter. I didn't expect anything. Dying people rarely give anything away. Only those who are recuperating. Dying people don't want to believe that they must die. That's why they don't do it. Then too, some don't do it out of spite. You wouldn't believe it, doctor, how terrible dying people can be! What they say sometimes before they die!''

Her red-cheeked childish face was open and clear. She did not pay any attention to what happened around her if it did not affect her small world. Dying people were naughty or helpless children. One took care of them until they were dead, and then new ones came, some of them became healthy and were grateful, others were not, and some just died. That's how it was. Nothing to disquiet one. It was much more important whether the prices at the sale at Bon Marché were reduced, or Cousin Jean was to marry Anne Couturier.

It actually was more important, Ravic thought. The small circle that protected one from chaos. Otherwise where would one be?

He was sitting in front of the Café Triomphe. The night was pallid and cloudy. It was warm, and somewhere lightning flashed noiselessly. Life crept more densely along the sidewalks. A woman with a blue satin hat sat down at his table.

"Will you buy me a vermouth?'' she asked.

"Yes. But leave me alone. I'm waiting for someone.''

"We can wait together.''

"Better not. I'm waiting for a woman wrestler from the Palais du Sport.''

The woman smiled. She was so thickly painted that one saw the smile only on her lips. Everything else was a white mask. "Come with me,'' she said. "I have a sweet apartment. And I am good.''

Ravic shook his head. He put a five-franc bill on the table. "Here. Adieu. And good luck.''

The woman took the bill, folded it, and pushed it under her garter. "Blue?'' she asked.

"No.''

"I am good against the blues. I have a very nice friend. Young," she added after a pause. "Breasts like the Eiffel tower."

"Some other time."

"All right." The woman got up and took another seat a few tables away. She looked at him again a few times, then she bought a sport paper and began to read the results of the races.

Ravic stared into the bustling crowd which incessantly pushed along past the tables. The band inside was playing Viennese waltzes. The lightning grew stronger. A group of young homosexuals, coquettish and noisy, perched at the adjoining table like a swarm of parrots. They wore beards, the newest fashion, and jackets too broad in the shoulders and too narrow in the waists.

A girl stopped at Ravic's table and looked at him. She seemed vaguely familiar to him, but there were many that he knew slightly. She looked like one of the dainty whores with the appeal of helplessness.

"Don't you recognize me?" she asked.

"Of course," Ravic said. He hadn't any idea. "How are you?"

"Fine. But don't you really know me any more?"

"I forget names. But of course I know you. It's a long time since we saw each other last."

"Yes. You gave Bobo a good scare that time." She smiled. "You saved my life and now you don't recognize me."

Bobo. Saved her life. The midwife. Now Ravic remembered. "You are Lucienne," he said. "Of course. Then you were sick. Today you are healthy. That's it. That's why I didn't recognize you right away."

Lucienne beamed. "Really! You actually remember! Many thanks for the hundred francs you got back from the midwife."

"That—oh yes." After his failure with Madame Boucher he had sent her something out of his own pocket. "Sorry it wasn't the whole amount."

"It was enough. I had given the whole thing up."

"Would you like to have a drink with me, Lucienne?"

She nodded and sat down cautiously at his side. "A Cinzano with soda."

"How are things with you, Lucienne?"

"I am doing very well."

"Are you still with Bobo?"

"Yes, of course. But he is different now. Better."

"Good."

There was not much to ask. A little seamstress had become a little whore. That was what he had patched her together for. Bobo had taken care of the rest. She no longer needed to be afraid of having children. One more reason. She was still at the beginning; her childlike quality still held attraction for elderly rounders—a piece of china that had not yet lost its luster through too much use. She drank carefully like a bird; but her eyes were already wandering. It wasn't exactly cheering. Nor a cause for great regret. Just a fragment of life, on the skids. "Are you content?" he asked.

She nodded. He saw that she really was content. She found everything quite in order. There was nothing to be dramatized. "Are you alone?" she asked.

"Yes, Lucienne."

"On such an evening."

"Yes."

She looked at him shyly and smiled. "I've got time," she said.

What's the matter with me? Ravic thought. Do I look so starved that every prostitute offers me a bit of commercialized love? "It is too far to go to your place, Lucienne, I haven't that much time."

"We could not go to my place. Bobo must not know anything about it."

Ravic looked at her. "Doesn't Bobo ever know anything about it?"

"He does. He knows of the others. He keeps track." She smiled. "He's still so young. He thinks I won't give him the money otherwise."

"That's why Bobo must not know anything?"

"Not because of that. But he would be jealous. And then he goes wild."

"Does he always get jealous?"

Lucienne glanced up, surprised. "Of course not. The others are business."

"So only when there isn't any money involved?"

Lucienne hesitated. Then she slowly blushed. "Not for that reason. Only if he thinks there is something else." She hesitated again. "That my feelings are in it."

She did not look up. Ravic took her hand, which lay forlornly on the table. "Lucienne," he said, "it's nice that

277

you remembered. And that you want to go with me. You are charming and I would like to take you with me. But I cannot sleep with anyone on whom I have once operated. Do you understand?"

She raised her long dark lashes and quickly nodded. "Yes." She got up. "Then I'll go now."

"Yes. Adieu, Lucienne. Good luck. Take care that you don't get sick."

"Yes."

Ravic wrote something on a slip of paper. "Get this in case you don't already have it. It's the best. And don't give all your money to Bobo."

She smiled and shook her head. She knew and he knew, too that she would do it nevertheless. Ravic looked after her until she disappeared in the crowd. Then he called the waiter.

The woman in the blue hat passed by. She had watched the scene. She was fanning herself with her folded newspaper and she showed a mouth full of false teeth. "Either you are impotent or a pansy, my dear," she said pleasantly in passing. "Good luck and my thanks."

Ravic walked through the warm night. Flashes of lightning swept over the roofs. The air was still. He found the entrance to the Louvre lighted. The doors stood open and he walked in.

It was one of the night exhibitions. A few of the rooms were illuminated. He walked through the Egyptian section, which looked like a huge lighted tomb. The stone kings of three thousand years ago squatted or stood staring motionlessly out of granite eyes at groups of sauntering students, women in last year's hats, and bored elderly men. There was a smell of dust, stale air, and immortality.

In the Greek section, in front of the Venus of Milo, stood a whispering group of girls who did not resemble her at all. Ravic paused. After the granite and green syenite of the Egyptians, the marble was decadent and weak. The soft, well-rounded Venus was a little like a housewife contentedly bathing; beautiful and without a thought. Apollo, the lizard-killer, was a homosexual who needed more exercise. But they were standing in rooms; that was what killed them. It did not kill the Egyptians; they were made for tombs and temples. The Greeks needed sun, air and columns through which shone the golden light of Athens.

Ravic walked on. The large hall with its staircase came steadily toward him. And suddenly, high above everything, rose the Nike of Samothrace.

It was a long time since he had seen her. The last time it had been on a gray day. The marble had looked dull and in the dirty winter light of the museum the princess of victory had seemed hesitant and freezing. But now she stood high above the staircase on the bow of the marble ship, illuminated by spotlights, gleaming, her wings wide spread, her garment pressed tight by the wind against her striding body, bright and ready for flight. Behind her the wine-colored Sea of Salamia seemed to roar, and the sky was dark with the velvet of expectation.

She knew nothing of morals. She knew nothing of problems. She did not know the storms and dark ambushes of the blood. She knew the victory and the defeat, and the two were almost the same. She was not temptation; she was flight. She was not enticement; she was unconcernedness. She held no secret; and yet she was more exciting than Venus, who by hiding her sex emphasized it. She was akin to birds and ships, to the wind, to the waves, and the horizon. She had no country.

She had no country, Ravic thought. But she did not need one either. She was at home on all ships. She was at home wherever there was courage and conflict and even defeat if it was without despair. She was not only the goddess of victory, she was also the goddess of all adventures and the goddess of refugees—so long as they did not give up.

He looked around. No one else was in the room any longer. The students and the people with Baedekers had gone home. Home—what other home existed for one who belonged nowhere, but the stormy one in the heart of another for a short time? Was not this the reason why love, when it struck the hearts of the homeless, shook and possessed them so completely—because they had nothing else? Had he not for this very reason tried to avoid it? And had it not followed him and overtaken him and struck him down? It was harder to rise again on the slippery ice of a foreign land than on familiar and accustomed ground.

Something caught his eye. Something small, fluttering, white. It was a butterfly that must have flown in through the open entrance door. It had come, perhaps from the warm rose beds of the Tuileries, startled out of its perfumed sleep by two lovers, then dazzled by lights which were unknown suns—many and bewildering—it had escaped into the entrance, into the sheltering dark behind the big doors, and now it fluttered about, lost and courageous, in the spacious room where it would die—tiring, sleeping on a marble cornice, on a window ledge, or on the shoulder of the radiant goddess high above. In the morning it would search for flowers and life and the light honey of blossoms and would not find them and later it would fall asleep again on millennial marble, weakened by then, until the grip of the delicate, tenacious feet loosened and it fell, a thin leaf of premature autumn.

Sentimentality, Ravic thought. The goddess of victory and the refugee butterfly. A cheap symbol. But what touched one more deeply than the cheap things, the cheap symbols, the cheap feelings, the cheap sentimentality? What had made them cheap? Their overclear truth. Snobbery vanished when things became a question of life and death.

The butterfly had disappeared in the semidarkness of the dome. Ravic left the Louvre. Outside the warm air met him, tepid as a bath. He stopped. Cheap feelings! Wasn't he himself at the mercy of the cheapest of all of them? He stared into the wide courtyard where the shadows of the centuries brooded and he felt suddenly as if fists were striking him. He almost staggered under the attack. The specter of the white Nike poised for flight was still before his eyes; but behind it another face emerged out of the shadow, a cheap face, not a precious face but one in which his imagination had become entangled like an Indian veil on a thorny rosebush. He tugged at it but the thorns held fast, they held the silk and golden threads, they were already knitted together so that the eye could no longer distinguish clearly between the thorny boughs and the shimmering fabric.

Face! Face! Who asked whether it was cheap or precious? Unique or existing a thousand times? One could pose questions beforehand, but when one was caught one no longer knew. One was imprisoned by love—not by the one person who happened to bear its name. Who could still judge, blinded by the fires of imagination? Love knew no values.

The sky hung lower now. At instants soundless lightning tore sulphurous clouds out of the night. Formless and with a thousand sightless eyes the sultry warmth lay upon the roofs. Ravic walked along the Rue de Rivoli. The shopwindows blazed under the arcades. A dense throng of people pushed its way along. The cars were a row of twinkling reflections.

Here am I, he thought, one among thousands, walking slowly past these windows filled with glittering junk and precious things, my hands in my pockets, an evening stroller—and my blood trembles within me, and in the pulsing gray and white labyrinths of two handfuls of mollusk-like matter, called a brain, an invisible battle is raging, making reality appear unreal and unreality real. I can feel arms touching me, bodies brushing against me, eyes scrutinizing me, I can hear the cars, the voices, the turmoil of palpable reality, I am in the midst of it and yet farther away than the moon—upon a planet, beyond logic and facts, something within me is crying a name, knowing it is not the name and nevertheless crying it aloud; crying it into a silence that always existed and in which many cries have died away and from which never an answer has come and, knowing this, it still cries, the cry of the night of love and of the night of death, the cry of ecstasy and of collapsing consciousness, of the jungle and the desert, and I may know a thousand answers, but this one is beyond me and I can never attain it.

Love! How much that word had to cover! From the softest caress of the skin to the most remote excitement of the spirit, from the simple desire for a family to the convulsions of death, from insatiable passion to Jacob's struggle with the angel. Here am I, Ravic thought, a man of more than forty years, trained in many schools, with experience and knowledge, who has been beaten down and has risen again, sifted through the filter of the years, having become more callous, more critical, colder—I did not want it and I did not believe it, I did not think it would come again—and now here it is, and all my experience is of no avail, all the knowledge makes it only the more burning—and what burns better in the fire of the emotions than dry cynicism and the stacked wood of the critical years?

He walked and walked, and the night was wide and resonant; he walked heedlessly, not knowing whether hours or minutes were passing, and he was not surprised when he found himself in the gardens behind the Avenue Raphaël.

The house in the Rue Pascal. The faint outlines of the floors, on top the studios, some lighted. He found the windows of Joan's studio. They were bright. She was at home. But maybe she was not at home and had only left the lights on. She hated to come back to dark rooms. Just as he did.

Ravic walked over to the street. A few cars were parked in front of the house. Among them a yellow roadster, an ordinary car dressed up like a racing car. That might be the car belonging to the other man. A car for an actor. Red leather seats, a dashboard like that in a plane with a profusion of unnecessary instruments—of course it must be his. Am I jealous? he thought, astonished. Jealous of the chance object to which she has attached herself? Jealous of something that does not concern me? One can be jealous of a love that has turned away, but not of that to which it has turned—

He went back to the gardens. The smell of blossoms came out of the dark, sweet, mixed with the odor of soil and cool greenery. The smell was strong as before a thunderstorm. He found a bench and sat down. This is not I, he thought, this belated lover sitting here on a bench in front of the house of the woman who has forsaken him and looking up at her window. This is not I shaken by a desire which I can thoroughly dissect and yet not master. This is not I, this fool, who would give years of his life to be able to turn time back and regain a blond nothing babbling blissful nonsense into his ear! This is not I, who—to hell with all pretenses—is sitting here, jealous and crushed and miserable and who would like to set fire to that car!

He lit a cigarette. The silent glow. The invisible smoke. The short comet's path of the match. Why did he not go up to the studio? What could happen? It was not yet too late. The light was still on. He would be able to master the situation. Why did he not get her out of it? Now that he knew everything? Get her out and take her with him and never again let her go?

He stared into the darkness. What good could it do? What would happen? He could not throw the other out. You could not throw anything or anybody out of another's heart. Couldn't he have taken her at that time when she had come to him? Why hadn't he done it?

He threw away his cigarette. Because it was not enough. That was it. He wanted more. It would not be enough even if she came, even if she came back and everything else was forgotten and drowned, it would never again be enough, in a strange and frightful way, never again enough. Something had gone wrong, at some point the ray of his imagination had failed to hit the mirror, the mirror that caught it and threw it back intensified into itself, and now the ray had shot beyond into the blind sphere of the unfillable and nothing could bring it back again, not one mirror or a thousand mirrors. They could only catch a part of it, but never bring it back; by now its specter moved forlornly through the empty heavens of love and only filled them with radiant mist which no longer had any shape and which could never again become a rainbow around a beloved head. The magic circle was broken, the lamentation remained, but hope lay shattered.

Someone came out of the house. A man. Ravic straightened up. A woman followed him. They were laughing. It was not they. One of the cars started and drove off. He took out another cigarette. Could he have held her? Could he have held her if he had been different? But what could be held? Only an illusion, little else. But wasn't an illusion enough? Could one ever attain more? Who knew anything about the black whirlpool of life, namelessly seething beneath our senses, which, out of empty uproar, turned it into things, a table, a lamp, home and You and love? There was only a foreboding and a frightening twilight. Was it not enough?

It was not enough. It was enough only if one believed in it. Once the crystal had burst under the hammers of doubt one could only cement it together, but nothing more. Cement it, lie about it, and watch the broken light that once had been a white splendor! Nothing came back. Nothing reshaped itself. Nothing. Even if Joan came back it would not be the same again. A crystal cemented together. The hour had been missed. Nothing would bring it back.

He felt a sharp, unbearable pain. Something rent him, rent inside him. My God, he thought, that this can make me suffer so. I observe myself over my own shoulder, but it doesn't change anything. I know if I should get it I would let it go again, but that does not quench my longing. I dissect it like a corpse on the table in the morgue, but it only becomes a thousand times more alive. I know that it will pass sometime, but that helps me not at all. He stared with strained eyes up at the windows, and he felt horribly ludicrous, but that did not change anything either.

Suddenly heavy thunder rumbled over the city. Raindrops splashed on the bushes. Ravic got up. He saw the street mottled with black silver. The rain began to sing. The heavy drops beat warmly against his face. And suddenly he no longer knew whether he was ludicrous, or miserable, whether he was suffering or not—he only knew that he was alive. He was alive! He was there, it held him again, it shook him, he was not a spectator any longer, not an onlooker from outside; the great splendor of uncontrollable feeling shot through his veins again like fire through a furnace; it scarcely mattered whether he was happy or unhappy, he was alive and he was fully aware that he was alive and that was enough.

He stood in the rain which was pouring down upon him like heavenly machine-gun fire. He stood there and he was rain and storm and water and earth; the lightning from the horizon crossed within him, he was creature, element; nothing any longer had a name and was thereby made lonesome, everything was the same, love, the pouring rain, the pale fires above the roofs, the earth which seemed to swell; there were no longer any frontiers and he belonged to all this and happiness and unhappiness were empty husks cast off by the overpowering sensation of being alive and feeling it. "You up there," he said to the lighted window and laughed and was not aware that he laughed. "You small light, you fata morgana, you face that exercises a strange power over me, on this planet where there are a hundred thousand other faces, better ones, more beautiful, more intelligent, kinder, more faithful and understanding—you, accident, thrown across my way at night, dropped into my life, you, thoughtless, possessive feeling that was washed ashore and crept under my skin while I slept, you, who know hardly more about me than that I resisted and who threw herself against me until I no longer resisted and who then wanted to pass on, I salute you! Here I stand and I never thought to stand like this again. Rain is running through my shirt and is warmer and cooler and softer than your hands and your skin, here I stand, miserable and with the sharp claws of jealousy in my stomach, longing for you, despising you, admiring you, worshiping you, because you cast the lightning that set me ablaze, the lightning hidden in every womb, the spark of life, the black fire, here I stand, no longer like a dead man on furlough with his small cynicism, sarcasm, and portion of courage, no longer cold: alive again, suffering if you like, but again open to all the thunderstorms of life, reborn into its own simple strength! Be blessed, Madonna of the flighty heart, Nike with a Romanian accent, dream and deceit, broken mirror of a dark god, be blessed, you, unsuspecting, whom I will never tell, for you would mercilessly make capital of it, but you have returned to me what neither Plato nor star chrysanthemums, neither flight nor freedom, neither all poesy nor all mercy, neither despair nor high and patient hope could give me: the simple, strong, immediate life that seemed to me like a crime in this time between two catastrophes! I salute you! Be blessed! I had to lose you in order to learn this! I salute you!''

The rain had turned into a glistening silver curtain. The bushes became fragrant. The smell of the soil was strong and grateful. Someone rushed out of the house opposite and put the top up over the yellow roadster. It did not matter. Nothing mattered. The night was there shaking rain down from the stars; mysterious and fructifying, it poured down on the stone city with its alleys and gardens, millions of blossoms held out to it their multicolored sex and conceived it; it flung itself into the millions of open arms of the trees and penetrated the soil for its dark nuptials with millions of waiting roots, the rain, the night, nature, growth, they were there unconcerned about destruction, death, criminals, false saints, victory or defeat, they were there as in every year, on this night he belonged with them; the shell had broken open, life stretched out, life, life, welcomed and blessed.

He walked quickly through the gardens and streets. He did not look back, he walked and walked, and the treetops in the Bois received him like a huge humming beehive, the rain drummed upon them, they swayed and answered, and he felt as if he were young again and were going to a woman for the first time.

Chapter 24

"WHAT SHALL IT BE?" the waiter asked Ravic.

"Bring me a—"

"What?"

Ravic did not answer.

"I didn't understand you, sir," the waiter said.

"Anything. Bring me something."

"Pernod?"

"Yes."

Ravic closed his eyes. He slowly opened them again. The man was still sitting there. This time there was no possibility of mistake.

Haake was sitting at the table by the door. He was alone and was eating. A silver plate with the two halves of a langouste and a bottle of champagne in an ice-bucket were on the table. A waiter was standing by the table, mixing a lettuce and tomato salad. Ravic saw all this overdistinctly as though there were a relief engraved on wax behind his eyes. He saw a signet ring with a coat of arms on a red stone when Haake took the bottle out of the ice-bucket. He recognized this ring and the chubby white hand. He had seen it in the confused nightmare of methodical violence when, after collapsing beside the whipping-table, he had been hurled back from unconsciousness into the glaring light—with Haake before him, carefully stepping back to protect his neat uniform from the water pouring down over Ravic—with his chubby white hand stretched out, pointing at him, and with his soft voice declaring: "That was only the beginning. It has been nothing so far. Now will you reveal the names to us? Or shall we continue? We still have many other possibilities. Your fingernails are still intact, I see."

Haake looked up. He looked Ravic straight in the eyes. Ravic needed all his strength to remain seated. He took his glass of Pernod, took a swallow, and forced his eyes to look at the salad plate as if the preparations interested him. He did not know whether Haake had recognized him. He could feel how, in a second, his back had become completely wet.

After a while he glanced at the table again. Haake was eating the langouste. He was looking at his plate. His bald head reflected the light. Ravic looked around. The place was crowded. It was impossible to do anything. He had no weapon on him and if he leaped at Haake, there would be ten people to pull him back the next moment. Two minutes later the police. There was nothing he could do but wait and follow Haake. Find out where he lived.

He forced himself to smoke a cigarette and not to glance at Haake again until he had finished it. Slowly, as if he were seeking someone, he looked about. Haake had just finished his langouste. He had the napkin in his hands and was wiping his lips. He did not do it with one hand; he did it with both. He held the napkin taut and touched his lips lightly with it; first one, then the other, like a woman removing lipstick. At that instant he looked straight at Ravic.

Ravic let his eyes wander. He sensed that Haake was continuing to stare at him. He called the waiter and asked for another Pernod. A second waiter was busy at Haake's table now. He cleared off the remainders of the langouste, refilled the empty glass, and brought a dish with cheeses. Haake pointed at a piece of melting Brie which was on a mat of straw.

Ravic smoked another cigarette. After a while, out of the corner of his eye, he again saw Haake looking at him. This was no longer accidental. He felt his skin contracting. If Haake had recognized him—he stopped the waiter as he was passing. "Can you bring the Pernod to me outside? I'd like to sit on the terrace. It's cooler there.'"

The waiter hesitated. "It would be easier if you'd pay here. There is another waiter outside. Then I can bring your glass outside to you."

Ravic shook his head and took a bill out of his pocket. "I can drink it here and order another one outside. Then there won't be any confusion."

"Very well, sir. Thank you, sir."

Ravic emptied his glass without haste. Haake had been listening, that he knew. He had stopped eating while Ravic had been talking. Now he went on with his meal. Ravic still kept quiet for a while. If Haake had recognized him, there was only one thing to be done; to act as if he had not recognized Haake and to continue to watch him from hiding.

After a few minutes he stood up and sauntered out. Almost every table outside was occupied. Ravic remained standing until he found a table from which he could keep an eye on a part of Haake's table in the restaurant. Haake himself could not see him; but Ravic would see Haake when he got up to leave. He ordered a Pernod and paid at once. He wanted to be ready to follow him immediately.

"Ravic—" someone said at his side.

He was startled, as if someone had struck him. Joan stood at his side. He stared at her.

"Ravic—" she repeated. "Don't you recognize me any more?"

"Yes, of course." His eyes were on Haake's table. The waiter was standing there and had brought coffee. He caught his breath. There was still time. "Joan," he said with an effort, "how do you happen to be here?"

"What a question! Everyone comes to Fouquet's every day."

"Are you alone?"

"Yes."

He realized that she was still standing while he was sitting. He got up in such a way that he could still look obliquely at Haake's table. "I have something to do here, Joan," he said hastily without looking at her. "I can't explain what. You must leave me alone."

"I'll wait." Joan sat down. "I'll see what the woman is like."

"What woman?" Ravic asked uncomprehendingly.

"The woman you are waiting for."

"It's not a woman."

"Who else?"

He looked at her. "You didn't recognize me," she said. "You want to send me away, you are excited—I know there is someone. And I'm going to see who it is."

Five minutes, Ravic thought. Perhaps even ten to fifteen for the coffee. Haake would smoke another cigarette. Maybe a cigar. He had to see that he was rid of Joan by then.

"All right," he said. "I can't prevent that. But sit down somewhere else."

She did not answer. Her eyes became sharper and her face tense.

"It isn't a woman," he said. "And if it were, what the devil business is it of yours? Don't make yourself ridiculous by acting jealous while you run around with your actor."

Joan did not answer. She turned in the direction in which he had been looking and tried to discover whom he had been looking at. "Don't do that," he said.

"Is she with another man?"

Suddenly Ravic sat down. Haake had heard that he intended to sit on the terrace. If he had recognized him, he would be suspicious and see where he was. In that case it would appear more casual and harmless to be sitting out here with a woman.

"All right," he said, "you may stay here. What you are thinking is nonsense. I'll get up at a certain moment and leave. You'll go with me to a taxi and you won't come along with me. Will you do that?"

"Why are you so mysterious?"

"I am not mysterious. There is a man here whom I have not seen for a long time. I want to know where he lives. That's all."

"It isn't a woman?"

"No. It is a man and I can't tell you anything more about it."

The waiter stood by the table. "What do you want to drink?" Ravic asked.

"Calvados."

"One calvados." The waiter shuffled away.

"Aren't you going to have one?"

"No, I'm drinking this."

Joan studied him. "You don't know how I hate you sometimes."

"That may be." Ravic glanced at Haake's table. Glass, he thought. Trembling, flowing, glimmering glass. The street, the tables, the people—all immersed in a jelly of quivering glass.

"You are cold, egotistic—"

"Joan," Ravic said, "we'll discuss this some other time."

She was silent while the waiter put the glass before her. Ravic paid at once.

"You got me into all this," she said challengingly.

"I know." For a moment he saw Haake's hand over the table, the chubby white hand reaching for the sugar.

"You! No one but you! You have never loved me and you played with me and you saw that I loved you and you did not take it seriously."

"That is true."

"What?"

"It is true," Ravic said without looking at her. "But it became different later on."

"Yes, later! Later! Everything was upside-down then. Then it was too late. It was your fault."

"I know."

"Don't talk to me like that!" Her face was white and angry. "You're not even listening!"

"I am." He looked at her. Talk, say something, no matter what. "Did you have a fight with your actor?"

"Yes."

"That will pass."

Blue smoke from the corner. The waiter was pouring coffee again. Haake seemed to be taking his time. "I could have denied it," Joan said. "I could have said I just came here by accident. I didn't. I was looking for you. I am going to leave him."

"That's what one is always going to do. It's part of it."

"I'm afraid of him. He threatens me. He wants to shoot me."

"What?" Suddenly Ravic looked up. "What was that?"

"He says he'll shoot me."

"Who?" He had only half listened. Now he understood. "Oh, I see! You don't believe it, do you?"

"He has a terrible temper."

"Nonsense! Whoever says such a thing never does it. Least of all an actor."

What am I talking about? he thought. What is all this? What does she want here? A voice, a face above the roaring in my ears. What does it matter to me? "Why are you telling me all this?" he asked.

"I'm going to leave him. I want to come back to you."

If he takes a taxi it will take me at least a few seconds until I can stop one, Ravic thought. By the time it gets started it might be too late. He got up. "Wait here. I'll be back at once."

"What do you want—"

He did not answer.

He crossed the street quickly and hailed a taxi. "Here are ten francs. Can you wait for me a few minutes? I still have something to do inside."

The driver looked at the money. Then at Ravic. Ravic winked. The driver winked back. He turned the bill around slowly. "That's extra," Ravic said. "You know why—"

"I understand." The driver grinned. "All right, I'll park here."

"Park so that you can get started immediately."

"All right, chief."

Ravic forced his way back through the crowd. Suddenly his throat tightened. He saw Haake standing in the doorway. He did not hear what Joan was saying. "Wait!" he said. "Wait! Just a moment! One second!"

"No."

She rose. "You'll regret this!" She was almost sobbing. He forced himself to smile. He held her hand tight. Haake was still standing there. "Sit down," Ravic said. "One second."

"No!"

Her hand strained in his grip. He let her go. He did not want a scene. She left quickly, making her way through the rows of tables close by the door. Haake followed her with his eyes. Then he slowly looked back at Ravic, then again in the direction in which Joan had gone. Ravic sat down. Suddenly the blood thundered in his temples. He took out his wallet and pretended to be looking for something. He noticed that Haake was slowly walking between the tables. He looked indifferently in the opposite direction. Haake had to pass the place he was looking at.

He waited. It seemed to take endless time. Suddenly he was seized by a hot fear. What if Haake had turned back? He quickly turned his head. Haake was not there any more. Not there any more. For a moment everything turned around him. "Will you permit me?" someone asked at his side.

Ravic did not hear. He looked at the door. Haake had not gone back into the restaurant. Jump up, he thought, run after him, still try to get hold of him. Then the voice was there behind him again. He turned his head and stared. Haake had come around behind his back and was standing now beside him. He pointed at the chair on which Joan had been sitting. "Will you permit me? There is no other table free."

Ravic nodded. He was unable to say anything. The blood was drained from his head. It ebbed and ebbed as if it would run under the chair and leave his body behind like an empty sack. He pressed his back close against the back of the chair. There stood his glass still in front of him. The milky fluid. He lifted it and drank. It was heavy. He looked at the glass. It was steady in his hand. The trembling was in his veins.

Haake ordered a fine champagne. An old fine champagne. He spoke French with a heavy German accent. Ravic called a newspaper boy. *"Paris Soir."*

The newspaper boy looked cautiously toward the entrance. He knew the old newspaper woman was standing there. He handed Ravic the newspaper, folded, as though accidentally, grabbed the coin, and quickly disappeared.

He must have recognized me, Ravic thought. Otherwise why would he have come? He had not counted on that. Now he could only stay and see what Haake wanted and act accordingly.

He picked up the newspaper, read the headlines, and put it back on the table. Haake looked at him. "Fine evening," he said in German.

Ravic nodded.

Haake smiled. "Keen eye, eh?"

"Apparently."

"I saw you while I was still inside."

Ravic nodded attentively and indifferently. He was strained to the utmost. He could not imagine what Haake's intentions were. The latter could not know that Ravic was in France illegally. But maybe the Gestapo had known even that. But for that there still was time.

"I recognized you at once," Haake said.

Ravic looked at him. "That scar," Haake said and pointed at Ravic's forehead. "Member of a student corps. Therefore you must be German. Or have studied in Germany."

He laughed. Ravic was still looking at him. This was impossible! It was too ridiculous! He breathed deeply in sudden relief. Haake had no idea who he was. He thought the scar on his forehead was a dueling scar. Ravic laughed. He laughed with Haake. He had to dig his nails into the palm of his hand to make himself stop laughing.

"Is that correct?" Haake asked with jovial pride.

"Yes, exactly."

The scar on his forehead. He had got it when they had

beaten him in the cellar at Gestapo headquarters before Haake's very eyes. Blood had run into his own eyes and mouth. And now Haake sat here, mistaking it for a dueling scar, and was proud of himself.

The waiter brought Haake's fine. Haake sniffed at it like a connoisseur. "That's one thing they have here!" he declared. "Good cognac! Otherwise—" He winked at Ravic. "Everything's rotten. A people of rentiers. They don't want anything but security and a good life. Helpless against us."

Ravic thought he'd be unable to talk. He thought if he talked he would seize his glass, smash it against the edge of the table, and dig the sharp splinters into Haake's eyes. He took the glass, carefully and with effort, emptied it, and put it quietly down again.

"What is that?" Haake asked.

"Pernod. A substitute for absinthe."

"Ah, absinthe. The stuff that makes the French impotent, eh?" Haake smiled. "Pardon me! Nothing personal intended."

"Absinthe is prohibited," Ravic said. "This is a harmless substitute. Absinthe is said to make one sterile, not impotent. That's why it is prohibited. This is anise. Tastes like licorice-water."

It worked, he thought. It worked and without much excitement either. He could answer, easily and smoothly. There was turmoil deep inside him, roaring and black—but the surface appeared calm.

"Do you live here?" Haake asked.

"Yes."

"Have you lived here long?"

"Always."

"I understand," Haake said. "A foreign German. Born here, eh?"

Ravic nodded.

Haake drank his fine. "Some of our best men are Germans born in foreign countries. Our Fuehrer's deputy, born in Egypt. Rosenberg, in Russia. Darré comes from Argentina. It's the political conviction that counts, eh?"

"Only that," Ravic replied.

"I thought so," Haake's face radiated satisfaction. Then he bowed slightly across the table, and it seemed as if he clicked his heels under the table at the same time. "By the way—permit me—von Haake."

Ravic repeated the ceremony. "Horn." It was one of his former pseudonyms.

"Von Horn?" Haake asked.

"Yes."

Haake nodded. He became more intimate. He had met a man of his own class. "You must know Paris well, eh?"

"Fairly."

"I don't mean the museums." Haake grinned like a man of the world.

"I know what you mean."

The Aryan superman would like to go slumming, and doesn't know where to go, Ravic thought. If I could get him into a hidden corner somewhere, a lonely bistro, an out-of-the-way brothel—he deliberated quickly. Some place where he wouldn't be disturbed and hindered.

"There are all sorts of interesting things here, eh?" Haake asked.

"You haven't been in Paris long?"

"I come here every other week for two or three days. Sort of a check-up. Pretty important. We have built up quite a few things here during the last year. It's working out wonderfully. I can't talk about it, but"—Haake laughed—"you can buy almost anything here. A corrupt lot. We know almost everything we want to know. We don't even have to look for information. They bring it themselves. Treason as a form of patriotism. A result of the party system. Each party betrays the others and their country for their own profit. Our advantage. We have a great many friends here of our political persuasion. In the most influential circles." He lifted his glass, examined it, found it empty, and put it down again. "They don't even arm themselves. They think we won't demand anything from them if they are unarmed. If you knew the number of their planes and tanks, you would laugh yourself sick at these candidates for suicide."

Ravic listened. He was all attention and yet everything swam around him as in a dream just before the awakening. The tables, the waiters, the sweet nocturnal commotion of life, the gliding rows of automobiles, the moon above the houses, the multicolored electric signs of the house fronts—and the garrulous manifold murderer opposite him who had ruined his life.

Two women in short tailored suits passed by. They smiled

at Ravic. It was Yvette and Marthe from the Osiris. They were having their day off.

"Chic, Donnerwetter!" Haake said.

A side-street, Ravic thought. A narrow empty side-street—if I could get him there. Or into the Bois. "Those are two ladies who live by love," he said.

Haake looked after them. "They're very good-looking. The people here know all about that, don't they?" He ordered another fine. "May I offer you a drink?"

"Thanks, I'd rather stick to this one."

"They are supposed to have fantastic brothels here. Places with performances and that sort of thing." Haake's eyes glittered. They glittered as they had years ago in the stark light of the cellar.

I must not think of that, Ravic thought. Not now. "Have you ever been in one?" he asked.

"I have been in several. For observation, naturally. To see how low a people can sink. But surely not in the right ones. Of course I've got to be careful. It could be wrongly interpreted."

Ravic nodded. "You needn't be afraid of that. There are places where tourists never come."

"Do you know about them?"

"Of course. Quite a lot."

Haake drank his second fine. He became friendlier. The inhibitions he had had in Germany fell from him. Ravic felt that he was completely unsuspecting. "I intend to stroll about a bit tonight," he said to Haake.

"Indeed?"

"Yes. I do it now and then. One should learn everything one can."

"Right! Absolutely right!"

Haake stared straight at him for a moment. Get him drunk, Ravic thought. If it won't work any other way, get him drunk and drag him off somewhere.

Haake's expression had changed. He was not tipsy, he was only lost in thought. "It's a pity," he said finally. "I would have liked to come with you."

Ravic did not reply. He wanted to avoid anything that might make Haake suspicious.

"I must go back to Berlin tonight." Haake looked at his watch. "In an hour and a half."

Ravic sat there completely calm. I must go with him, he

thought. Surely he lives in a hotel. Not a private apartment. I must go with him to his room and catch him there.

"I'm just waiting here for two acquaintances of mine," Haake said. "Should be here any minute. They are traveling with me. My things are already at the station. We are going straight from here to the train."

I've lost, Ravic thought. Why haven't I a gun with me? Why did I, idiot that I am, come to believe in recent months that what happened before was an hallucination? I could shoot him on the street and try to escape through a subway entrance.

"It's a pity," Haake said. "But perhaps we can make it next time. I'll be back again in two weeks."

Ravic breathed again. "All right," he said.

"Where do you live? I could call you up then."

"In the Prince de Galles. Just across the street."

Haake took a notebook out of his pocket and put down the address. Ravic looked at the elegant covers of flexible red Russian leather. The pencil was a thin gold one. What must be in there, he thought. Probably information that will lead to torture and death.

Haake put his notebook back into his pocket. "Chic woman you were talking to before," he said.

Ravic had to think for a second. "Ah so—yes, very."

"In the movies?"

"Something of that sort."

"Good acquaintance?"

"Just that."

Haake looked straight ahead, meditatively. "That's the difficulty here—to make the acquaintance of someone nice. One doesn't have time enough and does not have the right opportunities—"

"That can be arranged," Ravic said.

"Really? You aren't interested?"

"In what?"

Haake laughed in embarrassment. "For instance, in the lady with whom you spoke?"

"Not in the least."

"Donnerwetter, that wouldn't be bad. Is she French?"

"Italian, I think. And a few other races mixed in."

Haake grinned. "Not bad. Naturally at home we can't have that. But here one is incognito, to some extent."

"Are you?" Ravic asked.

Haake was taken aback for a second. Then he grinned. "I understand! Of course not for those in the know—but otherwise, strictly incognito. Besides, it just occurs to me—have you any contact with refugees?"

"Very little," Ravic said carefully.

"That's a pity! We would like to have certain—you understand, information—we even pay for it—" Haake raised his hand "—naturally that's out of the question in your case! Nevertheless, the smallest item of news . . ."

Ravic noticed that Haake went on looking at him. "It's possible," he said. "You can never tell—it may happen sometime."

Haake moved his chair closer. "One of my tasks, you know. Connections from the inside to the outside. Sometimes it is difficult to get at them. We have good people working here." He raised his eyebrows meaningfully. "With us it is something else, of course. It's a matter of honor. It's the fatherland, isn't it?"

"Of course."

Haake looked up. "My acquaintances are arriving." He put a few notes on the china plate after he had added up the amount. "It's convenient that the prices are always on the saucers. We might initiate that at home." He stood up and extended his hand. "*Auf Wiedersehen, Herr von Horn.* I am very pleased to have met you. I'll call you in two weeks." He smiled. "Discretion, of course."

"Of course. Don't forget."

"I never forget anything. Not a face or an appointment. I can't afford to. That's my profession."

Ravic stood before him. He felt as if he would have to push his arm through a wall of cement. Then he felt Haake's hand in his. It was small and surprisingly soft.

He stood there undecided for another moment and followed Haake with his eyes. Then he sat down again. Suddenly he felt himself trembling. After a while he paid and left. He went in the direction in which Haake had gone. Then he recalled that he had seen him and the other two step into a taxi. There would have been no point in driving after them. Haake had already checked out of his hotel. If he had happened to see him again somewhere he would only become suspicious. He turned around and went to the International.

"You were being sensible," Morosow said. They were sitting in front of a café on the Rond Point.

Ravic looked at his right hand. He had washed it with alcohol a number of times. He had felt foolish for doing it, but he could not help it. Now his skin was dry as parchment.

"You would have been crazy if you had tried anything," Morosow said. "Good thing you were unarmed."

"Yes," Ravic replied without conviction.

Morosow looked at him. "You aren't such an idiot that you want to be tried for murder or for attempted murder?"

Ravic did not answer.

"Ravic—" Morosow put the bottle down hard on the table. "Don't be a fantast!"

"I am not. But can't you understand that it sickens me to have missed this opportunity? Two hours earlier and I could have dragged him off somewhere—or could have done something else—"

Morosow filled the two glasses. "Drink this! Vodka. You'll get him later."

"Or not."

"You'll get him. He'll come back. That sort of fellow comes back. You've hooked him thoroughly. *Prost!*"

Ravic emptied his glass.

"I could still go to the Gare du Nord. To see whether he leaves."

"Of course. You could also try to shoot him there. Twenty years in the penitentiary at least. Have you any more ideas like that?"

"Yes. I could watch to see whether he really leaves."

"And be seen by him and ruin everything."

"I should have asked him at which hotel he was staying."

"And make him suspicious." Morosow refilled their glasses. "Listen, Ravic. I know you're sitting here now and thinking you've done everything wrong. Get rid of it! Smash something to bits if you feel like it. Something big and not too expensive. The palm garden at the International, for all I care."

"No point in that."

"Then talk. Talk about it until you get sick of it. Talk it out of your system. Talk yourself calm. You aren't a Russian, otherwise you would understand that."

Ravic straightened up. "Boris," he said. "I know rats must be exterminated and one should not get into a biting match with them. But I can't talk about it. Instead of that I'll think about it. I'll think how I can do it. I'll prepare for it like an operation. As far as one can prepare for anything. I'll get used to it. I have two weeks' time. That's good. That's damned good. I can get used to being calm. You are right. One can talk things to death and so become calm and deliberate. But one can also think things to death coldly, purposefully. I'll kill so often in my thoughts that it will be like a habit when he returns. One acts more deliberately and calmly the thousandth time than the first time. And now let us talk. But about something else. About those roses there if you like! Look at them! They are like snow in this sultry night. Like white foam on the restless surf of the night. Are you satisfied now?''

"No," Morosow said.

Ravic remained silent.

"I'll be satisfied when we've talked about it a hundred times," Morosow said.

"All right. Take a good look at this summer. The Summer of 1939. It smells of sulphur. The roses look like snow on a mass grave in the coming winter. We are a gay people in spite of it, aren't we? Long live the century of nonintervention! Of the petrifaction of moral instincts! There is much killing going on tonight, Boris. Every night! Much killing! Cities are burning, dying Jews are wailing somewhere, Czechs are perishing miserably in the woods, Chinese are burning in Japanese gasoline, the whip-death is creeping through concentration camps—are we going to be sentimental women when it comes to eliminating a murderer? We'll find and exterminate him, that's all, as we have had to do often enough with innocent people who only differed from us in the uniforms they wore—"

"All right," Morosow said. "Or rather better. Have you ever learned what can be done with a knife? A knife makes no sound."

"Don't bother me with that tonight. I must sleep somehow. The devil knows whether I'll be able to, in spite of my faking of being so calm. Can you understand that?"

"Yes."

"Tonight I'll kill and kill. In two weeks I'll be an automaton. The problem is how I can get through that time. Through the time until I can first sleep. Getting drunk won't help. Neither would an injection. I must fall asleep exhausted. Then it will be all right next day. You understand?"

Morosow sat in silence for a while. "Get yourself a woman," he said then.

"How could that help?"

"It can. It's always good to sleep with a woman. Call up Joan. She'll come."

Joan. Yes, she had been with him before. She had been talking about something. He had forgotten it. "I am not a Russian," Ravic said. "Any other proposals?"

"Simple ones. Only the most simple ones."

"That was no simple one."

"Good God! Don't be complicated! The simplest way to tear oneself away from a woman is to sleep with her again occasionally. Not to let your fantasy run wild with you. Who wants to dramatize a natural act?"

"Yes," Ravic said. "Who wants to?"

"Then let me telephone," Morosow interrupted him. "I'll get you something. I'm not a doorman for nothing."

"Stay here. It's all right this way. Let us drink and look at the roses. Dead faces in the full moonlight after machine-gun fire can look just as white as that. Once I saw that in Spain. Heaven is an invention of the Fascists, the metalworker Pablo Nonas said at that time. He had only one leg. He became somewhat embittered against me because I had not preserved his other leg in alcohol. He felt as though one-fourth of him had been buried. He did not know that the dogs had stolen and eaten it—"

Chapter 25

VEBER CAME into the dressing-supply room. He motioned to Ravic. They went out. "Durant is on the telephone. He wants you to drive over immediately. Something about a special case and particular circumstances."

Ravic looked at him. "That means he's bungled an operation and wants to pin the responsibility on me, eh?"

"I don't think so. He's very excited. Apparently he doesn't know what to do."

Ravic shook his head. Veber remained silent. "How does he happen to know that I am back?" Ravic asked.

Veber shrugged his shoulders. "I've no idea. Very likely through one of the nurses."

"Why doesn't he call up Binot? Binot is very capable."

"I told him that. He explained to me that this is a particularly complicated case. In your special field."

"Nonsense. There are very efficient doctors in Paris for every special field. Why doesn't he call up Marteau? He's one of the best surgeons in the world."

"Can't you imagine why?"

"Naturally. He doesn't want to disgrace himself in front of his colleagues. It is different with an illegal refugee doctor. He must keep his mouth shut."

Veber looked at him. "It is urgent. Will you go?"

Ravic tore open the strings of his gown. "Of course," he said. "What else can I do? But only if you come with me."

"All right. We can take my car."

They went downstairs. Veber's car stood glittering in the sun in front of the hospital. They got in. "I'll work only if you are present," Ravic said. "God knows otherwise this fellow might try to trap me."

"I don't believe he's thinking of anything like that just now."

The car started. "I've seen all kinds of things happen,"

Ravic said. "I knew a young assistant doctor in Berlin who had everything to make him a good surgeon. His professor was operating; half drunk; made a wrong incision; said nothing; let the assistant doctor take over; he did not notice anything; half a minute later the professor made a scene; held the young doctor responsible for the wrong incision. The patient died during the operation. The young doctor a day later. Suicide. The professor went on operating and drinking."

They were stopped at the Avenue Marceau; a line of trucks was rattling along the Rue Galilée. The hot sun shone through the window. Veber pushed a button on the dashboard. The top of the car moved slowly backward. He looked proudly at Ravic. "I had it put in recently. Automatic. It's magnificent what people can think of, isn't it?"

The wind blew through the open top. Ravic nodded. "Yes, magnificent. The latest thing is magnetic mines and torpedoes. I read about them somewhere yesterday. When they miss their target they turn back in a curve until they find it. We are a fabulously constructive race."

Veber turned his red face toward him. He beamed good nature. "You, with your war, Ravic! We are as far away from that as from the moon. All this talk about it is nothing but pressure politics, nothing else, believe me—"

The skin was bluish mother-of-pearl. The face was ashen. Around it, flaming in the white glare of the operating lights, a wealth of golden-red hair. It flamed around the ash-colored face with such intensity that it seemed almost indecent. It was the only thing alive, sparklingly alive, noisily alive—as if life had already left the body and was now clinging only to the hair.

The young woman lying there was very beautiful. Slim, tall, with a face that even the shadows of deep unconsciousness could not mar—a woman made for luxury and love.

The woman was bleeding only a little. Too little. "You opened the uterus?" Ravic said to Durant.

"Yes."

"And?"

Durant did not answer. Ravic looked up. Durant stared at him.

"All right," Ravic said. "We don't need the nurses just now. We are three doctors, that's sufficient."

Durant motioned and nodded. The nurses and the assistant doctor retired.

"And?" Ravic asked after they had gone.

"That you can see for yourself," Durant replied.

"No."

Ravic saw; but he wanted Durant to say it in front of Veber. It was safer.

"Pregnancy in the third month. Hemorrhages. Necessity to curette. A curettage. Apparent injury to the inner wall."

"Apparent?"

"You can see it yourself. All right then, injury to the inner wall."

"And?" Ravic continued to ask.

He looked at Durant's face. It was full of impotent hatred. He will always hate me for this, he thought. Particularly because Veber is listening.

"Perforation," Durant said.

"With the curette?"

"Naturally," Durant said after a while. "With what else?"

The hemorrhage had ceased completely. Ravic continued his examination in silence. Then he straightened up. "You perforated. You did not notice it. In doing so you dragged a coil of the intestine through the opening. You did not recognize what it was. Apparently you took it for a piece of fetal membrane. You scraped it. You injured it. Is that correct?"

Suddenly Durant's forehead was covered with sweat. The beard behind the mask worked as if he were chewing too big a mouthful.

"It could be."

"How long have you been working?"

"Altogether three-quarters of an hour before you came."

"Internal hemorrhage. Injury to the small intestine. Most acute danger of sepsis. Intestine must be sewn, uterus removed. Immediately."

"What?" Durant asked.

"You know that yourself," Ravic said.

Durant's eyes fluttered. "Yes, I know. I did not get you to tell me this."

"That's all I can do. Call your people in and go on working. I advise you to do it quickly."

Durant chewed. "I'm too much upset. Will you perform the operation for me?"

"No. As you know I'm illegally in France and have no right to perform operations."

"You—" Durant began and fell silent.

Menials, students who have not yet completed their studies, masseurs, assistants, here all these claim to have been great medical men in Germany—Ravic had not forgotten what Durant had said to Leval. "Monsieur Leval explained it to me," he said. "Before my deportation."

He saw Veber raise his head. Durant did not reply. "Doctor Veber can perform the operation for you," Ravic said.

"You've operated for me often enough. If the price—"

"The price makes no difference. I'm not operating any more since my return. Especially not on patients who have not given their consent for this kind of operation."

Durant stared at him. "You can't get the patient out of the anesthetic to ask her now."

"Yes you can. But you risk sepsis."

Durant's face was wet. Veber looked at Ravic. Ravic nodded. "Are your nurses reliable?" Veber asked Durant.

"Yes—"

"We won't need the assistant," Veber said to Ravic. "We are three doctors and two nurses."

"Ravic—" Durant grew silent.

"You should have called Binot," Ravic declared. "Or Mallon. Or Martel. All first-rate surgeons."

Durant did not answer.

"Will you declare in the presence of Veber that you made a perforation and that you injured a coil of the intestine which you mistook for a fetal membrane?"

It took some time. "Yes," Durant said then in a hoarse tone.

"Will you also declare that you asked Veber to perform a hysterectomy and an anastomosis with me as his assistant because I happened to be present?"

"Yes."

"Will you take full responsibility for the operation and its results, as well as for the fact that the patient was not informed about it and had not given her consent?"

"Yes, of course," Durant croaked.

"All right. Call the nurses. We don't need your assistant. Explain to him that you gave Veber and me permission to assist you in a complicated special case. An old promise you had given us, or something like it. You may take over the

304

anesthesia yourself. Is it necessary for the sterile nurses to prepare themselves again?"

"It's not necessary. The adjoining room is sterile."

"All the better."

The abdominal cavity lay open. Slowly and with utmost care Ravic drew the coil of the intestine out of the hole in the uterus and wrapped it, bit by bit, in sterile dressings to keep it away from the peritoneum till the injured spot was free. Then he completely covered the uterus with dressings. "Extrauterine, ectopic pregnancy," he murmured in Veber's direction. "See this—half in the uterus, half in the tube. One can't even blame him too much. A rather rare case. Nevertheless—"

"What?" Durant asked from behind the shield at the head of the table. "What did you say?"

"Nothing."

Ravic cut open the intestine and made the resection. Then he quickly began to sew the open ends. Side to side he opened the outer layers again, turned them, and sewed them together on the other side.

He felt the intensity of the operation. He forgot Durant. He tied off the tube and the blood supply and cut off the end of the tube. Then he began to remove the uterus. Why doesn't this bleed much more? he thought. Why doesn't something like this bleed more than the heart? When one cuts out the miracle of life and the ability to pass it on.

The beautiful person lying here was dead. She could live on, but she was dead. A dead branch on the tree of the generations. In bloom, but without the secret of the fruit. Out of woods that had since become coal, huge apelike men had fought their way through thousands of generations, Egyptians had built temples, Hellas had flourished; mysteriously the blood had continued to run upward, finally to create this human being who now was barren as an empty ear of corn, and would not pass her blood on to a son or a daughter. The chain was broken through Durant's clumsy hand. But had not thousands of generations worked on Durant too, had not Hellas and the Renaissance bloomed to produce his musty pointed beard?

"Revolting," Ravic said.

"What?" Veber asked.

"All sorts of things."

Ravic straightened up. "Finished." He looked into the

305

lovely pale face with the radiant hair behind the anesthesia shield. He looked into the pail in which lay the blood-smeared thing that had made her face so beautiful. Then he looked at Durant. "Finished," he repeated.

Durant stopped the anesthesia. He did not look at Ravic. He waited for the nurses to push the cart outside. Then he followed them without saying anything.

"Tomorrow he'll explain to her that he saved her life," said Ravic. "And ask five thousand francs more."

"He doesn't look like it at the moment."

"A day is a long time. And repentance is short. Particularly when it can be turned into business."

Ravic washed. Through the window by the white wash-stand opposite him he saw a window sill on which there were red geraniums in bloom. A gray cat was sitting under the blossoms.

He called up Durant's hospital at one o'clock that night. He telephoned from the Scheherazade. The night nurse told him that the woman was sleeping. She had become restless two hours before. Veber had been there and had given her a light sedative. Everything seemed in order.

Ravic opened the telephone booth. A strong scent of perfume struck him. A woman with bleached yellow hair rustled proudly and challengingly into the ladies' room. The hair of the woman in the hospital had been a genuine blond. Radiant reddish-blond! He lit a cigarette and went back into the Scheherazade. The eternal Russian chorus was singing the eternal "Dark Eyes." Tragedy for twenty long years ran the risk of being ridiculous, Ravic thought. Tragedy had to be short.

"Sorry," he said to Kate Hegstroem, "but I had to telephone."

"Is everything all right?"

"So far it is."

Why does she ask? he thought, irritated. With her everything is certainly not all right. "Have you what you want here?" He pointed at the carafe of vodka.

"No."

"No?"

Kate Hegstroem shook her head.

"It's the summer," Ravic said. "One shouldn't sit in night clubs in summer. In summer one should sit on the street.

306

Near a tree, however consumptive, with an iron fence around it if need be."

He glanced up and looked into Joan's eyes. She must have come in while he had been telephoning. Earlier she had not been there. She was sitting in the opposite corner.

"Do you want to go somewhere else?" he asked Kate Hegstroem.

She shook her head. "No, do you? To some consumptive tree?"

"At such places the vodka is usually consumptive too. This one is good."

The chorus stopped singing and the music changed. The orchestra began a blues. Joan rose and went to the dance floor. Ravic could not see her very well. Nor with whom she was. Only every time the spotlight brushed the dance floor with a pale blue, she emerged into the light and then disappeared again in the half-dark.

"Did you perform an operation today?" Kate Hegstroem asked.

"Yes—"

"What's it like to sit in a night club afterward in the evening? Is it as if you had returned to a city from a battle? Or from sickness to life?"

"Not always. Sometimes you are simply empty."

Joan's eyes were translucent in the pale beam of light. She was looking toward him. It is not the heart that stirs, Ravic thought. It's the stomach. A shock in the solar plexus. Thousands of poems have been written about it. And this shock does not come from you, you slightly perspiring, beautiful, dancing piece of flesh—it comes out of the dark rooms of my brain—it's only an accidental, loose contact that makes it sharper whenever you glide through that streak of light.

"Isn't that the woman who used to sing here?" Kate Hegstroem asked.

"Yes."

"Doesn't she sing here any more?"

"I don't think so."

"She's beautiful."

"Is she?"

"Yes. She's even more than beautiful. That's a face in which life is written for all to see."

"Maybe."

Kate Hegstroem studied Ravic from the corners of her

narrowed eyes. She smiled. It was a smile that might have ended in tears. "Give me another glass of vodka and let us go," she said.

Ravic felt Joan's eyes as he got up. He took Kate's arm. It was not necessary; she could have walked alone; but he felt it would do no harm for Joan to see it.

"Will you do me a favor?" Kate Hegstroem asked when they were in her room in the Hôtel Lancaster.

"Certainly, Kate," Ravic replied, preoccupied. "If I can."

"Will you come with me to the Monfort ball?"

He looked up. "What's that? I've never heard of it before."

She took a seat on a chair by the imitation fireplace. The chair seemed much too big for her. She looked very fragile in it, like a Chinese dancing-figure. The skin on her cheeks was tauter than ever. "The Monfort ball is the great social event of the summer in Paris," she said. "It takes place next Friday in Louis Monfort's house and garden. That means nothing to you, does it?"

"Nothing."

"Will you go with me?"

"Can I in that case?"

"I'll get you an invitation."

Ravic looked at her. "Why, Kate?"

"I'd like to go. And I don't want to go alone."

"Would you have to, otherwise?"

"I would. I don't want to go with any of the people I used to know. I can't stand them any more. Do you understand?"

"Yes."

She smiled. Even her smile was no longer the same, Ravic thought. It was like a thin glittering net under which the face hardly changed. "It is the last and finest garden party every summer in Paris," she said. "I have been there every time for the last four years. Will you do it as a favor to me?"

Ravic knew why she wanted to go with him. She would feel safer. He could not refuse.

"All right, Kate," he said. "You don't need to have them send me a special invitation. If they know someone is coming with you, that will suffice, I assume."

She nodded. "Of course. Thank you, Ravic. I'll call up Sophie Monfort tomorrow."

He got up. "Then I'll call for you on Friday. How will you dress?"

She looked up at him. The light was sharply reflected from her tightly combed hair. The head of a lizard, Ravic thought. The slim, dry, firm elegance of fleshless perfection which health can never achieve. "That's what I've not yet told you," she said after some hesitation. "It's a costume ball, Ravic. A garden festival at the court of Louis XIV."

"Great God!" Ravic sat down again.

Kate Hegstroem laughed. Suddenly it was completely free childlike laughter. "Over there is some good old cognac," she said. "Do you need a drink?"

Ravic shook his head. "What people can think up!"

"Every year they have something similar."

"That means I have to—"

"I'll take care of everything," she quickly interrupted him. "You don't have to bother about anything. I'll get you your costume. Something simple. You don't even have to try it on. Just give me your size."

"I believe I do need some cognac," Ravic said.

Kate Hegstroem pushed the bottle toward him. "Don't say no now."

He drank the cognac. Twelve more days, he thought. Twelve days until Haake would be back in Paris. Twelve days which had to be got through. Twelve days, his life had no more than twelve days, nor could he think beyond them. Twelve days, beyond them yawned an abyss. It made no difference how he killed the time. A costume festival—after all what was grotesque in these two weeks of uncertainty?

"All right, Kate."

He went again to Durant's hospital. The woman with the red-golden hair was sleeping. Thick beads of perspiration stood on her forehead. Her face had color and her mouth was slightly opened. "Fever?" he asked the nurse.

"One hundred."

"Good." He bent closer over the moist face. He could feel her breath. There was no longer ether in it. It was a breath, fresh as thyme. Thyme, he remembered—a mountain meadow in the Black Forest, creeping, breathless under a hot sun, somewhere below the shouting of his pursuers—and the intoxicating scent of thyme. Strange, how one forgot everything, only not the smells. Twenty years from now its smell would still snatch out of the dusty corners of his memory the vision of that day of his escape in the Black Forest. Not in twenty years, he thought—in twelve days.

He walked through the hot city to his hotel. It was almost three o'clock. He climbed up the staircase. A white envelope was lying in front of his door. He picked it up. It bore his name, but it had no stamp on it, nor any postmark. Joan, he thought, and opened it. A check dropped out. It was from Durant. Ravic looked at the figure indifferently. Then he looked at it again. He couldn't believe it. It was not the usual two hundred francs. It was two thousand. He must have been damned scared, he thought. Two thousand francs, voluntarily from Durant—that was the eighth wonder of the world.

He put the check into his wallet and placed a pile of books on the table by his bed. He had bought them two days before in order to have something to read in case he was not able to sleep. It was a strange thing about books—they were becoming more and more important to him. They were not a substitute for everything, but they reached into a sphere where nothing else could reach. In the first years he had not touched any books; they had been lifeless in comparison with what had happened. But now they had become a wall; if they did not protect, at least one could lean against them. They did not help much; but they kept one from final despair in a time that was racing back into darkness. That was enough. Once thoughts had been thought that were despised and ridiculed today; but they had been thought and they would remain alive and that was enough. Before he could begin to read, the telephone rang. He did not lift the receiver. It rang for a long time. A few minutes later when it was silent again he lifted the receiver and asked the concierge who had called. "She did not mention her name," the man declared. Ravic could hear that he was eating.

"Was it a woman?"

"Yes."

"With an accent?"

"That I don't know." The man continued to eat. Ravic called up Veber's hospital. No one had called him from there. Nor from Durant's hospital. He called the Hôtel Lancaster as well. He was told by the switchboard girl that no one had called his number from there. So it must have been Joan. Probably she had telephoned from the Scheherazade.

After an hour the telephone rang again. Ravic put his book aside. He rose and went to the window. He propped up his elbows on the window sill and waited. The soft wind brought up the scent of lilies. The refugee Wiesenhoff had replaced the withered carnations in front of his window with them. Now the house smelled like a funeral chapel or a cloister garden on warm nights. Ravic did not know whether Wiesenhoff had done it as an act of piety for old Goldberg, or merely because lilies grew well in wooden boxes. The telephone was silent. Tonight perhaps I'll sleep, he thought, and went back to bed.

Joan came while he was asleep. She turned on the ceiling light at once and remained standing in the doorway. He opened his eyes. "Are you alone?" she asked.

"No. Turn off the light and go."

She hesitated for a moment. Then she went to the bathroom and opened the door. "A fraud," she said and smiled.

"Go to the devil. I'm tired."

"Tired? What from?"

"Tired. Adieu."

She came closer. "You've just come home. I've called up every ten minutes."

She glanced at him. He did not say that she was lying. She had changed her dress. She has slept with that fellow, sent him home, and now she has come to surprise me and to show Kate Hegstroem, whom she believed to be here, that I am a damned whoremaster on whom women drop in at night and whom one had better avoid, he thought. He smiled against his will. Perfect action unfortunately compelled his admiration, even when it was directed against himself.

"Why are you laughing?" Joan asked sharply.

"I'm laughing. That's all. Turn out the light. You look ghastly in it. And go."

She paid no attention. "Who was the whore you were with?"

Ravic half straightened up. "Get out of here or I'll throw something at you."

"Oh I see." She studied him. "So that's it! It has gone that far—"

Ravic reached for a cigarette. "Don't make yourself ridiculous. You are living with another man and here you put on an act as if you were jealous. Go back to your actor and leave me alone!"

"That's something entirely different."

"Of course."

"Of course it is something different!" she burst out suddenly. "You know very well it is something different. It is something for which I am not responsible. I'm not happy about it. It has happened, I don't know how—"

"It always happens, one doesn't know how—"

She stared at him. "You—you were so sure all the time. You were so smug it drove one crazy! There was nothing that could make you lose your self-assurance! I hated your superiority! How often I hated it! I need enthusiasm! I need someone who is mad about me! I need someone who cannot live without me! You can live without me. You always could! You did not need me. You are cold! You are empty! You don't know anything about love! You were never altogether with me! I told you a lie before when I said it happened this way because you were gone for two months! It would have happened this way even if you had stayed! Don't laugh! I know the difference, I know all about it, I know that the other one is not intelligent and not like you, but he gives himself to me, nothing except me is important to him, he doesn't think of anything except me and doesn't want anything except me and doesn't know anything except me, and that's what I need!"

She stood before his bed, breathing heavily. Ravic reached for a bottle of calvados. "Then why are you here?" he asked.

She did not answer at once. "You know," she said then in a low voice. "Why do you ask?"

He filled a glass and held it out to her. "I don't want to drink," she declared. "What woman was that?"

"A patient." Ravic was not in the mood to lie. "A woman who is very sick."

"That's not true. Find a better lie. A sick woman is in the hospital. Not in a night club."

Ravic put back the glass. Truth often seemed so improbable. "It is true," he said.

"Do you love her?"

"What does that matter to you?"

"Do you love her?"

"What does it really matter to you, Joan?"

"It does! As long as you do not love anyone—" She hesitated.

"You called the woman a whore before. How could there be any question of love?"

"I only said that. I could see right away that she wasn't. That's why I said it. I wouldn't have come because of a whore. Do you love her?"

"Turn off the light and go."

She came closer. "I knew it. I saw it."

"Go to hell," Ravic said. "I'm tired. Go to hell with your cheap charade which you think is something that has never happened before—one man for intoxication, sudden love, or your career—and the other whom you declare you love more deeply and differently, as a haven for the times between, if that ass puts up with it. Go to hell; you have too many kinds of love."

"It isn't true, not the way you put it. It's different. It's not true. I want to come back to you. I'm going to come back to you."

Ravic refilled his glass. "It's possible that you would like to. But it is only an illusion. An illusion which you have produced to make things easier for yourself. You will never come back."

"I will!"

"No. At best for a short while. Then someone else would come along again who doesn't want anything but you, only you, and it would go on this way. A wonderful future for me."

"No, no! I'll stay with you."

Ravic laughed. "Joan," he said almost tenderly, "you won't stay with me. One can't lock up the wind. Nor the water. If one does, they spoil. Imprisoned wind becomes stale air. You are not made to stay anywhere."

"Neither are you."

"I?" Ravic emptied his glass. The woman with the red-golden hair at morning; then Kate Hegstroem with death in her belly and her skin like brittle silk; and now this one, inconsiderate, filled with greed for life, still alien to herself and yet more familiar with herself than any man could ever be, naïve and shrewd, faithful in a strange sense and as faithless as her mother, Nature, drifting and being driven, waiting to hold fast and leaving at the same time—"I?" Ravic repeated. "What do you know about me? What do you know about love that comes into a life in which everything has become questionable? What is your cheap intoxication compared to that? When falling and falling suddenly changes, when the endless Why becomes the final You, when like a

313

fata morgana above the desert of silence feeling suddenly arises, takes shape, and inexorably the delusion of the blood becomes a landscape compared with which all dreams are pale and commonplace? A landscape of silver, a city of filigree and rose quartz, shining like the bright reflection of blooming blood—what do you know about it? Do you think that one can talk about it so easily? That a glib tongue can quickly press it into a cliché of words or even of feelings? What do you know about graves that open and how one stands in dread of the many colorless empty nights of yesterday—yet they open and no skeletons now lie bleaching there, only earth is there, earth, fertile seeds, and already the first green. What do you know about that? You love the intoxication, the conquest, the Other You that wants to die in you and that will never die, you love the stormy deceit of the blood, but your heart will remain empty—because one cannot keep anything that does not grow from within oneself. And not much can grow in a storm. It is in the empty nights of loneliness that it grows, if one does not despair. What do you know about it?" He had spoken slowly, without looking at Joan, as though he had forgotten her. Now he looked at her. "What am I talking about?" he said. "Old stupid things. I've drunk too much today. Come, have a drink too, and then go."

She sat down on the bed and took the glass. "I have understood," she said. Her face had changed. Like a mirror, he thought. Time and again it reflected whatever one held before it. Now it was composed and beautiful. "I understood," she said. "And sometimes I have felt the same way. But Ravic, you have often forgotten me for your love of love and of life. I was a point of departure; and then you went into your cities of silver and you thought very little about me any more."

He looked at her for a long time. "Maybe," he said.

"You were occupied with yourself so much, you discovered so much in yourself that I remained on the fringes of your life."

"Maybe. But you are not the person on whom to build, Joan. You know that, too."

"Did you want to build?"

"No," Ravic said after some deliberation. Then he smiled. "When you are a refugee from everything that is permanent, you get into strange situations sometimes. And you do strange more, the spark of eternity! for whom am I saving myself? for what cheerless thing? for what dark uncertainty? Buried, lost, my life has only twelve more days, twelve days and behind it is nothing, twelve days and this one night, shining skin, why did you come on this night, torn from the stars and floating, clouded by old dreams, why did you break through the forts and barricades of this night in which no one is alive but us? "Joan," he said.

She turned. Her face was suddenly transfused by a wild breathless radiance. She let her things fall and rushed toward him.

Chapter 26

THE CAR STOPPED at the corner of the Rue Vaugirard. "What's the matter?" Ravic asked.

"A parade of demonstrators." The driver did not look back. "Communists, this time."

Ravic looked at Kate Hegstroem. Small and frail, she sat in her corner in the costume of a lady-in-waiting at the court of Louis XIV. Her face was heavily powdered. In spite of that it gave an impression of pallor. The bones stood out at the temples and cheeks.

"Not bad," he said. "July, 1939, a Fascist demonstration by the Croix de Feu five minutes ago, now one by the Communists—and we two in costumes of the great seventeenth century. Not bad, Kate."

"It doesn't matter." She smiled.

Ravic looked down at his escarpins. The irony of the situation was great. He didn't have to add the reflection that any policeman might arrest him.

"Shall I try another street?" Kate Hegstroem's chauffeur asked.

"You can't turn now," Ravic said. "There are too many cars behind us."

The demonstrators walked quietly through the street at right angles to theirs. They carried banners and placards. Nobody sang. A great number of policemen escorted the procession. At the corner of the Rue Vaugirard, unnoticed, stood another group of policemen. They had bicycles with them. One of them was patrolling the street. He looked into Kate Hegstroem's car. Without altering his expression he moved on.

Kate Hegstroem saw Ravic's look. "He isn't surprised," she said. "He knows. The police know everything. The ball at the Monfort's is the event of the summer. The house and garden will be surrounded by police."

"That puts me completely at ease."

Kate Hegstroem smiled. She knew nothing of Ravic's situation. "That many jewels won't be assembled very soon again in Paris. Real costumes with real jewels. The police won't take any chances. There will be some detectives among the guests too."

"In costume?"

"Possibly. Why?"

"It's just as well to know. I planned to steal the Rothschild emeralds."

Kate Hegstroem screwed the window down. "It bores you, I know. But that won't help you this time."

"It doesn't bore me, Kate. On the contrary. I wouldn't have known what else to do. Will there be enough to drink?"

"I think so. But I can give the head butler a hint. I know him fairly well."

One could hear the footsteps of the demonstrators on the pavement. They were not marching. They walked in disorder. It sounded as if a tired herd was passing by.

"Which century would you like to live in, Ravic, if you could choose?"

"In this one. Otherwise I'd be dead and some idiot would be wearing my costume to this party."

"I don't mean that. I mean, in which would you like to live your life over again."

Ravic looked at the sleeve of his costume. "Just the same," he said. "In ours. It is the lousiest, bloodiest, most corrupt, colorless, cowardly, and dirty so far—but nevertheless."

"I wouldn't." Kate Hegstroem pressed her hands together as if chilled. The soft brocade glittered at her slim wrists. "In this one," she said. "In the seventeenth. Or in an earlier one. In any—only not in ours. I have known this for only a few months. I never thought about it before." She pulled the window all the way down. "How hot it is! And how humid! Isn't the demonstration over yet?"

"Yes, that's the end coming over there."

A shot was fired; it came from the direction of the Rue Cambronne. The next moment the policemen at the corner were on their bicycles. A woman screamed. The crowd answered with a sudden rumbling. People were beginning to run. The policemen stepped on their pedals and rode into the crowd, swinging their clubs.

"What was that?" Kate Hegstroem asked, frightened.

"Nothing. A tire bursting."

The chauffeur turned around. His face had changed. "That—"

"Drive on," Ravic interrupted him. "You can get through now."

The intersection was free as if a gust had swept it bare. "Go on!" Ravic said.

Screams came from the Rue Cambronne. A second shot was fired. The chauffeur drove on.

They were standing on the terrace overlooking the garden. Every place was filled with costumes by then. In the deep dusk of trees roses were in bloom. Candles protected by shades gave a warm flickering light. In a pavilion a small orchestra was playing a minuet. It all looked like a Watteau that had come to life.

"Lovely?" Kate Hegstroem asked.

"Yes."

"Really?"

"Yes, Kate. At least from a distance."

"Come. Let's walk through the garden."

Under the high old trees an unreal picture unfolded. The uncertain light on the many candles shimmered on silver and gold brocade, on precious faded blue and pink and sea-green velvets, its soft illumination fell on full-bottomed wigs and bare, powdered shoulders around which played the delicate glitter of violins. Couples and groups wandered slowly through the alleys, hilts sparkled, a fountain splashed, and the trimmed boxwood hedges formed a dark stylized background.

Ravic noticed that even the servants were in costumes. He took for granted then that the detectives would be too. It wouldn't be bad, he thought, to be arrested by Molière or Racine. Or by a court dwarf, for a change.

He looked up. A warm heavy raindrop had fallen on his hand. The red sky had darkened. "It's going to rain, Kate," he said.

"No. That's impossible. The garden—"

"It is! Come quickly!"

He took her arm and hurried her to the terrace. Hardly were they there when it began to pour. The water streamed down, the candles went out in their chimneys, after a few seconds the table decorations hung like colorless rags, and panic broke out. Marquises, duchesses, and ladies-in-waiting

320

hours. Outside, the rain was coming down heavy and straight. The buildings opposite looked as if they were behind the water-flooded window of a florist's shop.

The car rolled up. "Where do you want to go?" Ravic asked. "Back to your hotel?"

"Not yet. But we can't go anywhere else in these costumes. Let's drive around for a while."

"Good."

The car glided slowly through the Paris night. The rain beat upon the top and drowned out almost all other noises. The Arc de Triomphe emerged, gray in the silver downpour, and disappeared. The Champs Elysées with its lighted windows slipped by. The Rond Point smelled of flowers and freshness, a gay-colored wave amid the uproar. Wide as the ocean dawned the Place de la Concorde with its Tritons and sea monsters. The Rue de Rivoli swam closer, with its bright arcades, a fleeting glimpse of Venice, before the Louvre arose, gray and eternal, with its unending courtyard, all its windows dark. Then the quays, the bridges, swaying, unreal, in the gentle rain. Lighters, a towboat with a warm light, as comforting as if it concealed a thousand homes. The Seine, the boulevards, with busses, noise, people, and shops. The iron fences of the Luxembourg, the garden behind them like a poem by Rilke. The Cimetière Montparnasse, silent, forsaken. The narrow old streets, pushed close together, houses, silent squares surprisingly opening themselves, with trees, warped façades, churches, weather-worn monuments. Street lights flickering in the rain, pissoirs rising out of the earth like little forts, the side-streets of hotels where one could rent rooms by the hour, and in between the streets of the past, in pure rococo and baroque, the fronts of their buildings smiling down, shadowy doors as in the novels of Proust—

Kate Hegstroem sat in her corner and was silent. Ravic smoked. He saw the glow of the cigarette, but he did not taste its smoke. It was as if he were smoking an insubstantial cigarette in the dark of the car, and gradually everything seemed to become unreal—this ride, this soundless car in the rain, these streets passing by, in the corner this silent woman in her costume across which reflections flitted, these hands already marked by death and lying motionless on the brocade as if they would never move again—it was a ghostlike ride through a ghostlike Paris, strangely transfused by half-finished thoughts and an unuttered and meaningless farewell.

He thought of Haake. He tried to deliberate what he would do. He thought of the woman with the red-golden hair on whom he had operated. He thought of a rainy evening in Rothenburg ob der Tauber with a woman he had forgotten, of the Hotel Eisenhut, and of a violin out of an unknown window. He recalled Romberg who was shot in 1917 during a thunderstorm on a field of poppies in Flanders—a thunderstorm that in ghostlike fashion had roared into the machine-gun fire as though God had become tired of man and had begun to fire upon the earth. He thought of an accordion, wailing and bad and full of unbearable yearning, played by a member of the marine battalion in Houthoulst; Rome in the rain flashed through his mind, a wet road behind Rouen; the endless November rain on the roofs of the barracks in the concentration camp; dead Spanish peasants in whose open mouths water had gathered; Claire's moist clear face before she died; the way to the university at Heidelberg with the heavy scent of lilacs—a magic lantern of the past, an endless procession of pictures from the past, gliding by him like the streets outside, poison and comfort in one—

He put out his cigarette and straightened up. Enough. Who looked back too much could easily run into something or fall off a cliff.

Now the car was climbing up the streets of Montmartre. The rain ceased. Silver clouds floated across the sky, heavily and hastily, like pregnant mothers hurrying to give life to a bit of moon. Kate Hegstroem had the car stop. They got out and walked around the corner and up a few streets.

Suddenly Paris lay below them. Widespread, flickering, wet, Paris. With streets, squares, night clouds and moon, Paris. The wreath of the Boulevards, the pale shimmering of the slopes, towers, roofs, darkness thrust against the light, Paris. Wind from the horizons, the sparkling plain, bridges shaped of darkness and light, a downpour of rain far over the Seine fleeing out of sight, the innumerable lights of cars, Paris. Defiantly wrested from the night, a gigantic beehive of buzzing life, built over millions of evil sewers, blossom of light above its subterranean stench, cancer and Mona Lisa, Paris.

"Just a moment, Kate," Ravic said. "I'll get us something."

He went into the nearest bistro. A warm smell of fresh

blood-sausage and liver-sausage struck him. No one paid any attention to his costume. He got a bottle of cognac and two glasses. The innkeeper opened the bottle and lightly inserted the cork again.

Kate Hegstroem was standing outside just as he had left her. She was standing there in her costume, a slender figure against the troubled sky—as if she had been left behind by some other century and were not an American girl of Swedish descent from Boston.

"Here, Kate. The best protection against coolness, rain, and the clamor of too great quiet. Let us drink to the city down there."

"Yes." She took the glass. "It's good that we have driven up here, Ravic. It's better than all the parties in the world."

She emptied her glass. The moon fell on her shoulders and her dress and her face. "Cognac," she said. "A good one too."

"Right. As long as you recognize that, everything is in order."

"Give me another. And then let's drive down again and I'll change and you too and we'll go to the Scheherazade and I'll plunge into an orgy of sentimentality and feel sorry for myself and take leave of all the wonderful superficialities of life, and from tomorrow on I'll read philosophers, write my will, and behave as befits my condition."

Ravic met the proprietress on the staircase of the hotel. She stopped him. "Have you got a moment?"

"Of course."

She led him up to the second floor and opened a room with a passkey. Ravic saw that it was still occupied by someone.

"What does this mean?" he said. "Why are you breaking in here?"

"Rosenfeld lives here," she said. "He intends to move out."

"I don't want to change."

"He intends to move out and has not paid for the last three months."

"His belongings are still here. You can hold them."

The proprietress contemptuously kicked a shabby suitcase that stood open beside the bed. "What is there in it? This has no value. Vulcanized fiber. Shirts frayed. His suit—you can see that from here. He only has two. You wouldn't get even a hundred francs for the lot.''

Ravic shrugged his shoulders. "Did he say he intended to leave?"

"No. But you can see something like that. I told him so to his face. And he admitted it. I've made it clear to him that he must pay by tomorrow. I can't go on like this with tenants who don't pay.''

"All right. What have I got to do with it?''

"The paintings. They belong to him, too. He said they were valuable. He maintains he can pay much more than the rent with them. Now just look at that!''

Ravic had paid no attention to the walls. He glanced up. In front of him, over the bed, hung an Arles landscape by van Gogh in his best period. He took a step closer. There could be no doubt, the painting was genuine. "Abominable, eh?" the proprietress asked. "These are supposed to be trees, these crooked things! And just look at that!''

That was hanging over the washstand and was a Gauguin. A naked South Sea girl in front of a tropic landscape. "Those legs!'' the proprietress said. "Ankles like an elephant. And that dull face. Just look at the way she is standing there! And then he has another one that has not even been finished.''

The one that had not even been finished was a portrait of Madame Cézanne by Cézanne. "That mouth! Crooked. And there is color missing on the cheek. With these he wants to cheat me! You saw my pictures—those were pictures! True to nature and genuine and correct. The snow landscape with the deer in the *salle à manger*. But this trash—as if he had done it himself. Don't you think so?''

"Well, approximately.''

"That's what I wanted to know. You are an educated man and you understand these things. Not even frames are around them.''

The three paintings were hung without frames. They shone on the dirty wallpaper like windows into another world. "If only they had good gold frames! Then one could take them. But this! I see that I'll have to keep this trash and I'll be taken in again. That's what happens when you are kind!''

"I don't think you'll have to take the paintings,'' Ravic said.

"What else can I do?''

"Rosenfeld will get the money for you.''

"How?" She looked quickly at him. Her face changed. "Are these things worth something? Sometimes just such things are of value!" One could see the thoughts leap behind her yellow forehead. "I could take possession of one of them without more ado, just for the last month! Which do you think? The big one over the bed?"

"None at all. Wait until Rosenfeld gets back. I'm sure he'll come with the money."

"I'm not. I am a hotel owner."

"Then why did you wait so long? You don't usually."

"Promises! The things he promised me! You know how it is here."

Suddenly Rosenfeld stood at the door. Silent, short, and calm. Before the proprietress could say anything else he took some money out of his pocket. "Here—and here is my bill. Will you kindly mark it paid?"

The proprietress looked at the notes in surprise. Then she looked at the paintings. Then back at the money. There was much she wanted to say—but she could not utter it. "You get some change back," she finally declared.

"I know. Can you give it to me now?"

"Yes, all right. I don't have it here. The cashbox is downstairs. I'll change it."

She left as if she had been gravely insulted. Rosenfeld looked at Ravic. "I am sorry," Ravic said. "The old lady dragged me up here. I had no idea what she had in mind. She wanted to know about the value of your pictures."

"Did you tell her?"

"No."

"Good." Rosenfeld looked at Ravic with a strange smile.

"How can you have such paintings hanging here?" Ravic said. "Are they insured?"

"No. But paintings don't get stolen. At most once every twenty years out of a museum."

"This place might burn down."

Rosenfeld shrugged his shoulders. "One has to take the risk. The insurance is too expensive for me."

Ravic studied the van Gogh. It was worth at least a million francs. Rosenfeld followed his look.

"I know what you are thinking. Who has this should also have money to insure it. But I haven't, I'm living on my pictures. I'm slowly selling them. And I don't like to sell them."

Under the Cézanne a spirit-cooker stood on the table. Beside it a box of coffee, some bread, a pot of butter, and a few paper bags. The room was poor and small. But from its walls shone the splendor of the world.

"I can understand that," Ravic said.

"I thought I could manage all right," Rosenfeld said. "I've been able to pay for everything. The railway fare, the ship ticket, everything; only not these three months' rent. I've hardly eaten anything, but I couldn't manage it. The visa took too long. I had to sell a Monet tonight. A Vertheuil landscape. I thought I would be able to take it with me."

"Wouldn't you have been forced to sell it somewhere else just the same?"

"Yes. But for dollars. It would have brought twice as much."

"Are you going to America?"

Rosenfeld nodded. "It's time to get away from here."

Ravic looked at him. "The Bird of Death is leaving," Rosenfeld said.

"What Bird of Death?"

"Ah yes—Markus Meyer. We call him the Bird of Death. He knows by smell when one has to flee."

"Meyer?" Ravic said. "Is that the short bald-headed man who plays the piano in the Catacombs from time to time?"

"Yes. We have called him Bird of Death since Prague."

"A good name."

"He always smells it. Two months before Hitler, he left Germany. Vienna three months ahead of the Nazis. Prague six weeks before they marched in. I've stuck to him. Always. He smells it. That's how I have saved the paintings. One could no longer take money out of Germany. The mark was blocked. I had a million and a half in investments. I tried to liquidate it. Then the Nazis came and it was too late. Meyer was smarter. He smuggled part of his fortune out. I hadn't the nerve. And now he's going to America. So am I. It's a pity about the Monet."

"But you can take the rest of the money you got for it with you. There are no blocked francs as yet."

"Yes. But I could have lived on it longer if I had sold it over there. This way I'll probably have to sacrifice the Gauguin soon."

Rosenfeld fumbled with his spirit-cooker. "They're the last ones," he said. "Only these three more. I must live on them.

A job—I don't count on one. It would be a miracle. These three more. One less is a bit of life less."

He stood forlornly in front of his suitcase. "In Vienna— five years, it was not yet expensive. I could live cheaply; but it cost me two Renoirs and a Degas pastel. In Prague I lived on and ate up a Sisley and five drawings. No one wanted to give anything for drawings—there were two by Degas, a crayon by Renoir, and two sepias by Delacroix. In America I could have lived longer on them a whole year. You see," he said sadly, "now I've only these three paintings left. Yester-day there were still four. This visa has cost me at least two years' living. If not three."

"There are many people who have no paintings to live on."

Rosenfeld shrugged his skinny shoulders. "That's no comfort."

"No," Ravic said. "That's true."

"They must get me through the war. And this war will last a long time."

Ravic did not answer. "The Bird of Death says so," Rosenfeld said. "And he is not even sure that America will remain safe."

"Where would he go then?" Ravic asked. "There is not much left now."

"He does not yet know exactly. He is thinking of Haiti. He doesn't believe a Negro republic would go to war."

Rosenfeld was entirely serious. "Or Honduras. A small South American republic. San Salvador. Perhaps New Zea-land too."

"New Zealand? That's pretty far away, isn't it?"

"Far?" Rosenfeld said, smiling sadly. "From where?"

Chapter 27

A SEA. A SEA of thundering darkness beating against his ears. Then a shrill ringing through the corridors, a ship marked for destruction, the ringing—and night, the familiar pale window intruding into the ebb of sleep, still the ringing—telephone.

Ravic lifted the receiver. "Hello—"

"Ravic—"

"What's the matter? Who is it?"

"I. Don't you recognize me?"

"Yes. Now. What's the matter?"

"You must come! Quick! Right away!"

"What's the matter?"

"Come, Ravic! Something has happened."

"What has happened?"

"Something has happened. I'm scared! Come! Come immediately! Help me! Ravic! Come!"

The telephone clicked. Ravic waited. The open-line signal buzzed. Joan had hung up. He put the receiver back and stared into the pallid night. Drugged sleep still hung heavy behind his forehead. Haake, first he had thought it was. Haake—until he had recognized the window and become aware that he was in the International, not in the Prince de Galles. He looked at his watch. The phosphorescent hands stood at four-twenty. Suddenly he jumped out of bed. Joan had said something on the evening when he had encountered Haake—something about danger, fear. If—anything was possible. He had seen the strangest things happen. He hurriedly packed up the most necessary implements and dressed.

He found a taxi at the next corner. The driver had a small griffon with him. The dog lay around the man's neck like a fur collar. It swayed when the taxi swayed. It drove Ravic mad. He would have liked to throw the dog onto the seat. But he knew Parisian taxi drivers.

The car rattled through the warm July night. A faint scent

of shyly breathing foliage. Blossoms, somewhere linden trees, shadows, a star-studded jasmine sky, in between an aeroplane with intermittent red and green lights like a sinister and threatening beetle among glowworms, colorless streets, buzzing emptiness, the singing of two drunks, and accordion playing in a basement, and suddenly hesitation and fear and driving, rending haste; perhaps too late—

The house. Lukewarm drowsy darkness. The elevator came creeping down. Creeping, a slow, lighted insect. Ravic had already reached the first landing when he changed his mind and turned back. The elevator was faster however slow it was.

These toy elevators of Paris! Flimsy prisons, creaking, coughing, open at the top, open at the sides, nothing but a bottom with a few iron grills, one bulb burnt out, gloomily flickering, the other one loosely screwed in—finally the top floor. He pushed the gate open, rang the bell.

Joan opened. He stared at her. No blood—her face normal, nothing. "What's the matter?" he said. "Where is—"

"Ravic. You came!"

"Where is—have you done something?"

She stepped back. He took a few steps. Looked around the room. No one there. "Where? In the bedroom?"

"What?" she asked.

"Is anyone in the bedroom? Is anyone with you?"

"No. Why?"

He looked at her. "But I wouldn't have anyone with me when you were coming," she said.

He was still looking at her. There she stood healthy and smiling at him. "How do you get such ideas?" Her smile deepened. "Ravic," she said and he realized, as if a hailstorm were beating against his face, that she thought he was jealous and was enjoying it. The bag with the instruments suddenly weighed a ton in his hands. He put it on a chair. "You damned cheat," he said.

"What? What has got into you?"

"You damned cheat," he repeated. "And ass that I am to fall for it."

He picked up his bag and turned toward the door. She was immediately at his side. "What are you going to do? Don't go! You can't leave me alone! I don't know what may happen if you leave me alone!"

"Liar!" he said. "Miserable liar! It doesn't matter that you are lying, but that you can do it so cheaply is disgusting. This isn't something to play with!"

She pushed him away from the door. "But why don't you look around? Something has happened! You can see for yourself! Look what he did in his rage! And I'm afraid he'll come back! You don't know what he can do."

A chair was lying on the floor. A lamp. Some pieces of broken glass. "Put on your shoes when you walk around," Ravic said, "so as not to cut yourself. That's all the advice I can give you."

Among the pieces of glass lay a photograph. He pushed the glass aside with his foot and picked up the picture. "Here—" He threw it on the table. "And now leave me in peace."

She stood before him. She looked at him. Her face had changed. "Ravic," she said in a low, restrained voice. "I don't care what you call me. I have lied often. And I'll continue to lie. All of you want it." She pushed the photograph aside. It slid across the table and dropped in such a way that Ravic could see it. It was not the picture of the man whom he had seen with Joan in the Cloche d'Or.

"Everyone wants it," she said, full of contempt. "Don't lie, don't lie! Only speak the truth! And when one does they—can't stand it. None of them! But I didn't often lie to you. Not to you. With you I didn't want to—"

"All right," Ravic said. "We don't have to go into that." Suddenly he was moved in a strange way. Something had touched him. He got angry. He did not want to be touched any more.

"No. With you it wasn't necessary," she said and looked at him almost beseechingly.

"Joan—"

"And I'm not lying now either. I'm not lying, not entirely, Ravic. I called you up because I was really afraid. Luckily I got him out the door. I locked it and he yelled and raged outside—so I called you up. It was the first thing that entered my mind. Is that so wrong?"

"You were damned calm and untroubled when I came."

"Because he was gone. And because I thought you would come to help me."

"All right. Then everything is in order now and I can leave."

"He'll come again. He shouted he would come again. He is sitting somewhere now and drinking. I know that. And

when he comes back drunk, then he isn't as you are—he can't drink—"

"Enough!" Ravic said. "Stop it. It's too absurd. Your door is all right. And don't do such a thing again."

She remained where she was. "What else can I do?" she burst out suddenly.

"Nothing."

"I call you up—three times, four times—you don't answer. And when you answer you tell me to leave you alone. What does that mean?"

"Just that."

"Just that? How—just that? Are we automatons one can turn on and off? One night everything is wonderful and full of love and then suddenly . . ."

She became silent as she looked at Ravic's face. "I was sure that was coming," he said in a low voice. "I was sure you'd try to make good use of it. It's just like you! You knew then that it was the last time and you should have left it at that. You were with me and because it was the last time it was the way it was and it was good and it was a goodbye and we were full of each other and that would have been in our memory; but you couldn't resist exploiting it like a businessman, turning it into a new demand, making of something unique, something that had wings, a creeping prolongation. And because I wouldn't have it, now you use this disgusting trick and one has to chew over a thing that even to speak of is shameless."

"I—"

"You knew it!" he interrupted her. "Don't lie again! I don't want to repeat what you said. I'm not yet able to do it! You knew! We both knew. You did not want to come back again."

"I did not come back again!"

Ravic stared at her. He controlled himself with an effort. "All right. Then you called—"

"I called you up because I was afraid!"

"Oh, God," Ravic said. "This is too idiotic! I give up."

She smiled slowly. "I too, Ravic. Don't you see that I only want you to stay here!"

"That's just what I don't want."

"Why?" She was still smiling.

Ravic felt beaten. She simply refused to understand him and if he began to explain to her, who knew where it would end? "It is a cursed corruption," he said finally. "Something you can't understand."

"I can," she replied slowly. "Maybe. But why is it different from last week?"

"It was the same then."

She looked at him. "I don't care for definitions."

He did not answer. He felt how she got the better of him. "Ravic," she said and came closer. "Yes, I said at that time it was the end. I said you would never hear from me again. I said it because you wanted me to. That I don't do it—can't you understand that?"

"No," he replied in a rough tone. "All I understand is that you want to sleep with two men."

She did not move. "No," she said then. "But even if that were true, how does it concern you?"

He stared at her.

"What does it really matter to you?" she repeated. "I love you. Isn't that enough."

"No."

"You don't have to be jealous. The others could. Not you. Nor have you ever been—"

"Really?"

"No, you don't even know what it means."

"Of course not. Because I don't make dramatic scenes like your young man—"

She smiled. "Ravic," she said. "Jealousy begins with the air the other breathes."

He did not answer. She stood before him and looked at him. She looked at him and was silent. The air, the narrow corridor, the dim light—suddenly everything was full of her. Full of waiting, of a breathless gentle compelling force, like the attraction of the ground for one leaning dizzily over the low railing of a tower.

Ravic felt it. He resisted. He didn't want to be caught by it. Now he no longer thought of going. If he went, this would pursue him. And he did not want to be pursued. He wanted to have a clear ending. Tomorrow he would need clarity.

"Have you brandy here?" he asked.

"Yes. What do you want? Calvados?"

"Cognac, if you have it. Or calvados if you like. It makes no difference."

She walked quickly over to the small chest. He looked after her. The light air, the invisible radiation, the allure, the

334

"here let us build our huts," the old, eternal deception—as though peace could ever come of the blood for longer than one night.

Jealousy. He didn't know anything about it? But didn't he know something of the imperfection of love? Wasn't that an older, less quenchable pain than the little personal misery, jealousy? Did it not begin even with the knowledge that one would have to die first, before the other?

Joan did not bring calvados. She brought a bottle of cognac. Good, he thought. Sometimes she shows some perception. He pushed the photograph aside to put his glass down. Then he took it up again. It was the simplest way to break the effect of a woman—to look at one's successor. "Strange, how bad my memory is," he said. "I thought the boy looked quite different."

She put the bottle down. "But that's not him."

"So—already someone else."

"Yes. That was the reason for everything."

Ravic took a gulp of cognac. "You are damned tactless. One should have no photographs around when the former lover comes. One never has photographs standing around. It's bad taste."

"It wasn't standing around. He found it. He searched around. And one does have photographs. You don't understand that. A woman understands. I didn't want him to see it."

"And now you've had a row. Are you dependent on him?"

"No. I have my contract. For two years."

"Did he get it for you?"

"Why not?" She was honestly surprised. "Is that important?"

"No. But there are people who get bitter about things like that."

She raised her shoulder. He saw it. A memory. A nostalgia. Shoulders that once had risen with her breathing beside him, softly, regularly, in sleep. A fleeting cloud of glittering birds in the reddish night sky. Far? How far away? Speak, invisible bookkeeper! Is it only buried, or are these really the last fleeting reflections? Who knows?

He picked up the photo that lay on the table. A face. Any face. One among millions.

"Since when?" he asked.

"Not long. We are working together. A few days ago. After you didn't—at Fouquet's—"

He raised his hand. "All right, all right. I know. If that evening I had—you know it isn't true."

She hesitated. "No—"

"You know it. Don't lie! Nothing of importance has such a short breath."

What did he want to hear? Why had he said that? Didn't he want to hear a lie after all? "It is true and it is not true," she said. "I can't help myself, Ravic. I am driven by it. It is as though I were missing something. I seize it, I must have it, and then it's nothing. And then I grope for something new. I know in advance that it will end the same way, but I can't leave it alone. It drives me and it tosses me aside; it satisfies me for a short time and then it lets go of me and leaves me empty once more, like hunger, and then it returns again."

Lost, Ravic thought. Truly and completely lost now. No more mistake, no entanglement, no awakening, no coming back. It was good to know that. It was good to know it when the vapors of fantasy should begin once more to dull the lenses of knowledge.

Gentle, inexorable, and hopeless chemistry! Blood that once had flowed together could never do it again with equal force. What still held Joan and from time to time drove her back to him was a part of him that she had not yet penetrated. Once she did penetrate it, she would be gone forever. Who wanted to wait for that? Who would be satisfied to? Who give himself up for it?

"I wish I were as strong as you, Ravic."

He laughed. Now this. "You are much stronger than I am."

"No. You can see how I run after you."

"That proves it. You can afford to do it. I can't."

She looked at him attentively for a moment. Then the radiance that had flitted across her face left it.

"You can't love," she said. "You never give yourself."

"You always do. That's why you always get saved."

"Can't you talk seriously with me?"

"I am talking seriously with you."

"If I am always saved, then why can't I get away from you?"

"You get away from me all right."

"Leave that. You know that has nothing to do with it. If I

had been able to get away from you, I wouldn't be running after you. Others I have forgotten. Not you. Why?"

Ravic took a sip. "Maybe because you couldn't get me completely under your feet."

She was taken aback. Then she shook her head. "I didn't manage to get them all under my feet, as you call it. Some not at all. And I have forgotten them. I was unhappy but I forgot them."

"You will also forget me. It's just too recent."

"No. You make me restless. No, never."

"You won't believe how much one can forget," Ravic said. "It's a great blessing and a damned misfortune."

"You still haven't told me why it is like this with us."

"This is something neither of us can explain. We could talk as long as we wanted. It would only get more confused. There are things that can't be explained. And some one can't understand. Blessed be the bit of jungle within us. I'll go now."

She stood up quickly. "You can't leave me alone."

"Do you want to sleep with me?"

She looked at him and said nothing. "I hope not," he said.

"Why do you ask that?"

"To cheer myself up. Go to bed. It's already light outside. No time for tragedies."

"You don't want to stay?"

"No. And I'll never come back."

She stood very quiet. "Never?"

"Never. And you'll never again come to me."

She slowly shook her head. Then she pointed to the table. "Because of this?"

"No."

"I don't understand you. We can, after all—"

"No!" he said quickly. "Not that. The formula of a friendship. The little vegetable garden on the lava of dead emotions. No, we can't do that. Not we. It may be possible with small affairs. Even then it's wrong. Love should not be polluted with friendship. An end is an end."

"But why just now—"

"You are right. It should have been earlier. When I returned from Switzerland. But no one is omniscient. And sometimes one doesn't want to know everything. It was—" He broke off.

"What was it?" She stood before him as though there were

something she could not understand and which she urgently had to know. She was pale and her eyes were translucent. "What was it with us, Ravic?" she whispered.

Behind her hair the corridor, dimly lit, swaying in the light as though it led far into a shaft where promises darkened, wet with the tears of many generations and the dew of constantly renewed hopes. "Love—" he said.

"Love?"

"Love. And that's why this is the end."

He closed the door behind himself. The elevator. He pressed the button. But he did not wait for the elevator to creep up. He expected Joan would follow him. He walked quickly down the stairs. He was surprised not to hear the door. He stopped at the second landing and listened. Nothing moved. No one came.

The taxi was still standing in front of the house. He had forgotten about it. The driver touched his cap and grinned confidentially. "How much?" Ravic asked.

"Seventeen francs fifty."

Ravic paid. "Don't you want to ride back?" the chauffeur asked, surprised.

"No. I want to walk."

"It's rather far, sir."

"I know."

"Then it wouldn't have been necessary for you to have me wait. Cost you eleven francs for nothing."

"That doesn't matter."

The driver tried to light a cigarette butt that stuck to his upper lip, brown and damp. "Well, I hope it was worth it."

"More!" Ravic said.

The gardens stood in the cold morning light. The air was already warm, but the light was cold. Lilac bushes, gray with dust. Benches. On one of them a man slept, his face covered with a copy of the *Paris Soir*. It was the same bench on which Ravic had sat during that rainy night.

He looked at the sleeping man. The *Paris Soir* rose rhythmically over the covered face as though the cheap paper had a soul, or as though it were a butterfly that would dart skyward at any moment with great news. The fat headline breathed softly: Hitler declares he has no more territorial claims, except the Polish Corridor. And beneath it: Presser kills husband with hot iron. A buxom woman in her Sunday dress stared out of the rotogravure. Next to her billowed a second photograph: Chamberlain declares peace still possible; a sort of bank clerk with an umbrella and a face like a happy sheep. Underneath his feet, in small print and somewhat hidden: Hundreds of Jews clubbed to death at the frontier.

The man who had protected himself with all this from the night dew and the early light slept soundly and peacefully.

He wore old, torn canvas shoes, brown woolen pants, and a torn jacket. All of this didn't concern him. He was so far down that it didn't concern him any more—as a deep-sea fish is not concerned with the storms above it.

Ravic walked back to the International. He was clear and free. He hadn't left anything behind. He had no need of anything either. He couldn't use anything now that would confuse him. He would move into the Prince de Galles today. Two days too early; but it was better to be ready for Haake too early than too late.

Chapter 28

THE LOBBY of the Prince de Galles was empty as Ravic came downstairs. A portable radio was playing quietly on the reception desk. A couple of scrub women were working in the corners. Ravic walked across quickly and inconspicuously. He looked at the clock opposite the door. It was five in the morning.

He went up the Avenue George V and over to Fouquet's. No one was sitting there. The restaurant had been closed for some time. He paused for a moment. Then he stopped a taxi and drove to the Scheherazade.

Morosow was standing in front of the door and looked at him questioningly. "Nothing," Ravic said.

"As I thought. You could not have expected it today."

"You could. Today is the fourteenth day."

"You can't count on one day. Have you been in the Prince de Galles all the time?"

"Yes. From morning up to now."

"He'll call up tomorrow," Morosow said. "He may have had something to do today, or may have left a day later."

"I have to operate tomorrow morning."

"He won't call that early."

Ravic did not reply. He was looking at a taxi out of which a gigolo in a white tuxedo had stepped. A pale woman with big teeth followed him. Morosow opened the door for them. Suddenly the street smelled of Chanel Five. The woman limped a little. The gigolo walked lazily behind her after paying for the taxi. The woman waited for him at the door. Her eyes were green in the light of the lamps. The pupils were contracted.

"At this time of day he certainly won't call," Morosow said as he returned.

Ravic did not answer.

"If you give me the key I can go up at eight," Morosow declared. "I can wait then until you get back."

"You must sleep."

"Nonsense. I can sleep on your bed if I want to. No one will call, but I can do it if it puts you at ease."

"I'll have to operate until eleven."

"All right. Give me the key. I wouldn't like you to sew the ovaries of a lady of the Faubourg St. Germain to her stomach in your excitement. She might vomit up a child. Have you the key?"

"Yes. Here."

Morosow put the key into his pocket. Then he took out a case with peppermint troches and offered them to Ravic. Ravic shook his head. Morosow took a few out and threw them into his mouth. They disappeared behind his beard like small white birds flying into a wood. "Refreshing," he declared.

"Have you ever sat in a plush hole the entire day and waited?" Ravic asked.

"Longer. Haven't you?"

"Yes. But not for something like this."

"Didn't you take anything along to read?"

"Enough. But I didn't read anything. How long will you be busy here?"

Morosow opened the door of a taxi. It was crowded with Americans. He let them in. "At least another two hours," he said when he came back. "You see what's on. The maddest summer for years. Everything filled to capacity. Joan is in there, too."

"Is she?"

"Yes. With a different man, in case you're interested."

"No," Ravic said. He turned, ready to leave. "Then I'll be seeing you tomorrow."

"Ravic," Morosow called after him.

Ravic came back. Morosow drew the key out of his pocket. "Here! You must be able to get into your room in the Prince de Galles! I won't see you before tomorrow. Leave the door open when you go out."

"I won't sleep at the Prince de Galles." Ravic took the key. "I sleep in the International. It's better if my face is seen as little as possible over there."

"You should sleep there. One doesn't live in a hotel where

one doesn't sleep. It's better so, in case the police inquire at the reception desk.''

"That's true. But it's also better to be able to prove that I've lived all the time in the International in case they do inquire. I've arranged everything in the Prince de Galles. The bed rumpled, the washstand, bath, towels, and everything else used so that it looks as if I'd left early in the morning.''

"All right. Then give me the key again.''

Ravic shook his head. "It's better they shouldn't see you there.''

"That doesn't matter.''

"It does, Boris. We don't want to be idiots. Your beard is not ordinary. Besides, you are right: I must act and live as if nothing in particular were the matter. If Haake really should call up tomorrow morning, then he'd call again in the afternoon too. If I didn't count on that I'd be a nervous wreck within a day.''

"Where are you going now?''

"To bed. We can't expect him to call at this time of day.''

"I can meet you somewhere later if you want me to.''

"No, Boris. I hope I'll be asleep by the time you're free here. I must operate at eight.''

Morosow looked at him doubtfully. "Good. Then I'll drop in on you tomorrow afternoon at the Prince de Galles. In case something happens before, give me a ring at the hotel.''

"Yes.''

The streets. The city. The reddish sky. Flickering red and white and blue behind the buildings. Wind playing around the corners of the bistros like an affectionate cat. People, fresh air, after a day lived through in a sticky hotel room. Ravic walked along the avenue behind the Scheherazade. The fenced-in trees hesitantly exhaled a memory of woods and greenery into the leaden night. Suddenly he felt empty and exhausted, ready to drop. If I'd let go of it, something within him thought, if I'd let go of it completely, forget it, strip it off as a snake strips off its outworn skin! What does it matter to me, this melodrama of an almost forgotten past? What does even this person matter to me, this little incidental instrument, this insignificant tool in a dark fragment of the Middle Ages, of a solar eclipse of Central Europe?

What did it still matter to him? A prostitute tried to tempt him into a doorway. In the dark of the door she opened her dress. It was made so that it opened like a robe when she undid the belt. The pale flesh glimmered indistinctly. Long black stockings, black sockets of eyes in whose shadows one no longer saw any eyes; frail, decaying flesh which seemed already to phosphoresce.

A pimp with a cigarette sticking to his upper lip leaned against a tree and stared at him. A few vegetable vans passed by. Horses, heads bowed, muscles working powerfully under their skins. The spicy smell of herbs, of heads of cauliflower which looked like petrified brains in green leaves, the red of tomatoes, the baskets with beans, onions, cherries, and celery.

What did it still matter to him? One more or less. One more or less out of a hundred thousand men who were just as bad or even worse. One less. He stopped abruptly. That was it! He was quite awake all of a sudden. That was it! That was what had made them grow, the fact that one got tired, that one wanted to forget, that one thought: What does it matter to me? That was it! One less! Yes, one less—it was nothing, but it was also everything! Everything! Slowly he drew a cigarette out of his pocket and slowly lighted it. And suddenly while the yellow light of the match illuminated his palms like a cave with gorges of lines in it, he became aware that nothing could keep him from killing Haake. Everything depended on it in a strange way. It was suddenly much more than just a personal act of vengeance. It was as if he would make himself guilty of an immense crime if he did not do it; as if something in the world would be lost forever if he did not act. At the same time he knew exactly that it wasn't so—but nevertheless and far beyond explanation and logic, the dark knowledge pulsed in his blood that he had to do it, as if invisible waves would emanate from it and far greater events happen later. He knew that Haake was only a small official of horror and not of much significance; but suddenly he knew too that it was infinitely important to kill him.

The light in the cave of his hands went out. He threw the match away. The dawn hung over the trees. A silver fabric, held up by the pizzicato of the awakening sparrows. He looked about in astonishment. Something had happened to him. An invisible court had held a sitting, and a sentence had been pronounced. He saw the trees with extreme clarity, the yellow wall of a house, the gray color of an iron fence beside

343

him, the street in the blue mist; he had the feeling that he would never forget them. And he knew that he would kill Haake and that it was no longer his own little affair, but far more. A beginning—

He passed the entrance of the Osiris. A few drunks staggered out. Their eyes were glassy, their faces red. Ravic glanced after them. They walked to the curb. There was no taxi there. They cursed for a while and then they walked on, heavy, strong, and noisy. They were speaking German.

Ravic had intended to go to the hotel. Now he changed his mind. He recalled Rolande's words that there had often been German tourists in the Osiris during the last few months. He entered.

Rolande was standing at the bar, cool, observant, in her black *gouvernante's* uniform. The music box blared resoundingly against the Egyptian walls. "Rolande," Ravic said.

She turned around. "Ravic! You haven't been here for a long time. It's good that you've come."

"Why?"

He stood beside her at the bar and looked around the place. There were no longer many customers there. They were hunched sleepily at the tables here and there.

"I'm leaving here," Roland said. "I go in a week."

"Forever?"

She nodded and took a telegram out of the neck of her dress. "Here."

Ravic opened it and gave it back to her. "Your aunt? She finally died?"

"Yes. I'll go back. I've told madame. She is furious, but she understands. Jeanette must replace me. I still have to break her in." Rolande laughed. "Poor madame. She wanted to show off at Cannes this year. Her villa is crowded with guests by now. She became a countess a year ago. Married a pimp from Toulouse. She pays him five thousand francs a month as long as he doesn't leave Toulouse. Now she's got to stay here."

"Will you open your café?"

"Yes. I run around all day ordering things. One can get them cheaper in Paris. Chintz for the curtains. What do you say to this pattern?"

She drew out of the neck of her dress a crumpled piece of

344

material. Flowers on a yellow background. "Wonderful," Ravic declared.

"I'll get it at a discount of thirty per cent. Last year's stock." Rolande's eyes radiated warmth and tenderness. "I'll save three hundred and seventy-five francs. Not bad, eh?"

"Marvelous. Will you marry?"

"Yes."

"Why do you want to marry? Why don't you wait awhile and attend to everything you want to do first?"

Rolande laughed. "You don't understand business, Ravic. It won't work without a man. A man belongs in it. I know what I'm doing all right."

There she stood, strong, secure, calm. She had thought over everything. The man belonged in the business. "Don't have your money put in his name right away," Ravic said. "Just wait to see how everything will work out."

She laughed again. "I know how it will work out. We are sensible. We need each other in the business. A man is no man if his wife has the money. I don't want a pimp. I must be able to respect my husband. I can't do that if he has to come to me every minute to ask for money. Don't you see that?"

"Yes," Ravic said, without seeing it.

"Fine." She nodded contentedly. "Do you want a drink?"

"Nothing. I must go. Just dropped in. I've got to work tomorrow morning."

She looked at him. "You are completely sober. Don't you want a girl?"

"No."

Rolande directed two girls with a light movement of her hand to a man who was sitting on a banquette, asleep. The others were romping around. Only a few of them were still sitting on the hassocks which stood in two rows along the middle walk. The others slid on the smooth floor of the corridor like children on ice in winter. Two of them at a gallop would drag a third in a squatting position through the long corridor. Their flying hair was disheveled, their breasts were swinging, their shoulders shone, their wisps of silk no longer hid anything, they screamed with pleasure, and suddenly the Osiris was an Arcadian scene of classic innocence.

"Summer," Rolande said. "One has to grant them some freedom in the mornings." She looked at Ravic. "Thursday is my last evening. Madame is giving a party for me. Will you come?"

"Thursday?"

"Yes."

Thursday, Ravic thought. In seven days. Seven days. That is like seven years. Thursday—it would be done by then. Thursday—who was able to think so far ahead? "Of course," he said. "Where?"

"Here. At six o'clock."

"All right. I'll be here. Good night, Rolande."

"Good night, Ravic."

It happened while he was applying the retractor. It happened swiftly, alarming and hot. He hesitated a moment. The open red abdominal cavity, the thin steam from the hot damp dressings with which the intestines were held up, the blood trickling from the delicate veins next to the clips—then suddenly he saw Eugénie looking at him with an inquiring glance, he saw Veber's large face, with all its pores and every hair of his mustache under the metallic light—and he collected himself and went on working calmly.

He sewed. His hands sewed. The incision was closing. He could feel the sweat running from his armpits. It ran down his body. "Will you finish?" he asked Veber.

"Yes. Is something the matter?"

"No. The heat. Not enough sleep."

Ravic saw Eugénie's look. "It can happen, Eugénie," he said. "Even to the righteous."

The room seemed to rock for a moment. A mad exhaustion. Veber went on sewing. Ravic automatically helped him. His tongue was thick. The palate was like cotton-wool. He breathed very slowly. Poppies, something in him thought. Poppies in Flanders. Red, open poppy blossoms, the shameless secret, life, so close beneath the hands with the knife; a trembling running down one's arms, the magnetic contact, from far off, from a distant death. I can't operate any more, he thought. This has to be settled first.

Veber painted the closed incision. "Finished."

Eugénie lowered the foot end of the operating table. The stretcher was rolled out noiselessly. "Cigarette?" Veber asked.

"No, I must leave. I've got to attend to something. Is there anything more to be done?"

"No." Veber looked at Ravic with surprise. "Why are you in such a hurry? Do you want a vermouth with soda or something else cold?"

"It's better the way it is now," Ravic said. "When I move out of here, Horn will no longer exist and there will be no papers."

"It would have been safer as far as the police are concerned. But they won't come. They don't come into hotels where one pays more than a hundred francs for an apartment. I know a refugee at the Ritz who's been living there without papers for the last five years. The only one who knows about it is the night porter. Have you thought over what you are going to do if the fellows here should nevertheless ask for papers?"

"Of course. My passport is at the Argentine Embassy for a visa. I'll promise them to call for it next day. Then I'll leave the suitcase here and won't come back. There is time for that. The first inquiry would come from the management, not from the police. I count on that. Only—then it would be all up, here."

"It will work."

They played until half past eight. "Now go and have a bite," Morosow said. "I'll wait here. Then I'll have to go."

"I'll eat here later."

"Nonsense. Go now and eat a decent meal. When that fellow calls you will probably have to drink with him first. In that case you'd better have had enough to eat. Do you know where you want to go with him?"

"Yes."

"I mean, in case he still wants to see or drink something?"

"Yes. I know a lot of places where everyone minds his own business."

"Go and have something to eat now. Don't drink anything, eat heavy, fat things."

"All right."

Ravic walked across to Fouquet's again. All this was not real, he felt. He must be reading it in a book or seeing it in a melodramatic movie, or he must be dreaming it. He walked by both sides of Fouquet's again. The terraces were crowded. He checked on each individual table. Haake was nowhere.

He sat at a small table next to the door so that he could watch both the entrance and the street. At an adjoining table two women were talking about Schiaparelli and Mainbocher. A man with a thin beard was sitting with them, saying nothing. On the other side a few young Frenchmen were discussing politics. One was for the Croix de Feu, one for the

Communists; the others made fun of both of them. In between they all studied two beautiful, self-assured American girls who were drinking vermouth.

Ravic watched the street while he ate. He was not stupid enough to disbelieve in accidents. Only in good literature are there no accidents; life was daily filled with the most absurd ones. He stayed at Fouquet's for half an hour. It was easier this time than at noon. Once more he walked around the corner along the Champs Elysées and then back to the hotel.

"Here is the key to your car," Morosow said. "I've exchanged it. Now it is a blue Talbot with leather seats. The other one had corded seats. Leather can be washed more easily. It is a cabriolet, you can drive with the top up or down. But always leave the window open. If you must shoot when the car is closed, shoot so that the bullet goes through the open window to avoid any bullet traces in the car. I've rented it for two weeks. On no account bring it back to the garage afterwards. Leave it in one of the side-streets. To air out. It is now parked in the Rue de Berri, opposite the Lancaster."

"Good," Ravic said. He put the key next to the telephone.

"Here are the registration papers for the car. I couldn't get you a driver's license. Didn't want to ask too many people."

"I don't need it. I drove the whole time in Antibes without one."

Ravic put the registration for the car next to the keys.

"Park the car in a different street tonight," Morosow said.

Melodrama, Ravic thought. Bad melodrama. "I'll do it. Thanks, Boris."

"I wish I could come with you."

"I don't. This is the sort of thing one does alone."

"Come to my place and wake me up if I'm no longer in front of the Scheherazade."

"I'll come in any case. No matter whether something happens or not."

"All right. So long, Ravic."

"So long, Boris."

Ravic closed the door behind Morosow. Suddenly the room was very quiet. He sat down in a corner of the sofa. He looked at the hangings. They were of blue material, with a border. He had come to know them better in these two days than any others with which he had lived for many years. He

350

knew the mirrors, he knew the gray velours on the floor, with the dark spot near the window, he knew every line of the table, of the bed, of the chair covers—he knew everything so exactly that it made him sick; only the telephone he did not know.

Chapter 29

THE TALBOT stood in the Rue Bassano between a Renault and a Mercedes-Benz. The Mercedes was new and had an Italian license plate. Ravic maneuvered the Talbot into the open. He was so impatient that he did not take sufficient care; the Talbot's back fender touched the left mudguard of the Mercedes and left a scratch. He paid no attention. Without pausing he drove the car down to the Boulevard Haussmann.

He drove very fast. It was good to feel the car in his hands. It was good against the dark disappointment that lay like cement in the pit of his stomach.

It was four o'clock in the morning. He had intended to wait longer. But suddenly the whole thing seemed meaningless. Very likely Haake had forgotten the little episode a long time ago. Or perhaps he had not returned to Paris at all. Just now they had other things to do over there.

Morosow was standing in front of the door of the Scheherazade. Ravic parked around the next corner and walked back. Morosow looked at him expectantly. "Did you get my telephone message?"

"No. Why?"

"I called up five minutes ago. A group of Germans is sitting inside. Four men. One of them looks like—"

"Where?"

"Next to the orchestra. It's the only table with four men. You can see it from the door."

"All right."

"Take the small table by the door. I've kept it free."

"All right, Boris."

Ravic paused at the door. The room was dark. The spotlight was on the dance floor. A singer was standing in it, wearing a silver dress. The small cone of light was so strong that one could not recognize anything beyond it. Ravic stared at the table next to the orchestra. It was not discernible. The wall of white shut it off.

He took a seat at the table next to the door. A waiter brought a carafe of vodka. The orchestra seemed to lag. The sweet mist of melodies was creeping, creeping, slow as a snail. *J'attendrai. J'attendrai.*

The singer bowed. Applause broke out. Ravic bent forward. He waited for the spotlight to be cut off. The singer turned to the orchestra. The gypsy nodded and took up his violin. The cymbals threw a few muffled notes into the air. The second song. *La chapelle au claire de lune.* Ravic closed his eyes. It was almost unbearable to wait.

He sat upright again, long before the song was ended. The spotlight was cut off. The lights on the tables came on, glowing. At the first moment he could see nothing but indistinct contours. He had stared into the spotlight too long. He closed his eyes and then looked up. He found the table at once.

Slowly he leaned back. None of the men was Haake. He remained sitting this way for a long time. Suddenly he was terribly tired. Tired behind the eyes. It drifted upon him intermittently in uneven waves. The music, the rise and fall of the voices, the muffled noise cloaked him in a haze after the quiet of the hotel room, and the new disappointment. It was like a kaleidoscope of sleep, like a gentle hypnosis, enveloping the brain cells, their sketchy thoughts, and their tortured vigil.

He saw Joan at some moment in the pale light-mist in which the dancing couples moved. Her open thirsty face was bent backward, her head close to a man's shoulder. It did not touch him. No one can become more alien than a person one has loved once, he thought wearily. When the enigmatic umbilical cord between imagination and its objects was torn, sheet lightning might still leap from one to the other, there might be fluorescence as if from ghostly stars; but it was dead light. It excited, but it no longer set fire—nothing any longer flowed to and fro. He leaned his head against the back of the banquette. The brief intimacy above abysses. The darkness of the sexes with all their sweet names. Star flowers on a bog which swallowed you up when you started to pick them.

He straightened up. He had to get out before he fell asleep. He called the waiter. "Check, please."

"There is nothing to pay for," the waiter said.

"How is—"

"You did not drink anything."

"Oh yes, that's right."

He tipped the man and left.

"No?" Morosow asked outside.

"No," Ravic replied.

Morosow looked at him. "I give up," Ravic said. "It is a damned laughable game of Indians. For five days now I've been waiting. Haake told me that he always stays for only two or three days in Paris. If that's so then he must have left again by now. If he was here at all."

"Go to bed," Morosow said.

"I can't sleep. Now I'll drive back to the Prince de Galles, get my suitcase, and check out."

"All right," Morosow said. "Then I'll meet you tomorrow noon there."

"Where?"

"In the Prince de Galles."

Ravic looked at him. "Yes, of course. I'm talking nonsense. Or am I? Maybe not."

"Wait until tomorrow night."

"All right. I'll see. Good night, Boris."

"Good night, Ravic."

Ravic drove past the Osiris. He parked the car around the corner. The thought of going back to his room in the International made him shudder. Maybe he could sleep a few hours here. It was Monday. A quiet day for brothels. The doorman was no longer outside. Hardly anyone would still be in there.

Rolande stood beside the door, keeping watch over the big room. The music box made a lot of noise in the almost empty place. "Nothing much going on tonight?" Ravic asked.

"Nothing. Only that bore over there. Lascivious as a monkey, but he doesn't want to go upstairs with a girl. You know the type. Would like to, but is afraid. Another German. Well, he has paid; it can't take much longer."

Ravic looked indifferently toward the table. The man was sitting with his back to him. He had two girls with him. As he leaned toward one of them, taking both her breasts in his hands, Ravic saw his face. It was Haake.

He heard Rolande speaking as if in a haze. He could not understand what she said. He realized only that he had stepped

354

backward and was standing by the door now so that he could just see the corner of the table without being seen.

Finally Rolande's voice came through the haze. "Some cognac?"

The squawking of the music box. Still the oscillation, the spasm in the diaphragm! Ravic dug his nails into his palm: Haake must not see him here. And Rolande must not notice that he knew him.

"No," he heard himself saying. "I've had enough. A German, you said? Do you know who he is?"

"No idea." Rolande shrugged her shoulders. "They all look alike to me. I think this one has never been here before. But don't you want to have a drink?"

"No. Only wanted to look in—"

He felt Rolande's eyes on him and forced himself to be calm. "I only wanted to hear when your party is," he said. "Will it be Thursday or Friday?"

"Thursday, Ravic. You are coming?"

"I'll be on time. That was all I wanted to know. Now I've got to go. Good night, Rolande."

"Good night, Ravic."

The lighted night, suddenly roaring. No buildings any more—a thicket of stone, a jungle of windows. Suddenly war again, a crawling patrol, along the empty street. The car, a shelter in which to take cover, the motor droning, lying in ambush for the enemy.

Shoot him down when he comes out? Ravic looked along the street. A few cars, yellow lights, stray cats. Under a street lamp in the distance someone who looked like a policeman. His own license plate, the noise of the shot. Rolande, who had just seen him—he heard Morosow's: "Risk nothing, nothing! It isn't worth it."

No doorman. No taxi. Good. There were few fares on Mondays at this hour. The moment he had thought this, a Citroën taxi rattled past him, and stopped at the door. The driver lit a cigarette and yawned audibly. Ravic felt his skin contracting. He waited.

He deliberated whether to step out and tell the driver that there was no longer anyone inside. Impossible. To send him away on some errand and pay him for it. To Morosow. He snatched a piece of paper out of his pocket, wrote a few lines, tore them up, wrote them again, Morosow should not wait for him at the Scheherazade, signed it with a fictitious name—

The taxi went into gear and drove off. He stared after it, but could not see inside. He did not know whether Haake had stepped in while he had been writing. He went into first gear swiftly. The Talbot shot around the corner after the taxi.

He could not see anyone through the back window. But Haake might be sitting at one side. He passed the taxi slowly. He could not recognize anything in the dark inside of the car. He fell back and again passed the other car as close as possible. The driver turned around and shouted at him. "Hey, you idiot, do you want to run into me?"

"There is a friend of mine in your cab."

"You drunken fool," the driver yelled. "Can't you see the car is empty?"

At that moment Ravic saw that the meter was not running. He made a sharp turn and raced back.

Haake was standing at the curb. He waved. "Hello, taxi."

Ravic drove close to him and stepped on the brake. "Taxi?" Haake asked.

"No." Ravic leaned out of the window. "Hello," he said.

Haake looked at him. His eyes contracted. "What?"

"I think we know each other," Ravic said in German.

Haake bent forward. The suspicion disappeared from his face. *Mein Gott—Herr von—von—*"

"Horn."

"Correct! Correct! Herr von Horn. Of course! What a coincidence! My good man, where have you been all this time?"

"Here in Paris. Come, step in. I didn't know you would be back so soon."

"I've called you up several times. Did you change your hotel?"

"No. It's still the Prince de Galles." Ravic opened the door of the car. "Step in. I'll take you along. You won't get a taxi very easily at this time."

Haake put one foot on the running board. Ravic could feel his breath. He saw the red, overheated face. "Prince de Galles," Haake said. "Damn it, that's what it was! Called you at the George V." He laughed loudly. "Now I understand. Prince de Galles, of course. Got the two mixed up. Didn't bring my old notebook with me. Thought I'd remember."

Ravic kept an eye on the entrance. It would be some time before anyone came out. The girls had to change first.

Nevertheless, he had to get Haake into the car quickly. "Did you intend to go in?" Haake asked in a jovial tone.

"I was thinking of it. But it's too late."

Haake blew noisily through his nose. "You said it, friend. I was the last one. They are closing."

"It doesn't matter. It's dull in there, anyway. Let's go somewhere else. Come on!"

"Is anything still open?"

"Of couse. The really good places are just starting now. This is only for tourists."

"Is that so? I thought—this was really something."

"Not at all. There are much better ones. This is nothing but a cat-house."

Ravic stepped lightly on the accelerator several times. The motor roared and died down. He had calculated right; Haake carefully climbed onto the seat beside him. "Nice to see you again," he said. "Really very nice."

Ravic reached across him and closed the door. "I am delighted, too."

"Interesting place here! A lot of naked girls. To think the police permit it! Very likely most of them are sick, eh?"

"One is never quite sure in such places."

Ravic let in the clutch. "Are there any places where one can be absolutely sure?" Haake bit off the end of a cigar. "I wouldn't like to go home with a dose. On the other hand, one lives only once."

"Yes," Ravic said and handed him the electric lighter.

"Where are we driving?"

"How about a *maison de rendez-vous* to begin with?"

"What is that?"

"A house where society ladies go to look for adventure."

"What? Real society ladies?"

"Yes. Women whose husbands are too old. Women who have boring husbands. Women whose husbands don't make enough money."

"But how—they cannot simply—how do they manage it?"

"These women come there for one or more hours. As if for a cocktail or nightcap. Some of them can be called up. It isn't a brothel in the same sense as these in Montmartre. I know a very nice house in the middle of the Bois. The owner looks the way a duchess should look. Everything is extremely distinguished, discreet, and elegant."

Ravic spoke slowly and calmly, breathing slowly. He heard himself talking like a tourists' guide, but he forced himself to go on speaking in order to grow calmer. The veins in his arms trembled. He held onto the wheel tightly with both hands to control the trembling. "You will be surprised when you see the rooms," he said. "The furniture is genuine, carpets and tapestry old, the wine select, the service exquisite, and you may be absolutely sure as far as the women are concerned."

Haake exhaled his cigar smoke. He turned to Ravic. "Listen, all that sounds wonderful, my dear Herr von Horn. There is only one question: certainly this can't be cheap!"

"I assure you it is not expensive."

Haake laughed hoarsely in some embarrassment. "It depends on what you mean by that! We Germans with our limited foreign exchange!"

Ravic shook his head. "I know the owner very well. She is indebted to me. She'll consider us special guests. When you come, you come as a friend of mine and very likely you will not be permitted to pay. A few tips, if anything at all—less than you paid for one bottle in the Osiris."

"Really?"

"You'll see."

Haake moved in his seat. "Donnerwetter, that's really something!" He smiled broadly at Ravic. "You seem to be informed! You must have rendered a good service to that woman."

Ravic looked at him. He looked straight into his eyes. "Sometimes places of this kind have difficulties with the authorities. Attempts at blackmail. You know what I mean."

"And how!" For a moment Haake pondered something. "Are you so influential here?"

"Not really. A few friends in influential positions."

"That's something. We could use you to good advantage. Couldn't we have a talk about it sometime?"

"Certainly. How long are you staying in Paris?"

Haake laughed. "I always seem to meet you when I'm just about to leave. I'm going at seven-thirty this morning." He looked at the clock in the car. "In two and a half hours. I wanted to tell you. Must be at the Gare du Nord by then. Can we make it?"

"Easily. Do you have to go to your hotel before that?"

"No. My suitcase is at the station. I left the hotel this afternoon. Saved a day's rent that way. With our foreign exchange—" He laughed again.

Suddenly Ravic realized that he too was laughing. He pressed his hands tightly on the wheel. Impossible, he thought, this is impossible. Something will still happen to interfere! Such a chance is impossible!

The fresh air made Haake feel the alcohol. His voice became slower and heavier. He fixed himself more comfortably in his corner and began to doze. His lower jaw dropped and his eyes closed. The car turned into the soundless darkness of the Bois.

The headlights flew like white specters in front of the car, plucking ghostly trees out of the dark. The odor of acacias rushed through the open window. The noise of the tires on the asphalt was gentle, incessant, as it if would never cease. The motor's familiar droning, deep and soft in the damp night air. The shimmer of a small pond on the left, the silhouette of willows showing brighter than the dark beeches behind them. Meadows covered with dew, nacreous, pale. The Route de Madrid, the Route de la Porte St. James, the Route de Neuilly. A sleepy house. The smell of the river. The Seine.

Ravic drove along the Boulevard de la Seine. Two barges floated on the moonlit water. A dog barked on the farther one. Voices came across the water. A light burned on the forward deck of the first barge. Ravic did not stop the car. He kept it at an even speed not to wake Haake and drove along the Seine. He had intended to stop there. It was impossible. The barges were too close to the bank. He turned into the Rue de la Ferme, away from the river, back to the Allée de Longchamp. He stayed on it beyond the Allée de la Reine Marguerite, driving carefully, and then turned into the narrower roads.

As he looked over at Haake he saw that his eyes were open. Haake looked at him. He had raised his head, without shifting, and was looking at Ravic. His eyes shone like blue glass balls in the faint light from the dashboard. It was like an electric shock. "Awake?" Ravic asked.

Haake did not answer. He looked at Ravic. He did not move. Not even his eyes moved.

"Where are we?" he asked finally.

"In the Bois de Boulogne. Very near the Restaurant des Cascades."

"How long have we been driving?"

"Ten minutes."

"It has been longer."

"Hardly."

"Before I fell asleep I looked at the clock. We've been driving more than half an hour."

"Really?" Ravic said. "I didn't think it was so long. We'll be there soon."

Haake's eyes had not left Ravic. "Where?"

"At the *maison de rendez-vous*."

Haake moved. "Drive back," he said.

"Now?"

"Yes."

He was no longer drunk. He was clearheaded and awake. His face had changed. His joviality and bonhomie had disappeared. For the first time Ravic saw again the face he had known, the face that had been engraved on his memory forever in the terror chamber of the Gestapo. And suddenly the uneasiness he had felt all along since he had met Haake disappeared, the feeling that he was going to kill a stranger who actually did not matter to him. In his car he had had an amiable drinker of red wine and he had searched in vain for reasons in that man's face, for the reasons that were uppermost in his mind no matter what he tried to think of. Now, suddenly, they were again the same eyes he had seen before him when he had awakened out of unconsciousness in an agony of pain. The same cold eyes, the same cold, low, penetrating voice—

Something in Ravic reversed direction abruptly. It was like a current changing poles. The tension remained; but the vacillation, the nervousness, and the uncertainty were converted into a single current which had only one aim, and nothing was left but that. Years fell into ashes, the room with its gray walls was back again, the unshaded white lights, the smell of blood, leather, sweat, pain, and fear.

"Why?" Ravic asked.

"I must go back. I'm expected at the hotel."

"But you said your things were already at the station."

"Yes, they are. But I've still got to settle something before I leave. I had forgotten all about it. Drive back."

"All right."

During the last week Ravic had driven through the Bois a dozen times during the daytime and at night. He recognized where he was. Still a few minutes. He turned to the left into a narrow road.

"Are we going back?"

"Yes."

The heavy aroma under trees through which no sun shone during the day. The denser darkness. The brighter gleam of the headlights. Ravic saw in the mirror that Haake's left hand was stealing away from the door, slowly, carefully. Right-hand drive, he thought, thank God this Talbot has a right-hand drive! He took a curve, held the wheel with his left hand, pretended to sway with the turns, then accelerated on the straight road, the car raced ahead and a few seconds later he stepped on the brake with all his strength.

The Talbot bucked. The brakes screeched. Ravic held one foot on the brake, the other was pushed against the floor for balance. Haake, whose feet had no support and who had not expected the jolt, shot forward from the waist. He could not get his hand out of his pocket in time and his forehead crashed against the edge of the windshield and the dashboard. At this moment Ravic struck him in the neck, just below the head, with the heavy monkey wrench he had taken from the right side-pocket.

Haake did not rise. He was slumped sidewise. His right shoulder kept him from slipping down. It jammed his body against the dashboard.

Ravic drove on at once. He crossed the avenue and dimmed the headlights. He drove on and waited to see if anyone had heard the screeching of the brakes. He deliberated whether to pull Haake out of the car and hide him behind the bushes in case anyone came by. Finally he stopped beside a crossroad, switched off the lights and the motor, jumped out of the car, lifted the hood, opened the door, and listened. If anybody came, he could see and hear him at a distance. Time enough then to drag Haake behind a bush and to act as if something were wrong with the motor.

The silence was like a noise. It was so sudden and inconceivable that it hummed. Ravic clenched his hands until it hurt. He knew it was his blood that was humming in his ears. He breathed deeply and slowly.

The humming grew into a roaring. Through the roaring he

heard a shrill sound which grew louder. Ravic listened with all his might. It grew louder, metallic—then suddenly he realized that it was made by crickets and that the roaring had ceased. There were only the crickets in the awakening day on a narrow strip of a meadow diagonally in front of him.

The meadow lay bathed in the early light. Ravic closed the hood. It was high time. He had to get through with it before there was too much light. He looked about. This place was not good. No place in the Bois was good. It was too light along the Seine. He hadn't counted on its being so late. He whirled around. He had heard a scraping and scratching, then a groaning. One of Haake's hands had crept out of the open car door and was scratching along the running board. Ravic realized then that he still held the monkey wrench in his hand. He seized Haake by the collar of his coat, lifted him so that the head came free and struck him twice. The groaning ceased.

Something clattered. Ravic stood still. Then he saw that it was a revolver that had dropped from the seat onto the running board. Haake must have been holding it before the brake had been applied. Ravic flung it back into the car.

He listened again. The crickets. The meadow. The sky that became lighter and seemed to recede. In a little while the sun would be out. Ravic opened the door, dragged Haake out of the car, pushed the front seat down, and tried to shove Haake onto the floor of the car between the back seat and the front seat. It would not do. There was not enough room. He walked around the car and opened the trunk. He emptied it quickly. Then he pulled Haake out of the car again and dragged him to the back. Haake was not yet dead. He was very heavy. Sweat ran down Ravic's face. He succeeded in squeezing the body into the trunk. He forced him in like an embryo, with the knees doubled up.

He took the tools, a shovel, and a car-jack from the ground, and put them in the front of the car. A bird began to sing in a tree near him. He was startled. It seemed louder than anything he had ever heard. He looked at the meadow. It had become still lighter.

He could not take any chances. He went back and half lifted the cover of the trunk. He put his left foot on the rear fender and kept the cover half open with his knee, just high enough to reach under it easily with his hands. If anyone came by, it would look as if he were harmlessly working at something and he could immediately let the cover drop. There was a long ride ahead. He had to kill Haake first.

The head was near the right-hand corner. He could see it. The neck was soft; the arteries still pulsed. He pressed his hands firmly around Haake's throat and held tight.

It seemed to take forever. The head moved a little. Only a little. The body tried to stretch out. It seemed trapped in its clothes. The mouth opened. Shrilly the bird began to warble again. The tongue was thick, with a yellow coating. And suddenly Haake opened one eye. It protruded, seemed to gain light and vision, seemed to free itself and to come toward Ravic—then the body yielded. Ravic still held on for a time. Done.

The cover slammed shut. Ravic took a few steps. Then he leaned against a tree and vomited. He felt as if his stomach were being wrenched out. He tried to check it. It did not help.

When he looked up he saw a man coming across the meadow. The man was staring at him. Ravic stayed where he was. The man approached. His gait was slow, unconcerned. He was dressed like a gardener or worker. He looked at Ravic. Ravic spat and took a pack of cigarettes out of his pocket. He lighted one and inhaled the smoke. The smoke rasped and burnt in his throat. The man crossed the road. He looked at the place where Ravic had vomited and then at the car and then at Ravic. He did not say anything and Ravic could not read anything in the man's face. He disappeared beyond the crossroad with slow steps.

Ravic waited a few seconds more. Then he locked the trunk of the car and started the motor. There was nothing more to be done in the Bois. It was too light. He must drive to St.-Germain. He knew the woods there.

Chapter 30

AN HOUR LATER he stopped in front of a small inn. He was very hungry, and his head felt numb. He parked the car in front of the building where there were two tables and a few chairs. He ordered coffee and brioches and went to wash. The washroom stank. He asked for a glass and washed out his mouth. Then he washed his hands and went back.

Breakfast was on the table. The coffee smelled like all the breakfasts in the world, swallows flew along the roofs, and the sun hung its first golden tapestries on the walls of the houses. People were going to work and a maid with skirt drawn up was scrubbing the floors behind the beaded curtains of the bistro. It was the most peaceful summer morning Ravic had seen in a long time.

He drank the hot coffee but he could not make up his mind to eat. He did not want to touch anything with his hands. He looked at them. Nonsense, he thought. Damnation, I'm not going to start getting complexes. I must eat. He drank another cup of coffee. He took a cigarette out of his pack and took pains not to put the end he had touched into his mouth. I can't go on this way, he thought. But nevertheless he did not eat anything. I must get entirely through with it first, he thought, and got up and paid.

A herd of cows. Butterflies. The sun over the fields. The sun on the glass of the windshield. The sun on the top of the car. The sun on the glittering metal of the trunk under which Haake lay—killed without having heard why and by whom. It should have been different—

"Do you recognize me, Haake? Do you know who I am?"

He saw the red face before him. "No, why? Who are you? Have we met before?"

"Yes?"

"When? Were we close friends? At Officers' Training School, perhaps? I don't remember."

"You don't remember, Haake? It was not at Officers' Training School. It was after that."

"After? But you've lived abroad. I have never been out of Germany. Only in the last two years, here in Páris. Perhaps we drank—"

"No, we did not drink together. And it wasn't here. In Germany, Haake!"

A barrier. Railroad tracks. A garden, small roses, phlox, and sunflowers. Waiting. A forlorn black train puffing through the endless morning. Reflected in the windshield, alive, the eyes that were now in the trunk jelly-like and filling with dust that sifted in through the cracks.

"In Germany? Ah, I understand! At one of the party rallies. Nuremberg. I think I remember. Wasn't it at the Nuremberger Hof?"

"No, Haake." Ravic spoke slowly into the glass of the windshield and he felt the black wave of the years coming back. *"Not in Nuremberg. In Berlin."*

"Berlin?" The shadowy face broken by reflections showed a trace of jovial impatience. *"Now let's hear it, my friend, let's hear the story! Stop beating about the bush and don't keep me on the rack any longer! Where was it?"*

The wave, up to his arms now, rising out of the earth. *"On the rack, Haake! Just that! On the rack!"*

A laugh, uncertain, wary. *"Don't make jokes, my friend."*

"On the rack, Haake! Do you know now who I am?"

The laughter, more uncertain, more wary, menacing. *"How should I know? I see thousands of people. I can't remember each individual. If you're referring to the secret police—"*

"Yes, Haake, the Gestapo."

A shrug of the shoulders. On his guard. *"In case you were ever questioned there—"*

"Yes. Do you remember?"

Once more a shrug of the shoulders. *"How should I remember? We have questioned thousands—"*

"Questioned! Beaten into unconsciousness, kidneys crushed, bones broken, thrown into cellars like sacks, dragged up again, faces torn, testicles crushed—that was what you called questioning! The hot frightful moaning of those who were no longer able to cry—questioned! The whimpering between unconsciousness and consciousness, kicks in the belly, rubber clubs, whips—yes, all that you innocently called 'questioning'!"

365

Ravic stared at the invisible face in the windshield through which the country landscape with corn and poppies and hedge roses silently glided—he stared at it, his lips moved, and he said everything that he had wanted to say and hadn't said and had to say.

"Don't move your hands! Or I'll shoot you down! Do you remember little Max Rosenberg who lay beside me in the cellar with his torn body and who tried to smash his head on the cement wall to keep from being questioned again— questioned, why? Because he was a democrat! And Willmann who passed blood and had no teeth and only one eye left after he had been questioned by you for two hours—questioned, why? Because he was a Catholic and did not believe your Fuehrer was the new Messiah. And Riesenfeld whose head and back looked like raw lumps of flesh and who implored us to bite open his arteries because he was toothless and no longer able to do it himself after he had been questioned by you—questioned, why? Because he was against war and did not believe that culture is most perfectly expressed by bombs and flame throwers. Questioned! Thousands have been questioned, yes—don't move your hands, you swine! And now finally I've got you and we are driving to a house with thick walls and we will be all alone and I'll question you—slowly, slowly, for days, the Rosenberg treatment, the Willmann treatment, the Riesenfeld treatment, just as you have demonstrated it to us! And then, after all that—"

Suddenly Ravic realized that the car was speeding. He let up on the accelerator. Houses. A village. Dogs. Chickens. Horses in pasture, galloping, their necks stretched, their heads lifted high, pagan, centaur-like, vigorous life. A laughing woman with a laundry basket. Bright-colored laundry dangling on the lines, flags of secure happiness. Children playing by the doors. He saw all this very clearly and yet as if separated from it by a glass wall, very near and incredibly far, full of beauty and peace and innocence, painfully strong and severed from him and now unattainable forever because of this night. He felt no regret—it was this way, that was all.

Drive slowly. The only chance of being stopped lay in speeding through the villages. The clock. He had been driving almost two hours. How was that possible. He had not been aware of it. He had not seen anything. Only the face toward which he had spoken—

St.-Germain. The park. Black trellises against the blue sky, and then the trees. Trees. Avenues of trees, a park of trees, looked for, desired, and suddenly the woods.

The car ran more silently. The woods rose, a green and golden wave, they flung open on the right and left, they flooded the horizon and embraced everything—even the swift, glistening insect zigzagging into them.

The ground was soft and overgrown with underbrush. It was far from the road. Ravic left the car at a distance of about a hundred meters so that he could see it. Then he took the spade and began to dig up the earth. It was easy. If someone came by and saw the car, he could hide the spade and return as a harmless stroller.

He dug deep enough to have sufficient earth with which to cover the body. Then he drove the car to that spot. A dead body was heavy. Nevertheless he drove only as far as the ground was hard so as to leave no tire marks.

The body was still limp. He dragged it to the hole and began to tear off the clothes and to pile them in heaps. It was easier than he had thought. He left the naked body there, took the clothes, put them into the trunk, and drove the car back. He locked the doors and the trunk and took a hammer with him. He had to think of the possibility that the body would be found by accident and he wanted to prevent identification.

For a moment he found it difficult to go back. He felt an almost irresistible impulse to leave the corpse behind, to step into the car and race off. He stood for a while and looked about. A few yards away two squirrels chased each other on the trunk of a beech tree. Their red fur shone in the sun. He continued to walk.

Bloated. Bluish. He put a piece of woolen cloth soaked with oil over Haake's face, and began to smash it with the hammer. After the first blow he stopped. It seemed to make a lot of noise. Then he immediately went on striking. After some time he lifted the piece of cloth. The face was an unrecognizable lump clotted with black blood. Like Riesenfeld's head, he thought. He felt his teeth set tight. It was not like Riesenfeld's head, he thought. Riesenfeld's head was worse; he was still alive.

The ring on the ring hand. He tore it off and pushed the body into the hole. The hole was a little too short. He bent the knees against the belly. Then he shoveled the earth on. It didn't take long. He stamped the earth flat and covered it with squares of moss he had already cut out with the spade. They fitted in. One could not see the edges unless one bent down. He straightened the underbrush.

The hammer. The spade. The piece of cloth. He put them with the clothes in the trunk. Then he walked back once more, slowly, looking for telltale signs. He found almost none. Rain and a few days of growth would attend to what remained.

Strange: a dead man's shoes. The socks. The underwear. The suit, less so. The socks, the shirt, the underwear—ghostlike, withered, as if they had died with the man. It was ghastly to touch them and to look for monograms and labels.

Ravic did it quickly. He cut them out. Then he rolled the things into a bundle and buried them. He did this more than ten kilometers away from the place where he had buried the corpse, far enough to prevent their both being found at the same time.

He drove on until he reached a brook. He took the labels he had cut out and wrapped them in paper. Then he tore Haake's notebook into small pieces and searched the wallet. It contained two one-thousand-franc notes, the railroad ticket to Berlin, ten marks, several slips of paper with addresses, and Haake's passport. Ravic put the French money into his pocket. He had already found a few five-frank notes in Haake's pocket.

He looked at the railroad ticket for a moment. To Berlin—it was strange to see that: to Berlin. He tore it up and put it with the other things. He contemplated the passport for a long time. It was valid for three years more and had a visa valid for almost two years. He was tempted to keep it and use it himself. It would have fitted into the kind of existence he led. He would not have thought twice except for the danger.

He tore it up. The ten-mark bill too. He kept Haake's keys, the revolver, the ring, and the receipt for Haake's suitcases. He wanted time to decide whether to call for the suitcases and thus wipe out every trace in Paris. He had found and torn up the hotel bill.

He burned everything. It took longer than he had thought, but he had newspaper with which to burn the pieces of cloth. He threw the ashes into the brook. Then he examined the car for blood stains: there were none. He washed the hammer and the monkey wrench carefully and put the tools back into the trunk. He washed his hands as well as he could, took a cigarette, and sat for a while, smoking.

The sun shone obliquely through the high beech trees. Ravic sat and smoked. He was empty and did not think about anything.

Not until he turned again into the road that led to the château did he think of Sybil. In the bright summer, the château stood white under the eternal sky of the eighteenth century. Suddenly he thought of Sybil and for the first time since those days he did not try to resist the memory, to push it aside and suppress it. He had never got further in his recollection than the day when Haake had her called in. He had never got further than the expression of horror and mad fear in her face. Everything else had been wiped out by that. And he had never got further than the news that she had hanged herself. He had never believed it. It was possible— but who knew what had happened to her before? He was never able to think of her without feeling a spasm in his brain that turned his hands into claws and compressed his breast like a cramp, making him incapable for days of escaping the red fog of powerless hope for revenge.

He thought of her now, and the circle and the spasm and the fog suddenly left him. Something had been released, a barrier had fallen, the rigid image of horror began to move, it was no longer frozen as it had been all these years. Her distorted mouth began to close, her eyes lost their fixity, and the blood gently returned to her chalk-white face. It was no longer an eternal mask of fear, it became again Sybil whom he had known, with whom he had lived, whose tender breasts he had felt, and who had moved through two years of his life like a June evening.

Days rose up—evenings—like distant, forgotten fireworks suddenly seen beyond the horizon. A bolted, locked, and bloodstained door of his past now opened easily and quietly and a garden was once more behind it—and no longer the cellar of the Gestapo.

Ravic had been driving for more than an hour. He did not drive back to Paris. He stopped on the bridge which crossed the Seine behind St.-Germain and threw Haake's keys, his signet ring, and the revolver into the water. He then put down the car top and drove on.

He drove through a morning in France. The night was almost

369

forgotten and lay decades behind him. What had happened a few hours ago had been indistinct—and what had been repressed for years arose enigmatically and came close to him as if no longer separated from him by a chasm.

Ravic did not know what was happening to him. He had thought he would feel empty, tired, indifferent, agitated; he had expected a feeling of disgust, silent justification, a craving for liquor, for getting drunk, forgetting—but not this. He had not expected to feel easy and released as if a padlock had fallen from his past. He looked about. The landscape was slipping by, processions of poplars lifted on high their torchlike green jubilation, fields with poppies and cornflowers lay outspread, from bakeries of the small villages came the smell of fresh bread, and children's voices in a schoolhouse rose to the scraping of a violin.

What had he been thinking before while passing here? Before, a few hours, ages ago? Where was the glass wall, where was the feeling of being excluded? Evaporated like mist in the rising sun. He saw the children again, playing on the stoops of the houses, he saw sleeping cats and dogs, he saw the bright-colored laundry hanging in the wind, and the woman was still standing in a meadow with clothespins in her hands, hanging up long rows of shirts. He saw it and he felt that he belonged to it, more so now than he had many years ago. Something in him melted and arose again soft and moist, a burnt-over field began to turn green, and a far distortion gradually swung back into a great balance.

He was sitting in his car, very quietly, he hardly dared move, not to frighten it away. It grew and grew around him, it circulated downward and upward, he was sitting still and did not believe it yet; nevertheless he felt it and knew that it had come. He had expected Haake's shadow to be sitting beside him and staring at him—and now his own life was sitting beside him, it had returned and was looking at him. Two eyes that had been wide open for many years in silent and inexorable entreaty and accusation were closed, a mouth had gained peace, and two arms stretched out in horror were finally lowered. Haake's death had freed Sybil's face from its look of death—for a moment it came alive and then began to grow indistinct. At last it could have peace and it sank back; it would never come again now; poplars and linden trees buried it gently, and then all that remained was summer and the buzzing of bees and a clear, strong, overwakeful tiredness, as if he had not slept for many nights and now would sleep very long or would never sleep again.

He parked the Talbot in the Rue Poncelet. The moment the motor was silent and he stepped out, he felt how tired he was. It no longer was the relaxed fatigue he had felt during the ride; it was a hollow empty craving for nothing but sleep. He walked to the International and it was an effort for him to walk. The sun lay like a beam on his shoulders. He remembered that he must give up his apartment in the Prince de Galles. He had forgotten about it. He was so tired that he wondered for a moment if he might not do it later. Then he forced himself to walk back and drive in a taxi to the Prince de Galles. He almost forgot to ask for his suitcase after he had paid his bill.

He waited in the cool hall. To his right, at the bar, a few people were sitting and drinking Martinis. He almost fell asleep before the porter came. He gave him a tip and took another taxi. "To the Gare de l'Est," he said. He said it loud enough for the doorman and the porter to hear it distinctly.

He had the taxi stop at the corner of the Rue de la Boëtie. "I've made a mistake by an hour," he said to the driver. "It's too early. Stop in front of that bistro."

He paid, took his suitcase, went to the bistro, and saw the taxi disappear. He went back, hailed another, and drove to the International.

There was no one downstairs except a sleeping boy. It was twelve o'clock. The patron was having lunch. Ravic carried the suitcase to his room. He undressed and turned on the shower. He washed himself long and thoroughly. Then he rubbed himself with alcohol. It refreshed him. He put the suitcase and the things which it contained away. He put on fresh underwear and another suit and went down to Morosow's room.

"I was just coming to see you," Morosow said. "Today is my day off. We could eat at the Prince de Galles—" He fell silent and looked more closely at Ravic.

"No need now," Ravic said.

Morosow looked at him. "It's finished," Ravic said. "This morning. Don't ask questions. I want to sleep."

"Is there anything more you need?"

"Nothing. Everything is done. Luck."

"Where is the car?"

"Rue Poncelet. Everything's in order."

"Nothing else to do?"

"Nothing. All of a sudden I have a terrific headache. I want to sleep. I'll come down later."

"Good. Are you sure there's nothing else to be done?"

"No," Ravic said. "Nothing more, Boris. It was easy."

"You didn't forget anything?"

"I don't think so. No. I can't go over the whole thing again now. First I must sleep. Later. Are you going to stay here?"

"Of course."

"All right. Then I'll come down."

Ravic returned to his room. He stood by the window for a while. The lilies of the refugee Wiesenhoff shone in the window box below. Opposite the gray wall with the blank windows. Everything had come to an end. It was right thus and good and had to be this way, but it had come to an end and there was no longer anything to do. Nothing was left. Nothing before him any more. Tomorrow was a word without meaning. Outside his window today fell sleepily into nothing.

He undressed and washed once more. He held his hands in alcohol for a long time and let them dry in the air. The skin around the joints of his fingers was taut. His head was heavy and his brain seemed to roll loosely inside it. He got out a hypodermic needle and sterilized it in a small electric boiler on a chair by the window. The water bubbled awhile. It reminded him of the brook. Of the brook only. He knocked off the heads of two ampules and drew their contents, clear as water, into the syringe. He made the injection and lay down in his bed. After a while he got his old bathrobe and covered himself with it. He felt as though he were twelve years old and tired and alone in the strange loneliness of growing and of youth.

He woke up at dusk. A pale pink hung above the roofs of the houses. Wiesenhoff's and Mrs. Goldberg's voices came from below. He could not understand what they said. Nor did he want to. He was in the mood of someone who has slept in the afternoon without being accustomed to it—severed from all connections and ripe for a sudden unmotivated suicide. I wish I could perform an operation now, he thought. A severe, almost hopeless case. It occurred to him that he had not had anything to eat the whole day. Suddenly he felt desperately hungry. The headache had disappeared. He dressed and went downstairs.

Morosow was sitting in his shirtsleeves at the table in his room, solving a chess problem. The room was almost empty. A military coat was hanging on the wall. In one corner was an icon with a light burning before it. In another stood a table with a samovar, in the third a modern refrigerator. It was Morosow's luxury. He kept vodka, food, and beer in it. A Turkoman rug lay by the bed.

Morosow got up without saying a word, brought two glasses and a bottle of vodka. He filled the glasses. "Subrovka," he said.

Ravic sat down at the table. "I don't want to drink anything, Boris. I'm damned hungry."

"Good. Let's go and have something to eat. Meanwhile—" Morosow rummaged in the refrigerator for black Russian bread, cucumbers, butter, and a small box of caviar "—have this! The caviar is a present from the chef of the Scheherazade. Trustworthy."

"Boris," Ravic said. "Let's not behave like actors. I met the man in front of Osiris, killed him in the Bois, and buried him in St.-Germain."

"Were you seen by anyone?"

"No. Not even in front of the Osiris."

"Nowhere?"

"Someone came across the meadow in the Bois. When everything was finished. I had Haake in the car. There was nothing to be seen except the car and me, vomiting. I might have been drunk or I might have become sick. Not an extraordinary incident."

"What have you done with his things?"

"Buried them. Removed the labels and burned them with his papers. I've still got his money and a receipt for his suitcases at the Gare du Nord. He had checked out of his hotel room by then and intended to leave this morning."

"Damn it, that was luck. Any traces of blood?"

"No. There was hardly any blood. I've given up my room in the Prince de Galles. My belongings are back here again. It's possible that the people with whom he had dealings here will assume he took the train. If we call for his luggage, there will be no trace of him left here."

"They'll find out in Berlin that he didn't arrive and they'll investigate back here."

"If his luggage isn't here, they won't know where he has gone."

"They'll know. He hasn't used his sleeping-car ticket. Have you burned it?"

"Yes."

"Then burn the receipt for his luggage too."

"We could send it to the checkroom and have them send his suitcases to Berlin or somewhere else, collect."

"That amounts to the same thing. It would be better to burn it. If you are too smart they might suspect more than this way. Now he simply disappeared. That can happen in Paris. They will investigate and, if they are lucky, will find out where he was last seen. In the Osiris. Were you in there?"

"Yes. For a minute. I saw him. He didn't see me. Then I waited for him outside. No one saw us there."

"They might inquire about who was in the Osiris at that time. Rolande will recall that you were there."

"I often go there. That doesn't matter."

"It would be better they didn't question you. Refugee without papers. Does Rolande know where you are living?"

"No, but she knows Veber's address. He is the official doctor. Rolande will leave her position in a few days."

"They'll know where she is." Morosow filled his glass. "Ravic, I think you'd better disappear for a few weeks."

Ravic looked at him. "That's easily said, Boris. Where to?"

"Any place where there is a crowd. Go to Cannes or Deauville. There's a lot going on there now and you can easily disappear in the crowd. Or to Antibes. You know it and no one asks for papers there. Then Veber and Rolande can always let me know if the police have been inquiring for you to question you as a witness."

Ravic shook his head. "The best thing is to stay where one is and to live as if nothing had happened."

"No. Not in this case."

Ravic looked at Morosow. "I won't run away. I'll stay here. That's part of it. Don't you understand?"

Morosow did not reply. "First burn the receipt for his luggage," he said.

Ravic took the check out of his pocket, lighted it, and let it burn over the ashtray. Morosow took the copper plate and threw the fine ashes out of the window. "So, that's done. You've nothing else of his on you?"

"Money."

"Let's see it."

He examined it. There were no markings on it. "You can easily get rid of that. What will you do with it?"

"I could send it to the committee for refugees. Anonymously."

"Change it tomorrow and send the money in two weeks."

"Good."

Ravic put the bills into his pocket. Folding them, he realized that he had been eating. He gave his hands a fleeting glance. What strange thoughts he had had that morning. He took another piece of the fresh dark bread.

"Where are we going to eat?" Morosow asked.

"Anywhere."

Morosow looked at him. Ravic smiled. It was the first time he had smiled. "Boris," he said. "Don't look at me as a nurse might, expecting me to have a nervous breakdown. I've wiped out a beast that deserved a thousand times worse. I have killed dozens of people who did not matter to me, and I was decorated for it, and I didn't kill them in fair fight, but sneaked up on them, spied them out from behind when they were unsuspecting, and that was war and honorable. The only thing that was repugnant to me for a few minutes was that I could not first tell Haake to his face, and that was an idiotic desire. He's done with and he will never again torture anyone, and I've slept on it and it is as far removed from me as if I were reading about it in the papers."

"Good." Morosow buttoned his coat. "Let's go. I need a drink."

Ravic looked up. "You?"

"Yes, I," Morosow said. "I." He hesitated a second. "Today for the first time I feel old."

Chapter 31

THE FAREWELL PARTY for Rolande began punctually at six o'clock. It lasted only an hour. Business started again at seven.

The table was set in an adjoining room. All the whores were dressed. Most of them wore black silk dresses. Having always seen them naked or in a few thin wisps, Ravic had difficulty in recognizing a number of them. Only half a dozen had been left behind in the big room as an emergency force. They would change at seven o'clock and be served then. None of them would come in their professional costumes. This was not madame's rule; the girls themselves wanted it this way. Ravic had not expected anything else. He knew the etiquette among whores; it was stricter than that of high society.

The girls had collected money and given Rolande six wicker chairs as a present for her restaurant. Madame had presented her with a cash register, Ravic with two marble tables to go with the wicker chairs. He was the only outsider at this party. And the only man.

The dinner started at five minutes past six. Madame presided. Rolande sat at her right, Ravic at her left. Then followed the new *gouvernante*, the assistant *gouvernante*, and the rows of girls.

The hors d'oeuvres were excellent. Strasbourg goose liver, pâté maison, and old sherry to go with it. Ravic was served a bottle of vodka. He loathed sherry. This was followed by a Vichysoisse of finest quality. Then by turbot with Meursault 1933. The turbot was of the same quality as that served at Maxim's. The wine was light and exactly young enough. Then green asparagus came after it, then roast chicken, crisp and tender, carefully chosen salad with a whiff of garlic, with it a Château St. Emilion. At the head of the table they were drinking a bottle of Romanée Conti 1921. "The girls don't

and hav
move into

appreciate it," madame declared. Ravic appreciated it. He was served a second bottle. In exchange he passed over the champagne and the mousse chocolat. Together with madame he ate a ripe Brie with the wine and fresh white bread without butter.

The conversation at the table was that of a boarding school for young ladies. The wicker chairs were adorned with bows. The cash register glittered. The marble tables gleamed. An air of melancholy pervaded the room. Madame was in black. She wore diamonds. Not too many. A brooch and a ring. Fine blue-white stones. No coronet, although she had become a countess. She had taste. Madame loved diamonds. She declared that rubies and emeralds were risky. Diamonds were safe. She chattered with Rolande and Ravic. She was well read, her conversation was amusing, light, and witty. She quoted Montaigne, Chateaubriand, and Voltaire. Her white, slightly bluish hair shimmered above her clever ironical face.

At seven o'clock, after the coffee, the girls rose like obedient young ladies at a boarding school. They thanked madame politely and took leave of Rolande. Madame stayed on for a while. She had an armagnac brought such as Ravic had never drunk before. The emergency brigade that had remained on duty came in, washed, less painted than when they were working, dressed in evening gowns. Madame waited until the girls were seated and eating turbot. She exchanged a few words with each of them and expressed her thanks that they had sacrificed the preceding hour. Then she said goodbye graciously. "I'll see you, Rolande, before you leave—"

"Certainly, madame."

"May I leave the armagnac here?" she asked Ravic.

Ravic thanked her. Madame left—every inch a lady of the highest rank.

Ravic took the bottle and sat down at Rolande's side. "When are you going?" he asked.

"Tomorrow afternoon at four-seven."

"I'll be at the station."

"No, Ravic. That cannot be. My fiancé will be here tonight. We'll leave together. You understand why you can't come?"

"Of course."

"We plan to pick out a few more things tomorrow morning everything sent off before we leave. Tonight I'll he Hôtel Belfort. Good, reasonable, clean."

377

"Is he staying there, too?"

"Of course not," Rolande said in surprise. "We are not married yet."

"I see."

Ravic knew that all this was not a pose. Rolande was a bourgeoise who had been in a profession. Whether it was a boarding school for young ladies or a brothel did not matter. She had completed her professional work; it was over and she was returning to her bourgeois world without taking a shadow of the other world with her. It was the same with many whores. Some of them became excellent wives. To be a whore was a serious profession, not a vice. That saved them from degradation.

Rolande smiled at Ravic, took the bottle of armagnac, and refilled his glass. Then she took a slip of paper out of her bag. "In case you'd like to get away from Paris someday— here is the address of our house. You can come any time."

Ravic looked at the address. "There are two names on it," she said. "One is for the first two weeks. It's mine. Afterwards, that of my fiancé."

Ravic put the slip into his pocket. "Thank you, Rolande. For the time being I'll stay in Paris. Besides, your fiancé would certainly be startled if I suddenly dropped in."

"You mean because I don't want you to come to the station? That's something else. This is only in the event that you have to get away from Paris someday. Quickly. In that event."

He glanced up. "Why?"

"Ravic," she said. "You are a refugee. And refugees are sometimes in difficulties. In that case it's good to know where one can live without having the police concerned about it."

"How do you know I am a refugee?"

"I know. I haven't told anyone. It's no one's business here. Keep the address. And in case you should need it some day, come. No one will question you at our place."

"All right. Thank you, Rolande."

"Two days ago someone from the police was here. He inquired about a German. He wanted to know whether he had been here."

"Really?" Ravic said attentively.

"Yes. He had been here last time you were in. P̶ you don't remember it any more. A stout bald-h̶

378

He was sitting there with Yvonne and Claire. The police asked whether he had been here and who else had been here."

"I have no recollection," Ravic said.

"I'm sure you didn't pay any attention to him. Of course I didn't say that you were here for a moment that night."

Ravic nodded.

"It's better so," Rolande declared. "This way one doesn't give the *flics* a chance to ask innocent people for their passports."

"Naturally. Did he say what he wanted?"

Rolande shrugged her shoulders. "No. And it's none of our business. I told him that no one had been here. That's an old rule of our house. We never know anything. It's better. Nor was he very much interested in it."

"Wasn't he?"

Rolande smiled. "Ravic, there are many Frenchmen who don't mind what happens to a German tourist. We have plenty to do for ourselves.

She got up. "I must go. Adieu, Ravic."

"Adieu, Rolande. It won't be the same here without you."

She smiled. "Not right away perhaps. But soon."

She went to say goodbye to the girls. On her way she looked at the cash register, the chairs and tables again. They were practical presents. She saw them in her café already. Particularly the cash register. It meant income, security, home, and prosperity. Rolande hesitated for a moment; then she could no longer resist. She took a few coins out of her pocket, put them beside the glittering apparatus, and began to work on it. The machine whirred, marked up two francs fifty, the drawer shot out, and Rolande put in her own money with a happy childlike smile.

Curiously the girls came closer and surrounded the cash register. Rolande registered a second time. One franc seventy-five.

"What can one get for one franc seventy-five at your place?" asked Marguerite, who was otherwise known as the Horse.

Rolande considered. "A Dubonnet, two Pernods," she said then.

"How much do you charge for an Amèr Picon and one beer?"

"Seventy centimes." Rolande registered zero francs, seventy centimes.

"Cheap," the Horse said.

"We've got to be cheaper than Paris," Rolande explained.

The girls moved the wicker chairs around the marble tables and sat down carefully. They smoothed their evening dresses and all sudden began to act like visitors at Rolande's future café. "We'd like to have three teas with English biscuits, Madame Rolande," said Daisy, a delicate blonde who was a special favorite of married men.

"Seven francs eighty." Rolande kept her cash register busy. "I'm sorry, but English biscuits are expensive."

At the adjoining table Marguerite, the Horse, raised her head after keen deliberation. "Two bottles of Pommery," she ordered triumphantly. She liked Rolande and wished to show her affection.

"Ninety francs. Good Pommery!"

"And four cognacs!" breathed the Horse heavily. "It's my birthday."

"Four francs forty!" The cash register clattered.

"And four coffees with meringues!"

"Three francs sixty."

The enchanted Horse stared at Rolande. She could think of nothing more.

The girls crowded around the cash register. "How much is it altogether, Madame Rolande?"

Rolande showed the slip with the printed figures and began to add them. "One hundred five francs eighty."

"And how much of it is profit?"

"About thirty francs. That's because of champagne. You make a lot of money on it."

"Good," the Horse said. "Good! That's how it should always go!"

Rolande came back to Ravic. Her eyes were radiant as only eyes can be when they are full of love or business. "Adieu, Ravic. Don't forget what I told you."

"No. Adieu, Rolande."

She left, strong, upright, clearheaded—for her the future was simple and life was good.

He was sitting with Morosow in front of Fouquet's. It was nine o'clock in the evening. The terrace was crowded. At a distance behind the Arc two street lights burned with a white and very cold light.

"The rats are leaving Paris," Morosow said. "There are

three rooms empty at the International. That has not happened since 1933."

"Other refugees will come and fill them."

"What kind? We have had Russians, Italians, Poles, Spaniards, Germans—"

"French," Ravic said. "From the frontiers. Refugees. As in the last war."

Morosow lifted his glass and saw that it was empty. He called the waiter. "Another carafe of Pouilly."

"How about you, Ravic?" he asked then.

"As a rat?"

"Yes."

"Nowadays rats too need passports and visas."

Morosow looked at him disapprovingly. "Have you had any up to now? No. In spite of that you have been in Prague, Vienna, Zurich, Spain, and Paris. Now it's time that you disappear from here."

"Where to?" Ravic said. He took the carafe which the waiter had brought. The glass was cool and frosted. He poured the light wine. "To Italy? The Gestapo would wait for me there at the frontier. To Spain? The Falangists are waiting there."

"To Switzerland."

"Switzerland is too small. I have been in Switzerland three times. Each time the police caught me after a week and sent me back to France."

"England. From Belgium as a stowaway."

"Impossible. They catch you in the harbor and send you back to Belgium. And Belgium is no country for refugees."

"You can't go to America. How about Mexico?"

"Overcrowded. And also that would only be possible with some kind of papers."

"Haven't you any at all?"

"I had some discharge papers from prisons where I had been under various names because of illegal entry into the country. That's not exactly the right thing. Of course I always tore them up right away."

Morosow was silent.

"The flight has come to an end, old Boris," Ravic said. "At some time it always comes to an end."

"You know what will happen when war is declared?"

"Of course. A French concentration camp. They'll be bad because nothing has been prepared in advance."

"And then?"

Ravic shrugged his shoulders. "One shouldn't think too far ahead."

"All right. But do you know what may happen in case everything goes to pieces here while you are sitting in a concentration camp? The Germans may catch you."

"Me and many others. Maybe. It may also be that they'll let us go in time. Who knows?"

"And then?"

Ravic took a cigarette out of his pocket. "We won't discuss it today, Boris. I can't get out of France. Everywhere else it's dangerous or impossible. Also I don't want to move on any more."

"You don't want to move on any more?"

"No. I have thought about it. I can't explain it to you. It can't be explained. I don't want to move on any more."

Morosow remained silent. He looked the crowd over. "There is Joan," he said.

She was sitting with a man, quite far away, at a table facing the Avenue George V. "Do you know him?" he asked Ravic.

Ravic glanced at them. "No."

"She seems to change rather fast."

"She runs after life," Ravic replied indifferently. "Like most of us do. Breathless, afraid of missing something."

"One can call it by a different name."

"One could. But it remains the same. Restlessness, old man. The disease of the last twenty-five years. No one believes any longer that he will grow old peacefully with his savings. Everyone smells the scent of fire and tries to seize what he can. Not you, of course. You are a philosopher of the simple pleasures."

Morosow did not reply. "She doesn't know anything about hats," Ravic said. "Just see what she is wearing! In general she has little taste. That's her strength. Culture weakens. In the end it always comes back to the naked impulse of life. You yourself are a magnificent example of it."

Morosow grinned. "Let me have my low pleasures, you wanderer in the air! Who has simple tastes likes many things. He'll never be left sitting with empty hands. Who is sixty and chasing after love is an idiot who hopes to win although the others play with marked cards. A good brothel sets your mind at peace. The house I frequent has sixteen young women.

There, for little money, I am a pasha. The caresses I receive are more genuine than those many a slave of love bemoans. Slave of love, I said."

"I understand, Boris."

"Good. Then let us finish this drink. Cool light Pouilly. And let us inhale the silver air of Paris while it is still free from pestilence."

"Let's do that. Have you observed that the chestnuts have bloomed for the second time this year?"

Morosow nodded. He pointed to the sky in which Mars twinkled above the darkening roofs, large and red. "Yes, and they say that that fellow up there is closer to our earth than he has been for many years." He laughed. "Soon we'll read that somewhere a child has been born with a mole like a sword. And that it was raining blood somewhere else. The only thing missing now is the enigmatic comet of the Middle Ages to make all the ominous signs complete."

"There is the comet." Ravic pointed at the electric signs over the newspaper buildings which seemed to chase each other without intermission, and at the crowd which was standing there, silently, their heads bent backward, staring at them.

They remained sitting for a while. An accordion player posted himself at the curb and played *La Paloma*. The rug peddlers appeared with silken Keshans over their shoulders. A boy sold pistachios at the tables. It looked as it had always looked—until the newspaper boys came. The papers were almost torn from their hands and a few seconds later the terrace, with all the unfolded papers, appeared as if buried under a swarm of huge, white, bloodless moths sitting on their victims greedily, with noiseless flapping wings.

"There goes Joan," Morosow said.

"Where?"

"Over there, at the corner."

Joan walked across the street to a gray open car which was parked in the Champs Elysées. She did not see Ravic. The man who was with her walked around the car and sat down at the wheel. He wore no hat and was rather young. He skillfully maneuvered the car out from between the others. It was a low Delahaye.

"Beautiful car," Ravic said.

"Beautiful tires," Morosow replied and snorted. "Iron man Ravic," he added angrily. "The detached Central

383

European. Beautiful car—accursed wench, that I could understand."

Ravic smiled. "What does it matter? Wench or saint—it's always what one makes out of it oneself. You with your sixteen women, you can't understand that, you peaceful patron of brothels. Love is not a businessman who wants to see a return on his investments. And imagination needs only a few nails on which to hang its veil. Whether they are of gold, tin, or covered with rust makes no difference to it. Wherever it gets caught, it is caught. Thornbush or rosebush, as soon as the veil of moonlight and mother-of-pearl has fallen on it, either becomes a fairy tale out of *A Thousand and One Nights*."

Morosow took a gulp of wine. "You're talking too much," he said. "Besides, all this is wrong."

"I know. But in complete darkness even a will-o'-the-wisp is a light, Boris."

The coolness came on silver feet from the direction of the Etoile. Ravic put his hand around the frosted glass of wine. It was cool under his hand. His life was cool under his heart. It was borne by the deep breath of night and with it came deep the indifference toward fate. Fate and the future. When had it been like this before? In Antibes, he recalled, when he became aware that Joan would leave him. Indifference that became equanimity. Like the decision not to flee. Not to flee any more. They belonged together. He had had revenge and love. That was enough. It was not everything, but it was as much as a man could ask for. He had not expected either one again. He had killed Haake and not left Paris. He would not leave it now. That was part of it. Who profited by chance must expose himself to it, too. That was not resignation; it was the calm of a decision beyond logic. Vacillation had come to a stop. Something was set in order. One waited, pulled oneself together, and looked around. It was like a mysterious assurance to which existence committed itself before a caesura. Nothing was of significance any longer. All rivers stood still. A lake lifted its mirror during the night and the morning would show whither it would flow.

"I must go," Morosow said and looked at his watch.

"All right. I'll stay on, Boris."

"To enjoy the last evenings before the *Götterdämmerung*, eh?"

"Exactly. All this won't come again."

"Is that so bad?"

"No. Neither will we come again. Yesterday is lost, and no tears or magic spells can bring it back. But today is eternal."

"You are talking too much." Morosow got up. "Be grateful. You are witnessing the end of a century. It has not been a good century."

"You also talk too much, Boris."

Standing, Morosow emptied his glass. He put it down as carefully as if it were dynamite, and wiped his beard. He was in civilian clothes and stood, huge and heavy, before Ravic. "Don't think that I don't understand why you won't leave," he said slowly. "I can understand very well your not wanting to move on, you fatalistic joiner of bones."

Ravic returned early to the hotel. He saw a little lost figure sitting in the hall, who, at his entrance, excitedly got up from the sofa with an odd movement of both hands. He noticed that one of the trouser legs had no foot. Instead a dirty splintery wooden stump showed underneath.

"Doctor, doctor!"

Ravic looked more closely. In the dim light of the hall he saw the face of a youngster, drawn into a broad grin. "Jeannot!" he said in surprise. "Of course, it's Jeannot!"

"Yes! The same! I have been waiting here for you the whole evening! It was only this afternoon that I got your address. I tried to get it several times before from that old devil, the head nurse in the hospital. But every time she told me you were not in Paris."

"I wasn't here for a while."

"Finally this afternoon she told me you were living here. So I came right away." Jeannot beamed.

"Is anything wrong with your leg?" Ravic asked.

"Nothing!" Jeannot patted the wo__ stump as if he were patting the back of a faithf__ __ out of __bsolutely nothing.
__ __is perfect." __

__. He looked for an __ __ you got what you
__ years and found it. __urance company?"
__lidified alcoh__ __ __ __ical leg. I got the
__uel, put it under the __ __ __: fifteen per cent.
__ickered. He threw a __ __ dairy shop. It's

small, but we make out. Mother does the selling. I do the buying and the bookkeeping. We have good sources. Straight from the country."

Jeannot limped back to the shabby sofa and fetched a tightly tied package in brown wrapping paper. "Here, doctor! It's for you! I've brought you this. It's nothing special. But all from our shop—bread, butter, cheese, eggs. When you aren't in the mood to go out it's quite a nice supper, isn't it?"

He looked eagerly into Ravic's eyes. "This is a good supper at any time," Ravic said.

Jeannot nodded, satisfied. "I hope you'll like the cheese. It's Brie and some Pont l'Evêque."

"That's my favorite cheese."

"Wonderful!" Jeannot vehemently patted the stump of his leg with pleasure. "The Pont l'Evêque was mother's idea. I thought you would prefer the Brie. Brie is more of a man's cheese."

"Both are first-rate. You couldn't have hit on anything better." Ravic took the package. "Thanks, Jeannot. It doesn't often happen that patients remember their doctors. Mostly they call on us to haggle about their bills."

"The rich ones, eh?" Jeannot nodded shrewdly. "Not us. We are indebted to you for everything, aren't we? If the leg had only been stiff, we would have received hardly any compensation."

Ravic looked at him. Does he perhaps believe I amputated his leg as an obliging act of service? he thought. "We couldn't do anything but cut it off, Jeannot," he said.

"Certainly." Jeannot winked. "That's clear." He pulled his cap lower onto his forehead. "Well, I'll go now. Mother will be waiting for me. I've been away from home for a long time. I got to talk to someone about a new Roquefort too. Adieu, doctor. I hope you'll like it!"

"Adieu, Jeannot. Thank you. And much luck."

"We'll have luck!"

The little figure waved and limped self-confidently the hall.

Ravic unpacked the things in his room old spirit-cooker which he had not used fo He found somewhere else a package of s a small pan. He took two squares of the boiler, and lit it. The small blue flame f piece of butter into the pan, broke two eggs, and mixed them. Then he cut the fresh crisp white bread, put the pan on the table, using a few sheets of newspaper as a pad, opened the Brie, got himself a bottle of Vouvray, and began to eat. He hadn't done this for a long time. He decided to buy more packages of solidified alcohol tomorrow. He could easily take the cooker with him into a camp. It was collapsible.

Ravic ate slowly. He tried the Pont l'Evêque too. Jeannot was right; it was a good supper.

Chapter 32

"THE EXODUS FROM EGYPT," said Seidenbaum, the Doctor of Philology and Philosophy, to Ravic and Morosow. "Without Moses."

He stood, thin and yellow, at the door of the International. Outside, the Stern and Wagner families and the bachelor Stolz were loading their things. They had hired a van together.

In the bright August afternoon a number of pieces of furniture were standing on the street. A gilded sofa with an Aubusson cover, a few gilded chairs to match, and a new Aubusson rug. They belonged to the Stern family. An enormous mahogany table stood there too. Selma Stern, a woman with a faded face and velvet eyes, watched over it as a hen over her chicks.

"Be careful! The top! Don't scratch it! The top! Take care, take care!"

The table top was waxed and polished. It was one of the sacred objects for which housewives risk their lives. Selma Stern fluttered around the table and the two furniture movers, who with complete indifference carried it out and put it down.

The sun shone on the top. Selma Stern bent over it, wiping it with a rag. She polished the corners nervously. The top reflected her pale face like a dark mirror—as if a thousand-year-old ancestress were looking questioningly at her out of the mirror of time.

The movers appeared with a mahogany buffet. It was also waxed and polished. One of the men turned around too quickly and one of the buffet's corners grazed the entrance door of the International.

Selma Stern did not scream. She simply stood there, petrified, her hand with the rag raised, her mouth half open, as if she had been turned to stone when about to put the rag into her mouth.

Josef Stern, her husband, short, with glasses, and a drooping lower lip, approached her. "Vell, Selmale—"

She did not see him. She stared into a blank. "The buffet—"

"Vell, Selmale. Ve hev our visas—"

"My mother's buffet. From my parents—"

"Vell, Selmale, a scretch. So vot, a scretch. The main ting is det ve hev our visas—"

"Det vill stay. You can never get it off any more."

"Madame," said the furniture mover, who did not understand them but knew exactly what was going on. "Pack up your stuff yourself. I didn't make the door so narrow."

"*Sales boches,*" the other man said.

Josef Stern came to life. "Ve are no boches," he said. "Ve are refugees."

"*Sales réfugées,*" the man replied.

"Look, Selmale, here ve are," Stern said. "Vot are ve going to do now? Vot a business you have made over your mahogany! Ve left Coblenz four monts too late on account you couldn't separate yourself from it. Ve hed to pay eighteen tousand marks more refugee tax! And now ve're standing here on de street and the ship von't vait."

He turned his head and looked at Morosow in distress. "Vot can ve do?" he said. "*Sales boches! Sales réfugées!* If I tell him now ve are Jews he would say *sales juifs*, and den everyting is lost."

"Give him money," Morosow said.

"Money? He'll trow it in my face."

"Not a chance," Ravic replied. "Anyone who curses that way is always open to bribes."

"It is against my character. To be insulted and to hev to pay for it on top of it."

"Real insults don't begin until they become personal," Morosow explained. "This was a general insult. Turn the insult against the man by giving him a tip."

A smile sparkled in Stern's eyes. "Goot," he said to Morosow. "Goot."

He took a few bills out of his pocket and gave them to the men. Both took them contemptuously. Stern contemptuously put his wallet back. The furniture movers looked at each other. Then they began to load the Aubusson chairs into the van. They took the buffet as the last piece, on principle. As they loaded it, they gave it a twist and its right side scraped against the van. Selma Stern quivered, but she did not say anything. Stern did not even notice it. He was checking over his visas and other papers again.

"Nothing looks so depressing as furniture on the street," Morosow said.

Now the belongings of the Wagner family were standing there. A few chairs, a bed which looked shameless and sad in the middle of the sidewalk. Two suitcases with clothing. Various hotel labels on the suitcases—Viareggio, the Grand Hotel Gardone, the Adlon Berlin. A rotary mirror in a gilded frame reflecting the street. Kitchen utensils—one did not know why such things were being taken to America.

"Relatives," Léonie Wagner said. "Relatives in Chicago have done all this for us. They sent us the money. And they got us the visa. It's only a visitor's visa. We must go to Mexico after that. Relatives. Relatives of ours."

She was ashamed. She felt like a deserter as long as she felt the eyes of those who remained behind resting on her. That's why she wanted to get away quickly. She helped to push her belongings into the furniture van. She would breathe freely as soon as she was around the next corner. And the new anxiety would begin. Whether the ship would leave. Whether she would be permitted to go ashore. Whether they would send her back. It had always been one anxiety after the other. For years.

The bachelor Stolz had little more than books. A suitcase with clothing and his library. First editions, old editions, new books. He was ill-proportioned, red-haired, and reticent.

A number of those remaining behind slowly gathered at the door and in front of the hotel. Most of them were silent. They merely looked at the things and the furniture van.

"Then *auf Wiedersehen*," Léonie Wagner said nervously. They had finished loading. "Or goodbye." She laughed in vexation. "Or adieu. Nowadays one no longer knows what to say."

She began to shake hands with a few people. "Relatives," she said. "Relatives over there. Naturally, we alone would never have been able—"

She soon stopped. Dr. Ernst Seidenbaum tapped her on the shoulder. "Never mind. Some are lucky, others not."

"Most of us not," the refugee Wiesenhoff said. "Never mind. Have a nice trip."

Joseph Stern said goodbye to Ravic and Morosow and some of the others. He smiled like someone who had perpetrated a fraud. "Who knows vot is vaiting for us? Maybe ve'll vish ve vere beck et de International."

Selma Stern was already sitting in the car. The bachelor Stolz did not say goodbye. He was not going to America. He had only papers for Portugal. He thought that too insignificant for a farewell scene. He simply waved his hand briefly as the car rattled away.

Those remaining stood around like wet chickens. "Come," Morosow said to Ravic. "Let's go! To the Catacombs! This calls for calvados!"

They had hardly taken their seats when the others came in. They drifted in like autumn leaves before a wind. Two rabbis, pale, with thin beards; Wiesenhoff, Ruth Goldberg, the chess automaton Finkenstein, the fatalist Seidenbaum, a few couples; half a dozen children; Rosenfeld, the owner of the Impressionists, who had not got away after all; a few half-grown youngsters and several very old people.

It was still too early for supper, but it seemed that none of them wanted to go up to the solitude of his room. They clung together. They were silent, almost resigned. They had all had so much misfortune, it hardly mattered any longer.

"The aristocracy has departed." Seidenbaum said. "Now those sentenced to death or to life imprisonment are meeting here. The chosen people! Jehovah's favorites! Especially for pogroms. Long live life!"

"There is still Spain," Finkenstein replied. He had the chessboard in front of him and the chess problem from the *Matin*.

"Spain. Naturally. The Fascists will kiss the Jews when they arrive."

The buxom Alsatian waitress brought the calvados. Seidenbaum put on his pince-nez. "Not even that is possible for most of us," he declared. "To get thoroughly drunk. To be free of one night of misery. Not even that. Ahasuerus' descendants. Even he, the old wanderer, would despair nowadays—he wouldn't get far now without papers."

"Have a drink with us," Morosow said. "The calvados is good. Thank God the landlady doesn't yet know it. Otherwise she'd raise the price."

Seidenbaum shook his head. "I don't drink."

Ravic looked at a man who was unshaven and kept taking out a mirror every few minutes eying himself in it, then studying a passport, and in a little while starting the perfor-

cathedral in Chartres have been packed up, too. I was there yesterday. A sentimental journey. Wanted to see them once more. They had already been removed. There is an airfield too close. New windows had been put in. Just as they did last year at the time of the Munich conference."

"You see!" Veber instantly seized upon this. "Nothing happened then. Great excitement, and then came Chamberlain with the umbrella of peace."

mance over again. "Who is he?" he asked Seidenbaum. "I've never seen him here before."

Seidenbaum drew in his lips. "That is the new Aaron Goldberg."

"How is that? Has the woman married again so soon?"

"No. She sold him the passport of the dead Goldberg. Two thousand francs. Old Goldberg had a gray beard; that's why the new one is growing a beard too. Because of the photograph on the passport. See how he pulls and pulls. He doesn't dare use the passport before he has a similar beard. It is a race against time."

Ravic studied the man, who was plucking nervously at his scrubby beard comparing it with that on the passport. "He could always say that his beard was burned off."

"A good idea. I'll explain it to him." Seidenbaum took off his pince-nez and swung it to and fro. "Macabre affair." He smiled. "It was mere business two weeks ago. Now Wiesenhoff is beginning to be jealous and Ruth Goldberg is confused. The demonic effect of papers. According to the paper he is her husband."

He got up and went over to the new Aaron Goldberg.

"I like 'demonic effect of papers.' " Morosow turned to Ravic. "What are you doing tonight?"

"Kate Hegstroem is leaving on the *Normandie* this evening. I'll take her to Cherbourg. She has her car. I'll drive it back and deliver it to the garage. She has sold it to the proprietor."

"Is she able to travel?"

"Naturally. It makes no difference what she does. The ship has a good doctor. In New York—" He shrugged his shoulders and emptied his glass.

The air in the Catacombs was sultry and stale. The room had no windows. An old couple was sitting beneath the dusty artificial palm. They were completely immersed in sadness which surrounded them like a wall. Both sat motionless, hand in hand, and it seemed as if they would never be able to get up again.

Suddenly Ravic had the feeling that all the misery of the world was locked into this ill-lighted basement room. The sickly electric bulbs hung yellow and withered on the walls and made everything seem even more disconsolate. The silence, the whispering, the searching of papers which had already been turned over a hundred times, the re-counting of them, the silent waiting, the helpless expectation of the end, the little

She is all right.

"It's simple for you, Ravic. But I am a Frenchman."

"I am nothing at all. But I only wish Germany were just corrupt as France."

Veber glanced up. "I am talking nonsense. I'm sorry. forgot to light his cigar. "There can't be war, Ra simply can't be! It's all barking and threatening. So will happen at the last moment!"

He remained silent for a while. The self-assurar

spasmodic acts of courage, life a thousand times humiliated and now pushed into a corner, terrified because it could not go on any farther—all of a sudden he felt it, he could smell the odor of it, he smelled the fear, the ultimate overwhelming silent fear, he smelled it and he knew where he had smelled it before, in the concentration camp as they drove the people in from the streets, from their beds, and made them stand in the barracks and wait for whatever was to happen to them.

Two people sat at the table next to him. A woman, with hair parted in the middle, and a man. A boy of about eight stood before them. He had been listening at the tables and now came over to them. "Why are we Jews?" he asked the woman.

The woman did not answer.

Ravic looked at Morosow. "I must go," he said. "To the hospital."

"I must go, too."

They walked up the stairs. "Too much is too much," Morosow said. "I, a former anti-Semite, tell you that."

The hospital was a cheerful place in comparison with the Catacombs. Here too was pain, sickness, and misery, but here at least it had some kind of logic and sense. One knew why it was this way and what was to be done and what not. These were facts: one could see them and one could try to do something about them.

Veber was sitting in his examination room, reading a paper. Ravic looked over his shoulder. "Fine state of affairs, isn't it?"

Veber threw the paper onto the floor. "That corrupt gang! Fifty per cent of our politicians should be hanged!"

"Ninety," Ravic declared. "Did you get more news about the woman in Durant's hospital?"

"She is all right," Veber nervously reached for a cigar.

had before was gone. "After all, we still have the Maginot Line," he said then, almost entreatingly.

"Naturally," Ravic replied without conviction. He had heard that a thousand times. Discussions with Frenchmen usually ended with this statement.

Veber wiped his forehead. "Durant has transferred his fortune to America. His secretary told me."

"Typical."

Veber looked at Ravic with weary eyes. "He isn't the only one. My brother-in-law exchanged his French bonds for American securities. Gaston Neré has his money in dollars in a safe. And dupont is supposed to have hidden a few sacks of gold in his garden." He rose. "I can't talk about it. I refuse. It is impossible. It is impossible that France could be betrayed and sold out. When danger threatens all will unite. All."

"All," Ravic said without smiling. "Even the industrialists and politicians who are doing business with Germany now."

Veber controlled himself. "Ravic—we'd better talk about something else."

"All right. I'm taking Kate Hegstroem to Cherbourg. I'll be back at midnight."

Veber breathed heavily. "What—what have you arranged for yourself, Ravic?"

"Nothing. We'll be sent to a French concentration camp. It'll be better than a German one."

"Impossible. France won't lock up any refugees."

"Let's wait and see. It's a matter of course and one can't say anything against it."

"Ravic—"

"All right. Let's wait and see. Let's hope you're right. Do you know that the Louvre is being emptied? They are sending the best paintings to central France."

"No. Who told you?"

"I was there this afternoon. The blue witch

"Yes. The umbrella of peace is still in London, and the goddess of victory is still standing in the Louvre—without a head. It will stay there. Too heavy to move. I must go. Kate Hegstroem is waiting."

The *Normandie* was lying at the quay, blazing in the night with a thousand lights. The wind came from the water, cool and salty. Kate Hegstroem drew her fur closer to her. She was very thin. Her face was almost all bone over which the skin was stretched, with frighteningly large eyes like dark pools.

"I'd rather stay here," she said. "Suddenly it's so difficult to leave."

Ravic stared at her. There lay the mighty ship, the gangway was brightly lighted, people streamed inside, many of them hurrying as if they were afraid of arriving too late at the last moment. There lay the shimmering palace, and its name was no longer *Normandie*, its name was Escape, Flight, Salvation; in a thousand cities and rooms and dirty hotels and cellars of Europe it was life's unattainable fata morgana for ten thousand people, and here beside him someone at whose vitals death was gnawing said in a thin and lovely voice, "I'd rather stay here."

All this made no sense. For the refugees in the International, for the thousand Internationals throughout Europe, for all the harassed, the tortured, the fleeing, the trapped, this would have been the Land of Promise; they would have broken down sobbing and kissed the gangway and would have believed in miracles if they had held the ticket that fluttered in the tired hand beside him, the ticket of a human being who in any case was traveling into death and who said indifferently, "I'd rather stay here."

A group of Americans arrived. Deliberate, jovial, noisy. They had all the time in the world. The consulate had urged them to leave. They discussed it. It was really a pity. It would have been fun to look on longer. What could happen to them, after all? The ambassador! They were neutral! It was really a pity!

The fragrance of perfume. Jewels. The sparkling of diamonds. A few hours ago they were still sitting in Maxim's, ridiculously cheap in dollars, with a Corton '29, a Pol Roger '28 as the climax—now on ship they would sit in the bar, playing backgammon, drinking whisky—

And in front of the consulate the long lines of hopeless people, the smell of mortal dread like a cloud above them, a few overworked employees, the court of last resort, an assistant secretary shaking his head again and again, "No, no visa, no, impossible," the silent condemnation of silent innocence; Ravic stared at the ship which was not a ship any more, which was an ark, the last ark about to glide off before the deluge, the deluge which one had once escaped and which now was about to overtake one.

"It's time to go, Kate."

"Is it? Adieu, Ravic."

"Adieu, Kate."

"We don't need to lie to each other, eh?"

"No."

"Follow me soon—"

"Certainly, Kate, soon—"

"Adieu, Ravic. Thanks for everything. I'll go now. I'll go up there and wave to you. Stay here until the ship sails and wave to me."

"All right, Kate."

Slowly she went up the gangway. Her body swayed ever so slightly. Her figure, slimmer than all the others beside her, clear in its structure, almost without flesh, had the black elegance of certain death. Her face was bold as the head of an Egyptian bronze cat—only contour, breath, and eyes.

The last passengers. A Jew, streaming with sweat, a fur coat over his arm, almost hysterical, with two porters, yelling, running. The last Americans. Then the gangway slowly being drawn up. A strange feeling. Drawn up, irrevocably. The end. A narrow strip of water. The frontier. Two meters of water only—but already the frontier between Europe and America. Between rescue and destruction.

Ravic looked for Kate Hegstroem. He soon found her. She was standing at the railing, waving. He waved back.

The ship did not seem to move. The land seemed to withdraw. Only a little. Hardly perceptible. And suddenly the blazing ship was free. It floated upon the dark water, against the dark sky, unattainable. Kate Hegstroem was no longer to be recognized, no one was to be recognized any longer, and those left behind looked at each other silently, embarrassed or with false gaiety, and then hurriedly or hesitatingly they went their ways.

He drove the car back through the night to Paris. The

hedges and orchards of Normandy flew past him. The moon hung oval and large in the misty sky. The ship was forgotten. Only the landscape remained. The landscape, the smell of hay and ripe apples, the silence and the deep peace of the inevitable.

The car ran almost noiselessly. It ran as if gravity had no power over it. Houses glided past, churches, villages, the golden spots of the estaminets and bistros, a gleaming river, a mill, and then again the even contour of the plain, the sky arching above it like the inside of a huge shell in whose milky nacre shimmered the pearls of the moon.

It was like an end and a fulfillment. Ravic had felt this several times before; but now it had become entire, very strong and unescapable, it penetrated him and there was no longer any resistance.

Everything was floating and without weight. Future and past met and both were without desire or pain. No one thing was more important and stronger than anything else. The horizons were in equilibrium and for one strange moment the scales of his existence were even. Fate was never stronger than the serene courage with which one faced it. If one could no longer stand it, one could kill oneself. This was good to know, but it was also good to know that one was never completely lost so long as one was alive.

Ravic knew the danger; he knew whither he was going and he also knew that tomorrow he would resist again—but suddenly in this night, in this hour of his return from a lost Ararat into the blood-smell of coming destruction, everything became nameless. Danger was danger and not danger; fate was at the same time a sacrifice and the deity to whom one sacrificed. And tomorrow was an unknown world.

Everything was all right. That which had been and that which was still to come. It was enough. If it were the end, it was all right so. He had loved somebody and lost her. He had hated another and killed him. Both had freed him. One had brought his feelings to life again; the other had eradicated his past. Nothing remained behind unfulfilled. No desire was left; no hatred, nor any lament. If this were a new beginning, then that was what it was. One would start without expectation, prepared for many things, with the simple strength of experience which had strengthened and not torn asunder. The ashes had been cleared away. Paralyzed places were alive again. Cynicism had turned into strength. It was all right.

Beyond Caen came the horses. Long columns in the night, horses, horses, shadowy in the moonlight. And then men, four deep, with bundles, cardboard boxes, packages. The beginning of the mobilization.

One could hardly hear them. No one sang. Hardly anyone spoke. They moved silently through the night. Columns of shadows on the right side of the road to leave space for the cars.

Ravic passed one after the other. Horses, he thought, horses. Like 1914. No tanks. Horses.

He stopped near a gasoline station and had the car refilled. There were still some lights in the windows of the village, but it had become almost silent. One of the columns was moving through it. People stared after it; they did not wave.

"I've got to go tomorrow," the man at the gasoline station said. He had a brown, clear-cut, peasant face. "My father was killed in the last war. My grandfather in 1870. I go tomorrow. It's always the same. We have been doing this now for a couple of hundred years. And it doesn't help; we have to go again."

His look embraced the shabby pump, the small house next to it, and the woman standing silently beside him. "Twenty-eight francs thirty, sir."

Again the landscape. The moon. Lisieux. Evreux. Columns. Horses. Silence. Ravic stopped before a small restaurant. Outside were two tables. The proprietress declared she had nothing left to eat. A dinner was a dinner, and in France an omelette and cheese were not a dinner. But finally she was persuaded and even provided salad and coffee and a carafe of vin ordinaire.

Ravic sat alone in front of the pink house and ate. Mist drifted over the meadows. A few frogs croaked. It was very quiet. But from the top floor of the house came the sounds of a loud-speaker. A voice. The usual voice, comforting, confident, hopeless, and completely superfluous. Everyone listened and no one believed.

He paid. "Paris will be blacked out," the proprietress said. "They have just announced it over the radio."

"Really?"

"Yes. Against air raids. As a precaution. They say on the radio everything is only a precaution. There will be no war. They are about to negotiate. What do you say?"

"I don't think there will be a war." Ravic did not know what else he could say.

"God grant it. But what's the use? The Germans will take Poland. And then they will demand Alsace-Lorraine. Then the colonies. Then something else. And always more until we give up or have to make war. And so it's better to do it right away."

The proprietress went slowly back into the house. A new column came down the road.

The red reflection of Paris against the horizon. Blacked out; Paris would be blacked out. It was natural; but it sounded strange: Paris blacked out. Paris. As if the light of the world were to be blacked out.

The suburbs. The Seine. The bustle of the small streets. Swinging into the avenue which led directly to the Arc de Triomphe, rising faint but still illumined in the misty light of the Etoile, and behind it, still shimmering, in full brilliance the Champs Elysées.

Ravic drove down the avenue. He drove on through the city and then he suddenly saw; the darkness had already begun to descend upon it. Like mangy spots on a shiny fur, areas of sick dimness appeared here and there. The multicolored play of the electric signs was eaten up by long shadows which crouched threateningly between bits of anxious red and white and blue and green. Some streets lay dead already, as if black worms had crept in and smothered all brightness. The Avenue George V no longer had any light; on the Avenue Montaigne it was just dying out. Buildings which had thrown nightly cascades of light toward the stars, stared now with bare dark fronts. One half of the Avenue Victor-Emanuel III was blacked out, the other half still lighted, like a paralyzed body in agony, half dead and half alive. The sickness spread everywhere and when Ravic came back to the Place de la Concorde, its spacious circle too had died meanwhile.

The ministries lay pale and colorless, the garlands of light had gone out, the dancing Tritons and Nereids of the white nights of foam had stiffened to gray shapeless lumps on their dolphins, the fountains were laid waste, the flowing water obscured, the once brilliant obelisk rose leadenly like a mighty threatening finger of eternity in the darkened sky, and everywhere, like microbes, crept out the small, dim blue, hardly visible electric bulbs of the air-raid alarm, and with a dirty glimmer spread like cosmic tuberculosis over the silently collapsing city.

Ravic returned the car. He took a taxi and drove to the International. At the door the son of the landlady was standing on a ladder. He was screwing in a blue bulb. The light of the hotel entrance had always been strong enough only to light up the sign; but now the small blue gleam was no longer adequate. It missed the first half of the sign. One could just make out the word "—national," and even that only with care.

"Thank God, you are here," the landlady said. "Someone has gone crazy. Number seven. The best thing would be to get her out of the house. I can't have lunatics in the hotel."

"Maybe she isn't crazy. Maybe it's only a nervous breakdown."

"It's all the same! Lunatics belong in an asylum. I've told them. Of course they don't want to. What trouble they cause! If she doesn't calm down, she must get out. It can't go on. The other guests have to sleep."

"The other day someone went crazy at the Ritz," Ravic said. "A prince. All the Americans wanted to move into his suite afterward."

"That's something else. That's becoming crazy from folly. That's elegant. Not crazy from misery."

Ravic looked at her. "You understand life, madame."

"I have to. I'm a good-natured person. I took the refugees into my house. All of them. All right, I made money out of them. A little. But a crazy woman that cries, that's too much. She must get out of the house if she doesn't calm down."

It was the woman whose son had asked why he was a Jew. She sat, squeezed into a corner of the bed, her hands to her eyes. The room was brightly lit. All the bulbs were turned on and, in addition, two holders with candles stood on the table.

"Cockroaches," the woman murmured. "Cockroaches! Black fat shiny cockroaches! There, in the corners, there they sit, thousands, innumerable, turn on the light, turn on the light, the light, or else they will come, light, light, they are coming, they are coming—"

She yelled, pressed into the corner, her arms braced in front of her, her legs pulled high, her eyes glassy and wide open. Her husband tried to take her hands. "But there is nothing, mamma, nothing in the corners—"

"Light, light! They are coming! Cockroaches—"

"We do have light, mamma. But there is light, only look,

even candles on the table." He took a flashlight out of his pocket and directed the beam into the bright corners of the brightly lit room. "Nothing is in the corners, look here, look how I shine the light there, there is nothing, nothing—"

"Cockroaches! Cockroaches! They are coming, everything's black with cockroaches, out of all the corners, light, light, they are creeping on the walls, they are falling from the ceiling!"

The woman's breath rattled and she raised her arms over her head. "How long has this been going on?" Ravic asked the man.

"Since it became dark. I was not in. I was trying again; I was told to go to the Haitian consulate, I took the boy with me; it was useless again, and when we got back, she was sitting there in the corner on the bed and yelling—"

Ravic had the needle ready. "Was she asleep earlier?"

The man looked at him helplessly. "I don't know. She was always quiet. We have no money for an asylum. We also have no—our papers are not sufficient. If only she would be quiet. But, mamma, everyone is here. I'm here, Siegfried is here, the doctor is here, no cockroaches are here—"

"Cockroaches," interrupted the woman. "From all sides! They smell! How they smell!"

Ravic gave her the injection. "Has she ever had anything like this before?"

"No. Never. I can't understand it. I don't know why she just—"

Ravic raised his hand. "Don't remind her of it. In a few minutes she will become tired and fall asleep. It could be that she dreamed of—and was startled. Maybe she will wake up tomorrow and not remember anything. Don't remind her of it. Act as if nothing had happened."

"Cockroaches," the woman muttered drowsily. "Fat, thick—"

"Do you need all this light?"

"We put them on because she kept crying for light."

"Put out the upper light. Keep the others on until she is sound asleep. She'll sleep. The dose is large enough. I'll look in on her tomorrow morning at eleven."

"Thank you," the man said. "You don't think—"

"No. These things happen often nowadays. Some caution during the next few days. Don't show your worries too much—"

Easily said, he thought, as he went up to his room. He turned on the light. A few books stood by his bed. Seneca, Schopenhauer, Plato, Rilke, Lao-Tze, Li Po, Pascal, Heraclitus, a Bible, other books—the hardest and the softest, many in thin-paper editions for someone who was on the road and could take little with him. He selected what he intended to take along. Then he looked through his other things. There was not much to destroy. He had always lived so that they could call for him at any time. His old blanket, his dressing gown—they would help him like friends. The poison in the hollow locket which he had previously taken with him into the German concentration camp—the knowledge that he had it and could use it at any moment had made the ordeal easier to stand—he put the locket into his pocket. Better to have it with him. It gave one reassurance. One could never tell what might happen. One might be caught again by the Gestapo. Half a bottle of calvados was still standing on the table. He took a drink. France, he thought. Five years of unquiet life. Three months in prison, illegal residence, deported four times, returned. Five years of life. It had been good.

Chapter 33

THE TELEPHONE rang. He lifted the receiver drowsily. "Ravic—" someone said.

"Yes—" It was Joan.

"Come," she said. She spoke slowly and softly. "Right away, Ravic—"

"No—"

"You must—"

"No. Leave me in peace. I am not alone. I'm not coming."

"Help me—"

"I cannot help you—"

"Something has happened—" Her voice sounded broken. "You must—right away—"

"Joan," Ravic said impatiently. "There is no more time for such play acting. You've done this to me before and I was taken in. Now I know about it. Leave me alone. Try it with someone else."

He hung up the receiver without waiting for an answer and tried to go to sleep again. He did not succeed. The telephone rang once more. He did not lift the receiver. It rang and rang through the gray, desolate night. He took a pillow and put it over the instrument. It continued its muffled ringing and then stopped.

Ravic waited. It remained silent. He got up and reached for a cigarette. It did not taste good. He put it out. The remainder of the calvados stood on the table. He took a swallow and put it away. Coffee, he thought. Hot coffee. Butter and fresh croissants. He knew a bistro that stayed open all night.

He looked at his watch. He had slept for two hours, but he wasn't tired any more. There was no point now in falling into a second deep sleep and waking up groggy. He went into the bathroom and turned on the shower.

A noise. The telephone again? He turned off the tap. A sound of knocking. Someone was knocking at his door. Ravic put on his bathrobe. The knocking became louder. It could not be Joan; she would have come in. The door was not locked. He waited a moment before going. If it were the police already—

He opened the door. Outside stood a man whom he did not know but who reminded him of somebody. He was wearing a tuxedo.

"Doctor Ravic?"

Ravic did not reply. He looked at the man. "What do you want?" he asked.

"Are you Doctor Ravic?"

"You'd better tell me what you want."

"If you are Doctor Ravic, you've got to come immediately to Joan Madou."

"Really?"

"She has had an accident—"

"What kind of accident?" Ravic smiled incredulously.

"With a gun," the man said. "It went off—"

"Was she hit?" Ravic asked still smiling. Probably a fake attempted suicide, he thought, to frighten this poor devil.

"My God, she's dying," the man whispered. "You must come! She's dying! I shot her!"

"What?"

"Yes—I—"

Ravic had already thrown off the bathrobe and reached for his things. "Have you a taxi downstairs?"

"I have my car—"

"Damn it—" Ravic flung his bathrobe over his shoulders again took his bag and reached for his shoes, and his shirt, and his suit. "I can put these on in the car—come—quickly."

The car shot through the milky night. The city was completely blacked out. There were no streets any longer—only a floating misty space out of which blue air-raid lights emerged forlornly and too late—as if the car were driving on the bottom of the sea.

Ravic put on his shoes and his other things. He squeezed the bathrobe in which he had run down, into the corner by the seat. He had no socks and no tie. He stared restlessly into the night. There was no point in asking anything of the man who was driving. He drove with full concentration, very fast and paying complete attention to the direction in which he was going. He had no time to say anything. He could only swing

404

the car around, make way for others, avoid accidents, and take care not to lose his way in the unaccustomed darkness. Fifteen minutes lost, Ravic thought. At least fifteen minutes.

"Drive faster!" he said.

"I can't—without headlights—dimmed—air-raid precautions—"

"Damn it, then drive with headlights!"

The man turned on the big lights. A few policemen shouted at the intersections. A dazzled Renault almost collided with them. "Go on. Keep going! Faster!"

The car stopped with a jerk in front of the house. The elevator was at the ground floor. Its door was open. Somewhere, someone was ringing for it furiously. Probably the man had not shut the door when he had rushed out. Good, Ravic thought, a few minutes saved.

The elevator crept upward. It stopped at the fourth floor. Someone looked through its window and opened the door. "What do you mean by keeping the elevator downstairs for such a long time?"

It was the man who had been pressing the button. Ravic pushed him back and closed the door. "Right away! We must go up first."

The man, outside, cursed. The elevator continued to crawl. The man on the fourth floor pressed the button furiously. The elevator stopped. Ravic flung the door open before the man downstairs could start any nonsense and get the elevator down again with them in it.

Joan was lying on her bed. She was dressed. An evening gown. High at the neck. Silver, with stains of blood. Blood on the floor where she had fallen. When the idiot had laid her on the bed.

"Be calm!" he said. "Be calm! Everything will be all right. It isn't very bad."

He cut the shoulder straps of the evening gown and carefully pulled it down. Her breast was uninjured. It was her throat. The larynx could not have been hurt; otherwise she would not have been able to telephone. The artery was uninjured.

"Are you in pain?" he asked.

"Yes."

"Very much?"

"Yes—"

"That will be over soon. . . ."

405

The injection was ready. He saw Joan's eyes. "Nothing. Only for the pain. It will stop at once."

He applied the needle and drew it out. "All done." He turned to the man. "Call up Passy 2741. Order an ambulance with two stretcher-bearers. Right away!"

"What is it?" Joan asked with an effort."

"Passy 2741," Ravic said. "At once! Go ahead! Start telephoning!"

"What is it, Ravic?"

"Nothing dangerous. But we can't examine it here. You've got to go to a hospital."

She looked at him. Her face was smeared, the mascara had run from her eyelashes and her lipstick was rubbed up on one side. One side of her face looked like that of a cheap circus clown, the other with the black smear under her eye like that of a tired, wornout whore. Over it her hair shone.

"I don't want to be operated on," she whispered.

"We'll see. Maybe we won't have to."

"Is it—" she stopped.

"No," Ravic said. "Not serious. Only we have all the instruments there."

"Instruments—"

"For the examination. Now I'll—it won't hurt—"

The injection had taken effect. Her eyes lost their anxious fixity, while Ravic cautiously examined her.

The man returned. "The ambulance is on its way."

"Call up Auteuil 1357. It's a hospital. I'll talk to them."

The man disappeared obediently. "You will help me—" Joan whispered.

"Of course."

"I don't want to have pain."

"You won't."

"I can't—I can't endure—" She became drowsy. Her voice died down. "I can't—"

Ravic looked at the wound where the bullet had entered. None of the large vessels was injured. He saw no wound where the bullet had left. He did not say anything. He applied a compress bandage. He did not say what he feared. "Who put you on the bed?" he asked. "Did you—"

"He—"

"Were you—could you walk?"

Alarmed, her eyes returned from veiled lakes. "What? Is

it—I—no—I could not move my foot. My leg—what is it, Ravic?''

"Nothing. I thought so. You'll be all right again."

The man appeared. "The hospital—"

Ravic quickly went to the telphone. "Who is it? Eugénie? A room—yes—and call up Veber." He looked toward the bedroom. Softly: "Have everything ready. We must go to work right away. I've ordered an ambulance. An accident—yes—yes—right—yes—in ten minutes—"

He hung up. He stayed where he was for a while. The table. A bottle of crème de menthe, disgusting stuff, glasses, perfumed cigarettes, abominable, all this was like a bad movie, a gun on the rug, blood here too, everything unreal, what makes me feel that? he thought. It is true—and now he also knew who the other man was that had called for him. The suit with those padded shoulders, that smoothly brushed pomaded hair, the slight smell of toilet water that had irritated him in the car, those rings on his fingers—it was the actor all right about whose threats he had laughed so much. Well aimed, he thought. Not aimed at all, he thought. Such a shot could have not been aimed, one could hit with such precision only when one had no such idea and did not intend to hit at all.

He went back. The man was kneeling by the bed. Of course kneeling, it could not be otherwise, talking, wailing, talking, syllables rolling from his tongue. "Get up," Ravic said.

The man rose obediently. Absent-mindedly he brushed the dust from the knees of his trousers. Ravic looked at his face. Tears! That too! "I did not intend to, sir! I swear I didn't mean to hit her, I did not intend to, an accident, a blind, unhappy accident!"

Ravic's stomach contracted. Blind accident! Soon he'll talk in blank verse! "I know that. Now go down and wait for the ambulance."

The man wanted to say something. "Go!" Ravic said. "Keep that damn elevator ready. God knows how we'll get down with the stretcher."

"You'll help me, Ravic," Joan said drowsily.

"Yes," he said without hope.

"You are here. I am always at peace when you are with me."

The smeared face smiled. The clown grinned, the whore smiled laboriously.

"Bébée, I didn't—" the man said at the door.

"Get out!" Ravic said. "Damn it, go, will you!"

Joan lay still for a while. Then she opened her eyes. "He is an idiot," she said with surprising clarity. "Naturally he didn't intend to—the poor lamb—only wanted to show off." A strange, almost impish expression was in her eyes. "I too never believed it—I teased him—into—"

"You must not talk."

"Teased—" Her eyes narrowed to a slit. "Now that's the way I am, Ravic—my life—he didn't want to hit—hit—and—"

The eyes closed completely. The smile died away. Ravic kept listening in the direction of the door.

"We can't get the stretcher into the elevator. It is too narrow. At best, half upright."

"Can you get it around the landings?"

The interne went out. "Maybe. We would have to raise it high. We'd better tie her down."

They fastened her. Joan was half asleep. At times she groaned. The internes left the apartment. "Have you a key?" Ravic asked the actor.

"I—no, why?"

"To lock the apartment."

"No. But there is a key somewhere."

"Look for it and lock the door." The internes were busy on the first landing. "Take the revolver with you. You can throw it away outside."

"I—I'll—I'll give myself up to the police. Is she seriously hurt?"

"Yes."

The man began to perspire. The sweat surged from his pores so suddenly, it seemed there was nothing else under his skin. He went back into the apartment.

Ravic followed the internes carrying the stretcher. The hallway was equipped with electric lights that stayed on only three minutes and then went out. On each landing there was a button with which to turn them on again. The internes got halfway down on each floor with relative ease. The turns were difficult. They had to raise the stretcher high above their heads and over the railing to get around. Their huge shadows danced on the walls. Where have I seen this before? I've seen this somewhere before, Ravic thought, disconcerted. Then it occurred to him. With Raszinsky, at the very beginning.

The doors opened while the internes called directions and the stretcher tore pieces of plaster from the walls. Curious faces appeared at half-opened doors, pajamas, mussed hair, sleep-puffed faces, nightgowns, purple, poison green, with tropical flowers—

The light went out again. The internes grumbled in the dark and stopped. "Lights!"

Ravic searched for the button. He touched a woman's breast, smelled stale breath, something brushed his legs. The light flashed up again. A woman with yellow hair stared at him. Her face hung in rings of fat, cold cream shone on it, and with her hand she held a crepe de Chine robe with a thousand coquettish ruches. She looked like a fat bulldog on a lace bed. "Dead?" she asked with glittering eyes.

"No." Ravic walked on. Something squeaked, spat. A cat jumped back. "Fifi!" The woman bent down, her heavy knees spread wide. "My God, Fifi, did they step on you?"

Ravic walked down the stairs. The stretcher wavered below him. He saw Joan's head, which moved with the movement of the stretcher. He could not see her eyes.

The last landing. The light went out again. Ravic ran up the first flight again to find the button. At that moment, the elevator began to hum and it glided brightly lit down through the quiet darkness as if it were descending from heaven. The actor was standing in the open wire cage. He glided noiselessly, irresistibly down past the stretcher, like an apparition. He had found the elevator waiting upstairs and had used it to catch up with them. It was sensible, but it produced a ghostlike and terrifyingly comic effect.

Ravic looked up. The trembling had left him. His hands no longer felt sweaty under the rubber gloves. He had changed them twice. There was no choice but to overcome it.

Veber stood opposite him. "If you like, Ravic, call Marteau. He could be here in fifteen minutes. You can assist him and he can do it."

"No, too late. I couldn't anyway. Looking on even less than this."

Ravic took a breath. He was calm now. He began to work. The skin. White. Skin like anyone's skin, he told himself. Joan's skin. Skin like any other. Blood. Joan's blood. Blood like any other's blood. Tampon. The torn muscle. Tampon.

Caution. Go on. A shred of silver brocade. Threads. Go on. The channel of the wound. Splinters. Go on. The channel leading to—leading to—

Ravic felt his head growing empty. Slowly he straightened up. "Here, look at that—the seventh vertebra—"

Veber bent over the incision. "That's looks bad."

"Not bad. Hopeless. There's nothing to be done."

Ravic looked at his hands. They moved under the rubber gloves. They were strong hands, good hands, they had operated a thousand times and had sewn ripped bodies together again, they had often been successful and sometimes not, and a few times they had made the almost impossible possible, one chance in a hundred—but now, when everything depended on them, they were helpless.

He could do nothing. No one could do anything. An operation was impossible. There he stood and stared at the red wound. He could have had Marteau called. Marteau would say the same thing.

"Is there nothing that can be done?" Veber asked.

"Nothing. It would only shorten her life. Weaken her. You see where the bullet lies. I can't even remove it."

"The pulse is fluttering, rising—one hundred thirty—" Eugénie said from behind the screen.

The wound grew a shade grayer. As if a breath of darkness had blown over it. Ravic had the caffeine needle ready in his hand. "Coramine, quickly! Stop the anesthetic!"

He made the second injection. "How is it now?"

"Unchanged."

The blood still had a leaden tinge. "Keep the adrenaline injection and the oxygen apparatus ready!"

The blood became darker. It was as if clouds floated outside and cast their shadows over it. As if someone were standing in front of a window drawing the curtains tight. "Blood," Ravic said desperately. "A blood transfusion. But I don't know her blood type."

The oxygen apparatus began to work. "Nothing? What is it? Nothing?"

"Pulse falling. One hundred twenty. Very weak."

Life came back. "Now? Better?"

"The same."

He waited. "Now? Better?"

"Better. More regular."

The shadows disappeared. The edges of the wound lost their gray color. The blood became blood again. Still blood. The oxygen was working.

"Her eyelids are fluttering," Eugénie said.

"It doesn't matter. She may wake up." Ravic applied the bandage.

"How is the pulse?"

"More regular."

"That was by a hair's breadth," Veber said.

Ravic felt a pressure on his eyelids. It was sweat. Thick drops. He straightened up. The oxygen apparatus buzzed. "Keep it going."

He walked around the table and stood there for a while. He did not think of anything. He looked at the tank and at Joan's face. It quivered. It was not yet dead.

"Shock," he said to Veber. "Here is a sample of her blood. We must send it out. Where can we get blood?"

"At the American Hospital."

"All right. We must try it. It won't help. Only prolong it a little." He watched the tank. "Do you have to inform the police?"

"Yes," Veber said. "I ought to. Then you'll have two officials here who will want to question you. Do you want that?"

"No."

"All right. We can think that over this afternoon."

"Enough, Eugénie," Ravic said.

Joan's temples had regained a little color. The gray white had a tinge of pink. Her pulse was beating regularly, weak and clear. "We can take her back. I'll stay here."

She moved. One hand moved. Her right hand moved. Her left did not move.

"Ravic," she said.

"Yes—"

"Did you operate on me?"

"No, Joan. It was not necessary. We have only cleaned the wound."

"Will you stay here?"

"Yes."

She closed her eyes and fell asleep again. Ravic went to the door. "Bring me some coffee," he said to the day nurse.

"Coffee and rolls?"

"No, just coffee."

He went back and opened the window. The morning stood clear and resplendent above the roofs. Sparrows were playing in the eaves. Ravic sat down by the window and smoked. He blew the smoke out of the window.

The nurse returned with the coffee. He put it beside him and drank and smoked and looked out of the window. When he turned back from the bright morning, the room seemed dark. He got up and looked at Joan. She was still asleep. Her face had been cleaned and it was very pale. Her lips were hardly visible.

He took the tray with the coffeepot and the cup outside. He put it on a table in the corridor. There was a smell of floor polish and pus. The nurse carried a pail with old bandages past him. Somewhere a vacuum cleaner was droning.

Joan became restless. Soon she would wake up again. Wake up with pain. The pain would increase. She might live a few more hours or a few days. The pain would be so strong that no injection would any longer be of much help.

Ravic went for the needle and ampules. Joan opened her eyes when he returned. He looked at her.

"Headache," she murmured.

He waited. She tried to move her head. Her eyelids seemed heavy. She moved her eyeballs with effort. "It feels like lead—"

She became wider awake. "I can't stand that—"

"It will be better soon—"

He gave her an injection. "It didn't ache so much before—" She moved her head. "Ravic," she whispered, "I don't want to suffer. I—promise that I won't suffer—my grandmother—I saw her—I don't want that—and it didn't help her at all—promise—"

"I promise, Joan. You won't have much pain. Almost none."

She set her teeth. "Will it help soon?"

"Yes—soon. In a few minutes—"

"What is wrong—with my arm—"

"Nothing. You can't move it. It will come back again."

"And my leg—my right leg—"

She tried to pull it up. It did not move.

"It's the same, Joan. Don't do anything. It will come back."

She moved her head.

"I just intended to begin—to live differently—" she whispered.

Ravic did not reply. There was nothing he could say. Maybe it was true. Who did not always intend that?

She tossed her head from side to side restlessly again. Her voice came monotonous and with effort. "It was good—you came. What—would have happened—without you?"

"Yes—"

The same thing, he thought in despair. The same thing would have happened. Any quack would have been good enough for that. Any quack. The one time when I most needed all that I know and have learned, it is in vain. Any penny-doctor could have done the same thing. Nothing.

By noon she knew. He had not told her anything, but suddenly she knew. "I don't want to be a cripple, Ravic— What's the matter with my legs?—I can't move either of them—any more—"

"Nothing. You'll be able to walk, as always, as soon as you get up again."

"As soon as I get—up again. Why are you lying? You don't—have to lie—"

"I'm not lying, Joan."

"You are—You have to—You mustn't—let me lie here— when I am nothing—but pain. Promise me that."

"I promise."

"When it's going to be too much—you'll have to give me— something. My grandmother—lay in bed for five days—and screamed. I don't want that, Ravic."

"You won't have it. You'll not have much pain."

"When it's going to be too bad—you must give me— something strong enough—Enough for ever. You must do it—even if I don't want you to—or am unaware—What I say now goes. Afterward—promise me."

"I promise. It won't be necessary."

The frightened look disappeared. All at once she lay there peacefully. "It's all right for you—to do it, Ravic," she whispered. "Without you—I wouldn't be alive anyway."

"Nonsense. Of course you would."

"No. From then on when we first met—I no longer knew where to—you gave me—this year. It has been a gift of

413

time." Slowly she turned her head toward him. "Why didn't I stay—with you?"

"It was my fault, Joan."

"No. It was—I don't know—"

Golden noon stood outside the window. The curtains were drawn, but light came through at the sides. Joan lay in a drugged half-sleep. There was already little left of her. These few hours had devoured her like wolves. Her body seemed to grow flat under the blanket. Its resistance ebbed. She floated between sleep and waking. Sometimes she was almost unconscious, sometimes quite clear. The pain became stronger. She began to groan. Ravic gave her an injection. "My head," she murmured. "It's getting worse."

After a while she began to talk again. "The light—too much light—it burns—"

Ravic went to the window. He found the shade and pulled it down. Then he drew the curtains closer together. Now the room was almost dark. He walked back and sat down beside her bed.

Joan moved her lips. "It takes so long—it doesn't help any longer, Ravic—"

"In a few minutes—"

She lay still. Her hands lay dead on the blanket. "I must—tell you—so much—"

"Later, Joan."

"No. Now—there is no more time. So much—to explain—"

"I think I know most of it, Joan—"

"You know?"

"I think so—"

The waves. Ravic could see the convulsive waves go through her. Both legs were paralyzed now. Her arms too. Her breast still rose.

"You know—that I always—only—with you—"

"Yes, Joan—"

"The other was—just restlessness—"

"Yes, I know—"

She lay silent for a while. She breathed with effort. "Strange—" she said then very clearly. "Strange—that one can die—when one loves—"

Ravic bent over her. There was only darkness and her face. "I was not good enough—for you," she whispered.

"You were my life—"

"I can—I want—my arms can never—embrace you—"

He saw how she struggled to lift her arm. "You are in my arms," he said. "And I in yours."

She ceased breathing for a moment. Her eyes were entirely in the shade. She opened them. The pupils were very large. Ravic did not know whether she saw him. *"Io ti amo,"* she said.

She spoke the language of her childhood. She was too tired for the other one. Ravic took her lifeless hands. Something in him was torn apart. "You have made me live, Joan." He spoke to the face with the fixed eyes. "You have made me live. I was nothing but stone. You have made me live—"

"Tu me ami?"

It was the question of a child that wants to go to sleep. It was the final weariness beyond all the others.

"Joan," Ravic said. "Love is no word for it. It isn't enough. It is a small part, only, it is a drop in a river, a leaf on a tree. It is so much more—"

"Sono stata—sempre conte."

Ravic held her hands, which no longer felt his. "You were always with me," he said and did not notice that all of a sudden he spoke German. "You were always with me, no matter whether I loved you, hated you, or seemed indifferent— that never changed anything, you were always with me—and always within me—"

Up to now they had always spoken to each other in a borrowed language. Now for the first time, without knowing it, each one spoke his own and the barrier of words fell and they understood each other better than ever.

"Baccio me."

He kissed her hot dry lips. "You were always with me, Joan—always—"

"Sono—stata—perduta—senzate—"

"I was more lost without you. You were all the brightness and the sweet and the bitter—you have shaken me and you have given me yourself and myself—"

Ravic watched her. Her limbs were dead, everything was dead, only her eyes were still alive and her mouth and her breath, and he knew that the auxiliary muscles of respiration would gradually succumb to the paralysis now, she could hardly speak any longer, she was gasping already, her teeth ground together, her face was convulsed, she still struggled to speak, her throat was in spasm, her lips trembled, the rattle, the deep ghastly rattle, finally a cry broke through. "Ravic," she stammered. "Help!—Help!—Now!"

He had the needle in readiness. Quickly he picked it up and inserted it under her skin. Quickly, before the next spasm came. She should not suffocate slowly, torturously, again and again, interminably, with always less and less air. She should not suffer senselessly. There was nothing but pain ahead of her. Perhaps for hours.

Her eyelids fluttered. Then they became still. Her lips relaxed. The breathing ceased.

He drew the curtains back and pulled the shade up. Then he returned to the bed. Joan's face had become fixed and alien.

He closed the door and went into the office. Eugénie sat at a table with the charts. "The patient in number twelve is dead," Ravic said.

Eugénie nodded without looking up.

"Is Doctor Veber in his room?"

"I think so."

Ravic went down the corridor. Some of the doors stood open. He walked on to Veber's room.

"Number twelve is dead, Veber. Now you can call the police."

Veber did not look up. "The police have other things to do now."

"What?"

Veber pointed at an extra edition of the Matin. German troops had invaded Poland. "I have news from the ministry. War will be declared today."

Ravic put down the paper. "This is it, Veber."

"Yes. This is the end. Poor France."

Ravic sat awhile. There was nothing but emptiness. "It is more than France, Veber," he said then.

Veber stared at him. "For me it's France. That's enough."

Ravic did not answer. "What will you do?" he asked after a while.

"I don't know. I'll join my regiment. Things here"—he made a gesture—"someone will take over."

"You'll stay here. In wartime, hospitals are needed. They will leave you here."

"I don't want to stay here."

Ravic looked about. "This will be my last day here. I think everything is in order. The uterus case is recovering; the gall-bladder case is all right; the cancer case is hopeless, a further operation would be useless. That's that."

"Why?" Veber asked in a tired tone. "Why will it be your last day?"

"They'll round us up as soon as war is declared." Ravic noticed that Veber was about to say something. "Let's not argue about it. They'll do it all right."

Veber sat down on his chair. "I no longer know. Maybe. Maybe they won't even fight. Just surrender the country. One no longer knows."

Ravic got up. "I'll be back in the evening, if I'm still here. At eight."

"Yes."

Ravic went out. He found the actor in the hall. He had forgotten him completely. The man jumped up. "How is she?"

"She is dead."

The man stared at him. "Dead?" He pressed his hand against his heart with a tragic movement and staggered.

Damned comedian, Ravic thought. Very likely he had played something of the kind so often that he fell back into a role when it really happened to him. But maybe he was honest and the gestures of his profession simply clung absurdly about his real grief.

"Can I see her?"

"What for?"

"I've got to see her once more!" The man pressed both hands against his breast. In his hands he held a light brown Homburg with a silk edge. "Don't you understand! I must—"

He had tears in his eyes. "Listen," Ravic said impatiently. "You'd better disappear. The woman is dead, and nothing will change that. Settle this affair with yourself. And go to hell! No one cares whether you get sentenced to a year in prison or dramatically acquitted. Anyhow in a few years you'll be using it to show off in front of other women to conquer them. Get out, you idiot!"

He gave him a push toward the door. The man he. moment. At the door, he turned around: "You unk. .st! *Sale boche!*"

The streets were full of people. They stood in clusters in front of the big running electric bulletins of the newspapers. Ravic drove to the Jardin de Luxembourg. He wanted to be alone for a few hours before he was arrested.

The garden was empty. It lay in the warm light of the late summer afternoon. The trees showed a first premonition of fall, not of the fall that withers, but of the fall that matures. The light was golden, and the blue was a last silk flag of summer.

Ravic sat there for a long time. He saw the light change and the shadows grow longer. He knew they were the last hours in which he would be free. The proprietress of the International could no longer shield anyone once war was declared. He thought of Rolande. Not Rolande either. No one. If he made an attempt to continue his flight now he would be suspected of being a spy.

He sat there until evening. He was not sad. Faces drifted past him. Faces and years. And then the last unmoving face.

At seven he departed. He was leaving the last remnant of peace, the darkening park, and he knew it. A few steps farther up the street, he saw the extra editions of the newspapers. War had been declared.

He ate in a bistro that had no radio. Then he walked back to the hospital. Veber met him. "Will you perform a Caesarean? Someone has just been brought in."

"Of course."

He went to change. On his way he met Eugénie. She was taken aback at seeing him. "Didn't you expect me any more?" he asked.

"No," she replied and passed him quickly.

The child squealed. It was being washed. Ravic looked at its red screaming face and the tiny fingers. We don't come into the world with a smile, he thought. He handed the child to the assistant nurse. It was a boy. "Who knows what sort of war he's in time for," he said.

He washed. Veber was washing at his side. "If it should turn out that you are arrested, Ravic, will you let me know right away where you are?"

"Why do you want to get into difficulties? It is better now not to know people of my type."

"Why? Because you are a German? You are a refugee."

Ravic smiled sadly. "Don't you know that refugees are always as stones between stones? To their native country they are traitors. And abroad they are still citizens of their native country."

"That makes no difference to me. But I want you to get out as quickly as possible. Will you give me as a reference?"

"If you want me to." Ravic knew that he would not do it.

"It is an abominable thought. What would you do there?"

"For a doctor there is something to do everywhere." Ravic dried his hands. "Will you do me a favor? Take care of Joan's funeral? There won't be enough time for me to do it."

"Naturally. Is there anything else to look after? Property or anything like that?"

"We can leave that to the police. I don't know whether she has any relatives. It is of no importance."

He put on his coat. "Adieu, Veber. It was a good time working with you."

"Adieu, Ravic. We still have to settle for the Caesarean operation."

"Lets count that off against the funeral. It will cost you more anyway. I'd like to leave you money for it."

"Impossible. Impossible, Ravic. Where do you want her to be buried?"

"I don't know. In any cemetery. I'll leave her name and address here." Ravic wrote it down on a bill pad of the hospital.

Veber put the slip under a crystal paperweight in which a silver sheep was cast.

"All right, Ravic. I think I'll be gone too in a few days. We would hardly have been able to perform many operations without your being here." He walked outside with him.

"Adieu, Eugénie," Ravic said.

"Adieu, Herr Ravic." She looked at him. "Are you going to your hotel?"

"Yes. Why?"

"Oh, nothing. I only thought—"

It was dark. A truck was standing in front of the hotel. "Ravic," Morosow said, coming out from a house entrance near the hotel.

"Boris?" Ravic stopped.

"The police are in the place."

"I thought so."

"I have Ivan Kluge's *carte d'identité* here. You know, the dead Russian. Still valid for eighteen months. Come with me to the Scheherazade. We'll change the photos. Then you can stay at another hotel as a Russian refugee."

Ravic shook his head. "Too risky, Boris. One oughtn't to nave forged papers in wartime. Better none at all."

"Then what will you do?"

"I'll go into the hotel."

"Have you thought it over carefully, Ravic?" Morosow asked.

"Yes, carefully."

"Damn it! Who knows where they will put you."

"At any rate, they won't deport me to Germany. That's over. They won't even deport me to Switzerland." Ravic smiled. "For the first time in seven years the police will want to keep us, Boris. It took a war to get that far."

"It's rumored they're going to set up a concentration camp at Longchamp." Morosow pulled at his beard. "For this you had to flee a German concentration camp—to get into a French one now."

"Maybe they'll set us free again soon."

Morosow did not answer. "Boris," Ravic said. "Don't worry about me. Doctors are needed in time of war."

"What name will you give them when they arrest you?"

"My own. I have only made use of it once here—five years ago." Ravic was silent for a while. "Boris," he said then. "Joan is dead. Shot by a man. She is lying in Veber's hospital. She must be buried. Veber has promised to take care of it, but I don't know whether he'll be called up before that. Will you look after it? Don't ask me any questions, say yes and be done with it."

"Yes," Morosow said.

"All right. Adieu, Boris. Take any of my belongings you an use. And move into my room. You always wanted my bathroom anyway. I'll go now. So long."

"*Merde!*" Morosow said.

"All right. I'll meet you after the war at Fouquet's."

"Which side? Champs Elysées or George V?"

"George V. We are idiots. Heroic snotty idiots. So long, Boris."

"Merde!" Morosow said. "We don't even dare to say goodbye decently. Come here, idiot."

He kissed Ravic on the right and left cheeks. Ravic felt his beard and the smell of pipe tobacco. It was not pleasant. He walked to the hotel.

The refugees were standing in the Catacombs. Like the first Christians, Ravic thought. The first Europeans. A plain-clothes man was sitting at a desk under the artificial palm, writing down the particulars about each person. Two policemen guarded the doors through which no one had any intention of fleeing.

"Passport?" the man in plain clothes asked Ravic.

"No."

"Other papers?"

"No."

"Illegally here?"

"Yes."

"Why?"

"I fled from Germany. It was impossible to obtain papers."

"Your name?"

"Fresenburg."

"First name?"

"Ludwig."

"Jew?"

"No."

"Profession?"

"Doctor."

The man was writing. "Doctor?" he said and held a slip of paper toward him. "Do you know a doctor who calls himself Ravic?"

"No."

"He is supposed to live here. We received a denunciation of him."

Ravic looked at him. Eugénie, he thought. She had asked him if he was going to return to his hotel, and she had been so surprised to see him still free.

"I told you that no one of that name lives here," declared the proprietress, who was standing by the door leading to the kitchen.

"Be quiet," the man said ill-humouredly. "You'll be punished anyway because you did not report these people."

"I'm proud of it. If humaneness is to be punished, then go ahead!"

The man looked as if he wanted to answer; but he stopped himself with a gesture of dismissal. The proprietress stared at him challengingly. She had protection and was not afraid.

"Pack your things," the man said to Ravic. "Take your underwear with you and something to eat, enough for a day. Also a blanket, if you have one."

A policeman came upstairs with him. The doors to most rooms stood open. Ravic took his suitcase and blanket.

"Nothing else?" the policeman asked.

"Nothing else."

"You are leaving the other things here?"

"I'm leaving the other things here."

"This too?" The policeman pointed to the little wooden Madonna that Joan had sent him at the International after they had first met.

"That too."

They went downstairs. Clarissa, the Alsatian maid, handed Ravic a package. Ravic noticed that the others had similar packages. "Something to eat," declared the proprietress. "So that you won't go hungry. I'm convinced there will be no preparations made where you're going."

She stared at the plain-clothes man. "Don't talk so much," he said angrily. "I didn't declare war."

"Nor did these people."

"Leave me alone." He looked at the policeman. "Ready? Take them away."

The dark crowd began to move. Ravic noticed the man with the woman who had seen the cockroaches. The man supported her with his free arm. Under the other he had a suitcase, and he held another in his hand. The boy also was dragging a suitcase. The man looked at Ravic beseechingly. Ravic nodded. "I have instruments and medicine with me," he said. "Don't be afraid."

They climbed into the truck. The motor roared. The car moved off. The proprietress stood in the doorway and waved. "Where are we going?" someone asked a policeman.

"I don't know."

Ravic stood beside Rosenfeld and the false Aaron Goldberg. Rosenfeld carried a roll under his arm. The Cézanne and Gauguin were in it. His face worked. "The Spanish visa," he said. "Expired before I—" He broke off. "The Bird of Death has gone," he said then. "Markus Meyer, yesterday to America."

The truck shook. They all stood tightly pressed against one another. Hardly anyone spoke. They drove around a corner. Ravic noticed the fatalist Seidenbaum. He stood pressed into a corner. "Here we are again," he said.

Ravic searched for a cigarette. He found none. But he remembered he had packed enough in his bag. "Yes," he said. "Human beings can stand a great deal."

The car drove along the Avenue Wagram and turned into the Place de l'Etoile. There was no light anywhere. The square was nothing but darkness. It was so dark that one could not even see the Arc de Triomphe.

About the Author

ERICH MARIA REMARQUE was born in Germany in 1898. His experience as a soldier in World War I led to his first and most celebrated novel, ALL QUIET ON THE WESTERN FRONT. Remarque left Nazi Germany in the mid-thirties and came to the United States in 1939. ARCH OF TRIUMPH, published by Appleton-Century-Crofts in 1946, was first reprinted as a Signet paperback in 1950.